I0721194

MELKORKA

Book 1

The Kaelandur Series

Thrice Nine Legends

Joshua Robertson

Copyright © 2014 by Joshua Robertson

Published by Crimson Edge Press, LLC
www.crimsonedgepress.com

All rights reserved. This book or any portion thereof may not be reproduced or used in any manner whatsoever without the express written permission of the publisher except for the use of brief quotations in a book review.

Printed in the United States of America

First Printing, 2015
Second Printing, 2017

ISBN-10: 1-945397-94-2
ISBN-13: 978-1-945357-94-3

Cover art by Winter Bayne.

Mapwork by Josephe Vandel.

Acknowledgement

For those that have crossed my path in this existence,
sharing thoughts about thinking over frothy brew, who have
tolerated me in all my frolicsome forays, who have whispered
words of affirmation when my mind riddled in antagonism,
and to my brother most of all.

There once was a time when the gods were gods without question. When men were men without example. When heroes were only the frivolous dreams of lurid mortality. It was a time when truths and untruths were indistinguishable, hatred and love were equally excusable, and life and death regaled all of humanity in the same breath. Myths of old were realized and legends were born from the very dust man was formed of, to be told and retold until the grace of time altered them beyond knowing or forgot them completely. Still, some tales were preserved deep within the hearts of mankind, for reasons that could not be fathomed. Perhaps bearing the fruit of some profound truth or kept alive merely by the strength of the men who lived them. Some tales would never be forgotten.

Table of Contents

Thrice Nine Legends Saga

ANAERFELL*

The Kaelandur Series
MELKORKA*
DYNDAER*
MAHARIA*

Short Stories
STRONG ARMED*
WHEN BLOOD FALLS*
THE NAME OF DEATH*

Additional Works

THE HAWKHURST SAGA*

**Published by Crimson Edge*
***Forthcoming by Crimson Edge*

MELKORKA

Book 1

The Kaelandur Series

Thrice Nine Legends

Joshua Robertson

Month of High Grass

Third of Warmth

124 CE

Chapter I

Branimir Baran cowered away from the copper ore heating in the open hearth. He could not keep his heart from beating in his chest, knowing this would be the first weapon to ever have been crafted at Melkorka. His masters, the Highborn, had never needed a corporal weapon before this day. Even a hundred years ago when they had defended against the demonic Bukavac that bled from the Crags of Kazimir, not a single Highborn had held a weapon. Then again, there was not an *Eretik*, or an evil magus, living among them a hundred years ago.

Even at a distance, the warmth of the hearth touched Branimir's cheeks. "Why does the law say to cut off *their* heads?"

He scarcely noticed he had actually said the words until Jhar Gurov responded with a throaty growl, "It says to decapitate them, crush their skull, and blacken their carcass! The law of men is clear enough about *Eretiks*! You would not understand, Kras. You are not like us."

Branimir turned his head away standing at half the height of the man. The words struck him. It was true he was not the same as the Highborn. Many would think he had demon blood running through his veins, considering his red skin, pointed ears, and pale eyes.

He absentmindedly grinded his crooked teeth, and pulled at his long, hooked nose. He supposed he was considered grotesque by human standards.

Regardless, Jhar's next words implied the man did not fully understand why they were crafting the copper blade either. "The real question is why we have to fulfill the law of the Northmen. This is not what it means to be a Highborn!"

A timeworn man, shrouded in murky robes, swayed in a wooden chair behind Branimir. The rockers of the chair creaked at every incline. The man's grey mane bobbed, including the braided tassels of the beard hanging from his pointed chin. He spoke smoothly in a strange accent, "A proper weapon for a proper beheading, so we are told, yes?"

"Weapon or not, we are not blacksmiths, Dorofej," Jhar said firmly grasping his waistband. Branimir took a slight step back toward Dorofej as though the wrinkled Highborn could protect him. Jhar had an expression that suggested he was on the verge of strangling something.

"We are never the things we ought to be, yes?"

Jhar gained momentum with his discourse, his voice drowning out Dorofej. "How does Kinhar expect us to make a dagger by hand? The Highborn do not make daggers! Never have!" The dark-headed man snorted hard enough to suck the layered soot from the wooden floor to his nostrils.

"And yet here we are, yes?"

"Yes. Here we are!" Jhar slurred in mocking tone. "We should at least be allowed to use magic to hurry things along!"

Dorofej looked to the fire as though he might have been measuring the weight of the suggestion. The old Highborn hovered over Branimir even when sitting hunched over in his rocking chair. Branimir scooted closer to him, his own heartbeat thumping loud enough to ring his ears. With a gulp, Branimir followed Dorofej's gaze to the hearth, hoping to find whatever calm the Highborn had suddenly found.

Branimir had to admit that there was something hypnotic

about the copper softening under the intense temperature of the kiln. Its glow was a cherry red with a black coating that slowly formed around its surface. It helped him breathe a bit easier.

Jhar paced around the room. He scrunched his face up, persisting in his rant. "If we must do this, would it have been that hard to find copper nuggets? Do we really have to sit here like fools watching the slag separate?"

"Found on the Seven Islands or Kalamaar, copper is not," Dorofej said. "Kinhar was lucky that he found it in Arkaim at all."

"He did not find anything! It was that new convert—that young woman—who he had fetch it for him like an inept hound."

Dorofej nodded again, his knees bending and extending, keeping rhythm with the chair. "Katerina, her name is, yes? Katerina Gajic from Arkaim. It was likely she would be sent, with her father being in the merchant trade and—"

"I don't need a story, Dorofej. It doesn't matter. He should have sent a Kras. Those little, red broods are the pawns, not the Highborn!"

"Too far a journey for a Kras, I would think. In the wake of the Crags, beyond the hills and the sea—"

"Dorofej!" Jhar said the man's name as though he were casting it into the fire with the burning copper.

The older man innocently raised his bushy eyebrows, his blue eyes widening momentarily at the younger Highborn. He seemed to finally take the hint of Jhar's irritation and mused, "Do not let my reasoning mind disturb your senseless repartee. By all means, let your tongue continue to twitch."

Jhar scowled.

Branimir watched and listened, finding a hint of hilarity in the situation. Any fear he had a moment ago finally fled as he covered his mouth to stop himself from cackling out loud.

He swallowed hard to stomach the laughter. Branimir had

been brought up like every other Kras that served at Melkorka. It was their duty to serve the Highborn from birth to death, following directions without question. It was a simple way to live. In fact, it had guided his bloodline for at least the past millennium. He was smart enough to not be caught with a fit of the giggles.

Again, Branimir focused on the copper in the fire. The residue from the ore separated to be collected from the natural element and then disposed. Soon, the metal would be ready to be crafted into a blade and then delicately sharpened.

"Kras," Jhar mumbled, "tell Kinhar that *kaelandur* will be ready by nightfall. He can have his execution then, if that is his wish."

Branimir stood up from the fire. Apparently, the Highborn had named the copper dagger to be formed. It would be called *kaelandur*.

He dipped his head slightly. "At once, Lord," Branimir wheezed between his crooked teeth and cracked lips.

"Killing one of our own and with a weapon. It is madness," Jhar blathered, his fingers twisting to fists, turning white.

Branimir made no comment. The statement was not directed toward him.

Instead, Branimir straightened his wool jacket and pulled the cuffs over his crimson-colored hands. Adjusting his black cloak, he headed toward the rickety door leading to the courtyard. Rays of sunlight pierced through cracks in the wood. The fresh smell of spring pressed against his nostrils.

He grinned behind his closed lips, knowing the Season of Frost was still a quarter of a year away. He still had time to enjoy the sun. The cold was the worst.

He had just taken hold of the latch when Dorofej whispered his name.

"Branimir."

He turned on command. Dorofej was the only Highborn who ever called him by name. "Yes, my Lord."

Dorofej leaned forward in his rocker, clearing his throat while turning his head to observe the younger Highborn. Jhar paid him no attention as usual. Dorofej took a slow breath before speaking in a soft tone. "It has been many years that you have served the Highborn at Melkorka, has it not?"

"Yes, Lord. Over five decades."

With the flames dancing behind him, Dorofej's blue eyes looked like stones frozen in ice. He peered toward the slave as if weighing his next words carefully.

Branimir waited. His time was not his to measure.

"You have never known of an *Eretik* being beheaded here at Melkorka prior to Nedezhda, yes?"

Branimir kept himself from gasping at the sound of the *Eretik's* name. No one at Melkorka had said Nedezhda Mager's name in two days. Chained in the dungeons, she was already forgotten by the Highborn.

Branimir had not questioned her fate. She was considered a traitor the moment she was found meddling with death magic and worshipping dark gods. Laws about such things were for the humans, not him.

Branimir shuddered, his hand quivered against the latch with each word. "I do not understand, my Lord. Do you ask whether I have known of *Eretiks* among the Highborn, or whether I have known of *Eretiks* who have come to Melkorka, or simply knowing of *Eretiks* losing their head altogether?" The penalty for questioning the Highborn was not pleasant, and ranged from a firm beating to missing appendages. The Highborn were not considered violent as humans were concerned, but the Kras were not regarded much more than a filthy throw rug. Beating out the crud was not only believed to be necessary, but commonplace.

The handle clicked noisily against the planks of the door. The fear churning in his belly practically bubbled.

"I mean what I ask and nothing more," Dorofej replied.

"No, Lord." Branimir gulped, choosing his words

carefully. "In my lifetime, or the lifetime of my lineage, there has never been an *Eretik* who has lost their head at Melkorka. My father would have told me."

Dorofej harrumphed, returning to his private thoughts. Branimir waited, frozen under the gaze of the Highborn. Several moments passed before Dorofej turned back to the fire.

"Odd for it to happen this day, it is."

The statement seemed to reflect Dorofej's conversation with himself, not meant to be heard by others. It was surely not directed toward Branimir, a lowly Kras.

The Highborn did have a funny way of constantly talking to themselves.

"Do as Jhar told you, Branimir," Dorofej said.

"Yes, my Lord." Branimir dipped his head again, and squeezed through the narrow door into the morning sunbeams. He sighed with a sense of relief.

The sun was high for it being only a few hours after morning meal. As was common in the Season of Warmth, the sun brightened the stronghold called Melkorka. The castle was considered great in ancient times, as well as now, even when compared to modern day manors in the cities on the mainland. Branimir had never been to the mainland, but he had overheard stories from the Highborn. He was quite sure nothing could ever be greater than Melkorka.

It was not an exceedingly large castle. In fact, it could easily be overlooked if not sought out. Melkorka did not oversee any city, village or hamlet. No monuments pinpointed its exact location. Melkorka stood alone, hidden and forlorn, like a lone warrior, dauntless and diligent.

Branimir had heard the stone structure was crafted from chiseled boulders nearly two thousand years ago. The massive rocks, the size of faerings, or long boats, were stacked in such a way that they almost appeared to have grown straight out of the hilltop. It was said that the heavy stones had been carried by an unknown means from the Crags of Kazimir to the south and east to build Melkorka. Although it was likely that the Highborn had used their magic, Branimir preferred the stories that suggested that giants had moved the chunks of rock. There was something thrilling about creatures who towered over humans.

His gaze drifted, seeing the few Highborn and fewer Kras. Of course, most of the Highborn would be in the keep, and there were not many Kras left at Melkorka. Not many at all.

The flapping tapestries atop the towers of the stronghold stole Branimir's attention. The symbol was circular with thick golden, dancing swirls strewn throughout. Such a sign was meant to represent the god, Dahz, the ruler of the golden sun and Protector of Men.

"Bran!" A comforting voice resounded as he made his way across the courtyard toward the keep. "Bran!"

Branimir turned to see another Kras come running from the guardhouse just inside the main gate. Mojmir Nok peddled his feet across the worn path inside the walls, barely making a sound. His scarlet skin glistened against the sunrays, a head of thin, black hair bouncing over his offset mouth. Mojmir was an odd creature to look at. Not because of his traits of being a Kras, but because he was missing his left eye. This gave more attention to his right eye. Its color was dark as pitch.

Mojmir squeaked again in his shrill voice. "Bran!"

Branimir raised his hand to quiet his friend. "What is the hubbub, Mojmir?"

"Andrik sent me. Kinhar is in the dungeon with … her … he wants you."

Branimir chewed the inside of his lip. Obviously, *her* could only be Nedezhda Mager, the *Eretik*. "Why me?"

Mojmir shrugged his shoulders.

Branimir turned to look at the housing unit he had just exited, holding Dorofej and Jhar. Similar stone houses with thatched roofs lined the inner side of the wall. They had just replaced the straw at the beginning of the season, and would have to change it again in a few months before the cold came.

He scratched his head. Being sent to Kinhar was one thing, but being summoned by him was another matter entirely. "I needed to speak with Kinhar anyhow."

Branimir turned from Mojmir without a farewell and quickly climbed the stone staircase that stood adjacent to the keep. He did not hesitate and entered through the sturdy wooden door. Mojmir had gone his own way after delivering the message. Even if Branimir had the option, he would not have asked Mojmir to join him. A Kras always had their orders to attend to and could not be distracted by idle chitchat.

Branimir stepped within the hall of the keep. It gave suggestion to the skeleton of the building's framework. The walls were the same stone as most of Melkorka, but the main flooring was made of beaten earth laid between the stone walls. There were two upper floors that had planks of timber covered with light layers of dirt in many areas. He tiptoed to the dungeon to the left and then right, following no more than a dirt trail that led at a harsh angle into the depths of the earth beneath the castle. The single path to the dungeon was much like the others, smooth and even from ages of being walked upon.

Branimir glided his hand along the smooth stone as he crept down into the dungeon, careful not to slip down the crevice. He cautiously placed each of his small feet in front of one another and inched twenty feet deep toward the dilapidated door that was supposed to hold prisoners securely beneath Melkorka.

Branimir approached the poor excuse for a door. He had been enslaved to the Highborn for his entire life. Never once had he tried to make an escape, nor had any Kras within Melkorka. It was likely that the Highborn would have their heads before they could dream up a scheme for escape. Branimir could as easily claim that no prisoner had ever runaway either, but then again, there had never been a prisoner at Melkorka in his lifetime.

Nedezhda was the first.

Branimir pushed open the door, afraid that it might crumble beneath his touch. When it did not, the Kras scooted inside the narrow opening.

Kinhar Sayan's voice was easily recognizable in a hollowed wheeze, "It pains me to have to sentence you to death, but there is no other way. You know the penalty of being an *Eretik*. I do not have to explain the law to you, Nedezhda."

Kinhar's coarse cloth outlined his frail frame. He was easily aged beyond that of the ancient Dorofej. Kinhar stood, stooped with his hand against the stone wall for support. His white hair fell to his heels, tied in knots to keep him from tripping over it. His upper lips and chin had flimsy hair of the same color that hung wildly over his mouth and chest.

He appeared to be more hair than man.

"I know your schemes, Kinhar. Taking my head this night will not silence your wickedness."

Nedezhda was sprightly, despite the chains that bound her body to the stone wall. A small etching of an eye scraped with a moon and a cross was engraved over her head. Branimir could only guess that the symbol prevented her from touching the craft, *Koldovstvo*. There was no evidence of torture to her flesh or mind, as she stared defiantly at Kinhar. Her light blue eyes were alarming, shining in the darkness, with a hint of knowing that made Branimir shiver and turn his head away momentarily.

"The evil traces of *Koldovstvo* flow deep in your veins, my poor girl. Madness has enveloped your mind and has led you to paranoia and delusion and—"

"I know what was said!" The woman's nose was small, but her nostrils flared with the intensity of a horrendous beast. "You spoke of the *Kadari*!"

Kinhar was poised as though her shouts were the quietest

of whispers. "Such faith I had in you, Nedezhda. The Highborn are the hand of the Lightbringer. We will be the deliverers of hope even when there is none to be had."

"The Highborn are to have no allegiance," she began.

"And yet, you have allied yourself with the heart of darkness, embracing its futility and uniting eternally with its acidic breath," Kinhar continued.

Nedezhda gave no sign of wavering to her elder. "Cut me down this night or the next, Kinhar Sayan, but know that my innocence will be avenged. The Highborn do not kill their own."

"The law must be upheld. It has been decreed that your actions extend beyond the privilege of breath. Dahz demands that Strega's breath be breathed by His brethren and not those that spit on righteousness."

"You speak of the gods as if they speak to you. You speak of good and evil as though it is defined by the divine. Any delusion that runs rampant in Melkorka is in your mind, Kinhar!"

"Bah!" The old man turned his crumpled face from the younger woman, taking notice of Branimir standing idly behind him.

Branimir recoiled at the man's sudden attention.

"Alas, you have come, Kras," Kinhar spoke steadily, turning his attention back to the *Eretik* with a snort. "See how the Kras knows their function without question, ever vigilant in their loyalty to those of exceptional power. The Kras to the Highborn is the Highborn to the Lightbringer, Nedezhda. Such simple logic you should have recognized early in your apprenticeship."

"Such loose connections are contrived by men absorbed with entitlement, taking advantage of the less fortunate," she flung back at him.

Kinhar shook his head in disbelief at the woman, returning focus to the Kras. "What news do you bring from

Jhar and Dorofej?"

"My Lord, *kaelandur* will be ready by nightfall."

"So, it is this night that justice will run its course in Melkorka?"

Branimir hesitated, uncertain if the question was meant for him. It was awfully difficult to know when the Highborn were speaking to one of their gods or themselves entirely. "Yes, my Lord."

Kinhar looked at Branimir, with a hint of surprise that he had spoken and then continued, "I have a task for you and the one-eyed one."

Branimir recognized the reference to Mojmir. "Speak it and consider it done, my Lord."

"Take this," Kinhar grabbed a hand full of Nedezhda's hair and tore it from her head. She screamed, blood immediately surfacing on her scalp.

Branimir winced, holding his small, red hand out to take the strands of hair from his Lord with as much eagerness as he could muster. "Yes, my Lord."

"Take this inland toward the Crags and set fire to it so that when the evening gale blows, the ashes are swept toward the shores of Strega's Deep. Make haste and do not let any Highborn go with you."

"You will bring death to the world," Nedezhda hissed.

Kinhar frowned at her.

Branimir winced at her words. He was inclined to ask Kinhar of the true purpose of the task, but he knew better than to question the Highborn.

He bowed his head in submission. "As you wish, my Lord. It will be done at once."

"By the time you return," Kinhar said with more ferocity than Branimir had ever witnessed from the old man, "the *Eretik* will have her neck severed and body bloodied in flame."

With the hesitation of a raindrop falling from a thatch roof, Branimir raised his pale eyes slowly to look at Nedezhda and quickly wished he had refrained. Her cold eyes were ignited with equal rage, stained with the shadow of an inescapable death, and were frozen to his own with timeless hatred.

Chapter II

In the dim light of the failing sun, the peaks of the adjacent Crags were a silhouette on the horizon, stretching toward the scattered clouds in the evening sky.

"Bran," Mojmir squeaked. "How far inland must we go before burning this hair? We've been walking for hours."

"Lord Kinhar did not say exactly," Branimir said. "I suppose this is far enough. The evening gale will be upon us shortly anyway."

Mojmir nodded, picking at the hole where his left eye should have been. "It has never been the same without it."

Branimir stared at his companion, unsure of how to respond to such a statement. "I suppose not."

Mojmir circled around in the dirt, walking without purpose as Branimir held Nedezhda's hair against the ground under his foot. He reached in his pocket for tinder, flint, and steel. In the meantime, Mojmir hopped and bounced about somewhat carelessly before finally sitting with his legs crossed. The other Kras stared toward the Crags. His hand petted the eye socket repeatedly as if mourning the loss of his full sight.

"What do you think it was like, Branimir?"

Branimir laid the tinder over the hair and clicked the flint and steel together creating a spark. "What are you talking about?"

"Farmas? Patul? Illuard? Faran? Eyanria?"

Branimir paused with his kin to look at the Crags of Kazimir. Mojmir spoke of the lost, underground cities of the Kras that once existed deep in the mountainside. They were not permitted to speak of such things around the Highborn. Branimir found himself hesitant, even now, but still said softly, "It was said that Eyanria had more gems than the Kras had pockets, with chests overflowing with trinkets, charms, and shiny stones."

"I would like to have a shiny stone."

"Me too, Mojmir."

"My father's father told me that Farmas was pretty."

"I did not know you had met your father's father."

"It was brief when I was a small child. I was surely the size of a pebble at the time."

Branimir raised an eyebrow at Mojmir, who did his best to keep a straight face before letting loose a gut-wrenching bellow of a laugh. Branimir could not help but join in with the foolish Kras.

"Don't say that around the Highborn. Their sense of humor is as keen as their taste in women!"

"Ha!" Mojmir gaped open his mouth, overly amused with himself. "In fifty years, I have yet to see one worth looking at!"

Branimir grabbed his stomach, falling backwards gleefully with an abrupt chuckle. "No wonder they never mate."

"Hold on a minute," Mojmir paused, taking a deep breath, becoming very serious. "I thought the Highborn came from lightning bolts from their gods. You mean they actually have mating rituals?"

Branimir stopped, his laughter silenced in an instant. He turned toward Mojmir. "You cannot be serious?"

Mojmir shrugged. "I've never seen a Highborn infant."

Branimir had to admit that he had never seen one either, but he knew humans did not descend from lightning. "I am not explaining to you how human pollen spreads."

"What does that mean, Bran?"

"It means…forget it."

"If you think so," Mojmir shrugged again. "Anyway, I would like to know what a Kras woman looks like."

Branimir stared blankly at Mojmir. "You had a mother?"

Mojmir returned the look of absoluteness, placing a finger on his nose. "And she was a mother, not a woman. Heh?"

"You have seaweed for brains, Mojmir."

Branimir could not condemn Mojmir for having such thoughts, as Branimir had thought such things himself in the late hours, in secret. Never had he met a female Kras outside of his own mother, or seen any real remnant of the Kras civilization. He had few answers and even fewer questions, because he had no basis of knowing where to begin.

The Kras would soon become extinct, forever removed from the world of men. Their underground cities were home to demons. Their riches had long ago been appropriated and traded by humans. And their fates were at the hands of the Highborn. Truly, the life of the Kras was forlorn.

As if remembering his task, Branimir struck flint against steel again, dropping spark to the tinder. The stench immediately touched his nostrils. He wiggled his hooked nose to take away the itch before giving breath to the flame. Stepping back from harm's way, the hair caught fire and singed to ash. As if prompted, the evening wind swept from east to west, picking up the scorched strands of hair and carried them toward Strega's Deep.

"What was that? Did you hear that, Bran?"

Mojmir jumped to his feet, continuing to look toward the Crags.

Branimir noticed the sun was nearly gone from the sky. It did not matter much to him. He and Mojmir could see as well in the dark as they could during the day. In fact, they did not know much difference except when the Highborn complained about it.

Branimir stepped carefully toward Mojmir with the grace of a fish in water, barely making a sound on the light pebbles beneath his feet. He was not sure he had heard anything.

Mojmir ran a thin hand through his black strands of hair, before touching the missing eye again. "Branimir! Did you hear it or not?"

Branimir grimaced. "I can't hear anything but the wind. May I add, it doesn't help with you and your hubbub, Mojmir."

In that moment, a definite howl resounded in the distance ahead of them, causing them both to drop to the ground on their stomachs, nearly simultaneously.

"That's not wind, Bran," Mojmir cried out again, attempting to scoot back the way they had come.

"Stay down, you fool!" Branimir instructed. "You aren't going to scoot all the way back to Melkorka."

Mojmir gave no argument, stopping instantly.

"We are safe if we do not move," Bran reasoned. "The light has dimmed and our clothes are dark."

"Unless whatever it is can see as we do."

Branimir bit his cheek. He had not thought about that.

"But," Mojmir lifted his eyebrows, surprised at his own thought, "we can always disappear from sight if needed!"

Branimir grinned enthusiastically in agreement. A Kras could always disappear when needed. "Good thinking."

"Okay, I am not moving. What do you see?"

"Give me a moment," Branimir replied, taking a slow breath. Ever so slightly, he raised his body from the dirt.

Branimir scanned the low hills between Melkorka and the Crags. The skies darkened but it did not impair Branimir's vision in the slightest. He could faintly see something moving on the horizon. Blinking a couple of times, he focused on the shadows dancing at the base of the mountains.

"What is it?" Mojmir wheezed. His single eye darted to Bran's face looking for some sort of answer.

Lightning ricocheted through the colorless clouds. And Branimir knew these were not storm clouds. This lightning was unnatural.

Again, the lightning flashed, illuminating the ground around the two Kras. Mojmir squeaked again pushing his body closer to the uneven ground, covering his single eye.

"Are one of the Highborn being born?"

"No. Bukavac," Branimir said with a trembling voice, ignoring the other Kras's ignorance.

"Demons from the Netherworld..." Mojmir croaked at a whisper, throwing his head up again. "That's not funny! You have never seen a Bukavac. How would you know?"

"Not hard to mistake! I have heard stories."

"What kind of stories?"

Branimir scoffed. "There aren't any good stories with Bukavac, Mojmir!"

Mojmir scrunched his nose, hesitantly keeping his eye on Branimir. His words were filled with distrust, "Well, how many are there?"

"More than I can count."

A beastly roar like no other sounded across the expanse. The ground shook beneath their feet. It was as though an army were marching on it. Mojmir's tone drastically changed with the realization that Branimir was speaking truthfully.

"They are giant." Branimir's words hung in the air for a moment before Mojmir said anything. Maybe demons had built Melkorka.

"Have... have they spotted us?"

"Not yet. Not...quite yet," Branimir said. "We must get back to Melkorka and tell the Highborn."

"If they see us, we are dead."

"Then don't get spotted!" Branimir mocked.

"But—"

"Shut it, Mojmir, and run!"

Branimir flung himself from the ground and scampered

northwest toward the castle. He could hear Mojmir panting behind him. He may be a dupe for running like a three-legged mule across open land, but it was far more foolish to be discovered with his face pressed to the earth.

Legend held truth in saying the Kras were fast. Not as quick as a horse or a dog, but quicker than a human. Branimir hoped they were faster than the demonic Bukavac too.

Chapter III

Branimir was relieved when Melkorka appeared before him. His feet ached and his legs burned from running, but he did not plan to stop until he was within the stronghold. The walls were gigantic compared to him, standing almost three times his height. The towers and keep were even grander in size. Yet Branimir was afraid that their height would be trivial when compared to the size of the Bukavac.

Melkorka was triangle-shaped, positioned on top of a narrow, flat hill. One tower provided a lookout at the gate and the other overlooked the ocean to the west and the hills to the north. Branimir was certain that no one was manning the towers. The Highborn would not waste their time idly guarding the landscape. Luckily, Melkorka was a solid structure, built to withstand the attack of small legions. The greatest defense for the castle was the steep slopes surrounding the hill. Historically, it had slowed enemies, lessening their numbers, preventing any army from overrunning the castle. In fact, he had heard stories of the Highborn defending against demons before, and winning.

Branimir hoped tonight would not be any different.

The tapestries hanging from the towers were likely too dark for any human to make out in the night, but he could see them clearly. They flapped fiercely in the lurching wind.

He did not understand why, but seeing the sun symbol on the fabric made his gut churn. Branimir knew the Lightbringer's crest had not always been honored at Melkorka. Before his father's death, the Highborn had held fidelity to no god.

The gods were the humans concern though; not his.

Branimir and Mojmir did not slow until they had made it through the aged wooden doors leading to the courtyard. At Melkorka's entrance stood Dorofej and Jhar. A few oil lamps lit the area to give some light to the humans. Thirty feet behind them was the outside staircase of stone that led to the keep.

Dorofej was speaking to Jhar as Branimir approached them. His robes were so thick that they easily hid his ripened body in shadows. It did not help that the attire was dyed with mixed shades of black and dark grey. Not only was the man heavily wrapped up in cloth, but also in his words. Dorofej did not show any indication of acknowledging him or Mojmir.

Jhar, on the other hand, noticed them immediately and interrupted Dorofej, "By the Nine Lands, Kras! You are back awfully fast. What is the rush?" Jhar wore similar attire as the elderly man, but strangely enough was the one that carried a walking stick. He slammed the base of the shaft against the ground as he finished speaking. Dust sprinkled into the air.

Dorofej grunted in surprise as the two tried to catch their breath. As expected, the old man spoke before either of the half-sized men had a chance. "Something is coming, yes?" Wrinkles of wisdom lined his eyes. "Look at them, Jhar. Mojmir is shaking right out of his red skin, he is!"

It was true. Mojmir's pint-size body trembled beyond control.

Lightning flashed.

"Speak to us," Jhar said in a demanding tone.

"Bukavac...from the Crags," Branimir said between heaves. "We must tell Lord Kinhar."

"It cannot be," Dorofej said, speaking over the top of Branimir's last words. He cleared his throat. "Eighty years, it has been, since any demon has come down from the mountaintops."

"Are you sure?"

Branimir nodded. "Twice your height, skin like ice, clawed and fanged like the Seamstress of Nightmares herself..."

"Enough, Kras." Jhar ordered.

Dorofej had a twinkle in his eye. "What would cause them to return to the world of the living, I wonder?"

Jhar scowled. "Her death, Dorofej. She has come for her revenge."

"Nedezhda?"

Jhar nodded as though the answer could not be more obvious. "*Kaelandur* took her life once already. And now, how will we defeat her when she is already dead?"

"Kinhar will know a way, yes?" Dorofej's lip curled under his white mustache.

"He better after playing with daggers." Jhar dipped his head, hitting the butt of his staff against the dirt again. The cloud of dust powdered the air over Branimir's head. Jhar peered at him. "How many Bukavac does Nedezhda bring?"

Branimir blinked, suddenly remembering his place among the humans, among the Highborn. "An army, my Lord." He watched each pinch of dust fall back to the ground. Branimir shivered under his cloak.

Dorofej licked his lips, dry and cracked. He did it carefully, meticulously—as though it were the last time to perform such a mundane task. His voice was steady. "Run along and inform Kinhar, you will. Be quick about it, yes?"

Mojmir and Branimir were well practiced in following instruction without questioning it. The Highborn had been sure of that. As Branimir scurried toward the entrance, the final words of the conversation effortlessly fell upon his ears.

"What will we do, Dorofej?"

"It is likely we will die. That will be another adventure entirely, yes?"

Branimir and Mojmir did not take any more time to scan the courtyard. It was silent, suggesting many of the Highborn were already in their beds. Branimir rushed up the staircase and through the wooden door leading into the keep.

For the second time that day, Branimir's feet fell over the beaten earth of Melkorka's halls. He headed the way carefully, avoiding the rotten timbers, with Mojmir close at his heels.

"Do you really think Nedezhda is back from the dead?" Mojmir asked.

"I know little about *Koldovstvo*."

"The human's craft? Me either."

"I don't think we are meant to." Branimir scrunched his shoulders. He might be able to manipulate his body to blend in with the world around him, but he could not manipulate the elements like a Highborn.

Branimir slowed his pace as they neared Lord Kinhar's chambers.

"Maybe she was not killed," Mojmir suggested. "I don't think you can return from the dead once you are…dead."

"Her head was chopped off, Mojmir." Branimir's tone was dry.

"Yeah, but maybe—"

"Shut it, Mojmir."

Kinhar's chamber was narrow and uneven with the north wall shorter than the south. It was evident that water dripped frequently in the room, causing mold and stalactites to form on the ancient stones. The smoke from the flames in a center fire pit touched Branimir's nostrils before escaping through a hole in the wall. He suddenly found himself distracted with thoughts of burning hair.

Lightning flashed again and Branimir jerked his head to the window. The southeast tower was visible but Branimir could not see much else. Several footsteps trudged across the ground below, accompanied by frantic shouting.

"You have returned. I hope that you did not tarry in your

task." Kinhar sat in his stitched robes hunched on a stone chair on a raised dais. Oil lamps sat on either side of the throne-like seat for better lighting. His hair was still knotted in the back, his beard shrouding his torso. Standing behind him was a man and two women.

Again, Branimir found it hard to look at the powerful Highborn, and distracted himself by drifting his gaze throughout the chamber. Dormant tables were misplaced throughout the room, awkwardly positioned with piles of scrolls and books strewn over them. The place was a mess.

"What do you mean?" Mojmir muddled.

"When burning the hair? Did you waste time?"

"We burned..." Mojmir tried again, "We...burned it..."

Branimir interrupted, "We did not tarry, my Lord."

"Do not lie to me, Kras, or I will have your head."

Branimir squinted, unsure of how he may have failed the Highborn.

"What have you come to tell me?"

"The Bukavac are coming from the Crags. Dorofej and Jhar say that Nedezhda has returned for revenge."

Sighing, Kinhar leaned forward, gripping an ash branch that suddenly seemed to appear from the sleeve of his filthy green and white tunic. He stood as straight as he could. The stave helped him maintain balance. Carefully, the old man hobbled toward the fire.

"My Lord," Branimir raised his tone, "Nedezhda has come back from the Netherworld. She will kill us all!"

"I am aware, Branimir Baran." Kinhar shuffled closer toward the fire pit, and sighed. "This should not have happened. This was only a sacrifice." The old man's voice was eerily calm at a whisper, but it was the use of Branimir's full name that gave him chills.

Branimir hung to Kinhar's words. Taking Nedezhda's head was meant to be a punishment, not a sacrifice.

"Falmagon, Katerina, Faina," Kinhar muttered to the

room. "Jhar and Dorofej will need your assistance. Help rouse those who are not already awake. The Bukavac have likely reached the outer walls by now."

Branimir gawked at the familiar Highborn making their exit from the room.

Falmagon was a young man with a pointed nose over a thick mustache. Like Mojmir, this human was also missing his left eye. The gaping hole in his skull was covered with a piece of cloth tied back under his scraggly, brown hair. He spoke with unyielding respect to the older Highborn, "As you wish, Kinhar."

The middle-aged woman, Faina, went to the window and peered out at the courtyard fifteen feet down. She glanced back to Kinhar, the firelight outlining the wrinkles at the corners of her mouth. Her gaze was undeniably filled with concern. Without a word, she leaped from the window to the ground below.

Katerina dipped her head but also held her tongue. The woman was the youngest Highborn at Melkorka, arriving only a few months ago from Arkaim. Her hair was dark brown much like her large eyes. She was too young to have ever seen one of the frozen demons, let alone battle against them. Of course, no one had fought the Bukavac in almost a century. It was no wonder Katerina stumbled over her own feet before squeezing through the door after Falmagon.

Branimir stayed with her until she faded from sight, paying less attention to Falmagon and Faina. Katerina often had shown kindness to him, even smiling in his direction from time to time. She held no smile now.

"Are you not going to join the battle, Kras? This moment will likely change the world. You may yet be recorded in the history of men."

Branimir mirrored Mojmir's blank stare. Kinhar could not be serious. Branimir would have less than nothing to offer against the giant demons of the Netherworld.

Mojmir was the first to break the silence. "Is that an order, my Lord?" The quiver in his voice was unmistakable.

Kinhar tilted his head for a moment as if hearing a whisper in his ear. "No, not at all. No, I do not command men or women, human or otherwise, to their death."

Branimir eyed the window, where the Highborn would engage in battle against the Bukavac. Victory or not, from the stories he had heard of demons, several Highborn would be die in this fight, and at the direction of their fearless leader.

With a gulp, Branimir decided to keep his mouth closed. Either the spearhead of the Highborn was speaking in jest, or he was delusional.

Mojmir was less wise. "You just chopped off Nedezhda's head."

Kinhar raised his thick brow in surprise at the Kras's boldness. A frown formed under the man's hairy face, disgruntled in trying to provide reason to a slave. Bran wondered if the explanation was for his benefit and not for Mojmir. "Nedezhda's choices led her to that fate. The command for her execution came down from Dahz the Lightbringer."

"The Sun God, the Protector of Men, told you to kill Nedezhda?" Mojmir scrunched up his face. The Kras was actually challenging the spearhead of the Highborn.

"Yes."

"What could she have—"

"Mojmir, shut it!" Branimir hissed between clenched teeth.

"If you had not killed her then the Bukavac would not have come!"

Branimir jumped at the crash of splitting wood. It sounded from outside, suggesting the wooden gates had been smashed. Shouts and cries of combat sounded through the window. Instant screams of men and roars of beasts followed.

"You will kill us all!" Mojmir cried out.

Branimir puffed out his cheeks and turned to hit Mojmir with his fist. The shorter Kras turned to look at him. Branimir hastily pointed to his good two eyes and then made a small fist.

Mojmir's mouth gaped open with confusion. He mouthed the single word. "What?"

"Who cut out your eye, Mojmir?" Branimir said just loud enough for his friend to hear.

"Uh…" He uncomfortably mumbled, twisting his neck to look back at Kinhar.

Kinhar was too old to make out their murmurs. He rambled, "Nedezhda defied the will of Dahz and used *Koldovstvo* as an *Eretik*. Any practice of death magic is an atrocity only to be punished with death. Her execution was judged correctly by the gods, as evidenced by her rise from the frozen Netherworld with these demon spawn." Kinhar's voice trailed. "This must be a test from the Lightbringer."

Mojmir bowed his head. "I see, Lord…um…Kinhar, my Lord. Forgive my stupidity."

"To forgive a fool is to be a fool!" Kinhar's voice was harsh, unbecoming of an old man. "I have no time to deal with it now. Move to the window, out of my way, and out of my sight. I have little time."

Branimir and Mojmir stepped away from the tables and fire pit, where Kinhar hurriedly began to dig through scrolls, searching for something. Branimir moved next to the single window in the room and stood up on his tippy-toes to peer outside.

Twenty of the Highborn were strategically placed across the courtyard and in the towers. Branimir could see fires from torchlight to light the grounds for the Highborn. He imagined most of Melkorka was darkened by the night, shadow on shadow. For him, he could see everything.

The wooden gates were destroyed as expected. The fallen Highborn were already speckled in heaps with dead Bukavac.

Bodies littered Melkorka. The numbers of the beasts were overwhelming though, pressing through the gates like flooding waters. He could not see the end to their army across the terrain beyond the gates. The Bukavac bled out from the Crags like a wound that could not be healed.

The demonic, man-shaped creatures were truly from horror dreams. Each Bukavac stood twice as tall as any Highborn. With a simple leap, any of them could reach the window ledge leading into the chamber where Branimir hid. Fortunately, none of their size would be able to fit through the opening without tearing out the stone wall.

"And to think I always wanted to see giants…" Branimir said to himself.

The faces of the Bukavac were etched in fanged snarls, teeth longer than Branimir's torso. Their weapons were not made from copper or bronze, but of a stronger substance that they gripped between their three fingers and thumb. These weapons had never been seen at Melkorka. Branimir did not know what they were, but they looked sharp and dangerous. He could only guess they had been forged in the Netherworld, the home of these demons.

The fires in Melkorka's courtyard reflected off the bluish-white bodies of the Bukavac, colored like snowfall on the Eve of Frost. The light illuminated their blue-grey eyes, like the precious gems of the underearth.

War cries echoed again and again across the demonic ranks. Screams of agony mixed with valiant shouts from the Highborn were nearly silenced in the uproar. Nothing was louder than the soul-shattering sound of death's undertone.

The lightening that once again ricocheted through the pastel clouds illuminated the battleground below and above. Branimir squeaked holding his body closer to the uneven wall in Kinhar's chamber. He could feel the broken rock crumble away from the aged stones as he pressed harder. His skilled ears heard them as they collided with the worn floor.

The few Highborn against hundreds of Bukavac crafted the energy of flame, stone, sky and sea. Waves from the Strega's Deep crashed into the courtyard. Fire and rock erupted from the ground. Still, the demons spread into Melkorka. Nothing could stop them. For every fallen Bukavac, three more seemed to take its place.

"Look, Bran!" Mojmir squealed, staring out the window with a pointed finger, "Lord Jhar and Lord Dorofej are still alive."

"Quiet, Mojmir," Branimir said softly, shadowing Mojmir's gesture. "You will draw attention to us."

Mojmir was right. The two Highborn were fighting against the Bukavac. Jhar and Dorofej stood with three other Highborn against the base of the east tower, facing more demons than they had fingers among the lot of them.

Jhar held the frontline, wielding his wooden staff between his left and right hand with exceptional speed. He frequently slammed the stick against the ground, causing the clouds of dust to rise into the air. These small particles circled around him and whirled like a sandstorm, with some of its pieces enlarging to the size of flagstones. The larger chunks of earth were then manipulated by Jhar with a wave of his hand, thrown into the Bukavac like a stone from a sling.

Branimir screeched as bodies exploded and limbs were severed. The death was rampant but he could not turn his eyes away. The magic was magnificent.

As more Bukavac filled the courtyard, Falmagon joined the five men, using his own crooked staff in a similar fashion. With his one eye, Falmagon peered decisively at the demons, striking his own staff into the dirt. Walls of earth erupted across the courtyard forcing the Bukavac to funnel to the tower and away from the keep where Branimir was hiding.

He could only think Falmagon tried to protect Kinhar.

Lightning zig-zagged again, but this time it struck at the ground. The bolt tore through one man near Jhar.

Branimir gasped.

The man's cry echoed above the sounds of battle as the tormenting fire ripped through his chest and out of his back. Blood sprayed from the gaping hole.

"Andrik…" Mojmir wept in recognition.

Dorofej's gritty voice was heard above the battle, echoing Mojmir's murmurs. "Andrik!" The old man sprang to the fallen Highborn burning from the lightning bolt. In a heap of his heavy enigmatic robes, he knelt in the pool of blood.

Branimir became fixated on the scene, watching in absolute horror.

"Leave him!" It may have been Falmagon who instructed Dorofej. Branimir could not be certain.

Dorofej ignored the words. His frail hands sank deep into Andrik's flesh, blood surged over his shaking hands.

Branimir tuned into Dorofej's whispered words despite the raging battle. They sounded ancient, flowing like a song. A glow of red and yellow glowed beneath Andrik's skin as Dorofej manipulated *Koldovstvo*. As the spell increased in complexity, a clear difference presented itself in Dorofej. The Highborn began to show signs of increased aging. Additional wrinkles formed under his eyes, and his hair lightened and lengthened. His skin sunk against his bones, and his voice rasped and croaked. Bran would not have been surprised if his very bone was turning to ash beneath the flesh.

"Dorofej!" Jhar pulled the old man away from Andrik's body. "You'll kill yourself!"

"No." Dorofej fought against Jhar's grip, but was too weak to struggle. His eyes scanned the body of Andrik. The flesh had mended considerably, but a gaping hole remained from chest to back. The damage to the body was too great.

"The man is dea—" Jhar began, before an arrow the size of his staff tore through his skull. The younger man's body collapsed on top of Dorofej, crushing the old Highborn to the ground.

"No!" Dorofej screamed.

"No!" Branimir echoed.

Mojmir grabbed him and pulled him away from the window. "*Koldovstvo* has its cost. Life for power."

"I know," Branimir teared up. "But, Lord Dorofej…"

"He was willing to pay the price."

Branimir pushed Mojmir off him and jumped back to the window. Dorofej was motionless under the body of Jhar. He could not believe it.

It was now Falmagon that took charge of the Highborn and directed the battle. The Bukavac began to bust through the walls of earth with their fists instead of following the path Falmagon had formed. Branimir saw Katerina and Faina near the one-eyed Highborn. It was evident Katerina had nearly exhausted herself; her features had drastically changed from a young woman to one closer to Faina's age.

"They are all going to die." Branimir quivered.

Mojmir asked the question needing answered, "But, if she has returned, where is Nedezhda?"

"Get back." Branimir grabbed Mojmir and pulled him down from the window. A Bukavac drew near the opening in the keep.

His question was forgotten.

Branimir peaked carefully at the glimmering beast. It was seemingly made of stone, iced over, standing just short of the ledge. The sharpened sword he carried would easily split Branimir in two, maybe three. Mojmir quickly disappeared entirely, his body fading so none could see him, save Branimir.

Branimir copied Mojmir's actions, physically vanishing from sight, as was the way of the Kras.

He was surprised by the overwhelming stench of burnt flesh reeking from the demon. The Bukavac seemed to be layer on layer of frozen skin. He turned to Mojmir ever so slightly, pleased to see his friend also was discontent with the smell.

Mojmir heaved a sigh as the Bukavac marched past. Mojmir waited several seconds after the demon was out of sight before reappearing.

"That was close," Mojmir said.

Branimir nodded and became visible once more.

Mojmir sighed looking across the courtyard, "Not many Highborn left."

Kinhar, whom Branimir had nearly forgotten about, barked at them, "If you two do not keep your mouths shut, I am going to cut your tongues out."

Branimir and Mojmir exchanged a simple look. The threat did not have to be repeated. Lord Kinhar continued to move around the room from table to table, muttering under his breath.

The battle continued in the courtyard of Melkorka, ever increasing in vigor and ferocity. As the Bukavac advanced through the corridors of Melkorka, across the courtyard, and within the towers, the body count seemed incalculable. Screams and shrieks were carried throughout the air. The cream-colored blood of the Bukavac mixed with the crimson blood of the Highborn. Death painted the grass and stone of Melkorka.

The footsteps outside of Kinhar's chambers were heard by Branimir several seconds before Kinhar lifted his head toward the wooden door. Branimir vanished again, hiding himself before the door opened. Mojmir followed suit.

Kinhar, on the other hand, balanced himself with his ash branch and hobbled back to the fire pit. He waited for the door to open.

Nedezhda came through the door delicately. Her grace was unexpected, considering all that had taken place in the courtyard thus far. But the door slowly opened, barely creaking. The undead woman stepped through as though she had been personally invited, and closed the door behind her.

In a moment of silence, as the living stared into the icy

gaze of the dead, Branimir considered Nedezhda, a shadow of her old self. Her eyes were still bright blue, and her nose was still diminutive above her wide mouth. Yet her hair had become disheveled and discolored with the consistency of algae on a pond's surface. Though, the black stitches circling her neck are what held Branimir's gaze. Her head must have been reattached to her body in the Netherworld.

"Death comes to all of us, Kinhar," She stepped a foot closer, smiling at the old man.

Her dark robe hung loosely over her pale flesh. The blood blotching her visible skin was clearly not her own.

"Killing me will be no easy task, Nedezhda," Kinhar raised himself up as best he could, his long white hair still fastened in knots behind his head. His lie was not convincing. "I was long prepared for your return, well before your beheading this evening."

"This evening?" Nedezhda paused, flicking her tongue against her lip. "I have been dead for years upon year, waiting in the Netherworld to return to Aenar. The valleys of the dead are overflowing with legions."

Kinhar harrumphed. "Even in death, you are a fool. The *Kadari* will strike you down still!"

Nedezhda looked amused. "At last, you speak of your little secrets? Though, it is too late! The *Kadari* and all of Aenar will be dust when I am through, Kinhar." She clenched her webbed fingers into fists at her side. Nedezhda's smile faded from her pastel face. She did not wane. Never had a woman been so full of hate.

Kinhar stood with his head high, showing no sign of defending himself. "You will not succeed, Nedezhda. Why do you come back from the Netherworld? Does Marheena banish you from her sight? Return to your Seamstress of Nightmares, accept your fate, and leave the living alone. Not even the Ash Tree can save you."

Nedezhda scoffed. "Banished? My army of Bukavac

grows with Marheena's blessing. I prepare the way for the Likhyi. I have defiled the roots of your petty tree, and I will cut down its girth in the Waters of Life. Humankind will suffer at my hand as I did at yours. I will steal away their breath."

"I will not allow it."

"You cannot stop the will of the gods, Kinhar."

"You are no god. You are an *Eretik*!"

"I am the hand of Marheena," Nedezhda said in a deadly whisper. "I am closer to the gods than you have ever been. I have done what no other has had the strength to do. You killed me because you feared my knowledge and my power." Nedezhda assailed upon Kinhar. "Now, in death, I am a Lord and you will be my slave."

She waved her right hand at Kinhar. Lightning blasted through the window, striking the ground in front of the old man. As he stepped back, Nedezhda waved her hand, using *Koldovstvo* to throw the frail body of Kinhar backwards near his makeshift throne. Kinhar took his time returning to his feet.

He sighed brushing himself off. "A simple spell for such a powerful *Eretik*," Kinhar said with amusement. He waved his own hands forward with a whisper and fire flung from the two oil lamps, raining toward Nedezhda. Yet, before a drop of fire touched her fair skin, a blue orb surrounded her and deflected the fire.

"You waste my time. Will you kill me again? I am already dead!" Nedezhda mumbled inconceivable words. A Bukavac's mighty fist slammed into the base of the window to the courtyard. The stones from Crags of Kazimir that formed the walls of Melkorka shattered.

Branimir and Mojmir flickered into sight for a brief instant before regaining their control and hiding again. The two Kras fled from the window and the Bukavac, hiding behind the powerful Highborn and his stone seat.

Kinhar smirked as he clamped his hands together firmly.

The Bukavac fell back from the window, its body smashing lifelessly against the ground. "You die as a demon, Nedezhda, and your soul is erased from existence."

"Only in the Netherworld! Kill me in this world all you want; I will simply return to the Netherworld. I can come fight you for eternity."

"And, for eternity, I will murder you," his aged voice cracked.

"Unlikely, old man."

A black blade erupted from the palm of Nedezhda. With a simple word, the blade swung toward Kinhar as though wielded by an invisible swordsman. Kinhar's eyes widened only briefly before he took the defensive. Kinhar barely dodged and ducked from the sword's attacks, watching Nedezhda from the corner of his eye. Nedezhda continued to manipulate the energy of the living world and in moments ice was plummeting from the ceiling.

Kinhar grabbed his staff in a firm grip and stumbled toward the fire pit, crying out in a language never heard by any man, dead or alive. He twisted and turned, all the while staying clear of the deadly blade from the Netherworld. A ball of ice smashed against his left shoulder. He fell to a knee, but pressed forward to the flames. Several scrolls from the tables were flung into the fire, turning the flames from plum and cerulean to scarlet and olive. In a final jaunt, Kinhar fell into the colored blaze.

A light brighter than high sun at midday, a hundred times over, flashed within the room. Thunder, greater than a thousand warhorses stampeding, resounded against the walls within Kinhar's chambers. *Koldovstvo* was ancient, as old as the gods themselves, known by many and mastered by few. Kinhar was a master.

The ice continued to fall. The black blade continued to strike. Yet, where an old decaying man once stood, there now stood a youthful man. The ash branch that was used as his staff was gone, but Kinhar stood, nearly limitless in his power. His long white hair was gone, replaced with thick black strands. His lip and chin were clean shaven as though hair had never touched his face. Where delicate muscles once barely framed his skin, muscle on muscle now bulged from the coarse cloth. If time could be measured without limitation, he looked to be a hundred years younger.

Without the limitations presented by old age, Kinhar effortlessly tumbled away from the falling balls of ice and spoke a word, raising three blades of his own around his body. The silver swords that he conjured defended against the black blade, giving him an opportunity to focus on his own casting, a lifetime of *Koldovstvo* was suddenly available to him.

Arrows of flame manifested from behind Kinhar and flew at Nedezhda swiftly. Nedezhda conjured small shields of stone and blocked the arrows. Kinhar called on the winds from the north and the waters from the sea, pulling their power into the small room, creating a storm any seafaring man would fear. Nedezhda transformed the wind into a breeze and the water to fog. Nothing could touch the dead sorceress.

She laughed, "You will kill yourself. The aging effects of magic only affect the living."

"So be it!" Kinhar said, already ten years older in a matter of minutes.

"So be it," Nedezhda repeated menacingly.

Nedezhda and Kinhar unleashed energy at one another while their swords danced about them. More lightning and fire fell along with ice and stone.

Branimir screamed among the madness.

The room was destroyed. Scrolls burned, embers floated and the tables were overturned or in ashes. The two, one living and one dead, attacked and defended. Their war was personal. It was eternal.

In the end, Branimir found himself huddled in the corner of the room, not knowing what to do but clutch Mojmir in terror when he heard footsteps racing outside Kinhar's chamber.

Faina burst through the door with far less subtlety than Nedezhda. She had more wrinkles on her face from using *Koldovstvo*. The redheaded woman immediately joined the fight, raising her finger at Nedezhda, repeatedly speaking words as song.

Nedezhda, taken by surprise, flung the black sword at Faina away from the silver swords.

Faina cried out in surprise as the blade plunged deep into her right shoulder, stopping *Koldovstvo* from flowing off her tongue. The blade dissolved into ashes. Blood spilled.

"No!" Katerina lunged into the chamber immediately after Faina.

She tried to grab Faina to pull her to safety, but Nedezhda was ready this time. She grasped a handful of Katerina's dark hair with a greasy, webbed hand. Poor Katerina, who had been a young lady only hours before, cried out. Her round, brown eyes widened with terror.

With a fitful cry, Nedezhda flung Katerina through the gaping hole in the chamber wall toward the Bukavac who continued to crowd the courtyard. The dark-haired woman was caught midair between two Bukavac and torn in half at the waist. No scream left her innocent lips. She was forever silenced.

Kinhar hurled his three swords through the air at Nedezhda, but not quickly enough. The woman dodged them effortlessly as they hit the stone wall behind her and fell to the ground.

"You kill your own brethren, Nedezhda!" Kinhar screamed.

"You killed me, Kinhar," she said.

"You disobeyed the law!" Kinhar roared, clenching his fists.

Nedezhda's face went from calm to fury. "Your law!"

The copper dagger called *kaelandur* suddenly plunged through the stitches of Nedezhda's neck, taking her life for the second time. Her head toppled to the floor, quickly obscured by her collapsing body. Pasty white blood poured across the old timber flooring.

Falmagon stood erect, holding *kaelandur* firmly in his right fist, the crooked staff held by his left. He used the dagger to motion at Kinhar before replacing it at his belt. The Highborn said nothing regarding Kinhar's change in appearance. "We must flee or we will join the dead."

"We cannot flee," Faina muttered, trying to pull herself up from the ground only to fall back to her knees. "This is Melkorka and Nedezhda will return shortly from the Netherworld. We must defend Melkorka! The prophecy..."

"No. Falmagon is right," Kinhar said. "The *Kadari* must find a way to kill Nedezhda permanently. Until then, we must find and protect the Ash Tree. If she destroys it then the entire world will die! This is our duty now."

Branimir shuddered. He did not know what the *Kadari* was, but he had heard of the Ash Tree. Legends said that it gave life to the world of the living and the non-living, sitting within the Waters of Life, stretching across all worlds.

The one-eyed Highborn sniffed. "Then you must lead us there, Kinhar."

"First, we go to Arkaim to see Erzebeth for guidance."

"Come! Dorofej has horses." Falmagon grabbed ahold of Faina's robes and pulled her to her feet. She used him as support, trying to ignore the blood flowing down her front.

"I'm weak..." Faina collapsed into Falmagon's shoulder. He caught her, sweeping her up into his arms.

"Dorofej is dead," Mojmir cried. The Kras came into view, materialized from his hiding place. Branimir joined him without a word.

"Dorofej took the tunnels north," Falmagon claimed assuredly. "He waits for our escape."

"I watched him die," Mojmir screeched in his squeaky voice. "We both did!"

"Bah!" Kinhar stormed up to Mojmir's side, grabbing him by his child-sized head. In a quick motion, he snapped the neck of the small creature.

The Kras fell to the ground dead.

Branimir froze in fear, staring at the lifeless body of his kin. He did not hear Kinhar speak to him the second time, or even third. The world spun, nearly knocking him to one knee.

"Answer me or your fate will be the same as his," Kinhar growled, obviously irritated by asking more than once. "Are you a fool, too?"

"No..." Branimir stammered, "No, my Lord." He could not bring himself to look at the face of the young Highborn, who had appeared to be only a few breaths away from death an hour ago.

"Good. Then you will continue to serve me. Say anything to Dorofej of the *Kadari* and it will be your death."

"Yes, Lord Kinhar," Branimir wept.

Kinhar turned his attention to his companions, "To the tunnels, Falmagon. Consider Melkorka fallen."

Branimir followed the Highborn obediently.

Chapter IV

Branimir was awakened by the red glare of the horizon against his eyelids. His body slumped against Kinhar's back as they trotted along the coastline on a brown horse. He rubbed his eyes wearily.

His first thoughts were of Mojmir. His second were of himself. Mourning the dead would not help him this day or the next; his father had told him that. Besides, Branimir was certain Mojmir's fate would prove to be one of luck compared to what he was about to endure. He was not sure how he could be so exhausted when he had not actually done any of the fighting.

Faina and Falmagon were riding to the left on their own horses. Faina was unconscious and slouched over with more blood on her robes than fabric. Falmagon led both mounts with a single hand, while keeping Faina on her horse with his other. His one eye was fixated on the sands ahead of them.

Dorofej marked the rear, still shrouded in his dark robes. The man was brittle, barely maintaining the strength to sit on his own brown horse. It was only hoped that some strength might return to the old man. The reigns were wrapped repeatedly around his wrists and the horn of the saddle, assuring that he stayed atop the animal.

Branimir did not think any of the three men had slept

during the night.

"When we reach Narthwich," Kinhar began, "We need to obtain a boatman to take us to Kalamaar."

"We need an herbal healer for Faina," Falmagon said. "She is fortunate to have stayed alive this long. Who knows the sorcery of the death blade that pierced her flesh? Dorofej cannot heal her with *Koldovstvo*. The old man is far too weak and we do not have the right bloodline."

"Even if with the strength, it is likely nothing can heal her beyond the Waters of Life, yes? And, we know not where to find such a thing, whether myth or truth is quite uncertain, it is."

Kinhar spoke over his shoulder, "It must be truth, Dorofej. Nedezhda seeks it with the purpose of destroying the Ash Tree. She said as much last night. We are charged with protecting this world and that means we must keep the Ash Tree safe! Erzebeth is in Arkaim. She will provide us the guidance needed to stop the *Eretik*."

"Kinhar, you do not know the way?" Dorofej wheezed. His voice was guttural, giving suggestion he barely had any life left within him.

The spearhead of the Highborn gave pause. "How could I know the way? No living man knows the way."

"Yet," Dorofej's bushy eyebrows lifted, "You have a youth about you that only the Ash Tree could provide. Only yesterday you had more wrinkles on your face than I do between my thighs, yes?"

"Watch your mouth, Dorofej," Kinhar glared threateningly under the dark locks that bespoke of the youth Dorofej perceived.

Dorofej pressed with a tilted chin. "Erzebeth is who precisely? In all my years, I have never heard her name mentioned in the halls of Melkorka."

"She is a friend. That is all you need to know."

"I see," Dorofej slumped back into his saddle in apparent defeat.

Kinhar did not seem to notice, and returned to his original point. "Regardless, Faina will not make it to the Waters of Life by any means. That type of luck is unheard of in history, myth, or legend."

Falmagon pulled the woman firmly onto her saddle as she began to slip. "Tell me, what can we do, Kinhar? I cannot carry her for eternity on her saddle."

"She should stay at Narthwich, and let Dahz decide her fate."

Branimir noticed Dorofej lift his hand to object before second guessing himself. The old man's eyes locked onto Branimir. The dissatisfied look on his face was unmistakable, even beneath the braided white beard shielding his thin lips.

"May Dahz look kindly upon her in this life and the next," Falmagon said.

They rode the rest of the distance in the company of the waves that crashed against the shoreline. The dark blue waters lashed against each other in an endless war.

Branimir knew a little about Narthwich. It was a worn city of few buildings against the coast that stood adjacent to the mainland of Kalamaar. The village was small, fitted for the poor fishermen residing there. Branimir could see the entire village from the hilltop, including the docks stretching into Strega's Deep. Long boats with oars and simple sails called faerings, built from the inland trees, lined either side of the wooden platforms extending over the water.

Kinhar led them down the hill at a gallop, unnecessarily demonstrating the calamity that had befallen them. There was more urgency in his actions in this moment than Branimir had witnessed in the past day, even when slinging magic against Nedezhda. The Kras held tightly onto Kinhar's robes as he raced down the hillside on the horse. Once within earshot, Kinhar raised his voice, shouting at the villagers to fetch Jarl Avar. Seeing the Highborn riding down the hillside set the people of Narthwich into action, not questioning the motives of the so-called guardians of the Seven Islands. The Highborn, although often secluded from civilization, were not strangers to the races of regular men.

Branimir had the fleeting thought that the people may think less of the Highborn if they knew the atrocities that had been committed. It was hard to be called guardian when responsible for unleashing the dead and worse upon the world.

"Jarl!" Kinhar halted the horses in front of the great hall that marked center to Narthwich. He used the common title for the chief of small settlements. The position was respectable, generally appointed by the King.

Immediately a man bounded from the door, holding hilt in hand to the copper sword at his belt. The Kras shifted his attention quickly away from the weapon that reminded him of *kaelandur*, the cause of all their problems.

The Jarl's hair was curled and wild, along with the scruffy beard that prickled his chin. The villagers that had run ahead had done well in conveying the alarm. The man looked like he had just been pulled out of bed.

"Highborn, I am Jarl Likshol Avar of Narthwich. We witnessed fires in the sky late last eve from Melkorka, knowing not what in the Nine Lands had befallen its stone walls. What has happened?"

"Bukavac have bled from the Crags and have taken Melkorka. We are all that remain."

Whispers erupted around them from the villagers who gathered around Kinhar on his horse and Jarl Avar. The seed of fear had been planted with such few words.

"Who are you exactly? Is that one of the demons on the back of your mount?" the Jarl asked cautiously, pointing at Branimir.

Branimir gasped in astonishment, keeping his hands from covering his face. Humans and Kras had shared the Seven Islands for centuries before being enslaved by the Highborn. He knew some may mistake him as a demon, but he expected those on the same island to know his kind.

"I am Kinhar Sayan of Melkorka, and—"

"Kinhar Sayan?" the Jarl pulled at his sword, "Although I know not the man, I am quite familiar with the name. Kinhar was known by my father thirty years ago, marking him a man much more aged than you."

Kinhar started again, "I—"

Dorofej interrupted, "You are as wise as your father, my Lord. I am Kinhar Sayan of Melkorka. This Highborn speaks in my stead to protect me from those who may wish an old man harm. Lies are not becoming of the Highborn, but such precautions must be taken after the loss we have experienced. You understand, yes?"

Jarl Avar released his hilt with a respectful nod. "What of the demon on the horse?"

Dorofej shook his head. "No, my Lord. That is a Kras, a loyal servant of the Highborn. You may never find a more loyal creature."

Again, whispers resounded in the crowd.

"My apologies," the Jarl faltered, sliding his hands to his waist. "I did not know the Kras were still in existence."

Dorofej nodded, taking a moment to look at Branimir, "He may very well be the last of their number."

Branimir choked at the statement. He turned from the Jarl and Dorofej, burying his face in the musty robes of Kinhar. The truth had not struck him until this moment and it made his heart hurt. He was the last of his kind.

"May your future deeds bespeak of your race as honorable and glorious, Kras," Jarl Avar stumbled for the right words.

Branimir steadied his voice as best as he was able. "My thanks, my Lord."

The Jarl dipped his head, as was custom, and turned back to Dorofej. "Demons from the mountains, you say? What numbers? Do they come this way?"

"Their numbers are unknown, Jarl. As for now, your

people are safe in Narthwich. There has been no sign of pursuit through the night, but the beasts must not be allowed to cross to Kalamaar."

"What do you need from us, Kinhar?"

Dorofej licked his lips, taking a moment to reflect on the leveled gaze Kinhar gave him. There was no mystery in its meaning. "Lady Faina Zholdan will be left in your care without charge. I say, she will likely pass in the night, and we would ask for a proper burial."

The Jarl signaled for two of the villagers to take Faina from the horse as Dorofej spoke. The redheaded woman was slumped into the arms of a mid-sized man who quickly carried her into the great hall. Branimir could not help but notice the villagers shrinking back from him as though he were a demon, too. Bran swore he could hear whispers in the gathering crowd about his skin and his ears.

Branimir tried to focus on the negotiation between Dorofej and the Jarl.

"A faering is requested to cross the pass to the mainland. Our horses can be payment, if that suits you well enough, yes?"

"For what purpose?"

Dorofej was quick of tongue. "Support from Arkaim and to inform the King, of course. The people of the Seven Islands must be protected from the shade of the Netherworld."

"Of course!" the Jarl exclaimed. "We will fetch rations for the journey. Delcho and Lel can take you across Strega's Deep."

Kinhar broke in, "That will be unnecessary."

"Nonsense! It is completely necessary. It will take half a day or more, depending on the Nine Winds. Let us pray that Strega's breath is strong in such desperate times.

"Indeed," Dorofej agreed.

"It is likely you will travel on land to Arkaim or find route on ship at Valishul upland. I can spare shana to help with any cost that you may endure. As I recall, the Highborn rarely have coin in their pockets."

Branimir's jaw nearly hit the horses back. Silver pieces, or shana, were scarce on the Seven Islands.

"Your generosity is well received, Jarl Avar. You truly are your father's son," Dorofej said sincerely. "Your benevolence is to be echoed to King Merreider Kar in Arkaim, it will."

Branimir watched incredulously as Dorofej spoke like a true Highborn. The knowledge under the wrinkled skin of the old man was astonishing. The mere happenstance that Dorofej would know the name of the King of Arkaim, when, to knowledge, he had not stepped foot from Melkorka in half a century was beyond Branimir.

The Jarl said, "You just be assured that you come back. Please do not leave my people at the hands of demons and worse."

"I say, our intent is to return, Jarl," Dorofej visibly shuddered. "But send a message along the Seven Islands to the other villages, you will. Jaoarr. Geirland. Refsstaoir. As far as Mjovadalsa if you can spare it, yes?"

The Jarl raised his hand to stop Dorofej, "You frighten my people, Kinhar. What are you expecting?"

Kinhar attempted to silence Dorofej. "He is fatigued. Prepare the faering and supplies so we can be on our way."

Dorofej's blue eyes locked onto the Jarl's with certainty beyond certainty. Branimir found himself squirming in the saddle, shivering well before the words escaped the old man's lips. "I expect death. Eternal war and death."

Chapter V

The faering rocked against the deep waters somewhere between Folkmar, home to Melkorka, and Kalamaar. Three of the Seven Islands of Forghar could be viewed from the aft. With Folkmar an hour behind them, appearing as a ghastly haze of smoke on the skyline, they rushed toward Kalamaar with the wind at their backs.

Branimir sat at the stern atop one of the four slats that provided seating across the deck. Kinhar, Falmagon, and Dorofej were scattered across the boat, partially asleep.

Branimir held his stomach with one hand, wishing he could join the Highborn and find some much-needed sleep. Instead, he leaned over the boat with his other hand caressing the white oak planks that overlapped on the clinker-built faering. He had never been on a vessel before, or even on the sea, despite living next to it his entire life. He was rapidly discovering that seafaring was not in his blood.

Along with exhaustion, Branimir's perception of the world around him was thwarted. The smell of saltwater and the sounds of slopping waves against the hull were overwhelming to his sensitive nose and ears. Not to mention, it was a constant reminder that if the faering upturned, Branimir would drown.

"Have another swig, Kras," the tall man from Narthwich called Lel slurred, stretching a clay jug toward him. It was as large as Branimir's head.

"Being drunk on mead will not settle my stomach or keep me afloat, Lord." Branimir decided to keep it to himself that the first drink and the second had done nothing more but burn his insides and make his eyes water.

"It just might! Get enough in your belly and you'll be rounder than a blowfish."

Branimir waved him off, feeling spew welling up in his throat.

"Kras, it is just honey and water. It will calm your nerves. Before you know it, the ocean will be riding you."

Branimir squinted at the seafaring man, swallowing vomit, looking for some hint of humor in the man's bloodshot eyes. "Excuse me, my Lord. What does that even mean?"

"Forget him, Kras," Delcho said, taking the jug from Lel and swallowing a mouthful of the dark liquid before continuing. "Mead turned Lel's mind to mush long before you were born."

Branimir looked at the two men, who may have been in their mid-years, if not younger. He was dumbfounded, "I am fifty-six-years-old, Lord." The humans obviously knew very little about the Kras. It was likely that he was the last one of his kind, just as Dorofej had suggested.

"Ha!" Lel croaked. "Fifty-six-years-old, you say, Kras? My oldest daughter hasn't had her first bleeding and she is bigger than you!"

"Yes, Lord. All the same, it is the truth."

"Sure it is."

"It is true!" Branimir squealed, hearing the ridicule in Lel's tone.

"Don't hold to a poor joke, Kras," Delcho belched. "The two of us hear the worst from seamen. Yury. Tyoma. Genrickh. We know lying when we hear it."

"That we do! Don't go joshing about—"

"Lord, I am not—"

Delcho hollered over the top of them both. "Spending all day working your shaft does not make you a jester, that's for sure! Every seafaring man knows that much."

"Nope. It sure does not."

"Craft, I mean," Delcho roared in laughter at himself.

"What?" Lel's eyes went crooked.

Delcho slapped his bare knee beneath his cutoff trousers. "I said working your shaft instead of craft."

Lel shrugged with a sudden gleam. "No matter. You don't become a jester either way."

Delcho laughed harder with Lel echoing his mirth.

Branimir was baffled, not sure how to respond. The two were intoxicated. Before he could say anything, he felt sick again and leaned over the side of the faering to empty what mead was left in his stomach.

Lel took the mead jug back from Delcho, "Genrickh was the worst. Remember that tale he told at Ida's about the rusalki supposedly slinking aboard his boat. Said the fish woman sang and danced and kissed him; and all sorts of rubbish. Even had the gall to say *on the mouth*! What woman, half fish or otherwise, would kiss a man as ugly as Genrickh Bershov on the mouth?"

Delcho jerked the jug back before Lel could get a drink. "Jealous, were you?"

Branimir found himself grinning at the jest as Delcho polished off the jug with a large gulp and swallow. With all that had happened, the Kras found himself feeling guilty for finding enjoyment in the company of the men, and attempted to appear more solemn.

Lel watched with longing as the mead was emptied, "Hey—"

"What are you two fools blathering about?" Kinhar pulled himself upright with the gunwale at the bow of the faering.

"Highborn," Delcho garbled, "We was just making conversation to pass the time. Did not mean to wake you."

Kinhar glowered under the thick black strands of hair that fell past his ears. His deep blue eyes seemed to be as shadowy as the waters they sailed upon. The coarse grey cloth of his robe clung to the muscle that bulged from his chest and arms. "You obviously do not have the sense to grasp the significance of what we are trying to accomplish here."

Delcho and Lel had blank looks about them.

Branimir watched in astonishment as Kinhar struck Falmagon upside the head to wake him. The one-eyed man grunted, sitting up quickly with his scraggily brown hair in knots.

"We cannot be to Kalamaar yet."

"No," Kinhar said. "These two half-wits have drunk themselves stupid, needlessly endangering the success of our journey."

"That is not true," Delcho muttered, suddenly very sober. "We have never sailed without mead, and we have always found our destination."

Lel grinned like a fool, speaking in turn with absolute honesty. "Yeah...eventually."

Kinhar's expression of disapproval deepened.

Branimir waited as Kinhar and Falmagon glared across the small vessel at Lel and Delcho. What felt like an eternity passed before Kinhar twisted his head to examine Dorofej. The old man did not budge in his black robes, and as if on cue, snorted in his sleep, giving sign that he was lost in a world of dreams.

"Falmagon," Kinhar spoke softly. "The faering will reach Kalamaar all the quicker if we lighten the load."

Falmagon did not say a word. Before Branimir could react, the one-eyed Highborn grabbed the two sailors with *Koldovstvo* and flung them into Strega's Deep, beyond the reaches of the boat, beyond the sound of their bloodcurdling screams.

Branimir squealed, jumping to his feet, witnessing the undeserved murder from the Highborn men. He had heard of mankind slaughtering their own race, but it was not the Highborn way. Mojmir was easily overlooked as a Kras, but these were of the same kin as the Highborn.

Dorofej shifted in his sleep.

"Stay seated, Branimir," Kinhar threatened between clenched teeth.

The Kras kneeled slowly back to the plank, swiftly recognizing how much was outside of his control. He had served the Highborn all his life. After that much time, Branimir's free will was practically buried in the grave. He had to remember his place in this tale, no matter how it unfolded. He was the Highborn's lackey.

"Yes, Lord," Branimir whispered.

Even in this moment, Branimir thought of Mojmir and the quick death he had received. He hoped that his foolish kin had found peace in the Beyond.

For the next two hours, Dorofej slept and Falmagon used *Koldovstvo* to blow the square sail in the center of the planks. The faering sped across the waves at impressive speed, with the oars staying tucked inside the hull without purpose.

Droplets of tears had come and gone from the pale eyes of Branimir. The two Highborn men ignored him in the corner of the boat as he wept with little control. Branimir desperately wanted to sleep, but was ever fearful that he may, too, be flung into the dangerous waters of the ocean. Try as he might, Branimir could find no reason as to why Kinhar would keep him living much longer.

Dorofej coughed and sat up from his resting place against the side. The man took his time scanning the boat, stroking the braided tassels of hair that formed his beard and the long stretches of his white mustache.

His eyes held all the innocence in the world as he acknowledged Falmagon and Kinhar with a dip of his head. Branimir caught a glimpse of a sliver of a smile beneath the overgrowth on his face. After several minutes, Branimir wondered if Dorofej was going to say anything at all.

When the old man finally loosened his tongue, his words were ungainly. "Dreamt of a woman with massive breasts. Barely could convince myself to wake, so enticing they were."

Falmagon hit the butt of his crooked staff against the white oak, peering eerily at Dorofej. "Keep those dirty thoughts to yourself, old man. What is wrong with you?"

"Like large buoys floating among the waves of this ocean. Must be my mind playing tricks on me, being on this boat, yes? Yet, unequivocally massive, they were! Enough of a teat to feed a throng of children, yes? I reached out to touch the nipple, to cop a feel, if you will, to receive the treasure of treasures, before waking back to this unsightly world." Dorofej shook his head miserably, and let out an elongated sigh. "As fate would have it, swallowed them whole before I could fondle such splendor, the ocean did."

"He is mad, Kinhar," Falmagon said.

"Speak plainly, Dorofej," Kinhar demanded crossly.

"A good pair of breasts are hard to come by is all—and when they are found—well, plundering them triumphantly is impossible, yes?"

"I have no idea how to respond," Falmagon muttered.

"Moreover," Dorofej scrunched his nose, his lip curling slightly, "Our vessel has grown lighter whilst I was inhibited, yes? Then again, I am old and my mind has begun to wilt. By chance, two men from Narthwich were never aboard this faering, yes? By chance, I am not on a faering at all, yes? By chance, I am truthfully lying in my stone bed at Melkorka covered in sheep fur, dreading to hear Jhar's twitching tongue at daybreak, yes?" Dorofej cleared his throat. "Dream and reality are equally misleading, it seems."

"Enough, Dorofej! When Falmagon and I awoke, the men were no longer aboard," Kinhar lied dryly, finding no humor with Dorofej. "We know not what their fate was."

"Is that so?"

"It is so," Falmagon supported Kinhar's untruth. His face looked to be chiseled from the Crags themselves.

The boat rocked as Dorofej hobbled over to a bench and slumped down next to the Kras. He unexpectedly grabbed Branimir by the shoulder. "Branimir Baran has been weeping, yes?"

Branimir quickly wiped his eyes, finding that his eyes were watering once more. He could not look at the old man. He feared to look at Kinhar or Falmagon. With all his heart, Branimir kept his gaze on the ocean that surrounded them.

Dorofej's blue eyes were penetrating and unrelenting on the back of his head.

"I have not, Lord," Branimir lied, too. "Just tired, I think." He did not need the wrath of any of the Highborn upon him, including Dorofej.

Dorofej snickered.

"He has every reason to weep after what happened at Melkorka," Falmagon challenged, hitting his staff against the baseboard again. "We all do."

Dorofej settled back against the stern. "Quite right you are, Falmagon Sej. Where has my mind gone… to question irregularity, especially in a dreadful world of relentless regularity, yes? The men from Narthwich surely fell overboard by accident, or felt elated to take a midday swim, or grew bird parts and flew straight to the Lightbringer, yes!"

Branimir held his head in his hands, tormented by the situation. He tried to focus his energy on keeping his lips sealed.

"We may never know," Kinhar sarcasm was teeming like poison from a viper.

"No, I suppose not," Dorofej finished with a hint of peril in his own words. "Then again, it may have been a pair of bounteous breasts that beguiled them to take a plunge, yes? Luck had it that we were *each* asleep, lest accompany them, we *each* would have."

No one said another word the rest of the way to Kalamaar.

Chapter VI

Evening had set in over Kalamaar after they had landed along an abandoned shore. Kinhar had led them northwest along the coastline in hopes of reaching Valishul. After two hours of steady walking, they still had not seen any sign of life.

Dorofej declared the massive mountains lining the length of the shoreline were also called the Crags of Kazimir, needing no other name, and fell inland for miles. History suggested that the Seven Islands had adopted the name from the mainland centuries ago. It was a suitable explanation, as the Crags maintained the same red rock and grew to greater heights on Kalamaar.

With the frequent ups and downs in the terrain, they attempted to steer clear of entering the mountain range. Unfortunately, thick grasses full of thorns and burrs grew between the Crags and the water's edge, keeping movement restricted. As night set in, their advancement was slowed even more. None of them could see past their feet, save Branimir.

He could see perfectly as though it were daylight, but he had never stepped foot on Kalamaar. This left him with little ability to lead the Highborn anywhere sensible or safe.

"Should have stayed in the boat and sailed it along the coast instead of walking," Falmagon reasoned after the first couple of miles.

"Too many rocks along the coast," Kinhar said.

"Unfortunate the men who had nautical knowledge vanished, lest they could have maneuvered about them, yes?" Dorofej scoffed as he took another step forward on his weakened knees, trying to wedge his way through the grasses.

Falmagon turned to face Dorofej at his rear, "Drop it, Dorofej. It is only two men."

"Two men, it is," Dorofej's bushy eyebrows angled in the dark, only visible by Branimir, "Two men who you disregard as though they were untimely flatus expelled through your pinned anus."

"We lost more at Melkorka, you fool," Falmagon said with a sneer. "The Bukavac are coming. Why would you cause ruckus over simple men? Our concern is greater—"

"Because I am Highborn, Falmagon!" Dorofej's chin quivered slightly, from pain or rage was uncertain. He took a deep breath and flattened his voice. "It is our duty to protect. Our vows, *Koldovstvo*, and all that we have rests on our decency, yes? If the Highborn lose their way, what way can there be? I say, for over a thousand years, goodness prevailed over the enemy."

Falmagon's crooked staff inched forward as he leaned toward the bearded Dorofej. His words lingered with his foul breath. "Olden ways for olden times, old man."

Dorofej considered Kinhar at the front. Even in the dark, it was evident that the spearhead of the Highborn had nothing to add to Falmagon's sacrilege.

"Your orations fall on deaf ears, Dorofej," Falmagon spat, saliva catching the end of his long hanging mustache. "In Narthwich, you incited fear and now deliver lectures on righteousness. Mend your own compass before piddling with mine!"

"He was trying to protect them." Branimir matched Falmagon's patronizing tone in a shrill voice.

As soon as the words were said, Branimir regretted it. His

chest tightened with the sudden thumping of his heartbeat.

Falmagon abandoned the argument with Dorofej and heatedly approached Branimir with his staff raised at waist level. Branimir dropped to his knees immediately, raised his hands defensively, and dipped his head so that it barely reached Falmagon's thigh. Branimir whispered apologies and mutterings of forgiveness, ending each befuddled breath with Lord.

"The world truly is truly falling to ashes when a Kras speaks against a Highborn," Falmagon said with vehemence. The man brought the staff down across Branimir's dipped skull without hesitation.

Branimir cried out, falling forward on his face against the sharp thorns in the grass. He could already feel blood gushing from the top of his head and down over his pointed ear. He rolled over, writhing in pain. A second strike hit him across the mid-section. The thwack that reverberated was mirrored with the sound of cracking ribs.

"My...Lord..." Branimir wheezed.

Falmagon raised the staff again.

"That will be enough," Kinhar stepped over Branimir's body protectively. "I will not have the Kras harmed beyond reprieve."

Salty tears blurred Branimir's vision, as he peeked at the Highborn for a sign as to why he should be kept alive when so many others would be killed. He was most surprised when his mouth formed the same question. "Why, my Lord? Why keep me alive?"

Kinhar glimpsed at Branimir, and then lifted his eyes to the other two Highborn.

Branimir followed the gaze to look at Falmagon mid-swing, and then Dorofej, who hurriedly averted his eyes.

"We will make camp here for the night," Kinhar forestalled the question. "Dorofej, tend to the Kras."

Within the hour, Branimir was sitting under the watch

of Dorofej near a crackling fire. With a flick of Falmagon's finger, and a few thrusts of his staff against the ground, rocks had surfaced for sitting, the grass was drowned with sand, and a fire was formed in the center of a stone pit.

"Lord Dorofej," Branimir started, looking to Dorofej who inspected the gashed wound above his temple. The bleeding had stopped, but the pain made his head throb against the old man's gentle touch.

Dorofej scanned the darkness outside the fire before responding, "Speak, Branimir, swiftly and softly."

"There are many things I do not understand."

"Recognizing your ignorance makes you wiser than most, it does." Again, the bearded man peered into the darkness. Perhaps, he was assuring himself that Falmagon and Kinhar were out of earshot. They had stepped away to find something more substantial to burn with the brush.

"*Koldovstvo* has the power to do many things, and yet we still sail on a boat, walk along the shoreline, and search for firewood. Why not just do what must be done to end this madness?" Branimir said.

"*Koldovstvo* must be balanced in its use or more madness there would be. The cost is frequently greater than its benefit," Dorofej paused to look at his wrinkled hands that ran through the thin hair of the Kras. As if remembering his place, he continued, "Simple tasks as lighting this campfire may cause a Highborn to lose minutes of their life, where walking across the sea would kill them."

"I have seen Highborn grow old when casting *Koldovstvo*," Branimir licked his cracked lips, trying to fully understand. He jerked away from Dorofej's light touch again. The pain in his head far outweighed the aching at his side. "But, I have also seen Kinhar grow young."

Dorofej grunted. "Best keep that to yourself unless you like holes in your skull, yes?"

Branimir shook his head, indicating not. Dorofej's fingers

scrapping against his wound caused him to retract once more. "Can you not just mend it, Lord Dorofej? Why pick at it with your nails?"

Dorofej tilted his head at the Kras. "I am not picking, Branimir Baran. I am harvesting dirt and grass from your brains to keep you from infection. Besides, Highborn do not heal Kras, and even if it were so, I am spent. *Koldovstvo* would drain my life permanently if I were to mend you, yes? Favor dying, I do not. Wear these wounds you must, yes?"

Branimir exhaled, cupping his chin in his hands while Dorofej continued to work. Branimir returned to the prior conversation. "How then does Falmagon uses *Koldovstvo* regularly, while barely growing old, even at Melkorka against the Bukavac."

"*Habërmani* is the name of the crooked staff he clings to, yes? The inner fires of *Habërmani* feed on *Koldovstvo*; lessening the effects of aging, it does. Yet drains him to some degree, it does. While in his possession, Falmagon will steal away from the natural balance of *Koldovstvo*, yes?"

"Where would he get such a thing? Do all Highborn have such tools to wield *Koldovstvo*?"

"Be best not to ask him, yes?"

"Do you?"

The flames flickered off Dorofej's icy eyes much like they had when he had helped melt the slag to craft *kaelandur* at Melkorka. "Best not to ask me either."

Branimir turned to face the fire. "My apologies, Lord Dorofej. I am not generally one to forget my place."

Dorofej cleared his throat. "I say, you will find you are not generally one to do a lot of the things in the coming months, but do them, you will."

"Months?" Branimir gasped, "Where are we going? What do you know, Dorofej?"

Dorofej's bushy eyebrows rose keenly.

Branimir stumbled with his speech. "Lord Dorofej, I

mean."

"For now," Dorofej said. "We will go to Arkaim to see this Erzebeth that Kinhar speaks of, yes?"

Branimir could hear movement, indicating Kinhar and Falmagon were returning to the campfire. He quickly twisted his head toward the Highborn at his back. "You know why they are keeping me alive, don't you, Lord Dorofej?"

Dorofej placed a hand on either side of Branimir's child-sized head. The strength in his clasp was unexpected as he forcibly straightened Branimir to stare into the flames.

The Highborn then leaned down, shrouded in his ominous robes, sharing insight that Branimir would have never considered. "Alive at my request, you are."

Chapter VII

Falmagon kicked Branimir in his side harder than necessary, waking him an hour before the sun peaked over the water's edge. Despite the rough awakening, Branimir was thankful the Highborn had not connected with his sore ribcage. He did not want to check with Falmagon standing around, but he was sure the swelling and bruising had gotten worse.

He groaned and sat upright. His head ached something fierce from the thrashing with *Habërmani*. Before he could lift his hand to touch the tender flesh, three dead rabbits flopped in his lap. Branimir sighed, taking the hint that he was meant to clean and cook them for the morning meal.

He spent the next half hour pulling fur from flesh and turning the meat over the fire, while Falmagon watched him like a guard over a thief. Branimir was not sure what to make of the Highborn's behavior, but he felt uneasy and unwelcomed. Up until now, he had little to no interaction with Falmagon. The one-eyed man was frequently gone from Melkorka, doing only the gods knew what.

If a thousand questions had sat idle in Branimir's mind the night prior, there were ten thousand more this morning. Branimir had known each Highborn to be secretive, as was their way, but he had assumed their confusing actions were due to his lack of understanding and position. After all, they were humans and he was a Kras. They were masters and he was a slave. He had never questioned their motives, always certain to act in accordance with their commands. Though, he had never been a pawn to be played in their schemes either. Even now, he could not be certain that was the case, but Dorofej wanted him alive and Kinhar had allowed him to live. None of it made any sense.

"You keep thinking that hard, and you are liable to have your brain bleed from your ears, Kras," Falmagon said. "If the Lightbringer wanted you to be thinking, you wouldn't be a slave."

Branimir kept his expression as blank as physically possible. His pale eyes did not flinch in the slightest. "Yes, my Lord."

Falmagon scoffed with a shake of his head. After another long look, he turned his attention from Branimir, seemingly bored in watching him cook.

As the sky lightened to a teal and pink, Falmagon began to dig through his pack, holding the supplies from Narthwich. He dumped it out on the ground, taking the inventory before they set off for the day. There were several wraps of dried meat and unleavened bread as well as a fishing line with hooks. There also were two coin purses of shana, a curved blade called a kinzhal, and a case of flint and steel.

While Falmagon scattered the belongings, Kinhar and Dorofej echoed each other's snores. Branimir ignored all three of the Highborn and scanned the landscape. He was not sure what he expected, but he knew he was a better lookout than any of the humans.

The Crags were larger than those on Folkmar, towering behind them. Branimir gazed up at the mountains, covered in light green grasses until the tips suddenly reddened at the end of the tree line. He had always felt comforted by the mountains, even near Melkorka, where demons apparently crawled to the surface from the depths of the Netherworld.

He pushed the thought from his head. The camp was safe between the Crags and Strega's Deep. The coastline stretched southeast, the way they had come, to the northeast, to the village of Valishul. Branimir hoped the morning walk did not take long; although, he suspected they would be boarding another ship for Arkaim. It was not an option he was particularly thrilled about.

The rabbits were nearly done roasting when a sound caught up with his pointed red ears. Jumping to his feet, he peered to the southeast, sniffing the air and squinting.

"What is it, Kras?" Falmagon hissed, noticing Branimir's quick movement. Falmagon may have been a brute, but, at least, he was intelligent enough to recognize the signs of a startled Kras.

"Bukavac." Branimir squealed, backing up toward the fire. "The demons have crossed the water in the night."

"Impossible." Falmagon said, sweeping the belongings into the pack, and snatching up his crooked staff, *Habërmani*.

"My Lord," Branimir stumbled with his words, "they are moving up the coastline."

Falmagon snickered. "Speak softly or I will have your head, Kras. How many?"

"Twenty or more."

Falmagon twisted his mouth beneath his mustache. "And Nedezhda?"

Branimir scanned the frozen bodies of the demons tearing across the terrain. The large beasts seemed to move in formation, padded armor against padded armor. Each icy fist held a labrys, a double-sided axe at the end of a shaft, stretching twice the length of a human.

"Nedezhda? Is she among them?" Falmagon repeated.

"I do not see her, my Lord." Branimir shivered. "What do we do?"

Falmagon tossed Branimir the pack. "Carry this and

douse the fire. We make haste to Valishul."

"We cannot outrun them!"

Falmagon raised his staff with the unspoken threat of being hit. "Do as I say, Kras."

The Highborn moved to the side of Kinhar and Dorofej, waking them in hushed voices while Branimir slung the pack over his shoulders and began kicking dirt over the flames. He was careful not to sling dirt onto the roasted rabbits.

"How could they have crossed the water? Strega would have drowned them." Kinhar spluttered, hearing the news. He stumbled about pulling on his robes and boots.

Dorofej casually slid on his first boot. "Tell me, why any god would interfere in the struggles of men, especially when facing demons?"

"For righteousness," Falmagon said bitingly.

Dorofej plucked his other boot off the ground and shook it at Falmagon mischievously. "Glory to be had, there is not, if gods relieve men of tribulations."

Falmagon angled his brow. "Don't lecture me, Dorofej."

A horn bellowed to the southeast and northeast, one after another. Branimir twisted in either direction. Fear enveloped him.

"The Bukavac come from the front and rear, my Lords," Branimir bawled. "They have found us out and are closing."

"We must fight," Falmagon declared, hitting the crooked staff against the ground.

"Three Highborn and a Kras," Dorofej shook his head. "After the numbers fallen at Melkorka? Fighting here would be fruitless, yes?"

"There is no choice!" Falmagon insisted.

"Opportunity lies in wait if you look for it, yes?"

"Bah! Stop speaking in riddles, Dorofej," Kinhar bellowed, grabbing his own pack off the ground. "Speak plainly."

"I am too feeble for fighting, and be plunging myself into the ocean to drown, I will not. I say, the Crags seem a worthwhile option."

Kinhar eyed the charging Bukavac who advanced on their position, agreeing, "We will not win a battle here. We should go through the Crags and circle around to Arkaim."

Dorofej smiled. "Go beneath, instead, I would recommend."

Falmagon gushed. "Who in their right mind would go under the Crags? Whatever you find in the depths of the Crags may very well contend with the Bukavacs at our backs."

Dorofej shrugged. "Battling the Bukavac will knowingly bring a close to our saga. Though, the battles yet to come have not been weighed, yes?"

"It doesn't matter, Dorofej," Falmagon argued. "Any entrance into the mountains is lost to the dead. It would take us a lifetime to find an opening, and even if we did, nothing would stop the Bukavac from pursuing."

Dorofej made his way to the dull fire pit and pulled a chunk from one of the rabbits. He peeled a piece of meat off and put it into his mouth. He chewed the meat and waited.

Falmagon glowered with hate. "I cannot take this infernal swine anymore." He slammed his stick into the ground again causing the rocks around the fire pit to rise into the air and fall again to the earth.

Branimir howled a ghastly cry as though he were on the frontlines of battle. It was a sound that had not been heard from a Kras in two thousand years or more.

Branimir stormed around the fire pit, shouting, "We do not have the time to argue or to feast on rabbits. Call stone and fire down on the enemy or flee." Branimir reached out and slapped the cooked rabbit out of Dorofej's lifted hand.

Dorofej stopped chewing to catch his jaw, watching the precious meat drop to the dirt as though it were his own heart.

Branimir, realizing his tactless action, dropped his hands to his sides and swiftly added, "My Lords."

Falmagon swung *Habërmani* and Branimir threw himself

to the ground, fearing the weapon was aimed for his skull once more.

Instead, the stones around the fireplace were thrown skillfully with *Koldovstvo* into the first Bukavac. The beast roared as the first struck it in the chest and the second across its frozen cheekbone. The Bukavac stumbled, but continued its charge.

The demon swung the labrys with the sharpened blade in full arc toward Falmagon, who fell on his back to dodge the blow. The Bukavac raised the double-sided axe over his head, ready to slice the Highborn in half from chin to gut.

Before the bluish-white demon could complete the attack, a ray of fire burst from Kinhar's hands into the Bukavac's eyes, colored like labradorites, blinding the beast. The Bukavac thrashed with its horns wildly and let loose another thunderous boom from his throat calling the attention of every demon within miles.

Habërmani struck the Bukavac repeatedly across the thighs, neck, and gut as Falmagon danced around the demon. The Bukavac, with fire in its eyes, swung wildly to hit the Highborn, crouching at half the height. Falmagon easily dodged the beast, and then finally hit the staff against the ground again. Rocks the size of Branimir's fists formed into stone spearheads. The stone pierced through the Bukavac a hundred times over and dropped the beast to the ground.

"This way. Come!" Dorofej shouted from several feet away. He had already begun making his way through the tall grasses up to the Crags of Kazimir. Branimir was not surprised to see the old Highborn holding another rabbit from the fire in his hand, a piece of the meat already hanging out from his thin lips.

Branimir scampered to his feet and ran toward Dorofej with Falmagon's pack held securely on his back. The Kras ignored the burrs and thorns that had haunted him the night prior, finding their irritation a minor payment for surviving the

Bukavac. Death by a demon's blade was not a fate he envied.

Kinhar hesitantly trailed behind with Falmagon at the far rear. The four of them said nothing as they abandoned the campsite and their destined path to Valishul. Branimir followed willingly as the Highborn forged another path. He could only guess it was fortune that pulled them down the path through the Crags with all other routes leading to death. Before long the tall grasses disappeared, and red rock and gravel was all that remained.

For half an hour, the four of them scampered like a dormouse dodging the deathly talons of a sparrowhawk. The sounds of the Bukavac giving chase never ceased. The echoes of their heavy footsteps and blood-hungry growls were lively upon the stone of the Crags.

Despite the Kras being quicker than humans, it soon became all Branimir could do to keep up with Dorofej, who had suddenly taken charge of their fates. The euphoric, old Highborn ran with increased urgency through the Crags, seeming to have ancient knowledge the speed and determination of the Bukavac.

Dorofej chortled like a madman as he twisted and turned past fallen rocks, loosened pebbles, and uneven paths that had not been traveled on for ages. He jumped and skidded through the terrain, full of vigor, as though he were half a century younger than he appeared.

"Where are you leading us, Dorofej?" Falmagon asked.

Dorofej paused for a moment to glance back at the younger Highborn before sticking his tongue out. The air was light and chilled, like dew from clovers in a dampened paddock. With a gleeful shout, he again picked up the pace with a sudden earnestness, rounding another crook in the mountain.

Two sarsen stones the size of the Bukavac stood polished against the mountain side. They were peculiar next to the red rock, but likely would be passed over if not sought out. Through the stones, one offset behind the right, was a gaping hole, pitch in color, leading into the depths of the mountainside. The dwelling was meant to be secluded, meant to be overlooked, meant to be forgotten.

Dorofej scarcely squeezed through the stones, making his way to the hole, small enough that he would have to crouch significantly to make his way inside the stuffy hole.

Branimir touched the smooth rock unnervingly as he passed through the crevice in the rocks.

"Quite fortunate there are no portly men in our fellowship, yes?" Dorofej said, still full of breath, urging them with a jerk of his head to follow. "Come."

Branimir was pushed to the front by Dorofej, to lead the way in the darkened tunnel as their guide. He had only made it a couple steps before Falmagon asked the question.

"What is this place?"

Kinhar gaped at the sarsen stones in wonderment and replied, "Dorofej has found the ingress to the Kras city of Illuard."

Branimir's knees buckled.

Chapter VIII

Pushing forward as though he had dug the tunnel himself, Branimir guided the Highborn down the dark path. Dorofej held fast to Branimir's small hand while the Highborn behind him held onto one another in a similar fashion. Unlike Branimir, the humans were sightless in the underground passageway, seeing nothing but darkness bounded in darkness.

Twice, Branimir had come to junctures in the tunnel where alternative tunnels had been dug out, forking wide in opposite directions. With simple explanation, Dorofej had wasted little time in directing Branimir down each path. Branimir was certain the old man had been here before.

Branimir recalled the conversation with Dorofej around the campfire about having an inquisitorial mind, and decided it was best to keep curiosity at sword's edge for the moment. He did not need holes in his skull.

The Kras was well-fitted in the smooth tunnel, having full range to walk upright. The walkway was worn with flat walls and ceiling, covered in a thick layer of dust. The Highborn behind him were not as privileged with their backs curved and necks bent; they still collided into the solid walls of earth on either side. Their muffled complaints harmonized with their stumbled footfalls as they descended into the depths of the mountainside.

After an hour or more, a dim, cloudy light brightened the end of the burrow. Thinking they had reached the outside, Branimir continued forward through the gap into the light. As he stepped out of the tunnel, he sauntered into a cave chamber the size of Narthwich, grander than Melkorka.

"The great hall of the Kras city of Illuard," Dorofej said from behind him, "distinguished as the *Eevaltti*, Hollow of Gravels, house of Electress Arabella, daughter to Atanasius Kulmata, Ninth Emperor of *Ojanen*, it is."

Light from a narrow, curved opening in the ceiling spilled with sparkling water, falling into a basin in the center of the cavern like a waterfall from the heavens. Mist bellowed from the gurgling basin fogging the cavern considerably. The smoky light shadowed columns formed from stalactites and stalagmites throughout the expanse.

"An empire long forsaken, long torn from the songs of skalds, and long forgotten by men," Kinhar added.

"Apparently, not all men," Falmagon muttered, eyeing Dorofej suspiciously. "How do you know of this place?"

Dorofej snorted, rubbing the mustache bristles from his inner nose. "From time to time, reminisce in the sound of songs once sung, my mind does."

"You mean, there is no one here," Branimir said disappointedly. "Where are the Kras?"

"I thought I had said you were the last of your kind." Dorofej offered without emotion, moving toward the basin.

Kinhar snickered.

Branimir looked at the spearhead of the Highborn, noting the odd behavior. He did not think he had ever heard the man scoff before.

"I expected…" Branimir did not know what he had expected.

"It is a ruin," Falmagon said. "Nothing more."

Branimir ogled as the Highborn scattered across the room, like newborns opening their eyes for the first time. The great hall was surrounded in multitudes of staircases sculpted from the mountainside led into more tunnels on several different levels. There were hundreds of them, each leading a different path, making up the city of Illuard.

The basin appeared to be naturally created, possibly from an underground waterway that flowed through the mountain, possibly creating this cavern thousands of years ago. Dorofej kneeled at the pool putting the liquid to his tongue and spitting on the ground.

"Bitter as acid, it is," he mumbled.

On the opposite side of the murky pool was a flattened surface with old stone tables thirty feet long covered with red chunks of stone and rusty pickaxes. Clay kilns were stretched around the tables, some collapsed or broken. Branimir could only assume they had been used to heat any ore found in the rocks, but there were no weapons or armor visible.

A treasure of the room was a ceremonial chair made of shiny stones, positioned inside an opening in the back wall on the opposite side of the cavern. Spinel, bloodstone, apatite, jade, and tanzanite were stacked together. The seat was clearly a masterpiece, far grander than Kinhar's stone throne back at Melkorka. The throne was built in the side of the mountain, in a cranny only large enough for a Kras to squeeze into, placed high enough in the wall to overlook the entire cavern with ease. In the depths of the edged rock, behind the grandiose throne, hung a tapestry. It was muddied and discolored beyond recognition.

Branimir found himself standing by the throne, stroking the gems gently, salivating from the lips. He had no memory of walking across the cavern, or climbing the small incline to the impressed cavity in the red rock.

His small hands traced each gemstone, each jewel, and each nugget, seared to the one next to it without hope of ever being removed from the throne. If his life were measured by feelings of ecstasy or absolute joy, in this moment, Branimir had just been born.

Dorofej's voice whispered from below. "Sat and watched over his people from *Oreg'henite*, Emperor Atanasius Kulmata would have."

Branimir did not respond. He couldn't figure out what words he wanted to say. The stones were so shiny.

"Branimir." Dorofej poked him in the side. The old Highborn's bushy eyebrows peeked over the edge from the level below with a coltish gaze.

"I want one," Branimir wheezed.

"Behind *Oreg'henite*, you will unearth the stone of stones. Quickly, now."

Branimir did not budge, still focused on the treasure before his eyes. He felt urged to sit in it, to feel the shiny stones all around him.

"Foolish, Kras." Dorofej pushed his finger harder into Branimir, striking his tender rib purposefully. "*Oreg'henite*, the throne is. Dig behind it, tear down the tapestry, and make haste," he urged through clenched teeth.

Branimir squealed in pain, turning to face Dorofej feeling the madness swell in his eyes. His first instinct was to strike out at the Highborn, but five decades of conditioning prevented him from acting on his natural disposition. He suddenly realized Dorofej could not do much more but poke at him. The Highborn could not fit behind *Oreg'henite*.

"What have you found, Dorofej?" Kinhar called from a distance.

"Dig." Dorofej whistled at Branimir. "I say, find me the moonstone, *Ojenek*. Fit in the palm of your hand, it will. Smaller than your fist, it is!"

Branimir bobbed his head.

"Dorofej?" Kinhar said again.

"*Oreg'henite*, the *Ojanen* Throne, Kinhar," Dorofej sung out in a bard's tone, causing a distraction away from Branimir. "Magnificent, yes? The Kras were slaves to their own before the Highborn, serving the Emperor night and day to find gemstones and precious rocks for the construction of *Oreg'henite* from Gjetvald Meas, the First Emperor of *Ojanen*, to the Ninth. It took era upon era to craft the chair. Still, Gjetvald had the most prevalent contribution, being the First to rule in *Eevaltti*, with each subsequent ruler adding bits more, yes?"

Branimir dug frantically behind *Oreg'henite* in the soft, muddied soil that lined its rear. His fingernails filled with red muck as he dug deeper and deeper into the earth.

"The Kras would sit beneath their ruler at these stone tables, breaking stone from clay, gem from stone, yes? An eternal search for jewels—to match their desire—in the depths of the mountains, they had."

Branimir's fingers touched a leather pouch, damp with decay. He pulled it free from the mud, ripped loose the leather binding, and dumped the contents into his hands eagerly. There, in his palm, was the bluish moonstone, sparkling as though it were filled with an inner fire, called *Ojenek*.

Branimir smiled wide. *Ojenek*, the jewel of an emperor, the talisman of the Kras, was held firmly in his grasp.

Falmagon raised next to Kinhar, passing through the columns, his single eye always watching and wary. "What did they discover in all their digging, Dorofej?" He clutched *Habërmani*, clearly showing he was aware of the significance of relics and *Koldovstvo* found within them.

"I found it!" Branimir yelped in delight, his little voice echoing from wall to tunnel like the uplifting exclamations of a hundred Kras cutting the sediment from their first shiny stone. He stood erect by *Oreg'henite*, jubilantly holding *Ojenek* in the air between his finger and thumb.

"Doltish, imprudent, Kras!" Dorofej's palm connected with his forehead. He shook his head, the tassels from his chin bouncing in defeat.

Before Kinhar or Falmagon could question the utility of

the moonstone between Branimir's crimson fingers, horrifying howls of awakened creatures reverberated into the cavern.

"The Bukavac have found us!" Falmagon cried out.

"Not likely," Kinhar said. "With their size, they would have never made it down here. This is something else entirely."

Small creatures, as large as a Highborn's forearm flew from out from the many tunnels, and circled wildly about the great hall in a fit of perceived madness. The forelimbs of the creatures served as wings, with a membranous skin that was too thin to see in the hazy cavern. The demonic looking creatures closely resembled bats apart from their spindly legs and miniature horned skulls.

Branimir did not hesitate in shoving *Ojenek* back into the leather pouch and stuffing it into the pocket of his trousers.

The ear-piercing screech of the flying demons did not match the howling heard moments before. Branimir covered his susceptible ears to block out the mishmash of noise erupting from the fanged mouths.

"What is this?" Branimir squealed, falling to his knees.

"Skyrz!" Kinhar bellowed over the insufferable noise. "They will fetch much worse with their clamoring."

Falmagon shrieked as a Skyrz swooped down and clamped onto his cheek. The claws of its feet tore into the flesh of Falmagon's neck as it extracted blood from the face of the Highborn ravenously with its hollowed fangs. Its wings beat violently about, maintaining its grip, while Falmagon lurched, pulling at the gristly body of the beast.

Dorofej sprang to Falmagon, grabbing the Skyrz by its gangling neck. Swiftly, Dorofej squeezed, crushing the bones and nearly severing the head. As the Skyrz dropped in a heap, the sharpened teeth were expelled from Falmagon and blood decanted from the bleeding puncture wounds in the Highborn's neck.

"Hold it fast." Dorofej said, tearing at the black fabric of his robes.

Falmagon clung to his cheek, dark blood oozing over his fingertips blending with the crimson liquid bleeding from the claw marks on his throat.

Another two Skyrz plummeted through the cavern pillars toward Dorofej and Falmagon, but were quickly met with fire flailing like whips from Kinhar's fingertips. As if being beckoned to war, the rest of the Skyrz about the room wheeled toward the Highborn with gnashing teeth and hollow eyes.

Dorofej shredded the end of his robe, and handed Falmagon the cloth.

Falmagon took it eagerly, holding it tightly against his cheek, blood swelling in his mouth. In his free hand, he used the crooked staff to keep another Skyrz from latching onto him.

Dorofej ducked a swooping Skyrz who collided with another string of fire unleashed from Kinhar.

"I will not waste my life with these demons!" Kinhar shouted above the echoing shrieks.

"Falmagon," Dorofej directed with an extended hand. "A weapon, if you will!"

The Highborn were distinguished for never crafting a manmade weapon, as it was against custom and tradition of their kind. *Kaelandur* had been the exception to this holistic practice. Outside of the occasional walking stick, not many tools of warfare would ever have reason to touch the hand of those blessed by *Koldovstvo*. Despite such truth, Bran was aware the Highborn would use *Koldovstvo* to construct armaments in times of distress.

Falmagon Sej, the Highborn Long-Walker, mumbled under his breath forcibly, crashing *Habërmani* against the cavern surface. The foggy mist spiraled and enveloped the man, taking hold as *Koldovstvo* pulsed through his veins. His brown hair, frayed and unraveled, blurred with his cloak as he shifted from shadow to shadow. With a stab of *Habërmani* into the nearest rock, two stone staves erupted and were supernaturally flung toward Kinhar and Dorofej.

The three Highborn formed a protective circle, standing back to back, each defensively holding a staff. The Skyrz clamored toward them. The movement in the dim light was difficult to make out as staves twirled and gloomy Skyrz lunged for flesh. Again and again, the Skyrz plunged to taste fresh blood and met a grueling strike. As more Skyrz surfaced from the depths of the underearth, another would fall dead at the feet of the Highborn, honored guardians of men, revered keepers of *Koldovstvo,* and esteemed wardens of Melkorka.

The continued wailing of howls that rebounded in the dark tunnels grew closer. The sounds went unheard by the frenetic Highborn that battled the Skyrz. It was Branimir's pinpointed ears stretching beyond the top of his hairline that caught the commotion.

Branimir was still crouched in hiding behind *Oreg'henite.* As the sound of the howls grew near, Branimir fuddled with the pack on his back that he had been holding for Falmagon. It suddenly struck him that where the Highborn had *Koldovstvo,* he had nothing in which to defend himself.

Compelled by terror instigated by the nightmarish baying, he reached inside the cloth pack and found the kinzhal. Branimir had never held a weapon before and was pleased that the curved dagger was so light in his grasp. He touched the blade carefully and yelped at its sharpness. It sliced through his red skin with ease, causing crimson liquid to drip. He quickly shoved his finger in his mouth, eyeing the blade with care. The dagger would make do.

"Dreka," Kinhar snarled.

At first, Branimir thought that the dark-haired man was shouting a battle cry, but soon realized he was referring to the demon that sprang from a tunnel above to the great hall. The howl was all too familiar, causing Branimir to duck behind the throne once more.

The Dreka was the size of Branimir with an oversized

head with goat horns breaking through the gray wrinkles of skin on its forehead. The Dreka had an elongated, thin body that wrapped behind it awkwardly, swaying and hunched over forebodingly. Yellow, molded eyes scanned the great hall as though the Dreka was the protector of Illuard, *Eevaltti*.

Branimir gaped like a child at the demonic beast that dwelled in the caves of the lost city of Illuard. The thin-lipped mouth of the Dreka was forced open by overlaying rows of sharpened teeth on the upper and lower gums. The Kras had never seen so many teeth on any one living creature. If such demons were common in mountains, Branimir understood clearly why his race was gone from existence.

The Dreka caught sight of the Highborn about the time that several more leaped from the holes in the walls. The first Dreka howled like a deep-throated wolf, springing to action on all four legs. It pounced about the ground with surprising agility, leaping from column to column like it was walking across a flat surface. The other Dreka, too many to count, joined the charge.

Falmagon dropped the cloth that prevented the gushing of blood from his face with a dark sneer. "No safer here than with the Bukavac!"

"Not the time," Kinhar crowed, dropping the stone slave and throwing up his hands defensively.

The Dreka leaped toward the spearhead of the Highborn, and was met with a gust of wind that sent it reeling backwards through a pillar of rock. The second and third demons met similar fates with the impact breaking skin and bone.

Falmagon used a similar method, pulling crumbled stone from the ground and flinging it at the enemy with *Koldovstvo*. Demon upon demon that assailed at Falmagon collided with rock and met their demise.

Dorofej kept his staff in hand, not risking his life in using *Koldovstvo*, as he had little to spare. The stone stave struck the nearest Dreka that approached him in the mouth, busting skin and shattering teeth. The Dreka spewed blood and attacked again, before Dorofej could bring his weapon down to shield himself. The cutthroat fangs ripped into his lower leg, tearing a chunk from his calf. Dorofej collapsed and the demon was immediately on his chest snapping at the throat behind his white beard.

"Dorofej!" Branimir screamed. In a moment, he found himself leaping from the cleft, fading from visibility, and blending into his surroundings. On light footsteps, he dashed forward with the swiftness of a Kras in its natural habitat. Through the broken columns, past the bitter basin, Branimir dodged the Dreka that bounded about the cavern in heated disarray.

Dorofej held the Dreka at a breath away, its saliva saturated in the old man's beard, when Branimir plunged the kinzhal between the horns on the beast's head. Blood churned over the blade and the creature fell limp.

"Branimir," Dorofej said with heavy breath.

"Lord Dorofej," Branimir acknowledged, pulling the blade free.

More Dreka spilled from the tunnels like a sea filling a void. Falmagon sounded above the demonic howls of the ferocious beasts. "There are too many. We cannot hold here!"

"May the Lightbringer help us," Kinhar proclaimed, pulling Falmagon to where Dorofej and Branimir lay in wait.

Tens of hundreds of Dreka seemed to fill the cavern, spilling over each other like rats over rotting meat. Kinhar, holding true to the Highborn way, threw up his arms, calling on *Koldovstvo*.

As the Dreka bounded to finish the three Highborn and single Kras, an invisible dome of force, created from the air they breathed, was fabricated around the Highborn men. The Dreka slammed into the wall repetitively, yapping and bawling in retaliation against the unseen energy that held them from their prey. Wrinkles immediately lined Kinhar's temples, his hair graying at the tips, age returning where it had previously been restored.

Branimir clung to Dorofej in disbelief as Kinhar lifted the lot of them above the cavern floor within the invulnerable globe. They sat upon nothing with demons hissing and screeching beneath them, leaping and clawing, intent on preventing escape from the forlorn city.

The edges of the protective orb collided with column upon column, destroying the fabric of their creation. Each column crumbled under the impact. Boulders the size of the sarsens at the entrance to Illuard flattened the enemy. The ceiling of the cavern fell away where water rained to the basin below. The Dreka found futility in their attempts and scampered back to the tunnels beneath.

Still, Kinhar lifted the orb through the ceiling. His features continued to change, bringing him closer to the man he had been at Melkorka, as opposed to the young man he had become. The ashen in his hair became more significant, wrinkles flooding his skin like fruit dried too long in the heat of the sun.

"Kinhar," Falmagon grabbed the Highborn in fervor, "If you defeat yourself, the war with Nedezhda will be lost."

The light of Dahz, the Lightbringer, had not yet gone astray, as the day had not come to an end, and shined on the group as they rose over the mountaintop from the cavern depths.

"Bless Dahz, the Protector of Men," Kinhar called to the heavens as though he were standing directly before the white castle of the Beyond. The protective orb lowered to the red rock atop the mountain, beyond the tree line and high grasses below. "Through the Lightbringer, I will preserve justice and the legacy of the Highborn. I will find a way."

As the protective orb dissipated from existence, the three humans collapsed on the ridge in exhaustion.

Branimir stood up determinedly, sliding the kinzhal into

his belt for safekeeping. He peered to the northwest toward Arkaim. Kalamaar stretched before them, shaded in gold and scarlet rays of the Sun God. There was no booming voice of Dahz the Lightbringer, and yet, Branimir knew that glory was to be had.

Chapter IX

Branimir poked at the fire lazily bumping his branch against the charred logs. It sparked atop the fading embers, looking to spread its flame. He understood the danger of allowing the fire to burn freely. As ravenous as power, a fire would devour whatever lay before it. Without proper tending, it would consume the whole world. Such lessons he had learned from Dorofej in the past two months, late in the evenings and early in the mornings, as they made their way through the Crags of Kazimir to Arkaim.

The journey to Arkaim had been more arduous than any would have predicted, laced with perils like poison on a dagger's edge. The mainland of Kalamaar was not well equipped for men to travel across with only a few scattered villages, making the opportunity to gain supplies or adequate rest minimal. Still, the most difficult of situations was what they had experienced at Illuard.

Branimir knew the battle had changed him. For once in his life, he felt brave.

"What do you want, Branimir?" Falmagon snorted, ripping the leg from the cooked hare and stuffing it in his mouth. It had taken nearly a week for Falmagon's face to heal from the Skyrz, leaving him with a nasty scar down the good side of his face. With the permanent imprint and the missing eye, the youngest of the Highborn appeared to be the most threadbare among them. His attitude, if it were conceivable, had taken a further turn for the worse.

Branimir looked away, not realizing he had been staring at the pink blemishes. He quickly clued in to his red skin, seemingly preoccupied with his hand and five diminutive fingers. His skin was flush with the color of the glowing cradle of the fire pit.

He could not help but notice that the one-eyed Highborn had called him Branimir instead of calling him a Kras. It was becoming a more common event in the past few weeks. Branimir was not sure if it was a gesture of respect or simply an attempt to break up the monotony. Being surrounded by one another for the past couple months had not been easy on any of them, especially after being drawn so far from their destination. The path through Illuard had only lengthened their journey to Arkaim.

Falmagon finished eating by throwing a bone into the fire. "Stare at me again before we reach Arkaim, red brood, and I will cut out your eyes to replace my own."

"Yes, my Lord," Branimir said.

Dorofej nudged Branimir with a nicker that may have been the underpinnings of a giggle. "Stare whilst he sleeps, you must. He does not have an eye to spare to keep open when resting, yes?"

Bran covered his lips with both hands to stifle a chortle. A month ago, Branimir would not have dared laugh at such an insult openly, but Dorofej had been somewhat protective of him since their escape of the underground, Kras city. The aged Highborn had not even asked for the moonstone, *Ojenek*, outside of telling Branimir to keep it safe. Falmagon and Kinhar seemingly had forgotten about it entirely.

Branimir touched the moonstone in his pocket lightly. He found himself slightly curious as to what exactly it was and why Dorofej had wanted it. He was not used to thinking about these types of things, but it did strike him once more that none of the Highborn around the campfire could have reached the moonstone in its hiding place. Branimir was the only one that could have fit behind the throne called *Oreg'henite*.

Dorofej widened his eyes playfully and sipped from his waterskin. It dribbled down his chin as he tried to hold back his own mirth.

Falmagon grabbed his crooked staff called *Habërmani* and stood with fury. "I have smashed your head in once, Kras. Do not think it will not happen again. Know your place!"

Dorofej waved indolently at the younger man. "Put your bent stick away, yes? I made the jest. Moreover, proven his worth in our company, Branimir has."

"Killing a single Dreka does not make him an equal to the Highborn, Dorofej."

"I did not suggest it did, Falmagon Sej, Highborn Long-Walker." Dorofej pulled up his robe, revealing the mended flesh of his lower leg, far more severe than the damage inflicted on Falmagon's face. "And yet, he measured his life against that of a Highborn, and chose the latter, yes? Deserving of veneration, the gesture is."

Branimir gleamed a bit at the old man's words.

Falmagon pulled at his mustache that hung over the brown scruff of a developing beard. "Are you going to refuse my right to thrash a slave, Dorofej?"

"The fortunes of men linger in the blight, from which alternative paths for your aggression you should consider, yes?" Dorofej dropped his robe.

Scowling, Falmagon sniffed. "I did not ask for your wisdom and you did not answer my question."

Dorofej separated his lips, taking a deep breath and looked long and hard at the one-eyed Highborn. Finally, Dorofej hobbled to his feet, clutching his waterskin in long, tangled fingers. Branimir could hear the old man's knees grinding, bone scraping against bone as he shuffled over to Falmagon. The elder hoisted himself as straight as a hanging man's rope, nose touching nose, with his shaggy eyebrows adding extra shadow to his visage.

Branimir cowered back, scooting away so that he would not be caught between the two. He found himself genuinely worried for Dorofej, but could not place how he should think or feel about the old Highborn protecting him.

From the angle, Branimir could not make out the expression of the old man, but he easily heard Dorofej's words. "Unblemished words, it is. Rest a finger on Branimir Baran and your blood it will be that I draft from my waterskin!"

With that, Dorofej lifted the sheep's bladder to his lips and sucked out the liquid and spat it out in Falmagon's face.

Falmagon shoved Dorofej with both hands, and the old man toppled to the ground in a heap. Dorofej grunted, landing rather awkwardly on his shoulder.

Dorofej retorted in feverish laughter, holding his stomach and lifting his waterskin off the ground protectively.

"Mad you are!"

"What has gotten into you, Dorofej?" Kinhar frowned from the fire pit. "What did you put in your waterskin?"

Dorofej hiccupped, rolling over onto his haunches, maintaining the waterskin being held in the air. "A bit of plum when we promenaded through Jh'tutar a fortnight ago, yes?"

"Wine? We were barely in the village for a half an hour," Kinhar started.

"All that was needed to taste the nectar of sweet plum," Dorofej tittered from the ground. "Like Falmagon's mother, it is."

He took another swig.

Falmagon's face turned as red as Branimir's skin.

"Leave him be, Falmagon. He is sloshed beyond reason," Kinhar said.

Branimir kept his hand over his mouth, holding back the merriment that welled up inside of him. Dorofej peddled about on the ground in attempts to stand once more, to move closer to the fire pit. After falling onto his buttocks more than once, he finally laid down. He murmured to himself, curling into a ball inside his dark robes.

"He is going to get us killed," Falmagon said to Kinhar, returning to the stone that he had been sitting upon.

"He has his own merits," Kinhar said.

"His capacity to wield *Koldovstvo*, to mend our wounds, to manipulate the elements, is restrained by his frailty. What use can Dorofej have besides slow our excursion? Already Nedezhda may have reached the Ash Tree while we have been wandering in the Crags."

Branimir licked his lips nervously. They had not discussed their quest of protecting the Ash Tree since Narthwich. For a moment, he had thought that the Highborn had forgotten their self-proclaimed quest.

"Dorofej has familiarity that is from beyond our time," Kinhar said wondrously, hearing the old man hiccup again in the dark. "From beyond my time. And, from where he obtained such knowledge, I must figure out before his death."

"He rambles."

"If you listen closely, Falmagon, there is truth in his words. If the *Kadari* are to flourish in the centuries to come, his truth must be ours."

Branimir's gaiety fled like shadow from flame as he grasped the intention of the Highborn. The name *Kadari* had been mentioned by these two back at Melkorka. He was too afraid to ask its meaning and decided to simply listen, while pretending not to listen.

"Once you learn it, I am going to kill the old cur," Falmagon avowed, pulling *kaelandur* from his robes wickedly.

Branimir stifled a yelp. He gaped at the copper dagger that had been forged at Melkorka. His jaw quivered at memory of it being forged by Jhar and Dorofej and then being used to slaughter Nedezhda. The weapon filled him with such distress that it was all he could do to stay seated and not flee from the campfire. From that time, it had remained hidden to the point that Branimir had forgotten that Falmagon carried it on his person.

"A fitting death," Falmagon cackled.

"Only if it is Dahz's will," Kinhar said. "The Lightbringer must guide us or we, too, will become misplaced."

Dorofej snuffled in his sleep, flopping sideways on the ground. A low toned gurgle sounded from his thin lips.

Falmagon harrumphed, pointing the weapon at Dorofej. "That pile of sheepdip? I guarantee you that the Lightbringer wills it!"

Kinhar curved his lips with amusement.

Branimir could not believe what he was hearing. These two men were leaps and bounds beyond the footpath of the Highborn. He understood that the Highborn were meant to protect humans, not meddle with life, and definitely not scheme to murder one of their own. He clamped his jaw hard and bit his cheek. This was unbearable.

"What of the red brood?" Falmagon shifted his gaze to Branimir.

He did not meet the Highborn's gaze, fixing his eyes to *kaelandur*. Although the world around him was as clear as day, he swore that it glistened against the dimming cinders.

His fingers trailed to the kinzhal tucked in his belt. It was unusual for a Kras to carry a weapon, but none of the Highborn had questioned it after he had killed the Dreka in the cavern. Even a couple months in his belt, the dagger was still sharpened. It hardly helped him feel at ease.

"Leave Branimir be. He has merit as well," Kinhar tossed a stone toward Branimir. It cracked him in the skull lightly. "Regardless of Dorofej's drunk blathering, the Kras knows to keep his mouth sealed. Is that not so?"

"Yes, my Lord," Branimir shuddered, keeping his eyes dropped. His hand fell away from his weapon.

"Kinhar, you have a funny way of measuring merit,

finding purpose in a half-dead carcass and a half-pint slave."

Kinhar rubbed his scalp. His gray hair had returned, leaving him rather flustered. He was not as aged as Dorofej, but the youth he had achieved at Melkorka had been lost at Illuard. "Bah! You undertook the *Kalamyr Oath*, as I did, pledging fealty to Dahz and the *Kadari*. Have some sense, Falmagon, and use what Dahz provides you. Dorofej is devoted by common name and the Kras by station. None could ask for better company, despite their lacking."

Falmagon grunted, signifying compliance. "I trust in you the utmost, Kinhar. You have not led me astray thus far." Falmagon returned the copper dagger to its hiding place.

"Trust in Dahz, the Protector of Men, before all else," Kinhar said.

"Even when the ritual failed us…" Falmagon said, squinting at Kinhar for guidance.

"True," Kinhar said, "the outcome was not what was expected, but I cannot say it was a failure. The Lightbringer simply tests our faith. We will defeat Nedezhda."

Falmagon ran his fingers over his mustache, studying Kinhar. As if making up his decision, he scooped up his hare again and used his teeth to pull the meat from the bone. "It'll be good to see Erzebeth."

Kinhar agreed, "Let us hope that she has the freedom to take leave with us. I will need Erzebeth to guide the way."

"Kinhar?" Falmagon paused chewing. His voice had more distress than what Branimir had ever heard in the tenor of the Highborn. "What are you saying?"

There was an unmistakable mist in the crook of Kinhar's eyes as he bore admittance to his companion across the burning residue. "I cannot seem to remember the way to the Ash Tree."

Kinhar stood up and sighed heavily, tears swelling. He swallowed hard.

"You were honest with Dorofej when you told him that

you did not know at Narthwich?

Kinhar grumbled in his throat.

"How long has it been?"

Branimir noticed Kinhar take his time in responding. The Highborn blankly looked at nothing. It was like his mind was wandering through a hundred memories of a hundred lifetimes in a single second.

Kinhar gulped. "I wish that I could tell you, Falmagon. I was young in my existence when I found my way, and timeworn when I finally returned to Kalamaar. I only know the Waters of Life and the Ash Tree are beyond Strega's Deep in a land far more dangerous than Kalamaar.

Kinhar continued, pacing about the fire. "Humans think they know the world. They believe they are powerful, and that they have the gift of wisdom unlike any other living creature. The human creature, in all its perfection, designed by the gods or nay, only sees what it wants to see."

Branimir's mind swelled. Not only was he attempting to understand the ramblings of a man who seemingly claimed to live the lifespan of a Kras or longer, but alleged that mankind, the master of the Kras, were ignorant despite their freedom and power.

Branimir had never known Kinhar to know humility in this way. Despite his professed connection with Dahz the Lightbringer, this measure of humbleness was incongruous with the spearhead of the Highborn.

"What do you see, Falmagon?"

Falmagon gnawed on the hare like a vagrant, talking with his mouth full. "I have journeyed all over Kalamaar and the Seven Islands at your direction from the time that you plucked me from Arkaim as a child. I did not ask for this life but I also did not question what was meant by being Highborn. I have done what was necessary for the world to be saved from itself, even when I did not completely agree with the path set before me. I have seen what some will never know. I have experienced what some will never have. I have more reason than most to lose my faith. Yet, even when my eye was torn from its socket at Jh'tutat, I found myself blessed, measuring godsend against calamity. There is not always goodness but there is justice. And, justice…righteousness…has many forms. Whether it is thought to be right or wrong, it is still necessary. If we forget justice then we forget reason, and then we forget what is meant by being Anshedar."

Branimir breathed deep, touching his head where he had received the beating from Falmagon on the shores of Kalamaar. The soreness was gone, but the memory of the harshness in the man remained. Yet, after Falmagon spoke, Branimir found himself finding appreciation for the Highborn Long-Walker. For once, he used the term for all humans—not Highborn or Northmen—but Anshedar. It was surprising that Falmagon found a connection with something greater than himself.

Branimir suddenly felt very isolated. He was not a part of anything larger than himself. He was alone in this world.

Kinhar paused in his movement. "You have the true sight of a leader, Falmagon Sej. You will shepherd the threshold of the *Kadari* in the upcoming era. I swear it."

Chapter X

Coming from a place where only a handful of people were ever gathered at one time, Arkaim was prodigious. Branimir gawked in fascination while trying to keep in pace with the long-legged Highborn that walked toward the capital.

"How big is this place?" Branimir asked.

Dorofej responded, "The largest city in the civilized world with nearly a thousand Northmen, Arkaim is. It is the home of Merreider Kal, Twelfth King of Kalamaar, Bearer of the *Svehla*, the Golden Scepter of Svarog, yes?"

Falmagon spit. "Fancy titles for a man who is hardly deserving of them. He spends more time traveling around to Jh'tutar, Valishul, and Jh'terin then caring for the people of Arkaim."

Falmagon headed up the party with his crooked staff repeatedly slamming into the ground, a sign of his irritability. Dust layered the lower seams on his brown robe. The attire had been bought with shana provided by Jarl Likshol Avar of Narthwich. In fact, the Jarl's coin had supported their travels tremendously while traipsing across Kalamaar.

Kinhar dipped his head in agreement, smoothing his own robes. He had bought himself a cream-colored cloth several villages back to replace the brittle pale robe he had adorned. The new, stitched robe was hardly worth the cost in Branimir's opinion. By and by, the two Highborn appeared to have an elevated station with the new attire.

It was only Dorofej who refused to change his mangled garb. That is, he and Branimir, who had not been given the option. Dorofej had said the dried blood and sweat gave his clothes character.

"A King has duty to his entire realm, to administer the law, yes? Occurring in more than just large cities, disease, murder, and squabbling does," Dorofej argued.

"He has Jarls in every village on the Seven Islands, across the countryside, and further down the coastline. The Jarls should travel to the King and take his law back to their domain, not the other way around," Falmagon said. He did not bother to look back at Dorofej to see the reaction to the reasonable suggestion, but Branimir did. Dorofej's face tightened in disapproval beneath his beard and mustache.

"Hopes of recompense in the hereafter helps man survive this difficult life, yes? Hope, like faith, is required to endure hardship, but it can be a fleeting." Dorofej took a breath before continuing. "If there is no sign of existing, a god will not have believers. It is the same, yes? An icon for hope and be seen, a King must be, lest the country will crumble."

Falmagon snorted in disapproval but said nothing.

As they neared, Branimir noticed that the construction of Arkaim was like other settlements in Kalamaar. The buildings were variable in size, built square from wooden frames, each layered with a straw roof. Steppingstone walls had just begun to be assembled around Arkaim to replace dug palisades that had probably provided its defense for the past century. Boulders, chiseled from the Crags, were laid about the terrain in heaps in preparation for stacking. The sight was exceptional to the eye; strange devices of harvested timber fastened with pulleys and levers and rope. Portions of the wall were scattered about the perimeter of Arkaim.

"Lucky, you are," Dorofej motioned to the flapping

tapestries of the golden scepter, *Svehla*, the signet of King Ker. "The banners are hung, meaning the King is within the city, yes? How wonderful it is that the Highborn Long-Walker can share his remarkable insight on leadership with royalty, yes?"

"Maybe I will." Falmagon shockingly showed considerable restraint.

"Enough already," Kinhar said as they passed through the wooden gates of the Arkaim.

The city was alive. Branimir kept his hand near the back of the black robes of Dorofej, as to not lose sight of the Highborn in the throng of people scattered about the city. If they caught him alone, Branimir feared they may beat him like Falmagon had with his crooked staff.

Branimir surveyed men and women as they muddled down the streets, accompanied by children who ran wildly about. Some children squalled at the sight of Branimir, taking off in the opposite direction. Some of the humans also took special notice of the Kras, and steered clear of the traveling fellowship.

Branimir was not quite accustomed to the reaction, but it was similar to how he had been welcomed within the hamlets of Kalamaar. These people must also believe that he was some sort of a demon.

The Kras had really been forgotten in the world of men.

Branimir pushed away his thoughts of being alone. He had to accept that he was the last of his kind. He did not want to think about what that meant for him.

"What news of the south?" A man shouted, raising his hand at them. "You haven't been to Arkaim since last harvest, Falmagon."

Falmagon stopped immediately and gestured in recognition, as though he had been looking for the yellow-toothed grunt standing at the edge of the street.

Falmagon led the group away from the red dirt road and

introduced the man. "Unnvar Grondahl. He drinks at the *Kal'bane* up the road here."

"Drink at it?" Unnvar hit Falmagon on the shoulder with a meaty hand. The human stood a head taller than the Highborn, with muscle as thick as an ox. "I own the alehouse, you lout."

Falmagon rubbed a hand through his greasy hair, a smile plastered on his face. "You wouldn't know it. Find you thrown in the streets more often than the drunks."

"My father always said if you were going to do something, to do it right!"

Falmagon threw his head back with a laugh that was outside of the man's regular character. He slapped Unnvar on the back in embrace. "Missed you, ole' chump. Good to see that you aren't settled in an urn."

Branimir kept quiet, but found himself surprised that Falmagon could be jolly with anyone.

"I'm fortunate of that. I hear those in the south aren't as lucky." Unnvar wiped slime from his nose to his pant leg, snot caught in a thick mustache. "Who travels in your company? Friends or chumps?"

"A mixture of both, I'm afraid," Falmagon said. "Kinhar Sayan, you have met before, though some time ago."

"Kinhar," Unnvar bellowed in near disbelief, "You don't look to have aged a day since we last met. How, under Dahz's light, have you done it?"

Kinhar nodded light-heartedly in relative familiarity to the burly innkeeper. "Abstinence from worldly pleasures?"

Unnvar scoffed. "I know abstinence from pleasure, but not from self-restraint like you insane Highborn. I'll tell you that. I've been wedded for fifteen years. Hasn't done a lick of good for my body?" Unnvar slapped his stomach that protruded slightly over the line of his trousers.

"That it has not," Falmagon agreed with a hoot, smile still coated, stretching the scar along his cheekbone. "The other is

Dorofej, and the Kras is Branimir Baran."

"Not a demon, then? Haven't seen your kind before, although Falmagon has talked about it, I suppose, more than once. I say, you fit the fireside story, though most would say the Kras are myth. A walking testimony you are, eh?"

Branimir dipped his head, unsure how to respond.

Unnvar coughed with another snort, quickly blowing his nose into his hand and wiping it on his clothing. "Well, enough of this. Come to the *Kal'bane* to fill your bellies and get a good rest. We can talk over some brew about the rumors of Netherworld demons raiding villages upon the Seven Islands and along the coasts. Gossip is that they come this way bringing mayhem and war. Arkaim is in all sorts of a fuss about the nonsense. Part of me thinks they are trying to construct that wall in defense, as if that won't take half their lives to do. Royals are as dumb as slaves sometimes."

Kinhar interrupted, "We have already lost much time, Unnvar. Your invitation is welcomed, but we *must* speak to Erzebeth."

"Erzebeth? Erzebeth Navenka?"

Kinhar nodded his head. "That is the one. It is important that we speak to her. Do you know her location?"

"That I do, regrettably. The woman has been imprisoned for the better part of a two months for thieving," Unnvar's face scrunched up. "Not a trade she will be practicing again, I am sure, if she is ever released."

"Ever released?" Branimir said in a higher pitch than he intended.

Unnvar shook his head. "Indeed. King Kar is under no compulsion to hold trial, especially after the punishment has already been inflicted. Erzebeth is chained in the jails, paraded about as a token and reminder to other thieves of Arkaim justice."

Kinhar's eyes narrowed, his voice was dangerously dark, "Justice? What did Merreider Kar do to her?"

Unnvar looked about the street, but the people were paid no heed to their conversation. "Severed her hand and hung it from her neck as a bloody token of her deed. It is a ghastly thing, rotten and beset with maggots."

Branimir's stomach churned. "What?"

"The Lightbringer have mercy…" Falmagon began.

"And, I'd be sure to address the King with his title when speaking his name, Kinhar. I have no personal qualm, and no disrespect, but as stealing takes the hand so does blasphemy steal the tongue. The King's blades are always sharpened and swift to deliver punishment."

Kinhar sneered. "I'll speak as I wish how I wish."

Unnvar contorted his face, clearly meaning to stay on good terms with the Highborn. "Be wary of your audience is all I am saying."

"Quite alright, Unnvar," Falmagon calmly whispered.

Kinhar dipped his head, apologetically. "Forgive my harshness. I forget myself as it has been a tiresome journey from Folkmar. All in all, Erzebeth must be retrieved at once, if we must level Arkaim, so be it. King Kar *will* take an audience with the Highborn."

Unnvar shook his head. "Luck is not so much in your favor, friend. You come to Arkaim during the Festival of Dahz."

"Great." Kinhar's scowl deepened. Falmagon looked equally distraught.

"The King does not see anyone this week," Unnvar said. "He is organizing the events in preparation for the Season of Frost, while we make wolf feasts to protect the herds."

"Wolf feasts?" Branimir pulled at his hooked nose with confusion.

His question was ignored, and instead the focus fell to Dorofej, who spoke with a smile. "After months of hearty travel, what is a week of rest, yes? By all means, lead the way to the alehouse and bring the plum whilst we wait."

Falmagon pulled at his mustache and mumbled under his breath. Even to Branimir's sensitive ears, the words were inaudible.

Chapter XI

Dorofej sipped the wine from the copper cup casually, his frosty eyes fixated on the clay hearth in the central of the one main room of *Kal'bane*. As with most housing units, the hearth served as a furnace for heat and a kiln to prepare meals.

Branimir did not have any alcohol, nearly afraid to have it touch his lips. He sat relaxed and cross-legged on one of the many beds that protruded into the main living area of the alehouse. The bed was made of straw and covered with blankets of sheep skin. The bedsteads at Melkorka had been naught but stone, meant to teach the value of simplicity to those who resided there, Highborn and Kras alike. This was, by far, the noblest bed Branimir had ever had the pleasure to rest upon.

Kinhar and Falmagon were not as concerned about having the malt. They each held a tankard in hand, enjoying the cheap drink served at the alehouse. Hours ago, supper of porridge and roasted lamb had been consumed. It had been a hearty meal, far better than anything that had touched their stomachs on the road or within the walls of Melkorka.

None of the Highborn paid much attention to Unnvar, who escorted the last of the townsfolk outside into the night before closing the wooden door over the fitted stone slab. The wooden bar was soon secured within the fitted holes of the door jambs. The innkeeper then took his time closing the wooden shutters that covered the two windows at the forefront of the building.

All in all, the alehouse was cozy, warmed by the inner fire, the smoke taking leave through a hole in the thatched roof. The structure had been built above the ground on midden, giving it more insulation and stability. In the winter months, it surely would fare well against the nipping winds of the North.

Unnvar moved idly past his family and children who filled several of the beds in the room, lifting his own tankard of ale. "Finally, we are alone. Again, I ask what news of the south? Of Melkorka?"

Falmagon, being most familiar with the man, spoke, a rueful look on his scarred face. "Melkorka has fallen, the Highborn nearly doused along with it."

Unnvar lowered his head. "I was fearful that it was true. Rumor rarely holds so much detail as to what had been shared…villagers flooding northbound with stories too similar…and when I saw you this day…I am thankful you did not share that lot, Falmagon."

Falmagon raised his drink. "It'll take more than the rise of demons to steal the charge I must see through."

"You were always the dour sort, even as a child, so grandfather had said. It is good that you have become Highborn. It suits you better than being a Northman."

Branimir rocked forward, hearing that Falmagon was not born Highborn. He had become it! What was it that made a human a Highborn opposed to a Northman? How had he not understood this earlier? The Kras piped up from the cot, speaking without thinking, "You are brothers, Lord Falmagon?"

Falmagon, for once, did not retort at the Kras. It was likely that the alcohol had calmed his tensions. "No, but kin still. His mother was my father's sister from what I know, each long dead and resting in tranquility in the Beyond."

"So, we pray," Unnvar said.

Kinhar, also impacted by the strong liquor that amassed in his belly, spoke in slur, "Just a boy child when our paths crossed. You were nearly an infant, barely able to walk. As an orphan being raised by a man who was too old to care for himself, I had little difficulty convincing your grandfather to let me take you to Melkorka. The craft of *Koldovstvo* was imprinted on your soul, marking you as a prodigy, to achieve greatness, even at such a young age. A gift bestowed on you by the gods as payment for stealing your parents away to the hereafter."

"Prodigy, indeed," Dorofej muttered with derision, heard only by Branimir. Dorofej gulped the rest of the wine in his clay cup. Branimir was not sure how the man could even taste the drink as fast as he was swallowing it. The wrinkled Highborn hurriedly filled it and gulped it down again before filling it once more.

Falmagon shrugged. "To be stolen to the Beyond is a boon I would wish upon any man as opposed to living this life."

Unnvar slapped his knee. "Hear, hear! Frailty, disease, death. What was Perom thinking when he created man into existence? What was Svarog thinking when he commended man to be created? What was Dahz thinking when he shielded man from annihilation? The will of the gods I will never understand. I suppose that is why they are divine and I am a Northman."

Dorofej again spoke in tones that only the Branimir could hear, sipping on his plum wine. "The only reason understanding evades you, it's not."

Branimir scratched his black hair. Dorofej was abnormally bitter as of late. But it was the mention of the handful of gods that caused Branimir's confusion. Overall, there were more gods than he would ever be aware. The Kras generally only heard of Dahz from the Highborn, particularly from Kinhar and

Falmagon. Though, as Nedezhda had clearly indicated before her execution, the Highborn were meant to hold allegiance to no specific deity. Branimir had a diminutive understanding of human law, but his family had served the Highborn over many lifetimes. The Kras had a basic interpretation of their beliefs, even when he did not understand their mannerisms. His father had told him of a time when Dahz's sigil had not hung on the walls of Melkorka.

A pounding on the wooden door interrupted Branimir's thoughts and the conversation of the men.

"Coming," Unnvar hollered, quickly glancing at his family that lay sound asleep before making his way to the door.

"Late hour for visitors," Kinhar commented, slumping back in his chair.

Falmagon took the interruption as an opportunity to refill his tankard. He offered the same to Kinhar.

Unnvar unfastened the door, cracking it slightly to peer out before opening it fully. An older gentleman dressed fairer than a peasant but not at the class of nobility, near Kinhar's age, stepped into the *Kal'bane*. At first, his face appeared relieved to see the Highborn but as he scanned the room, his face fell in dismay.

"Lubos, what can I do you for at this hour?"

"My daughter," the man was nearly weeping. "Where is she?"

"Your daughter?"

"That man," Lubos pointed at Falmagon accusingly, "He took her to Melkorka! It was his tongue that swayed her to become Highborn!"

Kinhar began, "I—"

Lubos didn't hear him. "I have heard the stories. I know Melkorka has been deserted and that the Highborn have run away to Arkaim. I have heard it as I have passed through every village this side of the cursed Crags. Where is my daughter, Highborn scum?"

Unnvar raised his hand, "My family sleeps, Lubos—"

"Where is she? Where is Katerina?"

Branimir scurried off the animal skin to the far corner, away from the enraged Northman, the merchant father of Katerina Gajic. The answer was already as obvious as it could be. There could be no painless way to say that which had no need to be said.

"Split legs from torso by the demonic Bukavac, she was. Her blood showered down like a mid-spring rain." Dorofej sniffed, his eyes remaining on the kiln.

Branimir gulped. The white-haired Highborn had chosen a method far less than accommodating.

Lubos's jaw fell, tears crashing to planks at his feet before words could be formed, "What—"

"I know," Dorofej inhaled again, licking the wine from his mustache, "a good pair of breasts is hard to come by, yes?"

Branimir could have sworn Dorofej nodded in agreement with himself.

"Dorofej!" Kinhar roared, suddenly very sober.

"Cursed Highborn!" Lubos lunged for Dorofej with outstretched hands.

Unnvar caught Lubos before he had taken two steps. He clenched him in his grizzly arms holding the man firmly against his massive chest and broad shoulders. If it were possible, it was likely that the merchant would have chewed through his flesh to free himself from Unnvar, living only to murder Dorofej.

Dorofej did not budge.

Lubos kicked wildly toward the tables and beds, off the walls, fighting as though he were an animal in a snare. It did not take long for Unnvar's wife and children to be awakened. The children, barely bigger than Branimir, cried out in panic. The wife hurried to crowd them into a corner protectively. Branimir listened to the woman's voice, squawking at Lubos and her husband to end their folly.

Lubos, try as he might, could not gain leverage against the massive innkeeper as he continued the endless struggle. Unnvar would have made an impressive blacksmith.

"Calm yourself, Lubos!"

Lubos's wails should have made his throat bleed. His tears could have flooded the caverns of Illuard. His wrath could have reached the far ends of the unmapped world. Branimir cried out in unison with the sound, covering his sensitive ears.

In short time, two sentries, with padded armor and copper swords pushed into *Kal'bane*, drawn by the lamenting shouts of the merchant.

"Unnvar! Labos!" the first sentry lifted his voice over the din. "What madness is this?"

Branimir moved his hands from his ears to his eyes, peeking in panic through spread fingertips.

"Die, Highborn!" Labos finally pulled an arm free, elbowing Unnvar in the side.

The innkeeper held his ground, "Take him away from here."

The guardsmen did not hesitate, determined to keep the peace. There was no oddity in removing a belligerent man, kicking and screaming, hard-set on fighting, from the alehouse.

They each took an arm of Lubos and pulled him from *Kal'bane*. The merchant, overcome with lunacy, continued to wrangle about. His expletives were heard as he was dragged down the dirt streets of Arkaim.

"It is a marvel that merchant would have any success in his trade with such manners, yes?"

Unnvar slammed the door shut. The house rattled.

"Do you desire death, Dorofej?" Falmagon heaved with clenched fists. "Look at the mark you leave on the Highborn! Have you no honor? Integrity? Decency? I thought you were Highborn!"

Branimir could not tell if Dorofej's face reddened from wine or temper. The clay cup dropped from his hand, shattering on the floor near his feet as he sprung from his chair and turned on Falmagon. "I am Highborn!" Dorofej's voice boomed grander than a thousand trumpets at war, the room darkening. It was as if some unmarked spell had been cast.

"My hand, you forced, in crafting *kaelandur* to spill Highborn blood, imposing your own justice outside of the King's law, naive or uncaring of the harm inflicted! Binding me to the fate of this warped tale, you do, endangering all Northmen and beyond! A timeless war, you have incited, while wearing a mask of purity with the divergence of a virgin harlot!"

"Nedezhda's blood is on your hands, as heavy as any Highborn, if not more." Falmagon squinted his single eye, revealing *kaelandur* from his brown robes. "Chance you'd like to taste its edge, too, Dorofej?"

Branimir whimpered. "No."

No one heard him.

The white-haired man was riled, hands shaking as he spoke, dark robes blending with the darkness that enveloped the room. "An impertinent, impenitent dupe, you are, Falmagon Sej. You are no more a prodigy than any other swine pulled from a sow's hind legs! I can only presume that your vast ignorance is caused by your ill-fit mother breeding out of season. You give sight to the dead!"

Falmagon charged with *kaelandur* toward the black-robed Highborn, but was quickly caught by an invisible strand of rope. The air wrapped around him, holding him steadily in place.

"Dorofej!" Kinhar barked, stepping between them. His hovering hand signaled he held the Highborn Long-Walker in place with *Koldovstvo*. "What do you mean he gives 'sight to the dead'?"

"There is good cause why Highborn do not craft manmade weapons," Dorofej's voice quivered, icy eyes locked on the copper dagger stretched toward him. He spoke as though his words were the last lungful of air in his body, chockfull with nightmarish foreboding.

"The Highborn are bound to *Koldovstvo*, through spirit and blood by the blessings of the divine, for Highborn, we are. With creation, we infect that which is touched, as we are all touched by the divine at our creation, and so, infected by their breath. With such contagion within us, the living are not easily destroyed, even after death, passing to the Beyond or the Netherworld, another life, another providence. So, it is the fate of the weapons that the Highborn create.

"*Kaelandur* cannot be damaged by any worldly means, and as it consumes life, the weapon will grow in strength, and the victims grow in resilience, tempted to use the weapon with unmeasured enticement. Falmagon's display of *kaelandur* has beaconed Nedezhda to Arkaim's gate!"

"Dahz save us." Unnvar dropped to his knees, any vehemence toward Dorofej was seemingly drained.

Kinhar cried out, "Why have you said nothing?"

"Carve our own fates, we must, and you are the spearhead of the Highborn, who should know these things, yes?" Dorofej answered. "And how could I know that you had *kaelandur* among you? Highborn only by name, it is, and torn asunder through secrecy, yes? Tell me what else you hide from me?"

Branimir wanted to scream out the word *Kindari*. He wanted to tell the secrets of Kinhar and the Ash Tree. But, more than anything, all Branimir could think was that Falmagon planned to kill Dorofej. His chest tightened as he restrained himself from speaking the truth.

Falmagon's deep voice croaked, realizing his fault, "Nedezhda's life has been appropriated twice by this blade, once in life and once in death."

Dorofej collapsed to the ground, the gloom flooding from the room as though it had never been. "Abandon hope, for thieved by halfwits, it has been."

As tears swelled in Dorofej's eyes, it was the weeping of Branimir that was heard. It was not the words he wanted to hear, but it spoke of the vainness of the Highborn's quest. In killing Nedezhda again, she had become more powerful.

Branimir saw Kinhar release Falmagon from the clutches of *Koldovstvo* and then join Dorofej on the floor in a heap. Only a few seconds elapsed before Kinhar spoke with intent to restore lost hope, to continue the tale. A single name was all that could be considered that might give way to the glory coveted. "Erzebeth. Erzebeth will know a way to make this right."

Chapter XII

The morning was filled with gloom. An overhang of clouds obstructed the sun from view. The world was so full of gray that it seemed the cold months were already upon Kalamaar.

"Bad omen," Unnvar said looking at the dark clouds that shadowed the crowd gathered in the town square. "By no means will the Season of Frost be mild this year."

Branimir trembled in the zephyr that blew southeast off the western coastline. The scent of saltwater and fish was stout this morning. Indeed, winter was already on the wind's breath.

"How long is this going to take? Do we really have to do this every day?" One of Unnvar's children pulled at their mother's long, layered skirts.

Branimir watched in amazement. He had seen many children in the past month as he journeyed through villages, but never in the context of parent to child. If only Mojmir were here now to see that the Highborn did not come from lightning bolts.

Dorofej whistled between his teeth, gripping his crumpled hand on Branimir's shoulder tenderly, as if reading his mind and giving comfort, like a grandfather over his grandchild. The two of them walked down the road still in the company of the other Highborn and Unnvar's family. The horde gathered from their homes around them, falling in step with other townsfolk who funneled to the center of Arkaim.

Branimir tried his best to ignore the idle chitchat among the commoners.

"I'll be done soon enough," Unnvar responded over the stirring hum. "The sacrifice has to be made each day during the Festival, or we will not receive Dahz's blessing."

The center of the town was marked by the front of the courtyard that led to King Kar's Manor House. The King's living quarters were multiple stories tall, which was unheard of anywhere outside of Arkaim. To see a building with multiple rooms that was not a castle, not Melkorka, Branimir was flabbergasted. King Kar had outdone himself when having it built.

Cheers and applause replaced the chatter among the crowd as a string of guards in layered armor, made of leather upon stitched cloth, made their way from the Manor House into the King's Courtyard.

Unnvar cheered in a booming tone, forming no words, along with the deafening crowd. He lifted one of his small children on his shoulders to see more clearly. Branimir looked at the small child in envy. All he could see was the back of Falmagon and Kinhar. They were fifty yards from the guards, at minimum, with people shoulder to shoulder every step of the way.

"Do not fret, Branimir." Dorofej shouted above the roar of the masses. "Missing much, you are not."

Branimir raised his head at Dorofej. "I do not even know what I am not missing."

As he finished his sentence, the townsfolk quieted down. Several looked toward him, stepping away. He knew how odd he may appear to them with his pale eyes, hooked nose, and blood skin.

Branimir stuck his tongue out at them in response. He

was accustomed to being treated unfairly, but the response of the Northmen was wearing on him.

"Branimir, mind yourself, yes?" Dorofej rustled through his fuzzy whiskers.

He turned his head away and frowned at the buttocks of the other Highborn, frustrated. "Yes, my Lord."

A voice at the front boomed, addressing the people of Arkaim with authority, "On this day, we offer the sacrifice to Dahz, the Lightbringer, Protector of Men, the White-Clad, who convinced Perom, the Creator, to make man in the image of the gods. Dahz carries *Mulafell*, the Hammer of Righteousness, steadfast while guiding his chariot, *Mioengi*, over the expanse, carrying the sun from our world to the Beyond."

Branimir pulled on Dorofej's black robes, feeling braver in raising questions with his curious mind. "Who is speaking, my Lord? What is he talking about?"

"The Viceroy, possibly," Dorofej said. "He speaks for the King when the King is not here and apparently when he is, yes? A reiteration of custom, and nothing more, the speech is."

An animal bleating rang from the King's Courtyard. Branimir heard it as clearly as Dorofej's words. He looked at the withered Highborn for explanation. "They are killing something, aren't they, my Lord?"

"Yes. I say, a red stag is being brought to the chopping block by rope. Large, beautiful, and magnificent, the beast is. Its blood will be drained from its neck, yes? An offering to Dahz, it is. Before the day is out, the stag will be dragged outside the palisades for the wolves to feast upon, yes?"

Branimir was dumbfounded. "They will waste the meat, my Lord?"

"This is the practice, the primordial custom, of the Northmen, yes? Passed down through word of mouth from father to son since the birth of man on Kalamaar, it has been.

All things have been done this way among humans. Tradition demands lavishness without question, even with the Kras, yes?"

The stag bellowed in the distance.

"My Lord, I would not know." Bran was growing tired of this feeling of emptiness, but could not seem to rid himself of it. At every turn was another reminder of his lonesomeness.

Dorofej grunted, and looked off in the distance, murmuring to himself as if being reminded of some faint thought or dream. Then, with frightening certainty, he said, "You may never know, yes?"

Falmagon turned his head. "Quiet yourselves, will you? This is not the time."

For once, Dorofej had no response for the one-eyed Highborn and sealed his lips with respect to the ceremony of the Festival of Dahz.

Branimir turned back to face the Highborn that stood before him. Kinhar had barely seemed to take notice of the Viceroy speaking, and looked through the people standing about.

The Viceroy continued his rhetoric. "Dahz the White-Clad, praise be sung for the life you gave, the sacrifice you undertook. The sustenance you provide in your holy light nourishes life, laying waste to our suffering. This stag is offered as sacrifice to cool your fury. Come, come quick to release us from the Frost."

The stag wheezed and bleated, grunted and bellowed in defiance to the sacred practice of the Northmen, as though it knew what was to come. Its hooves beat against the dusty ground, stamping and pawing for release, the rope tightened around its neck. A growl reverberated in the animal's throat, but the sentries held fast.

Branimir nearly had to cover his pointed ears as the dirges of the beast rose over the speech of the Viceroy. It was painful to hear, even after what he had witnessed at Melkorka and at Illuard.

Kinhar, apparently giving up in his search, turned to watch the ceremony.

A drum sounded in the King's courtyard, and those in the town square spoke in unison, a song repeated generation upon generation. Branimir was not sure why, but he was absolutely astonished to watch Kinhar, Falmagon, and even, Dorofej merge their own voices to recite the tale, told from grandfather to father to child for all of time.

White-Clad said unto Perom,
Before the Grandfather of Gods,
"The expanse above and under,
Beyond Thrice Nine Lands,
None is worthy of sacrifice,
Nor of praise to covenant.
Construct that which is worthy,
That will sheen in utmost glory."

Thunder-Bearer said unto Svarog,
Before the Lightbringer with Mulafell,
"O how unworthy must we be,
Without welcome, without veneration,
Across the expanse of neither here nor there,
All creation unworthy of covenant.
Bless me to make the worthy,
That will sheen in utmost glory."

Keeper of Kowin the Deathless,
Lord of Lords, said unto Perom and Dahz,
"Craft the Northmen, called Anshedar,
Craft the Highborn, called Anshedar,
Beyond the expanse of here nor there,
Impart unto them the covenant,
Give them charge; pray they are worthy,
To fulfill for all time, for glory."

Branimir heard the knife plunge into the thick skin of the stag. He did not have to see it. The bawling cries of the deer were silenced, its throat cut in this fruitless moment.

The townsfolk of Arkaim raised their hands, roaring in approval of the sacrifice, praying to Dahz the Lightbringer that it would be enough to lessen their struggles in the winter months to come. As was the circumstance every year, the Northmen yearned for a short winter.

"A vain deed," Kinhar said, turning to face the rest of them. His eyes scanned the clouded skies above. "Dahz has turned his eyes away from us this day. It is unlikely that the Lightbringer will be welcoming of this sacrifice."

Falmagon nodded. "I feel it, too. Our worthiness is to be tested. We are on our own in this quest."

Unnvar shooed his family back toward the alehouse, and huffed up at the three men in their robes. "Not completely. I have given it thought since our conversation last night, Highborn. I will accompany you, at your will, until this evil has been forced from Kalamaar and back into the trenches of the Netherworld where it belongs."

Dorofej watched the innkeeper's family depart. "Obligations here in Arkaim, you have, yes? What does your wife say?"

"I do not need my wife's approval, Dorofej. I choose my own path."

Branimir's jaw dropped. The innkeeper clearly had just sent his wife away before announcing his decision. The scowl beneath Dorofej's beard suggested he had come to the same conclusion.

"You know not what you ask, Unnvar," Kinhar replied.

"I know well enough what tales I have heard of Highborn

and what peril follows your number. Though, death in battle brings more glory to my family name than my throat being slit by demons while I sleep."

Dorofej said, "Chance of either fate is not altered by the road we travel, yes? Your throat still may find itself split open and your family name without honor, yes?"

Unnvar insisted, "Your numbers are lacking. I can offer more than what this Kras can provide, that much is for certain. Will you have me?"

"Fleeting, certainty is."

Falmagon ignored Dorofej's clashing comment. "I welcome you gladly among us, Unnvar, as kin and friend."

Kinhar nodded. "I do not contend with your words, Unnvar. If you wish to come along, I will not hold you from it. Though, our priority in this instance is to reach Erzebeth. You had said she would be here this morning?"

"I did." Unnvar nodded at the King's Courtyard at Kinhar's back.

The five of them, Branimir included, looked onward at the Courtyard expectantly. The town's people had meandered out of the square, back to their shops, to their homes, and to their daily obligations, leaving full view of King Kar's Manor House and courtyard.

The red stag lay bleeding, dead at the feet of the several guardsmen who had led it by rope to the slaughter. They worked idly to clean the yard, preparing the stag to be dragged to the wolves, and for another slaughter tomorrow morning.

The doors to the Manor House opened, and out stepped four guards, suited in their padded armor and equipped with copper swords. The woman, known as Erzebeth Navenka, trailed behind them into the King's Courtyard.

Even at a hundred yards, Branimir could see the prominent woman that Kinhar continuously spoke of as though she were a deliverer of their salvation, destined to pull them from the clutches of their own folly.

Erzebeth was a tall, slender woman with dark disheveled hair that hung to her shoulders, as unkempt as Falmagon's. Her eyes were blue like that of all the Highborn and Northmen, marking her among their kind. Her skin was exceptionally pale, more so than most of the humans upon Kalamaar. Though this may have been from residing in a cell for the past month. It was hard for Branimir to say.

The most distinguishing feature on Erzebeth was the decomposing hand that hung from her neck, missing from her right arm. Under her dilapidated white cloak, more rags than cloak, the severed hand hung loosely. The stub had been cared for with relatively decent precision, considering it being a penalty for a crime of thievery. Bone and flesh had been sewn shut and cauterized, seemingly healed as well as it could be.

"In the mornings she walks about the courtyard" Unnvar said. "As I said, a constant reminder to those that may employ thievery here in Arkaim."

"Why was her wrist mended? Why did they not let her die, my Lords?" Branimir asked.

"It is a greater punishment to live in dishonor and humiliation than to be allowed to die," Kinhar puffed, clearly upset after seeing Erzebeth in her deprived state.

"How long has she been put on display?" Falmagon shuddered.

"Since the hand was cut off," Unnvar answered.

"Bah! Enough of this." Kinhar scowled. "We have wasted enough time. The King will have counsel with the Highborn this very moment."

Kinhar stuffed his hands to his sides in fists, and entered the King's Courtyard without hesitation. Falmagon and Unnvar quickly jumped in step with Kinhar, warily watching the four guards and Erzebeth walking about the courtyard.

"This is unwise," Dorofej said from behind Branimir, "and yet, naught else can be done. Here we go, yes?"

Dorofej pushed Branimir forward to catch up with the other three men, and Dorofej hobbled along, covering the rear.

They had only taken three steps into the King's courtyard when Branimir noticed from the corner of his eye that Erzebeth had raised her head. The woman held her gaze longingly toward the men that approached the Manor House. Her eyes gave away her recognition of the men, and although not one of them returned the gaze, a glimmer of hope surfaced on her trodden face.

"Hold there," a guard jumped up from the slain deer. He ran forward and stepped in front of Kinhar.

The Highborn did not slow his pace and walked right around the man as though he had said nothing. In moments, the group was nearly halfway across the courtyard.

"I said 'hold' or you will be cut down!"

Branimir was the first to see the archers on either side of the Manor House. A quick count told him that there were nine, already with the arrows nocked on the luks, or shortbows.

Kinhar stopped. "I wish to see King Merreider Kar. He necessitates my counsel."

The guard moved his body in front of the gray-haired Highborn, taking a deep breath, seemingly outmatched with Falmagon and Unnvar on either side, but well protected by the archers at his rear. "King Kar does not receive *counsel* from anyone during the Festival, and when he does receive any *counsel*, he decides when it is necessary. Now, return the way you have come, or you will be cut down where you stand."

Kinhar's eyes were cold, staring into the guard's eyes for what felt to Bran like the entire harvest past. "You will take me to the King. I am Highborn, and I will give him *counsel* as I choose when I choose. If you refuse, I *will* cut you down!"

The man's eyes quaked in hesitation, the word 'Highborn' shaped his mouth, likely determining whether he should believe the threat or consider it rubbish.

The guards approached them as the door to the Manor House opened again. The Viceroy stepped forward, with a copper sword in one hand and a rod in the other, marking his position.

"I am Viceroy Stepan Komarov, the voice of King Kar. What is going on here? Who are you?" he demanded.

Kinhar put his hand on the guard and shoved him to the side, taking two bold steps toward the Viceroy, who lifted his sword in response. "Kinhar Sayan, Highborn from Melkorka upon the Seven Islands, and I will speak with the King, lest he wishes the destruction of all Arkaim and the end of whatever legacy he plans to bestow on his children, Viceroy Komarov."

Stepan kept his sword at the ready. "We were informed that Melkorka had fallen and that the Highborn were dead. I'd say you are a bit late to attempt such a ploy here."

"We are not all dead," Kinhar declared, taking another step toward the Viceroy. Falmagon stepped forward as well, leading with his crooked staff, *Habërmani*, holding his typical iron visage.

"Leave this place," the Viceroy said with poise, "and do not return."

"I will speak to Merreider Kar."

"What is this? You outwardly refuse to address the King by his title, and in front of the law at that!" the Viceroy exclaimed. "Sacrilege! Penalty by death!"

"Wha—"

Unnvar did not have a chance to finish his protest before archers released their sharpened projectiles. The arrows flew with precision from their luks toward the lot of them.

For once, Branimir was not surprised when the stone wall flung up, stopping the arrows and snapping them in half. As the wall fell away, as quickly as it had formed, the archers immediately reached for another round from their quiver. Kinhar swept his hand toward them, tearing the luks from their grasp one by one and flinging them back toward the town square. The guard that had stood nearest reached for his sword, but was struck across the jaw by *Habërmani*. He slumped to the ground in a heap.

Kinhar flew across the ground to the Viceroy's side, though his feet never moved, the wind carrying him a hundred paces in a heartbeat. His tone was as full of authority as it had ever been. "Do not speak to me of sacrilege. I am Highborn! I know what is sacred better than any Northmen. Now, show me to your King."

Stepan did not muddle over the demand. The archers had been disarmed and the guards would prove equally useless against such power.

He cleared his throat. "Follow this way, Highborn."

Kinhar pointed to Erzebeth with commanding authority. "The woman comes with us."

"I—"

It did not take more than a look from the spearhead of the Highborn to cut the Viceroy from any dispute.

"Very well. Bring her along," the Viceroy yielded.

"Dorofej and Unnvar remain here at the door," Kinhar ordered as they stepped toward the Manor House. "If any one of these men attempts to enter these doors before we have exited, Dorofej will use *Koldovstvo* to rip out the man's intestines."

Dorofej's bushy eyebrows could not have lifted any further off his forehead. "Kinhar, hardly do I—"

Kinhar kept his chin suspended, a sudden reminder of who held sway over the Highborn. "Will you not, Dorofej?"

Dorofej blinked several times before painting a wide grin on his face. His tone raised with unmatched giddiness as though ripping intestines from men was his favorite pasttime. "Like gutting a fish, yes?"

Color completely drained from the Viceroy's face. He gave further direction to the archers and sentries. "Yes, well, each of you stay out here, and wait for our return."

In a matter of moments, Branimir found himself being led into the Manor House. The Viceroy's footsteps were quickened as they made their way into the two-story building, hurrying to end this madness once and for all.

Kinhar and Falmagon walked ahead of Branimir. The Kras looked uneasily behind him at Erzebeth, her skin as white as frost.

The tall woman followed behind with her head lowered, her eyes averted from Branimir, and locked on the hand hanging from her neck. There was no mistake. The woman was actually smiling, a gleam in her eye.

Branimir winced.

They were led into a large room where the King's chair sat against the backdrop of violet tapestries. The signet of the King, the *Svehla*, was sewn with gold thread upon the fabric. It was the same as the banners outside the gates of Arkaim.

The chair itself was made from wood, possibly elm from the nearby forests, inscribed with circlets of an alloy in which Branimir was not familiar. It had a hint of the orange found in copper but with a darker brown color to it. Branimir was intrigued, as each circlet held a small diamond. He barely noticed King Kar sitting on his throne.

"King Merreider Kal, Twelfth King of Kalamaar, Bearer of the *Svehla*, the Golden Scepter of Svarog, I present Kinhar Sayan, Highborn of Melkorka from Folkmar, upon the Seven Islands of Forghar."

Branimir did as the Viceroy did, kneeling to one knee in respect of the nobility before him. As for Kinhar and Falmagon, their necks were as stiff as stale bread. Branimir could only guess that Erzebeth held a similar stature, as the Highborn men, snickering under her breath behind him.

King Kar sat with elbow on knee, a piercing gaze behind a flat nose and beneath a balding scalp. "What is the meaning of this, Stepan?" He waved off two servants that were near the throne. They bowed and made their way out of the room.

"It is the Festival of Dahz."

Viceroy Stepan Komarov stood. "I am aware, my King. These men—"

Kinhar interjected, "We must set aside custom for what comes, King Kar. Have you not heard of the battle at Melkorka? The Bukavac who march on Kalamaar? The hell that comes to claim the lives of Arkaim? Why do you not prepare for battle? Why do you waste hours slaying stags and feeding wolves?"

The King stood up from his throne with a clenched jaw. Irritation immediately lined the wrinkles in his forehead. His voice was unmatched. The King surely was accustomed to speaking to those lesser who flooded his courtroom. Smoothing the fur cloak, he rumbled, "What right do you have to speak to royalty in this way? The Highborn have an oath to protect the King and the law of men. Your twisted tongue does not mark you as Highborn. Such brashness in Arkaim will only end with your head on a wooden spike, Highborn or not."

Falmagon hit his crooked staff against the ground, but was stopped by Kinhar's hand.

Kinhar said, "Find forgiveness, King Kar. I know my place and my duty. I also know what evil comes, and that is why I speak with sureness, not to be confused with arrogance. My allegiance is to virtue and justice, as is yours, but war is coming."

King Kar plumped back down, his face softening considerably as though he may have accepted the quick apology. His beady eyes, sinking into his skull beneath the layers of age and fat, skimmed over the Highborn. He forced a grin with his gapped teeth. "Rumors of war and demons have haunted Kalamaar for as long as I can remember, even when my father reigned. Northmen are uneducated and full of superstition. For a month, the blathering of fools has been brought to my Manor House and Arkaim still stands."

"Now," the King pressed on without breath, "tell me who this other shabby peasant is, the imp kneeling behind you, and why you have my prisoner in your possession when she should be plodding in my courtyard, inhaling the stench of her own filth. Make haste, before I have you all gutted upon the palisades."

Kinhar's ears reddened. Curling his upper lip, and holding clenched fists. "Falmagon Sej, Highborn of Melkorka, and Branimir Baran, a Kras slave, also from Melkorka. We have traveled to Arkaim to—"

The King stood again from his throne, making his way toward Branimir. His spoke with amusement, "A Kras, you say? Well, that is something. No one has seen a Kras in two-hundred years, so they say. How can you be sure it is not a demon?"

Kinhar threw his head back and exhaled. "Branimir is not a demon. The Kras have served the Highborn for a long time, and have resided at Melkorka without interruption throughout that time. I am quite aware of what a Kras is, whether Northmen, nobility, or otherwise has seen one. Now—"

"I will keep him!" King Kar proclaimed. "He is already trained as a slave, you say? Most excellent."

"You cannot keep him. He is my property and must stay in my company."

The King did not appear to hear Kinhar. After a few more steps, he reached out and touched Branimir's red, pointed ear. The Kras kept his head stooped and shuddered again.

Bran was relieved that Kinhar was not planning on trading him off. He no longer had fear of being killed by the Highborn, especially with Dorofej among them. But, he had the sense Kinhar might risk anything to acquire Erzebeth. At first, Branimir thought Kinhar had dragged him into the Manor House for the sole purpose of trading him. Though, he now guessed it was to keep him from being alone with Dorofej.

"You cannot deny me what I want. I am the King."

"And, I am Highborn," Kinhar said.

King Kar raised his hand to strike Kinhar, but it was quickly held by a strand of air weaved from *Koldovstvo*.

Branimir found himself sneaking a glance at the woman. She stood with exceptional composure, her lips sealed.

"Careful, my King." The Viceroy warned meekly, taking a step backward. "The Highborn's power was displayed in your courtyard. And more wait outside."

"More of them?" King Kar said nervously, struggling against the unseen hand that grasped his wrist.

Kinhar let him loose with an untamed scowl.

The King stepped back, lowering his hand in bewilderment, as though he were seeing daylight for the first time. "You are Highborn, truly?"

Falmagon and Kinhar had such fury in their eyes that they could have instigated the sun to fall across the sky backwards.

Kinhar spoke as level as he could. "I am. We are all who remain from Melkorka. We have come a long way to receive returned service, from the royal family that we have, for so many millennia, protected, King Merreider Kal, Twelfth King of Kalamaar."

"What returned service? What is it that you require?"

"The release of Erzebeth Navenka into my custody."

The King frowned. "Why do you want her? She is a thief and as unrighteous as any Northmen can be."

"She has skills that we require, skills that will ensure the protection of this kingdom and future kingdoms of men. That is all that you need to know, King Kar."

The tides had quickly turned between the Highborn and the King of Kalamaar. Branimir did not understand how the craft of *Koldovstvo* held sway over men, even Kings, for that matter. The Kras had never known any other way, but to the Northmen, it seemed *Koldovstvo* was feared beyond any nightmare they could muster.

The King looked about his Manor House, considering the words of the Highborn. "I will trade her for the Kras."

Kinhar was quick in his response. "I said you could not have him. This is not a negotiation, King Kar. We are not bartering. If it were, I have already paid my dues in the deaths of the Highborn who fought against the Bukavac."

Curiosity touched the King's tongue. "What talents does this Kras have? Why would a slave be so important to you?"

Kinhar spoke carefully. "He is the last of his kind and must remain in my protection. If there were others, I would freely give him to you."

King Kar licked his lips again, and rubbed a hand over his smooth scalp as though it were flooded with hair. He finally conceded, and said, "Tell me of Dorofej then. What is the fate of the old man?"

Branimir could not stop himself from gaping like a fool. Was it true that Dorofej had left Melkorka and had known the King of Arkaim? He nearly fell over from where he kneeled.

Kinhar pursed his lips, eyes widening, nearly as speechless as Branimir. "He is outside your Manor House… in the courtyard."

"I will permit for you to take, Erzebeth. I have grown tired of her presence in my dungeon. But, I wish to speak with Dorofej before you leave. I want to hear of the Bukavac from him, a man who I can trust, a Highborn with who I am familiar."

Kinhar dipped his head. "As you wish, my King." The title was spoken with a hint of mockery, barely discernible, but caught easily by the ear of the Kras, who knew the spearhead of the Highborn too well. "Branimir, fetch Dorofej and make it swift."

Branimir had no qualms in following the simple order of the Highborn, as he had for the last half century.

Chapter XIII

Unnvar had shut down the *Kal'bane* upon their return. He then had sent his family outside of the home to make room for Kinhar, Falmagon, Erzebeth, and Branimir. The man worked quickly to close the shutters and door as the fellowship made their way into the alehouse.

Erzebeth stumbled into the large room and slowly removed the severed hand from her neck. As though she were seeing it for the first time, she laid it down on one of the crafted tables in the room. The decomposing appendage, gray, shriveled and wilted, had maggots tearing through it. Her eyes were glued to the hand that had once been attached to her wrist.

Branimir, second behind Erzebeth, crunched up his face in disgust, feeling his stomach churn. The hand alone was worse off than any corpse he had ever seen.

"Erzebeth," Kinhar said, his feet echoing on the baseboards. She said nothing. The gray-haired man approached her from behind, embracing the woman.

Branimir watched as Erzebeth shuddered.

She lifted her good hand and placed it on his before turning around and hugging the Highborn somewhat clumsily.

Her voice quivered, holding an accent that was beyond anything Branimir had ever heard, stranger than Dorofej's. "I knew not what my fate was, but the gods have looked after me. Never would I have thought you would come to liberate me in such a dark hour."

"If I had known, I would have come all the quicker."

Falmagon dipped his head from the door. "We both would have, Erzebeth. By *Mulafell*, we would have!"

Branimir raised an eye at Falmagon's use of the name of Dahz's hammer. It must be a form of Highborn swearing that he was not familiar with. He had never heard a Highborn curse before.

Erzebeth forced a smile at Falmagon, taking a deep breath between clenched teeth, and still clinging to the robes of Kinhar. Her teeth were yellow against pale lips, black strands of tattered hair, strung about her face as though she had been on a battlefield for months. In this moment, she appeared to be a savage, a stranger to civilization.

That strained smile only lasted a matter of seconds, before the tears burst and her mouth opened in lamentation. She buried her face into Kinhar's shoulder.

Branimir did not want to be rude, but he had to cover his ears from the overwhelming sound of her weeping. The wailing for her suffering, the mourning for her lost hand, the grieving for her lost time was strewn together in a pitfall of misery. In all Branimir's time, he had never seen a human so vulnerable, so forsaken, as Erzebeth was in the arms of Kinhar.

After several minutes, the bear of a man, Unnvar, became noticeably uncomfortable. He shifted about the room, and started to pace before muttering something about checking on his family. With that, he made his way out the door, shutting it quickly behind him.

Kinhar hushed the woman softly, rubbing her head in comfort, like a mother would with a child. Never had Branimir seen the man display such compassion.

As Erzebeth's sobbing visibly subsided, Branimir removed

his hands. He could not blame her, considering she may have been withholding such pain for a month or more.

Falmagon found a seat and held *Habërmani* in his lap, having less feeling in his voice than Kinhar. "How did this come to be?"

Branimir was not sure what the one-eyed Highborn was referencing, but assumed he meant the missing hand from the woman's arm.

She lifted her head, eyes drained. The shallow lighting in the room caused her eyes to appear brown, and then turned blue once again. Branimir seemed to be the only one who noticed.

"I was with…I was with Ragnarok…"

"Who is Ragnarok?"

Erzebeth paused before replying. "It is no matter now. He is dead. It is well enough to know I was with…him. It was the day before harvest and Pal'ka was taking place as custom."

Falmagon lowered his eyes, taking full meaning of what it meant to be *with* Ragnarok. Pal'ka was branded as a festival of fornication among the Northmen. It was a time when lovers intermingled for the pleasures of the flesh for blessing before the harvest.

"You always looked to Myestera for guidance." Kinhar spoke in reference to the festival that worshiped the Mother of the Stars, the Moon Goddess.

"And that day was no different, though I still do not understand what she aims to tell me."

"How so?"

"I'm trying to explain. Arkaim was enjoying the bonfires, filling their evening with drinking and dancing. The girls had made their wreaths of ferns, to learn how they might marry. Ragnarok had asked me to make a wreath too. He had given me his signet ring as a gift if I would only make a wreath. I had never made a wreath before but I wanted to please him, so I accepted the ring. Never had I wanted to please any man, the way that I wanted to please Ragnarok. Not for years…not since Meimer…"

She paused to cover her mouth in remembrance. When she raised her stub to her face, tears formed once more in her eyes.

"Branimir," Kinhar said. His hand was still placed upon Erzebeth as she spoke. "Some wine."

"I'm sorry," she apologized.

"It is quite alright. Continue when you are ready." Kinhar led Erzebeth to a table nearby, where they sat across from one another.

Branimir rushed to grab the jug of wine in the corner that Unnvar had, and filled clay cups for the humans. They paused as he filled a cup for each, serving the pale woman first. Again, he thought he saw remnants of brown in her blue eyes.

Erzebeth ignored the Kras, seemingly unsurprised by the Kras and his loyalty to the Highborn. She continued, "I made the wreath and tossed it into Strega's Deep. He had been with me and we watched it float out into the waters. We thought that we would watch it until the sun was gone, as was custom, but … but…

"What?" Falmagon insisted, suddenly appearing annoyed by the woman's emotional reaction to her memories.

Erzebeth breathed deep. "A beast, a serpent, lifted from the ocean and swallowed it whole."

"What are you speaking of?" Kinhar huffed. "A true serpent in Strega's Deep."

Erzebeth dropped her head into her hands, while Falmagon looked at her in amazement. His expression indicated that he thought Erzebeth had gone mad.

"Yes," Erzebeth said shrilly. "I know what it sounds like, but it is the truth. It was black and scaled unlike any beast I have ever have seen, its mouth cone-shaped and full of razor teeth. From the water depths, it rose, and down it plunged again, in a moment quicker than breath. But, not so quick that

I could not see it, nor Ragnarok."

Falmagon shook his head. "Did any other see it?"

"No," Erzebeth said, "Otherwise, I might still have my hand."

"I do not understand, my Lady," Branimir said. He could not help but be fascinated by the tale.

Erzebeth twisted sharply at Branimir, taken aback that he had spoken to her at all. Branimir nearly apologized for the question. Though, the look on Falmagon's face suggested Branimir was not the only one completely confused by the jumbled story.

Erzebeth explained further, "Ragnarok dived into the waters to fight the beast and to return my wreath, as he thought it was a bad omen. I screamed for him to stop, but the wool-headed man would not listen to me. He was slain by the beast, though I did not see it.

"My screams for Ragnarok were eventually heard by the guard when I stood on the shore. The curs thought my screaming was due to a quarrel between us. When his bloody limbs washed ashore the next day, they thought I had killed him for the worth of his signet ring I wore on my hand. They could not prove the murder, so the King chose to take my hand, labeling me thief."

Kinhar shook his head in bewilderment. "I am so sorry that this has happened to you, Erzebeth."

"I have seen men live and die. I grieve for Ragnarok, but I will heal in time. What I need is to understand what Myestera is trying to tell me."

"Clear, it is," Dorofej smacked his lips from the doorway with a half-wit smile. The door was already fastened behind him. None, not even Branimir, had seemed to hear him come into the alehouse, as though he had come through like smoke through the cracks. "The wreath, a symbol of forthcoming bethrothment, was on the water and then it was not, swallowed whole by a beast unsought, yes? Clear, it is, that you are *not* to be married."

Falmagon jumped up at the Highborn's face, whipping *Habërmani* defensively toward Dorofej. Yet when he saw it was Dorofej, he slammed the crooked staff down. "Your wisdom was not requested, old man."

Dorofej dipped his head half-heartedly. His words were crisp. "Freely, I offer it."

Kinhar moved from his table, and approached Dorofej, almost falling over his own feet. "Why did Merreider Kar want to speak with you? Why did you not say that you knew him, Dorofej?"

Dorofej's eyebrows reflected their own language, lifting and falling in deliberation. "Ah, I did not know I knew him, and I am still not sure how I do. Awkward when someone says they know you, and talks to you and you just cannot seem to place them, yes?" Dorofej shrugged his shoulders. "By and by, the King wished to speak of the weather at Melkorka."

Kinhar scowled. "I do not have patience for your riddles or your games. What did the King want?"

Dorofej grunted, stumbling past Kinhar and finding a seat at the nearest table. "If you must know, he wanted to know what happened with Lubos Gajic last night."

"What did you tell him?"

"Told him the Jarl of Narthwich would need help against the Bukavac as we had promised, I did. We did promise to tell King Kar of their plight and send aid, did we not? Keep our word, the Highborn must, yes?"

"What did you tell him about Lubos?"

"Ah, the simple truth. Exceedingly distraught by the death of his daughter, the merchant was."

"That is not the full of it, Dorofej."

"Perhaps, no, but my mind is a bit foggy on the issue, yes? Full as my belly with plum, my head was. Regardless, I'm afraid that it matters very little, yes?"

Branimir asked the question. "Why is that?"

"Given freedom this morning to go find his daughter's remains, Lubos was."

"There will be nothing worthwhile to find at Melkorka, if he even makes it there." Falmagon said in shock. "It has been too long."

"Comforted in knowing Katerina had a fitting death, the man can be. Much more proper than being left alive with a missing appendage, yes?" Dorofej smoothed out his robes, shrugging his shoulders with feigned innocence.

Bran was awestruck by the old Highborn's hateful words.

Erzebeth stood from her chair with a sneer. "Excuse me? Who is this old man?"

"Bah!" Kinhar threw his hands in the air. "He only aims to rile you up, Erzebeth. Ignore him! We all must."

The woman fumed across the room, her steps heavy, and stood over the long-bearded Highborn. Dorofej looked up at her, crossing one leg over the other. She growled at him. "Do not push me. I will tear you limb from limb."

Dorofej cleared his throat, leaning over his knees toward Erzebeth. "With just the one hand or should I expect gnashing of teeth?"

Erzebeth screamed, her eyes flashing blue to brown and back again. She raised her foot and slammed the heel into Dorofej's chest. The old Highborn busted through the back of his chair, toppling over himself twice over before landing sprawled out near Branimir.

Dorofej wheezed, rolling over on his knees with what little strength he had. His icy gaze locked onto Erzebeth as she approached him.

"Anshedar… you are not, yes?" He used the old term for human before they were separated between Highborn and Northmen.

If there was any response from the woman, Branimir

did not hear it. Erzebeth lifted another chair and slammed it down upon his head.

Bran squealed, rushing to Dorofej's side. His eyes fluttered and he fell into darkness in Branimir's arms.

Chapter XIV

Branimir sat among the shards of wood that were scattered across the floor. He lightly placed the damp wool cloth on Dorofej's head. The old man moaned and exhaled heavily but remained unconscious. The old Highborn was lucky he was not dead. The kick alone should have crushed his brittle chest, or at least, caused his heart to stop beating.

The swelling over his right eyelid was already turning purple. Blood had been wiped away from his temple and cheek. He had gotten the wound to stop bleeding, forming a dried barrier of blood for the time being. As for Falmagon, Kinhar, and Erzebeth, they had ignored him and Dorofej for the past half hour.

Branimir could only glare at the two men who were meant to be Dorofej's Highborn brethren.

Falmagon's voice echoed in the room from near the kiln. "What is this land called again?"

"Maharia," Erzebeth said.

"Maharia?" Branimir repeated beneath his breath as an echo. It had a strange sound to it.

"It is a month journey on the boat, but that is where we must go if you want to find the Ash Tree."

"I have never heard of Maharia. The Ash Tree must be on Kalamaar or the Seven Islands. This is where man was created. If there were land beyond the ocean, the Northmen surely would have found it. We all know the sea is endless, pouring off into nothingness, into the mouth of Strega himself," Unnvar claimed before gulping the rest of his drink.

"Maharia is very real, and so are the many lands beyond it," Erzebeth assured the innkeeper. "Maharia is a land much different from this one with beasts that are unlike anything you have seen. The road to the Ash Tree is well guarded and dangerous. Making it there alive will not be an easy task."

Unnvar gulped, squinting his eyes. "How do you know so much about Maharia, Erzebeth?"

Erzebeth did not respond.

But Kinhar did. "Erzebeth has been there before and can lead us there. She is the reason we have come to Arkaim."

"And I am thankful you did, Kinhar Sayan," Erzebeth picked something from her teeth roughly with her fingernail. "You risk much by sharing my name and my life with men hardly known to me. Knowledge of the Ash Tree is sought by every man living, seeking eternal life and the secrets of the gods. Men would easily kill to gain my knowledge!"

"These are trusted men, Erzebeth," Kinhar assured her with gentle eyes.

Erzebeth turned to look at Branimir, who continued to care for Dorofej on the floor. She may very well have been taking a glance at the old man, but Bran felt her eyes in his direction regardless.

"I hope you are right, Kinhar. Too much is at risk if they are not." She stared into the fire, the wild strands of her hair hanging over her eyes. "Let us hope they are."

Falmagon pulled at his mustache. "Will you come along as a guide?"

Erzebeth looked at her forearm that had been stitched shut, skin wrapped on top of skin. "I have good reason to travel there once again. You will be coming along with me and not the other way around, Falmagon."

Branimir wrinkled his nose, suddenly noticing that her severed hand was sweltering in the kiln. The burning flesh smelled acrid. He had not seen her throw it into the flames, but she must have.

Erzebeth added, "Though, I would be surprised if you all survive beyond the voyage." Her eyes glanced to Dorofej's body again. "It is a grueling journey and not suitable for most."

Branimir spoke up, feeling it necessary, "Dorofej is stronger than he looks, my Lady. He will keep up just fine."

"That is twice you have spoken to me without being spoken to," Erzebeth scolded. "Who keeps the reins on this Kras? I know enough of the Highborn and their kind to understand what is and what is not acceptable."

Branimir turned his face away.

Kinhar put his hand to his head. "Branimir has been allowed more autonomy in recent days, as he continues to prove his loyalty to the Highborn and serve us. His insights are worthwhile. Even now, he speaks truth. Dorofej has surprising fortitude despite his appearance and lack of manners. The question is who will take this journey to Maharia?"

Falmagon lifted his hand. "It is no question that I am with you in this tale until the end, Kinhar. Through blessing and misfortune, I will see this through."

"I gave my word that I would travel with the Highborn to save my family from a terrible fate," Unnvar spoke deeply, "but I fail to understand what need there is to go to Maharia and find the Ash Tree?"

Kinhar explained, "Nedezhda has said she will destroy the Ash Tree to destroy all life. We must find a way to stop her. We must protect the Ash Tree for all we are worth."

"I don't understand. Just go find her and kill her again. Strike the *Eretik* down," Unnvar said.

"Not that simple, Unnvar. Nedezhda cannot be killed without returning from the Netherworld again. We must find a way to destroy her soul and not simply the undead body she maintains. Not to mention, Nedezhda has unlimited access to *Koldovstvo* in battle. Even the Highborn are unmatched against her."

Unnvar scratched his head, and grunted. "You think to have a better chance at the Ash Tree?"

"The Ash Tree is surrounded by the Waters of Life. If we Highborn can stand within that pool during battle, we, too, can use *Koldovstvo* without the effects of aging or death."

Branimir promptly spoke again. "My Lords, you cannot battle Nedezhda for eternity within the Waters of Life, forever protecting the Ash Tree."

"We will if we must," Kinhar said sullenly.

Dorofej stirred on the ground.

Erzebeth thoughtfully shook her head. "That will not be necessary, I would not think. Though, the alternative brings more danger than any deed done by any man."

Branimir stared at Erzebeth in waiting for her explanation.

"The world has many exits to the Netherworld, but none of those openings provide passage both ways. The Crags of Kazimir near Melkorka, for instance, are only one of the exits from the frozen wasteland. The entrance to the Netherworld is at the Ash Tree, although you cannot exit the Netherworld from there."

"What are you suggesting?" Falmagon looked horrified.

Kinhar bellowed with equal confusion, "Why would we want to enter the Netherworld, Erzebeth?"

Erzebeth stared hard into the fire, as though she were reading from a scroll smothered in ink stains. "The soul can be eternally killed if it is taken in this life and the next. You could stop Nedezhda's ascent from the Netherworld if you can send her back to the Netherworld, follow her over, and defeat her in the frozen wasteland."

"In the realm of the gods?" Unnvar nearly fell back in his chair, the shutters shaking with his booming voice.

The sound jarred Dorofej into consciousness. He sputtered in surprise, trying to look around with little success. Dorofej had likely not been in this much pain since the Dreka nearly tore his leg off at Illuard.

"I thought you were dead, my Lord," Branimir whispered.

Dorofej's frosty eyes peered back through half-open eyelids. He lay his head back against the floor. "Not quite."

None of the others noticed Dorofej stirring. They were much too caught up in their musing.

"I did not say it was easy. I do not know what lies on the other side, nor would I know the way to return."

"By *Mulafell*," Falmagon gripped *Habërmani* until his knuckles were white.

Dorofej cleared his throat, forcing himself to sit up off the floor. It was a slow ascension. "What…what madness is being shared whilst I rest my eyes?"

Falmagon and Unnvar snickered and stared at the Highborn who had been matched by the woman only hours before.

Kinhar spoke with the leadership that gave him the title of spearhead. "We are going to Maharia, Dorofej, to protect the Ash Tree from Nedezhda. Erzebeth knows the way."

Dorofej snorted, the bristles of his mustache rippling, giving no suggestion of being shocked. "Indeed, she does."

Dorofej struggled to make it to his feet, clambering about, causing a rumpus as he scraped chair and table against the floorboards. The rest of the gathering, including Kinhar, raised their eyes in his direction. He waited until he was fully standing before he opened his thin lips again.

His words were blunt, in the way that was no less expected from him. "You are not Anshedar, nor from this age, yes?"

Erzebeth stood up, the blue eyes completely faded, leaving brown in their stead. Every other feature was remarkably the same, skin as pale as the first snowfall.

Unnvar and Branimir were the only two who moved backwards. Unnvar was taken aback enough to stand from his chair and skip backwards across the room nearly toppling over. Branimir simply stepped backwards and moved behind Dorofej. Branimir had known Erzebeth withheld something strange.

"I am Vucari of *Anaerfell*, beyond the shores of Maharia, Dorofej. You would not know my kind unless you had been to Rhian. I am a Warden of the Ash Tree."

Dorofej stood, shoulders broad, and faced the Vucari with a scowl. "Skin-switchers still walk on Maharia, yes?"

"I have not been to Maharia for half a century, but I imagine the Vucari remain among the forests, keeping a watchful eye on the Ash Tree."

Unnvar's voice did not quiver, but it did crack. "How have you remained alive so long, and still remain so young?"

"The same as I have," Kinhar said evenly, his eyes meeting each around the room. "The Ash Tree restores life and youth. Erzebeth has been a friend longer than any of you have been alive, including Branimir here. She and I have traveled the lengths of the world, and seen many things, including the Ash Tree."

Dorofej's eyebrows raised as the confession left the lips of the Highborn. "So, you have been to the Ash Tree, Kinhar."

"That I have, Dorofej, but it was a very long time ago. I do not remember the way any longer. I had brought its fruits, in the form of ash branches, with me back to Kalamaar and have used them with the power of *Koldovstvo* to sustain my life for years. The ash branch that was used in the battle at Melkorka against the *Eretik* was the last of its sustenance."

Dorofej goaded. "You seek the Ash Tree and the Waters of Life to replenish your life, yes? To share it with your prodigy, the Highborn Long-Walker, yes?"

Kinhar spoke carefully. "I seek the Ash Tree to stop Nedezhda from claiming the lives of the innocent. I seek the

Ash Tree to bring exaltation to the gods that give us life. I seek the Ash Tree for the Highborn. I seek the Ash Tree for the Northmen. And, I look to share the reaping of such a holy treasure with any who accompany me to righteousness and glory!"

Branimir could not help but wonder if that included him, the lowly Kras, as well.

Falmagon and Kinhar were quaking, their secrets seeping through to Dorofej's ears. There was no other way. The old man would eventually be able to put the pieces together, if he had not already. Branimir only hoped Dorofej would share what he was learning. In the meantime, Branimir gawked at Falmagon and Kinhar, who looked like children caught taking a pie off the shutter ledge.

"Will you accompany us to Maharia, Dorofej?" Kinhar asked.

Dorofej looked around the room, as though he were a blind man weighing silver pieces against cowries, before finally relaxing his face. "Not much of a choice, yes?"

Kinhar let loose a sigh of relief. "Then, it is settled. We will need to acquire a boat."

Dorofej scratched his white beard with care, tassels swaying. "By chance, have one, I do."

Falmagon stomped at the wooden baseboard, with an unexpected laugh, escalating to a hearty chuckle. "Of course you do, old man. Of course, you do."

Chapter XV

Within the hour, Branimir and the rest of the fellowship left the alehouse. Their quest had been defined.

Kinhar stepped lightly, leading the small group, with Falmagon and Erzebeth at his heels. The three were the most determined of the bunch, walking into the dirt streets of Arkaim. Their focus was purely on the docks where Dorofej said his boat, gifted by King Kar, awaited them.

Unnvar followed carrying two doloire, long-handled single-edged axes, on either side of his belt. His large frame filled the doorway, swallowing the light of the kiln, where his family huddled and prayed to the gods for their protection. His wife and children promised to tend to the alehouse and pray for Unnvar's return. Branimir did not believe Unnvar would return from Maharia. The demons were too many for a simple man to contend. But Unnvar insisted he had a duty to stand against evil, no matter the strength, to protect what life he had brought into the world. Come war and blood, Unnvar swore he would fight for his children to live and to see children of their own.

Dorofej and Branimir traipsed out of the wooden door behind Unnvar, as though they were being dragged by a noose around the neck. Bran's head hung low and his fingers trembled, realizing that he may not be the only slave in this tale. Dorofej was equally bound to the fate of the Highborn.

"Sound the alarm! We are under attack!" Sentries screamed near the gate of Arkaim. The sounds of clanging weapons and shrill cries echoed into the night.

"Nedezhda!" Kinhar hissed under his breath. "She has made it to Arkaim."

Branimir gasped, stepping back, eyes peering through the moonless night with ease. "I can see the Bukavac, my Lords. They come by the hundreds, maybe more."

"This is not our fight. Not here, Kinhar," Falmagon shook his shaggy head. "Let Arkaim fall as Melkorka did. We must flee to the boat to fight another day, and protect the Ash Tree."

"Falmagon speaks truth," Erzebeth said.

A group of sentries ran by the alehouse, shouting for the citizens to take cover. One stared at the Highborn as he passed. His face held the features of a young man, barely knowing his first love, if any love at all. His death was nigh. His copper sword would be useless against the thick skin and the strong metal blades of the Netherworld monsters.

Unnvar grunted in surprise. "I pledge my life to your cause, and you would leave my family and my people to die? The Northmen cannot fight against these demons. We are not Highborn."

Dorofej pulled a dark hood up over his head, completely shrouded in murky robes. "Unnvar, contend against this evil, we cannot either. Maybe it was *kaelandur*, maybe it was our sin in killing the *Eretik*, or maybe it is our very existence on Aenar. No matter the reason for our suffering, Nedezhda is far stronger than any could have thought possible, yes? Fight here and all mankind is lost or to the Ash Tree, we flee."

"We haven't the time to discuss, my Lords," Branimir squealed.

The Bukavac tore down the streets of Arkaim. Like a stampede of cattle, their blue skin blended in the night, lighted by torchlight. Their hands gripped weapons of the deep, forged by demon and devil, designed by the Mistress of Nightmares, Marheena, the Frozen Goddess.

The first carried a large spiked ball at the end of a long leather cord. The weapon circled over the Bukavac's head, sweeping through the air like an extension of its strapping arm. It roared with its charge, leading the many at its rear.

As Unnvar stepped backwards, Falmagon stepped forward. Wielding the crooked staff, which gave him power beyond the other Highborn, Falmagon slammed his weapon against the ground with ire. Dust surfaced and fluttered around his brown robes in half speed.

Branimir could have counted every speck.

The dust turned to boulders. One after another, the Highborn Long-Walker launched the stones at the frozen demons from the Netherworld. The common maneuver from Falmagon was worthwhile. Chunks of earth crashed into the Bukavac, smashing in their heads before they reached him. Yet, a few Bukavac smashed through the solid rock and charged.

In desperation, Falmagon furiously continued to wield *Koldovstvo*. Boulders were shattered, stone walls were torn down, and rock was fragmented. In short time, the young man's hair began to show signs of recession, his face wrinkled at the cheekbone. *Habërmani* could not contain *Koldovstvo* flowing through his veins.

"We must go," Branimir shouted over the din.

Falmagon's throat reverberated louder with cries of battle. It was the sheer robustness of a man meant to lead armies and destroy wickedness that caused Branimir to shudder and back away slowly. Falmagon's single eye was feral, holding the might of a thousand men behind its gaze, the sway of the gods.

Branimir slipped into the shadows, disappearing. He scooted back to the alehouse in hiding. This was how his people had survived as long as they had. Battling demons was for those who manipulated *Koldovstvo*. Their chance to escape without a battle was gone.

Another spiked ball on the end of a cord split the air toward Falmagon. At the last moment, he fell to his back with a thud, barely dodging the deadly blow aimed for his chest. Another Bukavac stormed toward him while the first spun the strange weapon to deliver a second attack.

The Bukavac who came next wielded a one-handed weapon with thick metal spikes on the opposite side of a mallet. Branimir cringed at the sight. The armament could batter the insides of an enemy to mush. The mallet came down toward Falmagon but was deflected mid-swing by Unnvar who grabbed the handle with a single hand.

The beast of a man stood a head shorter than the massive demon who growled ferociously at the unshaken Northman. The innkeeper roared back with equal ferocity, bringing his doloire from his slide and slicing the demon across the neck with the blade.

Where the bluish-white blood of the demon should have bled, Branimir was surprised to find that Unnvar's handaxe snapped against the harsh skin of the demon. It was like frozen rock, unbreakable against the soft copper.

The devastation only lasted momentarily as Unnvar dropped the handle and pushed with all his strength against the Bukavac. The demon slid inches, wrestling against Unnvar for control of the mace. Branimir had never seen such strength in a man.

"For Dahz the Lightbringer and glory!" Kinhar bawled. The spearhead raised his hands to the sky. As the Bukavac brought the flail down to strike Falmagon, a bolt of lightning tore from the heavens and ripped through its skull and chest. The weapon fell to the earth among the remains of the scorched carcass of the demon.

More Bukavac filled the streets.

Branimir, in fear, peeked through his fingers, knowing nothing but panic. He was motionless in his hiding spot.

"Victory here we will not find," Dorofej said, pulling Falmagon to his feet.

Falmagon ignored the old man. "Unnvar!"

The Bukavac and Unnvar continued to push back and forth on either side of the mace. From the road, another Bukavac charged with the intent of crushing Unnvar where he stood.

Erzebeth pushed pass Falmagon to intercept the attack. In a moment, her body shredded away and a bestial form rose from the remains. Where skin and blood fell, fur and muscle erupted into a creature similar to a great bear. The brute animal rose to the height of the Bukavac with strength of equal measure. Brown eyes of the Vucari remained, as well as a missing limb from the right arm, but it was no matter. Erzebeth, in the form of the beast, was powerful, unstoppable.

The bear collided with the Bukavac and its weapon fell to the ground. Erzebeth tore her teeth into the Bukavac's shoulder, breaking through with ease. The light liquid flowed across her gums as the demon roared, grabbing the Vucari in rage. It tried to tear apart the jaw of the bear, but her grip was locked.

Kinhar threw fire at the Bukavac. The blaze ruptured the gut of the demon struggling with Erzebeth. She crashed to the ground with the beast and tore out its throat, silencing its roar.

To her left, Unnvar finally yanked the mace from the hands of the other Bukavac, and smashed in its head with a final blow.

Fire and stone, sea and sky flowed together through the darkness of the night. The Bukavac laid waste to Arkaim from palisade to seashore with ease, striking down sentries and civilians with little resistance. The sounds of blood gurgling in the throats of children, and women shrieking as their stomachs were torn from breast to belly, filled Branimir's sensitive ears.

At Melkorka there had been a battle. At Arkaim, it was a massacre. Branimir had no time to process the horror.

"Branimir," Dorofej cried, searching the streets, "Let us flee."

At command, Branimir reappeared and rushed to the head of the group. Through the smoke-filled streets, the Highborn, innkeeper, and the Vucari, still in her bestial form, sped through Arkaim behind Branimir. He was exceptionally quicker than the lot of them, dodging obstacles in the road with ease. The docks were near but the enemy was closing.

"Falmagon, there," Kinhar directed. "And there!"

The one-eyed Highborn responded by throwing up a series of rock walls in front of the Bukavac that tore through the streets. Using *Habërmani*, he did his best to funnel the enemy away from them, to keep them safe. The endless casting of *Koldovstvo* was becoming costly to him though, his hair turning gray.

Though, Falmagon had little choice if they were to survive this night. He was the only one who had the power to see them through to the docks. He was the only one who could withstand the constant flow of *Koldovstvo* and pave their path to Maharia.

Another Bukavac approached and was torn down by Erzebeth. The claws ripped through its face, its brains spilling out from the shredded, frozen flesh.

"You are hurt," Falmagon cried to the Vucari after the demon had fallen. She rumbled in response, stumbling at the speed of Dorofej. She had a gash across her belly and another across her right arm.

"No time to bandage her. We must hurry," Unnvar growled, the mace heavily swaying in his hands.

Dorofej hopped over broken timber. "We cannot get on a boat for Maharia without provisions, yes? Starve to death, we will."

"We have not the time to find supplies," Kinhar muttered.

"We will have to make do."

Dorofej grunted in condemnation.

Falmagon scowled. "Come, Dorofej! Hurry before Nedezhda—"

The light striking in front of Falmagon cut him off. He reeled backwards, clinging to *Habërmani* tightly in his hand.

The *Eretik*, Nedezhda, stood with an army of Bukavac between them and the docks. Branimir could see every stitch connecting her head to her neck. Her thin lips curled. "Where is *kaelandur*? Give it to me, Highborn!"

Branimir hissed the thought haunting his mind, "You should have never killed her."

Erzebeth let loose a guttural roar from her throat, drowning out his words. She dropped to all fours, baring her teeth at the undead *Eretik*.

Kinhar growled. "Bah! What do you want the weapon for, Nedezhda?"

"Found your wrinkles so soon, Kinhar?" she cackled hatefully. "Give me *kaelandur.*"

"Why do you want it?" Kinhar repeated.

"Marheena desires it. *Kaelandur* was crafted for a destiny beyond what any of you can foresee. It will rip through the fabric of this world, laying waste to man, and preparing the way for the Likhyi."

"The Likhyi," Dorofej gasped from the rear. "The gods desire nothing, yes? I say, even the Frozen Goddess wants nothing from men," Dorofej said, pulling Branimir behind him. "Destiny is an untruth of men and demons alike to give life purpose outside of their charge."

"You know little, Dorofej, and even less of men. Most of all, you know nothing of those who reside in your company," Nedezhda said.

Dorofej's could not keep the smirk from his face. His voice was nearly as mocking, "Do I not?"

"Stop this, Nedezhda," Kinhar bellowed.

Nedezhda folded her arms. "Are you afraid of your secrets being revealed, Kinhar? You could not silence me in life. What madness would give you reason to try now?"

"I will cut off your pretty head a thousand times over to keep your mouth shut," Kinhar rushed at the undead woman, his fists glowing with a bluish glint of light.

Nedezhda met him with the Bukavac at her back.

Branimir vanished.

Kinhar flung blue flame from his fists at the demonic woman. Nedezhda dodged the fire, her bright blue eyes seemingly seeing *Koldovstvo* before it was cast. Her discolored hair, like moss against the tree's edge, clung to her face as she raised stone and fell water from the sea upon the Highborn.

Erzebeth and Unnvar were caught in the first wave that crashed down. Erzebeth was swept away and thrown through the side of a wooden structure. The impact knocked her unconscious returning her to human form. Unnvar, on the other hand, was able to withstand the impact, preventing himself from a similar fate.

Falmagon focused on the Bukavac, using his crooked staff to mold stone as though it were clay. Weapons slashed and crashed against his flesh, his face aged, and his skin tore. The man was being ripped to shreds, skin falling from bone, and yet he stood with all the poise of a Highborn.

Despite holding hate against those he called master, Branimir wept from the shadows. The salty tears burned his eyes.

Kinhar aged rapidly, rarely able to attack against Nedezhda. The undead woman was not affected by *Koldovstvo*, having the ability to mend the elements together with ease. Stone walls blocked fire. Protective orbs of air defended against frozen daggers of ice. Rocks rained from the heavens to collide with earth raised from Kinhar's feet.

The Highborn weakened in moments, collapsing to his knees as his bones grew brittle. He continued to craft

Koldovstvo, even after his eyes sunk into his skull, even after his breath had grown weak.

The end was nigh for all of them.

"Kinhar!" Dorofej screeched, helpless as the Bukavac descended upon him. The old man had found a makeshift stave from a broken branch that he swung wildly at the menacing demons.

Kinhar faced Nedezhda on his knees. The saltwater from Strega's Deep crashed around him, muddying the streets of Arkaim. Branimir's heart hurt in his chest as he watched a Bukavac advanced behind Kinhar, sinking a blade through the back of his head.

Branimir stared with blurred vision.

Life fled from Kinhar's blue eyes, blood pouring from his mouth and head. His body hung limp, held in place only by the metallic blade of the demon at his back. When the Bukavac yanked the sword clean, Kinhar's body fell for the last time.

The corner of Nedezhda's lips twisted into a smile.

"No!" Falmagon wailed. He raced to Kinhar's body, his wrinkled hands clinging to the bloodied, cream-colored cloth. The robe darkened further in a pool of Kinhar's blood.

Unnvar stumbled back to the battle, falling to Falmagon's side. He lifted the demon's mace he had carried and buried it into the Bukavac's skull behind Kinhar.

No more had the demon crumpled that Branimir helplessly watched another Bukavac slam a maul against the innkeeper's head. Blood gushed.

Unnvar joined Kinhar in the mud.

Falmagon, in his overwhelming misery, barely saw his kin collapse. Through the haze of tear upon tear, Falmagon did not see the hammer collide into his head either. He dropped over Kinhar's body.

Branimir's stomach churned, but he stayed hidden. He ignored the urgency to run to Dorofej. At one time, he may have felt pity for the Nedezhda, but she was no better than the men who had first killed her.

Nedezhda raised her hand and the Bukavac stopped their assault. The woman approached Dorofej, who sunk to his knees in defeat.

"Where is *kaelandur*?" she said. "Tell me, and I will let you live."

Dorofej hid his emotion, gazing into the eyes of Nedezhda. "You make me an offer you have no intent of holding to, yes?"

"I will keep my word, Dorofej." Nedezhda kneeled, returning the emotionless façade. "It is more than what Kinhar and Falmagon would have done."

"What do you speak of, Nedezhda?" he asked.

"You really do not know?" the pale woman laughed at the old man. "You are Highborn and yet know nothing of their scheme? You crafted the weapon that killed me, and know not why I was killed?"

Dorofej licked his thin lips patiently.

Nedezhda looked amused. "I will let you live and tell you of their secrets, if you give me *kaelandur*. Give me the weapon that delivered my death."

Dorofej stared across the bare streets and the burning city as he weighed the offer. His voice was silent but heavy on Branimir's ears as he gave up the copper dagger to the hand of Marheena. "Falmagon carries it."

Nedezhda rose to her feet. She gracefully walked through the mud, and then searched the body of the one-eyed Highborn. In a matter of moments, she held the copper dagger. With a satisfied grin, she held the weapon high in the air as though it were a rod that controlled all living creatures.

The Bukavac, her army, roared in approval. The sound of the demons echoed throughout the city of Arkaim.

Dorofej lowered his head.

Nedezhda tucked *kaelandur* into her belt, and glided back over to the old man. Her eyes narrowed. "Kinhar and

Falmagon intended to fortify the *Kadari*. Both have recited the *Kalamyr Oath*. My death was their needed sacrifice, cloaked as righteousness, labeling me *Eretik*, and *kaelandur* their talisman. They mean to destroy the name of the Highborn, and bring one religion to the world. They want every living creature to worship the Lightbringer."

Dorofej could not silence his gasp.

"But it is no longer important. You are the only Highborn left in this world, and the world will decay at my hand. The Ash Tree will be destroyed through the taint of *kaelandur*, and the Likhyi will be released."

"What dark magic do you wield that could destroy the Ash Tree with a copper weapon, Nedezhda?" Dorofej shuddered, masking his thoughts with a simple misdirection.

"Don't insult me, Dorofej. You know as well as I that this weapon is touched with *Koldovstvo*. I could not have returned to this world without magic being melded into this blade. The Bukavac will find the Ash Tree and I will do Marheena's bidding."

"This cannot be the will of Marheena." Dorofej's blue eyes twinkled as he dropped his gaze.

Branimir's mind riddled. Jhar was responsible for the *Eretik's* return. He had used magic to make *kaelandur*.

Nedezhda signaled the demons to follow and soon Dorofej was left alone, kneeling in the ruins of Arkaim.

The old Highborn's voice could be heard reciting prophecy.

The Lightbringer will wed,
The Countess of the deep,
The Kadari reigns.
A Defender will be slain,
The Harbinger will ascend,
The Kadari reigns.
The Serpent of the Empress returns,

The last word slid off of Dorofej's tongue like the last rain drop of spring falling before summer's heat. He buried his head in his hands, looking more defeated than any man, dead or alive.

Branimir approached slowly, revealing himself from the darkness. "What does it mean, Dorofej? What does all of this mean?"

Dorofej looked upon him, his eyes weeping for all of humanity, all living creatures. "It means our suffering has only begun, Branimir Baran. Darkness swells in demon and man alike, yes?" The old Highborn pulled at the braided tassels on his chin. "Yet we may have the advantage if Nedezhda does not know the location of the Ash Tree, yes? Swift, we must be!"

Branimir looked to the Highborn Long-Walker. Falmagon's hand twitched.

Chapter XVI

Smoke from Arkaim rose with the morning light of the sunrise. Fires still burned the city to ashes with very few alive in its wake. The world looked to be in ashes, without hope, without direction.

Only a handful of buildings still stood throughout the expanse of the city. The palisades were torn down, the gates broken open, and the streets littered with the bodies of its many citizens. Nothing seemed to stir, a thousand dead, fallen where they had stood.

Branimir stood at a distance, reflecting on Kinhar's body that lay upon a stack of charred wood near the water's edge. His gray hair had turned white. His furrowed skin, pale and bruised, already showed signs of decay. The body had little to no blood left, drained through the gaping hole in his skull. The spearhead of the Highborn was truly gone from the world of men.

Falmagon was close. His brown hair had turned to gray. He limped forward using *Habërmani* as a walking stick. He swayed with dizziness and slight confusion as he approached the corpse of his friend. The wound on his head was clotted in blood, and gave indication that he was lucky to be standing at all. If that were not enough, his right leg was in shambles, torn from the blades of the demons, wrapped in bloodied cloth. His left leg was not in much better condition.

Falmagon lowered his single eye, sunken behind swollen, purple flesh. "By *Mulafell…*"

Falmagon's hand shook as he reached to touch the man, balancing himself with the crooked staff. Branimir could feel the man's suffering. He could barely believe Kinhar could be dead? The man had lived lifetimes upon lifetimes and now his spirit had fled to the Beyond? It was unthinkable.

Falmagon's fingers hovered over Kinhar's blood-stained lips as though he hoped for breath to stir. For a moment, the Highborn Long-Walker could only stare at him with tears in his eyes. His teeth bared and nostrils flared as he tried to fight those tears back. He choked with a strangled throat.

Branimir folded his arms, and gulped. Watching Falmagon in anguish did not make him feel good. He almost felt like he were watching Kinhar die all over again.

With a cry of frustration, Falmagon pulled away and gripped his tangled hair. He screamed at the sun, at Dahz, at the Lightbringer who was the Protector of Men. There were no words in his roar.

At the end of his breath, the weakened man lowered his head, shaking in rage and fear.

"We will make this right, Falmagon," Erzebeth said, approaching him and placing her hand on his trembling shoulder. She stood slumped, holding him for support. Her other forearm clung to her midsection, seemingly holding her guts in her body even without her hand. The cloth that wrapped around her repeatedly covered the thick stitches that had been sewn to bind the deep wound. She, surprisingly, showed no signs of aging from using whatever magic had turned her into a bear.

Falmagon shook his head despairingly, "We have lost. *Kaelandur* has been taken. Kinhar is gone. What more is there to do?"

Dorofej held a torch in his hand, the flame searing,

"Plenty, there is. Travel to Maharia and defend the Ash Tree, we will. Take back hope for the Northmen, we will. We are Highborn and glory is to be had, yes?"

"Yes," Erzebeth agreed, her eyes locked onto the body of Kinhar.

Falmagon bobbed his head, his voice shaky. "You are right, Dorofej. It is what must be done. Even with Kinhar dea—dead, we must press forward."

Branimir felt his heart flutter, rocking back on his heels. Dorofej rallied those who stood against him for a purpose greater than himself. The man held more goodness in him than any Highborn.

"I will not accompany you," Unnvar said from the far rear where he sat slouched in the dirt, holding his dented head. Blood still oozed from the broken skin. He had said nothing for most of the morning, except a grunt when asked if he would live. "My family is dead. My King is dead. My people are dead. There is no reason for me to go to Maharia. There is nothing left to save."

Falmagon did not look at his kin. "There are plenty of Northmen left in Kalamaar worth protecting, Unnvar."

The innkeeper twisted the heavy mace in his hand, a weapon never seen by man. The metal was solid, stronger than anything crafted by a Northman in the history of the world.

Dorofej hummed in agreement. "Speaks the truth, Falmagon does. Yet Unnvar must remain here in Arkaim and rebuild, and tell what he has seen. Convinced to join our cause, he should not be."

Unnvar scowled with hatred, looking around at the dead flooding the deserted streets. "I will not stay behind to do the work of the Highborn. I stay behind to die in peace. Why would I ever do as you ask, Highborn?"

"Because," Dorofej said, "You will take the title of King of Kalamaar, Unnvar Grondahl, yes? Others worthy of the cause, there are not. And there is none other to walk away from this defeat, yes?"

Branimir was equally confused.

Unnvar balked, staring at the ashes of the city. "What are you talking about, old man? I am not nobility. I am not a King! I am a simple innkeeper."

"You are a warrior, yes?"

"I—"

"You will find the King's body, take the crown and you will place it on your head, yes? You will rebuild Arkaim and you will give hope to the Northmen on Kalamaar. The Jarls will follow you just as they did the King throughout Kalamaar to the Seven Islands. This day is not your day to die."

Dorofej spoke with the authority of a thousand kings, looking down upon the over-sized man that piddled in the dirt.

"Kings are not made in this way, Dorofej," Falmagon said flatly, finding little strength to argue his point.

"Are they not?" Dorofej asked.

Erzebeth coughed, holding her stomach. She finally swallowed her pain long enough to speak. "Kings come about in many ways, Falmagon. Unnvar will do as well as any other and someone must lead. He has seen and survived the demons. That is bold enough to give people reason to follow him."

Branimir tilted his head at the notion, repeating the thought in his head. Kings come about in many ways. If he was the only Kras left in the world, maybe he could also be King.

Falmagon snorted. "The Highborn should guide the way for the Northmen."

Unnvar pulled himself to his feet. "The Highborn, Falmagon? Bah! I would have thought you would be raised better, but your mind was fouled at Melkorka! Can you not see? The Highborn have only brought death upon the people they swore to protect. If I lead it will be without the wisdom of the Highborn! Such men should be banished from Kalamaar."

Falmagon raged. "The Highborn uphold justice!"

The innkeeper sneered, his voice menacing, "You uphold nothing. Nothing!"

Branimir jaw quivered, frightened by the larger man who screamed at them. "I don't understand. Why are you so angry, Unnvar? Men have always known war."

The large man turned on him. "Are you so different that you cannot see the truth of it? The Highborn have led the world to ruin. They killed these people! This is greater than any war. This is eternal death."

"We did not," Falmagon said. His voice fell to a whisper. "We will fix this."

"You brought the demons to Arkaim," Unnvar said.

"It was a mistake," Branimir said. "This has all just been a terrible mistake."

Unnvar pointed the mace at Branimir. "If you believe that, Kras, then you are a fool."

Branimir's lip trembled, not knowing what to say.

Dorofej tried to ease the tension. "So be it."

Falmagon huffed, gripping his staff until his knuckles turned white. "What do you mean by that?"

"So be it." Dorofej repeated in a softer tone. "Go, Unnvar, and give your family name the glory you seek, yes?"

Unnvar turned as red as Branimir. He looked at each of them as he made his first decree as King of Kalamaar, "Yes, well. Get what supplies you can muster and leave this land. Go to your precious Ash Tree and do what you must do."

Dorofej dipped his head in acknowledgment. "As you wish, King Grondahl."

Unnvar gripped the mace, his weapon and scepter, and left them where they stood without another word.

Falmagon stared in bewilderment, "Are you out of your mind, old— Dorofej?"

Dorofej waited for no ceremony, throwing the torch down

on the body of Kinhar. "I think not, Falmagon Sej. You and I are all that left of those who wield *Koldovstvo*. The Highborn will die along with us. Return to Kalamaar or Melkorka, we likely will not."

Falmagon watched Kinhar's skin cling to bone under the heat of the fire that spread over the timber. "No, Dorofej, you are wrong."

Dorofej's jaw fell, realizing that the man spoke beyond rashness. "What do you know, Falmagon?"

"Kinhar…" Falmagon hesitated. "Kinhar spoke of more Highborn at a place called Shayol Domier."

Dorofej's breath fled from his lungs. "Impossible."

Kinhar's body burned, finalizing his passage into the Beyond. The stench of his seared flesh lingered on the wind.

Branimir chocked on the smell.

"Falmagon speaks the truth," Erzebeth said, ignoring the reeking of death. "I have been there with Kinhar, though it was many, many years ago. The stronghold is located on Maharia, deep in the southern forests known as the Dyndaer. Kinhar helped build the city with a man named Moreth several hundred years ago."

Branimir's hands shook. "If there are more Highborn… are there more Kras? Did Kinhar take the Kras to Shayol Domier?"

He was not alone!

Dorofej's repetition of the name outweighed the questions of the slave. "Moreth?"

"Moreth Eanbald," Erzebeth clarified, "He is the Vicar of the…of…"

"Are there more Kras?" Branimir tried again. He had to know.

He was ignored.

"The *Kadari*," Dorofej finished with a snarl, curved beneath his white mustache.

"Y-yes," Erzebeth admitted.

Branimir gaped, his mind riddled with more questions. Was the Vucari a member of this religious sect, too? He wanted desperately to know more about this *Kadari* and why Dorofej held such bitterness toward them.

Dorofej's eyes turned to Falmagon, who met the gaze with equal caution. "Asked once, I have, of what secrets were being kept. I fear that it would be pointless to repeat the question, yes?"

Branimir bit his tongue.

The two old men clearly loathed one another, but were bound by their duty as Highborn. They had little choice but to work together to stop Nedezhda's schemes.

They should have never killed her.

Falmagon responded to Dorofej, ignoring the indictment. His words implied that he was taking charge as the new spearhead of the Highborn. "We sail to Maharia."

Chapter XVII

Branimir's small, crimson knees sunk into the cool sand of the shoreline that led into the unexplored lands called Maharia. He lay on the wet, dark earth that seemed to stretch for eternity. He had never been so thankful to have solid ground under his feet.

The clouds were thick overhead, blocking any attempt that the sun may have to warm him, but he barely noticed. Even though the breeze off the water was shrill, tearing through his red skin like ice, Branimir clung to the sea-stained sand.

The ground was hardening, close to freezing, giving sign to how much time had passed since the four of them had sailed from Arkaim. They had spent nearly two months on the boat through sunshine, rain, and storm. Branimir never wanted to touch foot on a faering again. He may very well have to make his home in Maharia.

"I nearly thought I would never see land again," Falmagon wheezed with a half-smile plastered on his face. He pulled the faering onto the beach with a rope, while clinging to his crooked staff. Once it was secure, the aging man collapsed onto the dirt and rolled over onto his back.

It was amazing that none of them had died on the long voyage in the small faering, especially when considering the wounds of Falmagon and Erzebeth before leaving Arkaim. Fortunately, the Vucari had found enough herbs in Arkaim that she could tend to their injuries. Her knowledge of the medicinal properties should have given her the title of herbal healer. Alas, most of their suffering had to be withstood, as supplies ran low and food became scarce. Branimir only knew that somehow they had managed to overcome the impossible.

Dorofej joined Falmagon on the sands of Maharia, "Much too long of a journey, yes? I fear, forgotten how to walk, I have. I say, a decent meal would be warmly welcomed." Any disdain for Falmagon was gone from the old man's voice for the time being. The Highborn, although confined on the boat together, had barely spoken. Time had been the remedy for their anger.

The two Highborn had little choice but to get along with one another. Dorofej and Falmagon had a similar quest with similar limitations. The Highborn Long-Walker's age was not as great as Dorofej, but it was beyond anything he had ever known. Falmagon's hope was the same as Dorofej's, to reach the Waters of Life to restore his youth.

"Rabbit stew," Branimir said, rubbing his hands together at the thought.

"Anything but fish," Erzebeth muttered, joining Falmagon in the sand with her arms folded to stay warm in the cool breeze.

Falmagon laughed.

Branimir chuckled to himself, realizing it had been a very long time since any of them had even broken a smile.

Kinhar's death had not been forgotten, but it was not talked about among the fellowship. Branimir had tried once and was shushed by Dorofej before Falmagon lectured Branimir on manners and respect. None had said a word about the death of the spearhead again. Branimir assumed none of them ever would.

"We are going to need to find shelter, yes?" Dorofej interrupted the mirth before it could fully begin.

Branimir nodded, standing fully to take a good look at

Maharia in the dimming light. He assumed the comment was a request for him to find something suitable.

To the east and north were grasslands, rising and falling over high hills that blocked his vision of the land beyond. A few trees dotted the hills, but not anything significant. To the south, nearly half a day's travel, were the remnants of a small mountain range that stretched along the coastline. He heard birds and small critters making movement in the grasses.

"There is no sign of a settlement," Branimir said, somewhat relieved. "Actually, I do not see any sign of movement. It seems safe enough."

Erzebeth pulled herself to her feet, pushing her hair behind her ears, brown eyes scanning the land as though it were a home she had long forgotten. Branimir nearly took offense as though the Vucari did not trust his judgment, but kept his lips sealed.

Her eyes locked onto the mountain range, and she shook her head upsettingly. "We are leagues away from the Ash Tree. It is to the south beyond those mountains. It'll be weeks before we reach it."

"Traveling through the mountains does not sound appealing," Falmagon added.

"No," Dorofej scowled, "it does not. Maybe we should take the boat along the shore, yes?"

Erzebeth nodded. "I would advise not to travel inland too far. Taking the faering along the coast is probably the quickest way to travel, but there are likely jagged rocks among the waters. It will not be safe either."

Branimir gripped his chin with both hands. He was lucky to not have drowned in the last two voyages. He did not want to push his luck.

"I am not sure getting back on a boat is any more appealing than the mountains," Falmagon groaned, placing his head in his hands.

"I agree," Branimir said.

"I don't see many other options for us," Erzebeth said. "Maharia is a hundred times larger than Kalamaar. Traveling to the Ash Tree is not going to be a quick venture. We are lucky Falmagan and Dorofej have made it this far at their age."

Falmagon snapped, "You would not have made it this far without me, Erzebeth. I risked much to keep you alive at Arkaim."

The Vucari lifted her hands. "I am not your enemy. I am just telling you what you should already know."

Falmagon snorted.

Dorofej interjected, seemingly having no desire to pay attention to Falmagon's cantankerous behavior. "Decide, we must. Land or water?"

Branimir raised his hand as though they were taking a vote. "Land. We may take more time, my Lord, but I prefer the shelter of the mountains against the nipping wind. The gale will only grow colder with the Season of Frost."

Erzebeth flared her nostrils. Clearly, she was still not sympathetic to him speaking his mind. "The red brood makes sense. We may all catch sickness on the sea if this cold increases, which will leave us nowhere. Besides, I have been relatively relieved that the serpent was not seen in the weeks at sea. I would prefer not to test my luck on the water. It may still be lingering in the depths."

"Glad we agree," Branimir murmured.

She glared at him, and he hurried to turn his eyes to Falmagon.

The Highborn Long-Walker wrapped his brown robes tightly around himself, and snorted again. "Dahz knows I have no interest in being on that boat. But, Dorofej, hear me when I say that I equally have no desire to go trudging about in underground caverns."

Dorofej dipped his head. "I hear you well and clear, Falmagon. It is decided then, yes? Let us make for the mountains before we lose the light, yes?"

Branimir said, "We will not make it before dark."

Dorofej started toward the peaks. "Make it as far as we can, we will."

Erzebeth pulled herself to her feet to follow. Branimir watched her head south for a moment, waiting for Falmagon. The Highborn grumbled, but eventually started after them, and Branimir trailed behind.

The four of them traveled over the grasslands and toward the mountains for several hours without anyone saying much. The land seemed to be completely barren, as though it were a man without a tongue. Erzebeth kept them close to the water's edge, maintaining that they must stay away from the inland.

Falmagon gripped *Habërmani* firmly in his right hand, using it as a walking stick as he scanned the horizon around them. The waters of the ocean were an eerie sight, hazed and dark as far as the eye could see. The terrain appeared as though it had not been touched by any man or beast in a thousand years.

"Maharia truly is barren," Falmagon growled in a harsh voice.

"I would not be so sure," Erzebeth said. "This land is never what it seems to be. It is best to remain vigilant."

Falmagon did not argue with the Vucari, who had more experience upon Maharia than any of them. The gale that lifted from the north made the world of the west seem even more ominous. Without doubt, Bran thought, Maharia was cursed.

The screeching howl that erupted from the ocean water lifted with a gust of wind. Each of them sprang backwards, but none as quickly as Branimir.

"What was that?" he hissed.

The sound rumbled again. It was shrill, riding the wind like the deafening cries of battle.

"Stay behind me." Falmagon said, pulling Erzebeth to his rear. He raised *Habërmani* defensively, scanning the surface of the ocean for the monster that could have made the sound.

"It must be the beast," Erzebeth said hastily, swatting Falmagon's hand away.

Dorofej squinted at the water.

Branimir squeaked again, "If so, where is it?"

Nothing stirred.

Erzebeth stood with composure, finally pointing out to the clashing waves. There was no light from the sky, the clouds still fully blocking the sun's rays. But beneath a ripple of a wave there was a vision of the creature. It glistened against the water's edge, a dark blue hint to the scales that lined its massive body.

A monstrous creature was nearly concealed within the waters. It was serpent-like, swaying like a snake on the surface of a pond. The bluish color of its skin was veiled to near perfection against the shade that loomed over Strega's Deep. A red, fiery tongue lashed against the waters as it took scent of the wind. The beast was larger than the Manor House in Arkaim.

"Our position, it has not found," Dorofej said.

"If it were to find us, we would be dead within an instant," Erzebeth said. "It is best that we move forward."

Falmagon nodded. "You will get no argument from me."

Branimir stepped further back from the ocean, feeling his hands shake slightly at the sight of the beast. "Move forward and inland."

Falmagon agreed, "The Kras may be right, Erzebeth. I would rather not contend with the creature if it can be helped. It would tear us to shreds with little effort."

Erzebeth frowned, looking back toward the hills to the west. "Very well, but there are equally dangerous creatures inland."

Dorofej said, "There is no other way, yes? I say, I fear we will find good reason why humans do not traverse these lands."

Erzebeth wrinkled her nose, rubbing the nub of her severed hand. "No place is truly safe from wickedness, Dorofej. But, you are correct. Whatever hardship you may have experienced before in Maharia will seem little in comparison to what lies ahead."

As they moved away from the ocean, Branimir secretly wished they would stop condemning their journey with a foretelling of suffering.

Chapter XVIII

Branimir's fingers traced over the *Ojenek* that he had retrieved at Illuard. The bluish-white stone was smooth, with the interior reflecting a dark blue as though it were filled with an inner fire. Branimir has spent much of the past month looking at the stone as they traveled on the faering. Before that time, he had nearly forgotten he had kept it in his pocket.

Dorofej seemed to notice his movement by the small fire they had built along the coastline. "It is safe, Branimir, yes?"

He looked to the mountains, still a quarter day away in travel, and then back to the old Highborn. "Yes, Dorofej, but what is it for?"

Dorofej scrunched his nose. "Let us hope that need of it, we will not have."

Branimir nodded, figuring that the man's wisdom was far greater than his own, especially in the matter of shiny stones from abandoned, underground cities. Bran immediately thought of *Oreg'henite* within the Kras city of Illuard. If he were ever to be a King, he would want a similar throne made of shiny stones.

"What are you two whispering about?" Falmagon asked from across the fire.

"Nothing of interest," Dorofej said offhandedly, looking to the stars, and then to face the fire.

Falmagon grunted.

Branimir believed Falmagon had completely forgotten about the *Ojenek*.

Erzebeth approached the fire and sat between Falmagon and Branimir. "Nothing for supper. Maybe I can find something in the morning."

"We should have stopped sooner for hunting," Falmagon said. "We are not going to be able to stay on foot through the mountains on empty stomachs. Food will be more scarce once we reach them."

The woman sighed. "The weather is growing cold, Falmagon. Animals are not going to stay this far north regardless during this time of the year. We must find the strength to make it to the Dyndaer."

"The forest?" Branimir clarified, doing his best to become familiar with the names of things in Maharia. He found it interesting that anything had a name in an unexplored land, but Erzebeth suggested the Vucari had traveled over this land nearly as long as humans had lived on Kalamaar.

"Yes, Kras. The Dyndaer is a dark forest that most would avoid if given the chance, but the Ash Tree lies within."

"Do you know where exactly it is?" Branimir asked.

Erzebeth glowered at the Kras. "We would not be here if I did not."

Branimir lowered his head.

A couple minutes passed and Erezbeth spoke once more, "We have gained enough warmth for the night. It is time to douse the fire."

"Are you kidding me? We will freeze out here without a fire." Falmagon parted his mouth as though he were swallowing a river.

Branimir could not help but agree with the Highborn Long-Walker, feeling the chill of the frost on his skin even though he sat by the flame. The Season of Frost had begun and it would only become colder as the days carried forward.

The days may be tolerable for a few months, but the nights would already be dropping below the level of comfort.

The Vucari attempted to keep the sneer from crossing her lips. "You must make do with your bedroll. It is not safe to have fires burning at night. You will draw unwanted attention."

Branimir twisted his head around, peering across Maharia. It may have been darkness for his companions, but he could see the land clearly. The sound of waves crashed in the far distance. The world was as still as a sculptor's muse.

Falmagon spoke Branimir's thoughts. "Attention from what, Erzebeth? There is nothing out here but us and the moon."

Branimir looked up at the pale moon, barely giving off enough light to consider it worthwhile. It might as well be hidden from sight all together.

"Maharia is much different than Kalamaar and the Seven Islands, Falmagon. Much of the land is ruled by Czern, the God of Darkness. The Grey-Clad, as he is called, wanders the night stirring evil with his breath. The Light that fights against his breath will draw him and bring evil with it."

"I know of Czern," Dorofej nodded. "The brother of Dahz, yes? He wears the stone crown of sacrifice called *Maelifell*, it is."

"By *Mulafell*," Falmagon muttered, using the name of Dahz's hammer to curse once more. It was becoming a habit for the one-eyed Highborn.

Branimir shivered in the cold.

"Myestera," Erzebeth pointed to the moon, "does what she can to watch after Czern, to place restraint on his mischief. But, she has little power in Maharia. She grows weakest in the Season of Frost."

Falmagon breathed heavily. "The Lightbringer needs to keep his brother inhibited, lest we freeze to death before reaching our mark. It seems that even the gods are working against our quest."

Dorofej pulled at the tassels of hair that hung from his chin. "Interest in our quest, the gods have not, I assure you, Falmagon. They continue on in existence regardless of the existence of man."

"Blasphemous words, Dorofej." Falmagon scoffed.

"Hardly, I think. Words that speak against your reasoning do not evoke blasphemy any more than a boy with a sword makes him a man, yes?"

"And yet, you made Unnvar a King."

Dorofej laughed out loud at the comment, rephrasing the statement with what appeared to be a cheer. "And yet, Unnvar is a King. Ha!"

Falmagon shook his head, likely reminding himself that arguing with Dorofej rarely rendered an efficacious ending.

"He will be lucky if a Jarl does not run him through after he makes such a claim," Falmagon said in finality.

The Vucari stood, holding her severed limb against her body and quickly kicked dirt over the embers. The flames died in the covering of dust.

Branimir pulled his cloak and blanket around his small body, eyes unaffected by the impending darkness. He watched as Falmagon and Dorofej adjusted themselves awkwardly, trying to find comfort in the dim light.

The Vucari did not seem to be affected by the loss of light. She shifted easily back to her place of rest, pulling her own blanket around her shoulders. She licked her lips in the dry air as though she were thinking deeply before turning her eyes to look at Branimir.

The Kras froze realizing she could see him as easily as he could see her in the darkness. Her brown eyes seemed to glow to the Kras, staring intensely as though they were looking at the very fabric of his soul. Branimir met the gaze bravely, fearful of maintaining the look and equally scared to turn away. The moment could have lasted the entirety of the night if it were not for Dorofej, who interrupted the awkwardness.

"Erzebeth Navenka, tell me of the Vucari, yes? I would like to learn of your people and their existence here on Maharia. How you came to be, as it were."

Erzebeth turned her head to Dorofej, who lay on his back with his closed eyes facing the moon above. "Okay. I will humor you for the evening, if it is truly your desire."

Dorofej smiled. "What I truly desire is plum wine, but that nectar seems far from accessible this moment. Thus, it must be knowledge, my second favorite mind-altering sap, to intoxicate my senses, if you please."

"So be it." Erzebeth laughed, with a nod of her head.

"You are out of your mind, Dorofej. Make as much sense as a half-witted mule," Falmagon muttered, falling back to the ground, and covering himself with his blanket.

Erzebeth ignored him. "The Vucari were initially said to be born from the breath of the animals, the first creatures to crawl upon the earth and fly through the wind. Our savants would later say Wolos called us into this world."

"Wolos?" Branimir scrunched his nose. He could not keep up with all the gods the humans kept going on about.

Dorofej cleared his throat. "The Horned God, Branimir, with far too many roles to go into right now, yes? Please, Erzebeth, continue with your history."

The Vucari woman sighed. "We were the first with mind and heart, caring for the living and breathing of the world. The Vucari did not originate from Maharia in the time before time, but came from the northern isle that long ago lost its name, but should be remembered as Rhian. I remember the ice-tipped mountains, known as *Valarun,* stretched across the expanse of the frozen world, beyond any realm that any man or beast has ever seen. Hidden within *Valarun* was the mountain city of *Anaerfell,* my home."

A moment of silence passed then Erzebeth continued.

"I left *Anaerfell* when the savants spoke of the Ash Tree hidden deep in the forests to the south. I left with many of my own kind, destined to find this mystical tree of the gods, a tree that gave eternal life to those who tasted its fruit. We were informed that Wolos, the Protector of the Eternal Spring, had charged the Vucari to become the enduring Wardens of the Ash Tree, to protect it from any evil. We had not known that evil was among our own ranks. We could not have known what destiny would wrought—"

Dorofej jolted upright, "What do you mean, Erzebeth?"

"I mean what I say, Highborn. The Vucari whom I traveled with became twisted in thought, their minds torn from a path of virtue. The Vucari were hungry for absolute power and found it through the consumption of the Ash Tree. With eternity in their hands, the Vucari quickly learned the craft of *Koldovstvo*, but differently than what the Highborn typically master." She paused, staring at Branimir for a moment, as if expecting something from him. Yet he had the impression she was purposefully leaving out the full history.

"That is how you turn into animals?" Branimir wondered, filling the void of silence. "All Vucari change shapes then?"

"I suppose so, yes," Erzebeth continued "though not all use it for the same purpose. Those who were meant to protect the Ash Tree from evil used it to bring hardship and pain upon those who lived in this world. Though, not even the Vucari were the first to be corrupted by their duty. Yet they scattered across Maharia, never again to return to *Anaerfell*. The home I once knew has long been in ruins."

"In light of their evil, what did you do, Erzebeth?" Branimir asked.

"I had no choice but to follow the example of my people, if anything, to maintain a sense of what it meant to be Vucari. I took the fruit of the Ash Tree and consumed it. I found my youth again through the lake that surrounds the mystical tree. And then, I set out to find those of goodness to help me maintain the balance of the world. It was in that search that I found Kinhar."

"What happened to the other Vucari over the decades, Erzebeth? Are they here in Maharia?" Branimir asked. He secretly wondered again if the Kras could also be here in Maharia.

"I could not know. It has been half a century since I have come to these lands. Last I knew, they were still the Wardens of the Ash Tree, or at least, viewed themselves as such. They will kill any living creature before they reach the tree, keeping the secrets for themselves. They are cruel, unkind creatures. I assure you the Vucari are far more ruthless than any human I have come across…" Erzebeth again paused. "Though humans are not the foulest of living beings."

Branimir scratched his thin, black hair, missing her suggestion. "How is it that you and Kinhar reached the tree and took branches back to Kalamaar?"

Erzebeth pulled at her hair nervously. She seemed to be caught up in the moment, not recognizing that he was asking the question. "I am Vucari. At the time, there was very little that prevented me from being accepted with my own kind. I fear times have changed."

Falmagon responded, "Let us hope it is not the case."

Dorofej grunted in what may have been agreement.

"How about you, Dorofej?" Falmagon said.

Dorofej smacked his lips. "What do you mean?"

The Highborn Long-Walker clarified, "How did you become a Highborn? I have never heard the story of your coming to Melkorka. Kinhar never spoke of it."

Branimir noticed the hint of sadness in Falmagon when saying the dead Highborn's name.

"I imagine he would not have, yes? To share the story, he would need to have known it," Dorofej replied.

"How would he have not? Was he not the first Highborn?" Branimir asked foolishly.

"Ha!" Dorofej laughed out loud. "Is that what you believe? There have been those who have known the craft of

Koldovstvo long before Kinhar Sayan."

"Alright, Dorofej," Falmagon licked his lips. Branimir realized he was trying to pry the secrets from Dorofej that Kinhar had long wanted to know. "How did you become Highborn?"

Dorofej put his finger to his nose with a chuckle. "To tell that story, I would have to know."

"You mean you do not know?" Branimir wrinkled his nose.

The old Highborn shrugged beneath his heavy, black robes. "I do not remember."

Falmagon snorted in frustration. "That is ridiculous."

Branimir watched the one-eyed Highborn fumble about awkwardly near his bedroll, clearly frustrated at Dorofej's insistent mystery about himself.

Erzebeth said, "You must know something, Dorofej."

"I could tell a story, yes? I know many stories," answered Dorofej.

"Would you?" Branimir smiled widely, clapping his hands together.

Dorofej began with boom, his voice full of strength and vigor, like a minstrel speaking outside of song. "A straw house, there once was, which none visited due to the lingering of a she-wolf. To escape the squall and downpour one night, a brave warrior went into the straw house and made a fire. He also slept beneath a pile of rubble. From his place beneath the rubble, he could watch the door and innards of the straw house without being seen, you see? By and by, the she-wolf came and warmed near the fire, not knowing that the warrior was hiding within."

"You are trying to impart your wisdom on us again, Dorofej, aren't you?" Falmagon asked distastefully.

The old Highborn ignored him. "The she-wolf stood like a woman and her skin fell away, yes? The wolf skin was hung on a peg and she was no longer a wolf, but a damsel, full of beauty never before seen by the warrior. Fell asleep in short time by the fire, the damsel did. The warrior was overwhelmed with wanting, he was. Leaving the rubble, he stole the skin and hid it away from the damsel."

"A terrible thing to do!" Erzebeth said with a knowing look.

"Isn't it though?" Dorofej lifted his bushy eyebrows, "When morning came, the damsel screamed at the sight of the warrior, and searched for her skin, but to no avail. After time, the pair married, and had some children, you see."

"That does not make any sense, Dorofej. Why would the damsel marry the warrior that stole her skin and her identity?"

Dorofej raised his finger as if Falmagon understood the point of the fable, but he continued the story. "That his mother was a she-wolf, the oldest child soon learned. The knowledge ate away at the child for some time, yes? While out in the field with his father, finally asked about his mother's skin, he did. The father shared the hiding place with the child and the child with his mother."

"Then what?" Branimir said when Dorofej had paused for more than a second.

"Then the she-wolf took her skin, went away, and was never heard of again. The warrior was filled with grief for the rest of his days."

Branimir wrinkled his forehead, along with Falmagon. "I don't get it."

Falmagon reiterated, "If there is a lesson in all that rubbish, it is truly lost."

Erzebeth tried to interpret. "It is an old story with similar versions among the Vucari. The she-wolf was not the one who was caught, but instead, the warrior. We are blinded by desire, sometimes not knowing the control it can possess. Whether it is good or evil, we crave what we should not have. The gods, as represented by the child, will intervene to save us, but we still choose our own response. In this case, the warrior chose grief."

"One of many interpretations," Dorofej indicated with a dip of his head. "Also, it has been said before that the she-wolf is our soul and the gods are the warrior, stealing away our true identity in this life. Fate, chance, or luck, it is, as signified by the child that sets us free from the sway of deities, yes?"

"Freedom by death," Erzebeth concluded.

"Nothing but a bunch of drivel," Falmagon said. "Enough already. We need rest. I imagine tomorrow will be trying."

As they lay down, a resounding howl echoed in the night. Branimir nearly sprang out of his bedroll. The image of the she-wolf was fixated in his mind. The Highborn and Vucari ignored the sound, turning under their own blankets. A shiver struck his spine that was beyond the cold. Branimir could not help but think that Falmagon's words had just sealed their fate.

Chapter XIX

Erzebeth had been unsuccessful in finding them food again. After taking less than an hour to grab their things, they set off toward the mountains with empty stomachs. Branimir's stomach growled several times before the sun peaked over the landscape, but he knew that he was not alone. The Kras could easily hear the bellies of his companions making similar noises of irritation.

A cold mist sat upon the shriveled grass in the early morning hours. The mountains to the south were still barely visible above the fog, but they were fading from sight. Branimir glanced about feeling a cold emptiness inside. At first, he thought it was from the poor night's rest that he had received, but he was uncertain. All he knew was that something did not feel right.

By and by, the morning hours escaped them and he forgot about his uneasiness. The group walked in silence, lost in their own thoughts. After two months on the faering, none had much to say to any one of the other. Whether there was more to be asked, or shared, was beside the point. To Branimir, it seemed that each had said all they wanted to say to any other, except for him.

Branimir always had a question. He found enjoyment in expanding his mind with knowledge.

"Erzebeth, what is the name of these mountains?" he asked.

"I do not know that they have ever been named," she replied with a sigh.

"That is funny. I would think something as apparent as mountains would be quick to be called something."

"I am afraid they are nameless."

Branimir hummed to himself, pulling at his hooked nose in thought.

Falmagon addressed him. "What is wrong with you?"

Branimir shrugged his little shoulders. "Homesick, I guess, my Lord. We have been gone from Melkorka for a very long time."

The Highborn Long-Walker tilted his head with a strange sense of understanding. "You get used to it after a while. Before long, no place is home."

Branimir shivered at the thought. Not having a home had to be a terrible feeling. Though, he supposed that he never had a home outside of Melkorka. The castle was never really *his*, but the Highborn's.

"I have an idea. We should name them," he said with a bounce. His mind immediately went to the memory of his father. "Let's call them the Hrani Highlands."

"The mountains?" Dorofej questioned.

"Yes!" Branimir exclaimed with excitement.

"You cannot just name mountains," Falmagon said.

"I believe he just did," Erzebeth hooted.

Branimir smiled widely nearly causing his cracked lips to bleed. The idea that the mountains were named after his family, his father, gave him a sense of security.

Dorofej chuckled at the sight for what seemed to be hours, his laugh echoing throughout the newly named Hrani Highlands.

The day pressed on.

Branimir had barely noticed they had gone into the

mountains before they were deep within the shadowed peaks. The Hrani Highlands were marked with frequent ups and downs as though they were oversized hills. The rise of the mounds behind them blended into the green-laced mountains so perfectly that there was barely distinction between the two.

At the high points, the Kras looked back over his shoulder toward the way that they had come. He quickly found that he was looking over the expanse of Maharia for miles upon miles. Hills stretched as far as he could see to the north and the west. Branimir could easily see the ocean to the east as the fog lifted near midday. The waters stretched for what seemed like an eternity. Branimir almost thought that he would be able to see Kalamaar from the heights of the mountains. It was a foolish notion.

It was around the third uprising that Branimir turned to glance back the way they had come when something caught his eye in the distance. In fact, it was a lot of somethings, and they were moving across the hills at an exceptional pace. By the time he noticed the creatures, they were already nearing the mountains.

Branimir was not afraid at first, but his voice still squeaked. "What are those?"

Falmagon twisted around, peering at the hundreds of creatures galloping across the hills toward them. "Horses?"

Dorofej's face turned paler than death.

"Those…those aren't horses, Falmagon." Erzebeth started to back up. "Those are Svet! Run! Run for all you are worth!"

Erzebeth took off through the mountains to the south with exceptional speed. Dorofej followed, clearly aged since the last time they had to run from an enemy. His movements were slow and his pace was excessively unproductive.

"What are Svet?" Falmagon screamed as the Vucari pulled away from them. The one-eyed Highborn pushed pass Dorofej, trying his best to catch up with the woman who was becoming smaller in the distance.

Branimir kicked his feet up pushing past both Highborn. The Kras were known for their ability to run fast, especially when afraid. He had the impulse to catch up with the Vucari, but felt he could not leave the Highborn behind.

"We must move faster, my Lords," Branimir urged. "I—"

He stopped, seeing the Vucari woman leap over a hill in front of them. In mid-air, she transformed her skin from human to wolf. The clothing and flesh fled from her body like the skin from a snake. Gray fur laced over her features. He could not see for certain, but he was sure her brown eyes had changed to yellow.

Branimir had thought only he could see her at the distance, finding himself more than puzzled when Falmagon spoke up. "By *Mulafell*, did you see that? She just left us! We saved her just to be left behind like the scraps from supper."

Dorofej lagged. "She is a survivor, yes? You'd likely do the same if you knew what we know."

Falmagon replied fiercely, "What is it that you know?"

Dorofej amended himself hastily, "What she knows, I mean."

The younger Highborn harrumphed and pushed forward, following Branimir who led the way with a wave of his hand.

"Come on," he said.

The three of them ran through the green mountains, not having any idea where they were going but always heading south. The Highlands were extensive, extending and broadening across Maharia down the coastline of the large land mass. If there was an end to this world, Branimir figured the three of them were not going to reach it any time soon.

It did not take long for Dorofej, and then Falmagon, to lose their breath, walking and stopping to regain some energy. They ordered Branimir ahead many times to find Erzebeth, or at least a cave for hiding. For the next hour or more, Bran found nothing. He and the Highborn men pressed onward.

After time, the sounds of hooves upon the rock reached Branimir's ears.

"They are growing closer, my Lords," he said.

Falmagon gripped his crooked staff. "We must make a stand, Dorofej."

The old man shook his head, clinging to the rocky wall. "Too many, Falmagon, there are. It would be a futile attempt, yes? Besides, you and I are far too weak to wield *Koldovstvo* without inviting our deaths, yes?"

"These Svet may kill us regardless," Falmagon argued.

"No, I think not. At least, not immediately, I am sure of it."

"You speak outside of your knowing, Dorofej. These Svet are as unknown to you as they are to me. Do not act as though you have wisdom where there is none to be had!" Falmagon heaved. "*Habërmani* will give me enough strength to lay waste to these Svet, and still we will make it to the Ash Tree."

Dorofej scowled. "I say, will you then defend against the Vucari who Erzebeth claims guards it or powerless, will you be?"

Falmagon cried out in frustration, his hands spread open to the heavens. Branimir had never been one to know power. He could only imagine what it meant to hold so much power and be able to do nothing with it.

Dorofej moved forward with a bound and slapped the one-eyed man across the cheek. "Screaming like a lunatic will only give away our position, you fool!"

Falmagon growled, raising *Habërmani*. "Keep your hands to yourself."

"Bah!" Dorofej turned on his heel, his black robes consuming what heat there was to gather, sweat glistening on his brow. "Branimir!"

"Yes, my Lord," Branimir said automatically.

"You must remain in service to us in this moment, yes? Require it desperately, we do."

"Of course, my Lord," Branimir looked with uncertainty at the Highborn. "What is it you need from me?"

"You still have *Ojenek*, yes?" Dorofej asked.

"Of course." Branimir pulled the moonstone from his pocket. The blue stone shined as though it were freshly polished.

"The gem from Illuard?" Falmagon said with confusion lacing his brow. "What good does that do us?"

"Quiet your tongue, Falmagon Sej, or I would cut it out," Dorofej screeched with a mad gleam in his eye.

Falmagon did not test the old man, holding his lips fast together.

Dorofej turned his attention back to Branimir. "Hold to it and follow wherever the Svet take us, you will. You must find a way to free us before—"

Branimir interrupted, "I do not understand, my Lord! How am I to free you?"

"There is no time. Go!" Dorofej pushed Branimir away from him.

Branimir rocked backwards, hearing the stamping of hooves, like an army of horsemen coming down upon them. They were closing quicker than a pack of wolves on their prey.

"Hide, Branimir," Dorofej said. "Hide yourself!"

Branimir vanished, heartbeats before the first Svet rose over the hill to the north.

The Svet stood over a foot taller than any man, and likely weighed six times as much. The head, arms, and chest of the Svet were that of a human with the rest of the body, including four legs, hindquarters, and a tail like that of a horse. Hair grew down the neck and back like the crest of a horse. The mane was as black as the dark skin and penetrating eyes of the creature, more beast than man. Erupting from the forehead were massive horns that jutted forward made for ramming or impaling an enemy.

Branimir was terrified.

The beast barely wore anything but the skin on its back. Due to the long hair, Branimir was unsure if it was man or woman. That is, until a female galloped up beside the first, her chest bare like that of a female human. Her mane was brownish in color, distinguishing her from the male. There was no sense of modesty, exposing all that there was to be exposed.

"Centaurs?" Falmagon said disbelievingly. "The monsters of fairytales?"

Dorofej stayed quiet, lifting his arms and exposing his hands, showing he was harmless.

Both Svet, male and female, raised bows that resembled the luks made by Northmen, their arrows pointed with stone and aimed at the Highborn. Extra arrows were held in a quiver hanging on the right side of a makeshift leather belt.

"Die, Vucari," the male snarled between fanged teeth, his ears were like that of a horse, twisted backwards behind his horns.

Branimir gasped realizing that every single tooth was sharpened, made to the tear flesh.

Falmagon and Dorofej said nothing. Branimir noticed Falmagon's face was twisted in confusion, whereas Dorofej held a façade carved in stone.

"We should take them back, Asgrim, for the herd," the female Svet said.

"Not alive," the Svet called Asgrim responded. "They are in our lands and deserve death. They threaten what is sacred."

"You know the meat would spoil if we kill them now."

Asgrim turned toward the female and bared his fangs. She responded with equal ferocity, a growl reverberating in her throat.

Several more Svet approached from behind the first two. Each creature was equally dark of skin with coarse hair that thickened near the hoof. Each Svet had different colored crests down their human backs, and clutched the weapon of an archer.

The first over the ridge stopped at the sight of the Highborn and said, "Do not leave them standing there. They will use their magic, Asgrim."

Asgrim responded to the other male, "Felitch insists we keep them alive and return to Sorod."

"Gah! So be it. But if it must be that way, do not leave them awake," the centaur responded.

Asgrim growled, rushing forward toward Dorofej and Falmagon, stomping his feet, throwing up dust. He towered over both old men with a fierce gaze.

Falmagon stared in astonishment at Asgrim.

The male Svet moved forward cautiously toward the one-eyed Highborn, licking his lips. "I do not like the way this one looks at me. It is as though it thinks it were my equal."

Falmagon kept his gaze steady as if trying to understand what the Svet was saying.

More centaurs lined the hills behind the others. There seemed to be hundreds of the horse-like creatures. Their faces etched in brutality and hate. Dorofej and Falmagon were heavily outnumbered.

Branimir gripped the moonstone, hoping for a miracle to happen.

"Careful, Asgrim," Felitch warned. "He may be preparing to change."

Asgrim roared, slamming his luk against Falmagon's head, and then did the same to Dorofej. Both old men fell to the dirt unconscious.

Satisfied, Felitch dipped her head and snorted through hollowed nostrils, larger than that of any human. "The High Priest can bless the meat when we return to Sorod."

Asgrim grabbed Dorofej's body and slung it onto Felitch's back. Falmagon was then picked up by Asgrim and placed on his own back.

Asgrim stamped its feet again, seemingly in agreement

with Felitch. His voice was deep. "For glory! For Rujan! We ride!"

As the many Svet rode back north, Branimir sprinted after them. He would not abandon the Highborn. He was Kras and they were his Lords.

Chapter XX

The day had come and gone. The night rose with Myestera, the Moon Goddess, shining dimly overhead. Out of the Hrani Highlands and over the adjacent, unnamed hills, Branimir ran northwest after the mass of centaur archers. He sped as fast as he was able, chasing after the Highborn like he had been ordered to do. In his heart, he gravely feared failure. To be trapped in this strange land without a master, to live anywhere without a master, would leave him without purpose.

As the Svet pulled leagues away, Branimir found himself blubbering, tears blurring his vision as he ran. The cold wind stung his eyes, the tall grasses whipped against his red skin. It was no matter. Branimir quickly found that the centaurs were far superior in speed compared to the Kras.

Still, he was not completely hopeless. The centaurs left clear marks of their path, tearing down the terrain like a sickle against the crop. The heavy hooves of the creatures pummeled the grasses back into the earth, giving Branimir direction to run, even after the sight of the Svet was long lost.

Branimir could not have guessed how many hours he ran. His legs continued to fall in rhythm against the ground long after he lost feeling in his feet. His arms had grown weak, the muscles in his shoulders and back aching as though he had spent a lifetime lifting rocks. His head ached, ears frozen against the coolness of the northern wind. Whatever gods the humans prayed to did not look positively down on him in this moment. He fought against negative thoughts. He fought against fate. Branimir took every feeling within his being—hate, love, sadness, fear—and pushed himself beyond his limitations.

Branimir refused to abandon Dorofej.

The moon had passed through the sky, nearly indicating the next dawn, with light barely illuminating the far horizon. Delusional with exhaustion, Branimir stumbled in the grass, and fell to his knees. His pale eyes scanned the world around him seeing nothing different than he had for the hours prior. Hill upon hill stretched in every direction. The mountains, the Hrani Highlands, were but a shadow in the distance.

The sounds of war cries reached his delicate, pointed ears. Branimir heard the noise like a whisper in a dream. He barely believed it to be real, but it gave him the strength to return to his feet.

He pushed onward, faltering over hill and hill again. The sounds of battle, high-pitched howling, and fierce cries of warring beasts echoed through the hills. Soon, he learned the battle he heard was real, and not just in his head.

Branimir's chest heaved with heavy breaths, his small hand clutching the kinzhal tucked in his belt. He again became invisible to the world around him for protection, and advanced. The crumpled grasses crunched under his light footsteps with every step as he moved over another hill.

The sight in the hazy pastels of the waking world filled him with untamed horror.

The Svet, monstrous creatures beyond anything that Branimir could have ever imagined, were an intimidating force alone. The many archers circled, bare chests and fanged teeth exposed, thundering with the ferociousness of a thousand demons. A hundred stood in defense with half more lying dead in the grasses, their shredded bodies a token of their bravery. Crimson colored the grass more than the green that should have painted each blade of the earth.

The arrows of the Svet were fired with the precision of skilled combatants toward monstrous wolf-men that attacked relentlessly. The wolves, layered in shaggy gray hair from snout to paw, walked upright on their hind legs with strength comparable to the mighty centaurs. The creatures leapt about the battle scene with impressive quickness, claws slashing and teeth gnashing. Their fangs buried into the dark flesh of the Svet over and over again. The roars and howls of the beasts were more ferocious than the wolves of Kalamaar.

Though, the Svet barely seemed intimidated. Branimir awed at the centaurs, who stood their ground against the enemy. If it were him, he would have fled from the wolf-like creatures. Yet as one Svet fell, the next would take its place. They were a single unit battling against the multiple foes. Stone arrow after stone arrow tore through the wolf-men, tearing down their ranks in equal measure.

He found comfort that he was hidden, and searched for Dorofej and Falmagon. He hoped that neither had been caught by a loose arrow or worse. It only took a few minutes before Branimir decided neither Highborn was on the battlefield. If either man was among the ranks, he had fallen permanently or was unconscious under the bodies of those who were dead. Then again, it was quite possible that the two men were laying within the ranks of the Svet behind the massive bodies, hidden from the sight.

He had to be certain.

Ever slowly, Branimir walked through the battlefield, creeping toward the raging onslaught like an insect on a spider's web.

"Come! We feast on Vulkodlak tonight!" a Svet cried from the ranks, dark hair flailing off his back, firing a series of arrows from the quiver at his side.

A female Svet near him laughed, catching a wolf-man by

the neck as it jumped at her. She crushed the larynx in her hand before pulling it close and ripping a chunk of flesh from the side of its neck with her teeth.

Branimir turned his eyes away before the bile in his stomach emitted from his mouth.

Branimir scurried over the many dead bodies and frayed limbs. Death cries echoed. Branimir could not help but think back to the battle of Melkorka, the battle of Illuard, and the battle of Arkaim. His life had been haunted by death.

Branimir ran under the crushing hooves of another large Svet who wrestled with a Vulkodlak. The wolf-man held the arms of the Svet at bay. Each gnashed teeth at the other, before the Vulkodlak thrust forward and locked jaws on the bicep of the Svet. The arm was torn from socket by the massive fangs and the Svet screamed. The Vulkodlak had drool drip from its blackened lips, mixing with the blood drawn from its enemy.

The Svet male responded with head-butt to the beast, causing it to drop the hunk of meat from its mouth. The Vulkodlak was barely fazed, leaping onto the upper body of the Svet and burying its teeth into the centaur's face.

As the two crumbled to the ground, Branimir rushed forward to avoid being crushed. Either of these monsters would make quick work of him if he were captured.

Unseen, he kept moving to and fro through the battle avoiding collision with either warring party.

Svets flung arrows from their luks as their circle grew smaller and smaller. Bran noticed that even in the face of defeat, not one Svet backed down from the battle. As apparent friend or even loved one met their death, the Svet fought onward with the vicious, relentless retaliation.

"War and glory!" a male shouted from the ranks.

"For Rujan!" cried a female with a voice as deep as the man.

"For Rujan!" the rest echoed. The bawling of the Svet resounded repeatedly as they matched brawn against brawn.

Branimir squirreled through the front legs and haunches of the Svet, eventually making it to the inner circle of the holding.

He gasped in surprise. The Highborn were not in the inner circle of the Svet. They were nowhere to be found.

Branimir wanted to cover his eyes, but instead covered his ears as the din of victory sounded among the many centaurs. The remaining Vulkodlak retreated across the hills to the south.

Branimir was overwhelmed with emotion and utterly exhausted. He had told Dorofej that he would remain loyal and free them. His stomach gurgled. He felt feverish.

Hope was lost.

A female voice, deep and sturdy rose behind. Branimir felt something grip his shirt tightly, lifting him directly off the ground. "Hold on! What is this?"

Branimir squealed. He twisted and fought as he flew off the ground in the grasp of one of the mighty Svet. He had forgotten to concentrate and had become visible.

He was lifted past the Svet's firm, small breasts, marked with dark nipples before catching sight of her face. Her black eyes peered at him under two curved horns, smaller than the male Svet, but threatening still. "Is this a polevik?"

He furrowed his eyebrows in confusion. He had never heard of this thing called a polevik.

"No. Its color is too wrong to be one of those broods," said a male harshly, fangs clicking together as it spoke.

"I just want to know if I can eat it. What is it?" she snorted through her nostrils, and twitched her ears.

Branimir frantically jerked against the grip of the beast. He squeaked, kicking his legs. "You cannot eat me! I am a Kras!"

"Gah!" she screamed, nearly throwing him. "It understands me. And, it speaks our language."

"What sorcery is this?" the male Svet gasped, rearing

back, lifting his forelegs in the air like a horse throwing a rider from its back.

Several Svet gathered to look at the sight. Grumbles, growls, and snarls resounded through the ranks.

Branimir stopped twisting, his hands flying to the fingers of the Svet, fearful of being thrown from such a great height. "Of course, I can understand you. Why would I not be able to?"

The Svet glared, and spoke more from surprise than purpose. "Our language is our own, small beast. Nothing but a Svet speaks Svet!"

Branimir looked as staggered as the Svet who surrounded him, completely speechless. He understood them as well as any other.

The male who spoke next. "Take him to the High Priest for blessing, and be told if you can eat him."

"You cannot eat me," Branimir cried.

The woman nodded with a dangerous smile of sharpened teeth, her angled ears twitched again. "Gather what of our dead you can muster. There will be a great feast. Praise Rujan!"

The other centaur replied, "He truly smiles on us this day!"

"Don't eat me!" Branimir wept in frustration. He struggled against the overpowering creature; yet he was no match for the strong grasp of the Svet. "Don't eat me," Bran repeated fervently.

The centaur frowned and hit him over the head.

As the world darkened, Branimir had made up his mind. He wanted to return to Melkorka. He did not like this place called Maharia.

Chapter XXI

Branimir awoke with his hands bound behind his back, bouncing slightly on the back of the female Svet who had captured him. He was slung over the hide awkwardly on his side. His first thoughts were to remain still. He feared to move a muscle, thinking that the Svet may whack him over the head again to keep him unconscious.

His head throbbed, swollen and tender from being struck by the centaur. A boulder may have well had been dropped on his head. His vision was blurred momentarily, but the world eventually came into sight.

He found himself in a meadow a score of miles west of the battlefield where Vulkodlak and Svet had fallen. He found himself being taken into what appeared to be a centaur city. There were more Svet here than there had been humans at Arkaim. Their numbers stretched for miles. This Svet settlement was larger than Branimir could have ever guessed, stretching across the hills with man-horses and woman-horses scattered across the terrain like sand upon the water's edge.

The structures built for the Svet were odd compared to the structures built for men. Each building towered as though towering trees had been cut in half, shaved clean of their bark, and then a wooden flat roof leveled, stacked, and placed overhead. There were no walls on any of the buildings, but simply four corners that were spread at length from each other, fastened by the stilted roof. Each makeshift home gave enough room for many Svet to lie under at one time. In the center of each wooden structure was a fire pit that roared. It was surprising that the fire did not burn down the building. If anything, the homes appeared to be half-constructed stables without stalls.

The streets in between each housing unit were worn and hardened from constant movement upon its surface. Even now, Svet after Svet traipsed down the streets with heavy hooves, plodding the dirt deeper into the earth. The grasses within the settlement, if there ever had been any, were nonexistent compared to the tall grasses that surrounded in the hills.

Branimir struggled to keep his eyes open as they passed by a massive bonfire. Many of the centaurs gathered around the flames, pulling their dead near. Branimir watched, mortified, as the Svet would approach the dead and nod as though identifying the deceased, and then cut off the head of their own with a massive curved axe.

The blade reflected off the fire, showing that it was not copper, but something different. The color very much resembled the metal seen at King Ker's Manor House, a mixture of copper and a stronger element.

Human head after human head fell away from the bodies of the half-horses. And then, the bodies were thrown on the fire to be thoroughly roasted.

Branimir wanted to shake his head, or turn away from the sight, but remained fixated. Still, he feared to budge. He had great sight of the Svet gathering their own from the fire, and tearing into the meat. They were feasting on their own dead.

"A great victory this day!" A Svet cried riding up to the female who carried him across the city.

"Many died, giving us nourishment, bringing glory to the clan," the female said assuredly with a dip of her head in return. She continued to push forward barely looking at the male that had approached.

He pursued. "Melyena, you were battle hardened against the Vulkodlak, so I hear."

The female snorted with what may have been a giggle, turning her eyes to the male, her fawn-shaped ears wiggling excitedly. "Wish I could say the same for you, Asgrim. Running with your tail between your haunches is not the Svet way."

"Bah!" Asgrim pushed her lightly, throwing his head back at the jest, "You know what I was after. The Vucari had to be brought to the temple. Their kind have not been seen this far north for decades. Questions need answered before we skin them!"

Melyena sighed with a smile, her ears calming, "Make your excuses. You missed battle, hardly honorable!"

Branimir dared not move his head, but peeked at the male Svet that had approached. It was definitely the beast that had taken Kinhar and Dorofej. His strapping chest was as solid as stone, as were the gigantic, muscular arms. The Svet could break him with threat.

He could not believe his luck that he had come to the same place as the Highborn. He found himself thinking that they were still alive.

Asgrim ignored her. "What is this *thing* on your back? It is too red to be a polevik, though it is about the same size."

Branimir shut his eyes quickly, playing as though he were still unconscious.

"It called itself a Kras."

Asgrim poked Branimir. "Must be lying. I have never heard of such a thing."

"It is a strange creature," she admitted.

Asgrim leaned forward and inhaled deeply as though he were sniffing the skin right off Branimir. The brown, coarse hair on Melyena's back waved slightly in the heavy snort. Asgrim then blew out disgusted, snot spewing onto Branimir.

Branimir held his body still, but could not stop from scrunching his face in disgust.

Asgrim did not seem to notice. "It definitely doesn't smell like a polevik. But, you smell nice."

"I will rip out both of your hearts, Asgrim. Keep your hands to yourself," she said with crude humor. Branimir wondered what she meant by both hearts.

Asgrim laughed, shoving her again with a wink. "You stole my hearts a long time ago, Melyena." He suggestively raised his eyebrows.

She snorted, turning her head with embarrassment.

"In all truth, I wonder what this thing tastes like. I bet it tastes no different than a polevik."

Melyena shrugged her shoulders, the luk on her back shifting, the string taut between her naked breasts, "I'll tell you after the High Priest blesses my capture. I found it. I get to eat it. You get to watch."

Asgrim growled. "What if the High Priest doesn't let you eat it?"

"It is my right, Asgrim."

"Not if the Oracle says otherwise."

Melyena twitched her ears with aggrevation. "Why would he consult the Oracle?"

"The two Vucari captured and this … thing … all in one day," Asgrim shrugged. "I am no High Priest, but it seems like something one would consult the Oracle about."

Melyena shook her head. "No. No. I will receive my blessing and be roasting this little red creature by nightfall. You will see. I bet it is made of the most delicate meat."

It took everything in Branimir's power to keep himself from leaping from the Svet's back and scampering away as fast as he could.

"Ha! Doesn't appear to have much meat worth mentioning," Asgrim said. "But Melyena always gets her way, doesn't she?"

The female Svet raised her dark eyes, her nose uplifted making the large nostrils swell. "Yes, Asgrim. I do."

The two Svet trotted along for some time in silence through the city. The centaurs who passed by stared at Branimir on Melyena's back, sometimes asking questions, sometimes saying nothing at all. There was not a single centaur who did not take at least one look at Branimir.

Bran could not say he was shocked by the interest, considering the men of Kalamaar and the Seven Islands, a place that he called home and knew of his people, had reacted in a very similar way. He could not expect the Svet to not be curious about him. Their confusion told him what he had dreaded all along. He really was the last living Kras.

Melyena and Asgrim stopped near a large structure with significantly more poles upholding the roof than the other makeshift buildings. It was about four times the size of most of the structures they had passed. Several centaurs walked underneath the shelter, with more surrounding the edges, peering past one another, as though they were eager to get inside. Most held weapons. A constant growl like a pack of wolves feasting on their prey, flowed through the spectators outside the place.

A stone table sat in the center, lit by torchlight. The dirt floor was compiled of piles of skulls, with a lone pile of decaying Svet heads. Branimir could not keep himself from shuddering at the hollowed eyes, gaping mouths, and the pool of blood collecting underneath.

"These Vucari smell strange," a dark-haired male said with a throaty rumble. The Svet had a light-colored mane down his crest and matching tail, a tan color to him that offset him from most of the centaurs who Branimir had seen. "I wonder if they are Vucari at all, or something else?"

"What else could they be, Saint Isaak?" a female shouted from the side.

The Svet male shook his head, responding off-handedly,

"If I knew that, I would tell you."

"Isaak, where is the High Priest," Melyena said. "I want his blessing on my capture." She trotted into the holding, displaying Branimir on his back.

Branimir squeezed his eyes closed.

Isaak gawked. "What demon have you brought into the temple, Melyena? Your father will have your hide!"

"It is not a demon, Isaak," she said willfully.

"Saint Isaak," he corrected. "You will address me with reverence, Melyena Rogov."

"Saint Isaak," Melyena smiled. "Where is my father?"

"The High Priest visits the Oracle to find meaning of the Vucari advancing into our lands before the Season of Frost. They may be planning to use the cold against us, believing they are superior in the frigid weather. War may be coming!"

Growls erupted around the temple from Svet that watched the exchange. Branimir peeked to see the female centaur from the Highlands stepped out of the midst.

"Asgrim and I captured these two with ease after one of their own shapeshifted into a wolf and fled. It is clear what they are, Saint Isaak."

"Is that so, Felitch?" the Saint asked. "Then why did they not also change and outrun you in the mountains?"

"Our numbers were too great. They were filled with fear!" Asgrim bellowed, stepping behind Melyena.

"Don't be foolish," Isaak said with a pointed finger.

Asgrim sprang forward, grabbing the hand with a meaty fist. "Foolish, is it? I can smell the fear off your holy skin. If given the chance, you are the one who would bolt; or perhaps, you would stand and fight me to the death?"

Isaak tried to pull away. "Your hand should not touch me. I am of the temple, Asgrim," Isaak cried out.

Asgrim snarled, baring ith his sharpened fangs. "I will do as I wish. I will not have any Svet question my honor."

"What honor can be found in injuring a temple priest?"

Isaak asked.

"Injure? I would kill you, Saint Isaak. What honor is there in keeping a priest who dribbles hateful words from his tongue and against his own kind?"

"Let him be, Asgrim!" a voice barked.

Branimir slowly turned his head to keep from drawing attention. He saw the massive Svet who stepped into the temple. It stood a head taller than Asgrim, horns twice as large, with a white cloth draped over its back. Dark colored hair fell from the top of its head past the barrel of its body, shrouding the animal ears that perched with authority. The beast was magnificent.

"High Priest," Asgrim bowed his head, releasing the Saint immediately.

"Father," Melyena dipped her head in respect.

"What is that *thing* you carry, Melyena? Does it come with these—these creatures?" The High Priest waved his hand at the two Highborn men who were heaped on the ground. They were stripped naked, dropped near the skulls and the stone table.

Branimir jerked at the sight of Dorofej and Falmagon, searching for any sign of breath in their chest.

"I think not," Melyena said, grabbing Branimir by his leg and twisting him about to display him to the High Priest. He struggled slightly, but remembering the throbbing in his head, stopped abruptly. "I caught it after the battle with the Vulkodlak in the meadows, sneaking among our ranks."

"Quite a distance from the mountains then."

"Yes, father."

Branimir swayed upside down by the ankle, considering the dark eyes of the High Priest, seemingly in charge of the settlement. The male Svet held sway over the strong warrior, Asgrim, who remained silent.

Branimir had no idea how he was going to save Dorofej and Falmagon. He had to do something.

"As is my right, father, I wish to eat him with your blessing," Melyena said.

The High Priest leaned forward, sharp teeth spread slightly in consideration at the request. "I am not certain it is safe to stomach the creature. It may make you ill, daughter."

There were murmurs within the tent.

"I do not want to be eaten!" Branimir finally shouted louder than expected. His shrill voice silenced the Svet throughout the tent.

The High Priest stumbled backwards, his rear colliding with the stone table, knocking it over and causing it to split down the middle. He spun around anxiously, his hand reaching for a weapon he did not carry. When he found that he was without arms, he roared, ears lifting from the bulk of hair.

There was a similar response from those who watched, suddenly searching for their weapons. When the stone table broke, gasps of astonishment echoed, followed by gruff growls that gave hint to an army ready to go to war at first suggestion.

Branimir froze, lips pressed, hands clinging to his shirttail as they stayed bound behind his back.

Melyena did not budge, dropping her head as though someone had revealed a great secret.

"It speaks. It speaks Svet." The High Priest squinted his eyes at Branimir.

"Yes, father," Melyena said, "and seemingly understands us as well."

"Of course, I understand you," Branimir muttered, struggling against the female Svet's hold.

The Svet High Priest ignored Branimir, easing forward. "You knew this, Melyena, and chose to keep it from me after all that has happened this day."

"This is not related," she said.

"Bah! Do not lie to your father." The large Svet stomped forward, clacking his hooves against the hardened dirt. He lifted a hand as though he might strike his daughter. Almost colliding with Branimir, the High Priest invaded the space of his daughter with Branimir hanging inches from his chest.

Branimir gagged, turning his head. The smell of horse and manure overwhelmed his senses.

"Can I eat him or not?" Melyena hissed.

"No!" Branimir shouted.

The High Priest looked down at Branimir, "You understand us? You speak our language? How is this possible?"

Branimir trembled, but he kept his voice steady. If anything, he had plenty of practice in serving the Highborn and speaking when he was afraid. "I am not sure what you speak of, honestly, my Lord. I hear no difference in your dialect than my own, and I hear myself speaking in my own language."

"He attempts to deceive us," Saint Isaak said. "He dishonors Rujan with his demon lies in our temple."

The High Priest lifted his hand. "Quiet, Saint Isaak, or I will have Asgrim finish what he had started."

Asgrim grinned, tilting his head toward the Saint. "Say another word. I beg you."

The High Priest shot a look of disdain at the strong warrior, silencing him as well, before turning back to Branimir. "What are you? Where do you come from?"

"I am Branimir Baran, a Kras, from Melkorka, upon the Seven Islands of Forghar, on the island of Folkmar, near the island of Kalamaar. It is a small place compared to Maharia, my Lord," Branimir rattled as quickly as he could spit out the words.

Wrinkles formed around the High Priest's eyes as he tried to make sense of the new words and places. "Is that so? Are there more of your kind at Melkorka?"

Branimir shook his head. "No, my Lord. I am afraid I am the last of my kind."

The High Priest twisted his head to see the broken stone

table and growled fiercely. "Leave us. All of you, leave us!"

Melyena protested. "Father! He is mine by law!"

"And bound to him, you may be, my daughter! For now, you leave us, so we may speak in private. Am I understood?" he replied with a darkened gaze.

Melyena rumbled, showing her fangs. Asgrim placed a hand across her chest with an unheard whisper, and Melyena took a breath. Reluctantly, she handed Branimir to the High Priest, who gripped the other leg as though he were grabbing a burning branch.

Branimir blinked his eyes several times as he was passed off from one beast to the other. He had no chance of leaving the camp alive.

Melyena, Asgrim, Felitch, and even Saint Isaak removed themselves from the temple with the several dozen Svet who had crowded on the sides. Objections and criticisms, and even whispers of conspiracy were shared among the large man-horses and woman-horses. Branimir did not know what to make of all of it.

The High Priest did not loosen Branimir's bindings, but he did put him down carefully on the ground. Branimir, even seated, barely reached the Svet's knee, and would probably stand just under the foreleg if he was standing at full height.

"Do not run. We will run you down if you do, Kras."

Branimir nodded. "I know." He did not have to be threatened by the Svet. After running across the countryside, he was easily convinced at the speed of the Svet. Besides, with his throbbing head, he was sure that he could not concentrate long enough to stay invisible to escape Sorod. Even if he could, he would have no idea where to go without the Highborn.

"Are you familiar with the Svet, Kras?" the High Priest asked.

"No, my Lord," Branimir said, continuing to give title the Svet as he was accustomed. "Your kind is not found on Kalamaar or the Seven Islands."

The High Priest nodded, deep in thought. "Then you are not familiar with our prophecies?"

Branimir shook his head, black hair clinging to his crimson forehead.

"We have many, but one," the High Priest's hoof scraped against the broken stone table.

Branimir wrinkled his nose. "What does it mean, my Lord?"

"I do not know, Kras, but you speak in the tongue of my people. You have also instigated the breaking of the *Solheimasandi*. This sacred stone table has been among the Svet for age upon age, crafted and carried from the dark mountains of the west before my grandfather came to the Hyaendi Hills."

Branimir rocked backwards, utterly confused by the High Priest. "I did not break the table, my Lord. You ran into it."

The High Priest's throat rumbled and softened, "Things happen for a reason, Kras. Do those where you come from not believe in fate."

"I suppose some do, my Lord."

The High Priest dipped his head, ears lying flat behind his massive horns. He tilted his head as if listening to the wind, in deep thought. After several moments, he shook his head. It was either in response to an unheard voice, or perhaps not hearing anything at all. Regardless, his face was clearly painted in frustration.

Seeing the ferocious, barbaric nature of the Svet, Branimir decided it was wise to remain silent. He peered at Dorofej and Falmagon again. Each had a significant bruising on their face where they had been struck by the heavy hand of Asgrim yesterday. It was likely they had been hit several more times to keep them unconscious. If that were the case, they were lucky their faces were not complete mush.

Branimir noticed each of them had a steady rise and fall to their chest. He sighed in relief.

"What are you doing in the Hyaendi Hills, Kras? Why have you come to Maharia from Melkorka?"

Branimir compressed his cracked lips, and wrinkled his nose. The question was more complex and difficult than any question he had ever been asked.

Several minutes may have passed before the High Priest growled impatiently. "What is your answer, Kras?"

"These two," Branimir pointed at Falmagon and Dorofej, "journey with me. I need them to complete my quest."

Branimir cringed, wondering if he had just incriminated himself permanently to whatever fate befell the two Highborn lying amongst the decaying skulls.

The High Priest kept his jaw locked, but his eyes were full of bewilderment. It was evident he had expected an answer that would lead him to deep deliberation, but nothing linking Branimir with the bodies at his hooves.

The patience and understanding of the High Priest was unlike any other who fell among the ranks of the Svet civilizations. "These are Vucari from the Dyndaer, and not from the place you call Melkorka?"

Branimir said, "They are not Vucari, my Lord."

"What are they then?" he replied.

Branimir was not sure why he answered with the ancient name of humans instead of referring to them as Highborn or Northmen. It was likely a question he would reflect on for the years to come. "They are Anshedar, my Lord."

"Anshedar..." the word slid off the pointed tongue of the High Priest as though it were a word that could move mountains, carve oceans, and even change the arrangement of seasons. He said it again. "Anshedar."

"Yes, my Lord."

Dorofej stirred. Branimir heard him snort as he twisted slightly on the ground.

"What is your quest, Kras?" the interest of the High Priest was exceptional. Branimir had a sense of calmness rush over him, hearing the soft tone of the great Svet that stood before him.

Branimir swallowed, finding honesty to be the best course to follow. "We seek the Ash Tree within the Dyndaer to—"

"What?" the High Priest roared, clamoring forward, nearly squashing the Kras where he sat. "What did you say?"

The rage that filled the Svet came without warning, sending Branimir reeling backwards into a pile of skulls. They collapsed down on his little body, hitting him in the head over and over again.

"What did you say?" The High Priest grabbed him by his throat and lifted him off the ground, nearly killing him from the mere grip.

The voice boomed with the ferocity of a thousand beasts followed by a thousand demons, carrying through Sorod like war drums. Branimir's ears hummed.

He wriggled, choking against the grip.

The High Priest cried out again, not noticing he was strangling Branimir, "Answer me!"

"The Ash Tree," Branimir croaked. "We ... protect it ... demons ..."

The Svet let loose Branimir, falling back on his haunches in a daze.

Branimir had no ability to even wave his arms with them tied behind his back, and fell four times his height to the ground with a thud. His body cracked against the solid earth.

The air was stolen from his lungs, a sharp pain tearing through him from chest to spine.

The High Priest spoke to himself. "I stand at an impasse, to follow tradition and eradicate those who tread on my lands or welcome blood and death by the beasts of the Netherworld. If the Kras speaks truth, I will welcome the destruction at my doorstep. Or, I can let this Kras and the Anshedar complete their quest, holy or not, futile or not, and forsake my people. I will lose any authority as High Priest, and worse yet, the admiration of my daughter. What choice will bring glory to Rujan? What choice will bring glory to the Svet?"

Branimir rattled for air, trying to understand the Svet through his panting. He crawled up to his knees and fell over with his cheek against the dirt.

Dorofej moved again followed by a groan from Falmagon.

The High Priest raised his horse body and stepped toward the two Highborn with a shake of his head. He looked at Branimir with an empty gaze. Then, with a quick stamp of his front foreleg, he connected hoof to human forehead, sending each Highborn spiraling back into sleep.

Branimir dropped his head in defeat, jaw quivering. He heard the High Priest approach him slowly, halfheartedly.

Branimir did not even feel the hoof strike him. In seconds, he joined his masters in the shadow of dreamless dreams.

Chapter XXII

The Kras did not know how long he had been unconscious. His head was flooded with aches and twinges, his own blood caked to his black hair. The dirt room, although massive, had little to no ventilation, like an underground tomb. There was no sign of the outside world, no view of the sun, stars or otherwise. He gasped for fresh air.

Night swept through Sorod, the centaur city, like locusts on the summer crop. Loud banter, singing, dancing, and feasting could be heard among the Svet throughout the city. The ground above Branimir shook under their falling hooves. The Hyaendi Hills, as they were called, reverberated with sound of the countless Svet. It seemed their voices and songs and praise would be heard for time without end.

"Oh," Branimir groaned, grabbing his stomach with both hands. To his recollection, he had gone nearly three days without food or drink, and his stomach had finally decided to remind him of it. It growled and tore at his insides as though it were intent on eating his guts. In the half decade he had been enslaved to the Highborn, Branimir had never known such treatment, nor had he been in such pain, even when Falmagon had beaten him with *Habërmani*.

With sudden awareness, Branimir jumped up and looked at his hands. He was not bound. He was free.

The moment only lasted a moment before his knees gave way and he weakly collapsed again to the ground.

"Branimir, come eat," Dorofej's voice echoed off the solid dirt walls.

He looked to Dorofej, who stood at a wooden table at the opposite side of the room. Falmagon stood next to him, stuffing his face with meat. He was relatively pleased to see that each of them had reunited with their robes, covering their aged nakedness. Though, Bran nearly fell backwards upon seeing the High Priest standing across from them, an enthralled look on his flattened face.

"What is happening, Lord Dorofej? What is with all the noise?" Branimir murmured, moving toward the table, the only object in the square room. On all fours, he crawled, barely finding any strength to stand. Besides the table, the room was completely bare, one door on one wall made of wood, large enough for the Svet to pass through.

"Celebrating victory and worshipping Rujan, the Four-Faced God of War, the Svet are," Dorofej explained. "Expect peace and quiet, I would not."

The High Priest spoke after listening to Branimir's speech and Dorofej's answer. The old Highborn lifted his hand as though he were about to provide solution to a grave concern.

Branimir stopped moving in astonishment. The words of the Svet were completely garbled nonsense, full of grunts and harsh consonants. It was absolute gibberish.

Dorofej must have used *Koldovstvo* to make the High Priest a babbling idiot. He and Falmagon must be holding him captive in this hole in the ground.

Branimir screeched in fear. "Where are we, my Lords? What have you done?" The stomping of hooves, thousands of them, echoed from above. The Svet were likely going to come crashing through the wooden doors in the room at any moment and slaughter them all.

He noticed the swollen faces of the Highborn, regardless

of the dim torchlight eating at the air of the room. Each Highborn had a large lump with a hoof imprint upon the wrinkles of their foreheads. Branimir could not believe they were not as distressed as he was from the massive blow. If they were even close to being distraught, Falmagon and Dorofej hid it well.

Dorofej held up his hand teasingly and opened it slowly, revealing the moonstone, the *Ojenek*, in his palm.

Branimir instinctively checked his pocket and sure enough, Dorofej had swiped it from him while he was unconscious.

Dorofej handed it to the High Priest, placing the small stone in his massive hand delicately. The stone continued to flicker as though an inner fire were deep within its core. The towering, Svet male looked at the stone in amazement.

"You say this stone allows me to understand the language of any creature, as though I am speaking in their tongue and them in mine?" the High Priest asked.

"Is it not so?" Dorofej said simply.

Branimir's jaw dropped. He now understood why he could speak Svet. He had been carrying *Ojenek*.

Falmagon shoved the meat into his mouth again without manners. "It is about time I can understand you two. Been cackling and coughing for a half an hour back and forth, leaving me in the dark, hearing nothing but rubbish! Why did you not just give it to him to begin with?"

"It was not the way that things could be done, yes?"

Falmagon harrumphed and took another bite, "Dorofej, why did you just not talk to the brute who brought us here in the first place? We could have explained ourselves and been on our way!"

"My apologies, High Priest," Dorofej started, as he explained his reasoning to Falmagon, "but the Svet are not accustomed to hearing explanations, especially from those who resemble the Vucari, yes? Explained what we could not, Branimir did. The Kras paved the way, yes?"

The High Priest nodded. "That he did, Dorofej. I fear if you would have spoken directly to Asgrim, he would have killed you on the spot. Such a thing would have been greatly feared. Besides, the Svet are not generally aware of the prophecy of our people. They are not gifted with the knowledge of the Oracle. Moreover, Rujan does not speak directly to them."

Branimir wondered at Dorofej. It was like he knew what was going to happen before it happened.

"Prophecy? Oracle? Rujan?" Falmagon muttered. "You speak outside of our knowing, High Priest. We are not from these lands."

He finally made it to the table, looking at *Ojenek*. Branimir repeated what the High Priest had told him earlier. "The 'talisman of treasures gifted'.

The High Priest nodded. "Yes, Kras. That is exactly what this is, and I accept the gift graciously as it should be done."

Branimir almost wanted to scream. The shiny stone was supposed to be his!

A warning look from Dorofej held him at bay. "High Priest, yours to keep, it is."

Branimir watched Falmagon rip another bite from the bone he gripped in his fist. "Do you know what you are eating, Lord Falmagon?"

Falmagon arched his eyebrows at the Kras in exasperation. "Meat."

Branimir winced, but found himself quickly devouring his own hunk of meat attached to bone. Some type of rib, he guessed, maybe from the fallen Svet or Vulkodlak. He did not want to think about it. He was too hungry to have to think about it.

"I imagine you exchange the stone for your freedom, so that you may continue your journey," the Svet said to the old Highborn.

Dorofej did not flinch. "Give nothing to the Svet, do I, for they take what they want. It is my hope the Oracle and

Rujan see to it that we may continue our journey. We have traveled a great distance for a cause affecting the entire world, Kalamaar and Maharia alike."

Branimir took another bite from the red meat, feeling his strength begin to return to him. It was startling as to what energy could be gained through a few simple bites.

"You are wise beyond your years, Anshedar. You speak as though you are familiar with the Svet."

Dorofej dipped his head. "I am familiar enough to know the bounds of my choice, yes?"

"Hmm," the High Priest moved away from the table. "I must consult with Oracle to decide the best course of action. I cannot decide, and should not decide, on my own. Remain here."

The High Priest galloped full speed toward the southern wall of dirt, solid in appearance. The wall waved like an ocean, and the Svet disappeared into its depths.

"By *Mulafell*," Falmagon said, watching in astonishment. "Even in all my years with *Koldovstvo*, there are still things that I cannot believe."

"Quite a sight, yes?" Dorofej agreed.

"Where did he go?" Branimir questioned.

Dorofej explained, while chewing on the red meat lay before them. "The Svet worship the god called Rujan, a god who is quite similar to Svathevit, who is worshiped by the Highborn and Northmen, yes? Rujan is a God of War and Glory, said to have a face on each side of his head to be watchful and vigilant in battle, he is."

Falmagon pulled at his gray beard. "Just like Svathevit. That must be more than a coincidence, a god having the same characteristics of another god from across the world. What can that mean?"

"More common than we might think, yes? Our level of understanding can be most frustrating at times, I would think," Dorofej continued, "Rujan is everything to the Svet. I say, they worship him with all of their being and communicate with him through the High Priest, who is given secrets to accessing the Oracle."

"Through that wall?" Branimir scrunched his face. "Is it a person? A thing?"

Dorofej shrugged with a chuckle, causing the tassels of his beard to bounce. "That is for the Svet to know, I suppose. Some say the High Priest travels directly to the Beyond or perhaps the Golden City, *Iriy*, to converse with Rujan about matters related to their fate, or so they say."

Falmagon suddenly dropped his hand holding the meat, and stepped back, his single eye peering at Dorofej, as though he were looking at him for the first time. "Who says, Dorofej? My education was the same as yours at Melkorka and none knew of the Svet. Even Kinhar, living a thousand years, who shared more with me than any other, never told me of the Svet."

Dorofej did not blink, scratching his beard in consideration. "The only Highborn to have been to the Ash Tree, Kinhar was not. Nor, living lifetime beyond lifetime, he has not been."

Falmagon spewed the meat from his cheek onto the table, a wild look filled his visage like a rabbit who had just stepped into a snare. "But—"

Branimir could not believe it, though he might have guessed it, if he had spent the time to consider the possibility. There was more to Dorofej than an old man.

Dorofej raised his hands ruefully. "It was not, and likely still is not, for you to know, Falmagon Sej. Young and rambunctious, you are, without understanding, I am afraid."

Falmagon did not hear him, slamming his fist down on the table. "How old are you exactly, Dorofej? You ridicule men of their secrets while holding your own."

The old Highborn lifted his shoulders, seemingly without a reasonable response. "I lost track centuries ago—"

"Centuries?" Falmagon stammered. "By *Mulafell* and all that is righteous. Centuries!"

Dorofej took another bite of the food on the table.

Branimir awed at Dorofej while trying to keep from giggling at the one-eyed Highborn. Falmagon could not make a coherent thought, let alone a sentence.

Without warning, the High Priest burst back through the wall. He stamped his feet against the ground, and shook his head as if shaking a ringing from his ears. It was likely he had just escaped the eternal cries of suffering souls in the hereafter.

Falmagon did not even look up, staring at Dorofej with his mustache separated from beard, as though they may never reconnect. Branimir nearly laughed out loud at the exasperated facial expression. He covered his face with his hands.

Dorofej remained unaltered, facing the High Priest, speaking before swallowing, "I say, what word does the Oracle give, High Priest?"

"What did I miss?" the overbearing Svet asked after looking at Falmagon's gawking face and Branimir's half grin, barely hidden by small, cupped hands.

"Imagine they have finally ate their fill is all, yes?"

The High Priest licked his lips. "Good! The Vucari are delicious when tenderized correctly. I was hoping you found it tasteful."

Branimir's smile had never fled from his face so quickly. "Vucari? What do you mean Vucari?"

The High Priest grinned. "Yes, we caught a female Vucari shortly after finding you. She was without a hand, but there was no sign of disease."

Dorofej's composure broke as he gripped the table, face pale as a winter sky. He spit the meat out of his mouth as though it were poisoned.

Falmagon immediately fell to his knees, gagging and vomiting. His fingers dug into the dirt with every convulsion.

Branimir dropped the meat that he held in his hand immediately, his eyes tearing up. Never had there been a fouler trick!

They had eaten Erzebeth!

The High Priest twitched his ears, gawking at them with confusion. "What has happened?"

It was Dorofej who finally found the strength to speak. "What of the Oracle?"

The High Priest winced, but answered, "You are free to continue to your quest on one condition."

"Please, tell me, what is that?" Dorofej said.

"Rujan desires a Svet to accompany you to add our lineage to this tale. The Svet will share in the glory."

Chapter XXIII

It was mid-morning when the High Priest gathered the elders to the temple to make the announcement. Dorofej and Falmagon stood boldly among the Svet with Branimir meekly standing in front of them. It was not a ceremonious occasion but it was one worth mentioning.

"Brethren of Rujan, we have been tasked to send one of our own to journey with the Anshedar and the Kras, last of his kind, for the glory of the Svet. The Oracle has spoken!" The High Priest shouted to all those who were gathered.

An elder cried from the crowd, speaking in a tongue that Bran could not understand without the *Ojenek*.

The High Priest raised his hand. "These are not simple trespassers deserving of death, Augastaoir. These are warriors who come to battle against demons that delve in the Deep."

Another elder interrupted with laughter, making comments in the Svet tongue pointing at the Highborn and then the city. He lifted his hands up, indicating the Svet were stronger and more powerful than the 'warriors' who stood before them.

Branimir could not blame them for doubting the two old men and a half-man, without weapon or army at their backs. The Svet had every right to laugh. Even Branimir wondered how they were going to accomplish something that the Svet could not rightly do on their own.

"No Svet will touch the Anshedar," the High Priest boomed.

The garbled argument came again from the Svet called Augastaoir.

The High Priest interrupted the objection. "This quest has been sanctioned by the Oracle. Listen, I questioned the decision of aiding these strangers too, but I do not disregard the wisdom of Rujan! Do you? If so, speak so that we may call you blasphemer and give you the death that you seek. Then ,you can face Rujan in the hereafter!"

The roar of the crowd fell silent.

Branimir could only wonder what death a blasphemer would receive in this barbaric culture.

The High Priest continued, his ears flicking irritably at the many Svet that questioned his judgment and that of their god. "I will not ask any of you to accompany them on this journey. The Vulkodlak still threaten our lands and we must protect them. The beasts grow stronger with each passing moment, more daring, threatening our lives and our way of life.

"There has already been word that Fenna and Kilmuir called for reinforcements. Belgorad has had none to send and so we must rely on our own to defend against the wolf-men. I would not risk the livelihood of our own."

There were shouts across the crowd, but there was no indication to Branimir as to whether they were positive or negative based on the dialect. The language was so harsh, and the body language so foreign, he could not make sense of the guttural sounds that erupted from the throats of the Svet.

"It is for that reason that I will send my daughter, Melyena Rogov, to accompany them into the Dyndaer to see their task through," the High Priest said. "My own blood will be put at risk at the command of the Oracle."

As shouts erupted, the color in Branimir's face drained. It was just his luck that the one centaur that wanted to eat him would join them.

Asgrim pushed through the crowd, screaming at the High Priest. His voice was like thunder, bellowing through the temple and beyond.

"I will not stop you, Asgrim Garoar. You are a strong warrior and would fight alongside her well. However, you would be desperately missed in the war against the Vulkodlak. Your luk and labrys is greatly needed against the wolf-men."

Melyena stepped into the temple as well, placing a hand gently on Asgrim's shoulder. She spoke softly.

Branimir tried to make sense of the conversation between the two centaurs. The large male Svet snarled harshly at her with a whip of his head, his dark hair flipping around his face fiercely. She reared up slightly and hissed between her sharpened fangs before turning away. Asgrim slammed his hoof against the ground, and then grunted at the High Priest once more.

The High Priest responded with a dip of his head. "It is settled. Asgrim and Melyena will accompany the Anshedar and Kras. Let it be sung for ages to come."

Another roar sounded from among the crowd. It was strange that it erupted from the rear of the group instead of the front where the High Priest spoke. Branimir tried to peer through the centaurs to make sense of the noise. He could not see anything.

The High Priest cried out, spinning around to address all the Svet. "To arms. We are under attack!"

"What?" Falmagon cried, obviously as confused by the back and forth as much as Branimir. The words from the High Priest were unexpected.

The High Priest turned toward the Highborn. "The Vulkodlak have come into the city. You must go! You must flee!"

Falmagon shouted with the intensity of a thousand men at the High Priest. "Where is my staff? We cannot leave without it!"

"What staff?"

"It has a crook that bends at the top. It was with me when Asgrim brought me to Sorod," Falmagon explained in desperation. "Where is it?"

"Asgrim, this Anshedar is looking for the staff he carried. Where has it gone?" the High Priest said as Melyena and Asgrim trotted toward them.

The sounds of battle echoed in the distance. The Svet's fingers twitched, looking toward the beginnings of the battle.

Asgrim responded hastily, loosening a glimmering two-sided axe from his belt. His voice was deep and hurried, making no sense to Branimir.

Melyena retrieved the luk from her back and nocked an arrow. Her eyes scanned her quiver to make count of the rest.

"What did he say?" Falmagon demanded, folding his fingers into a his fist.

The High Priest turned back to Falmagon with hesitation. "He said that they burnt it. He also said if you want a real weapon instead of a stick, we have bronze weapons at the armory."

Bronze. The metal was called bronze, not copper.

Falmagon's cry was like a madman watching his own child dismembered. He launched himself at Asgrim with outstretched hands. "Burnt it!"

Asgrim bared his teeth at Falmagon.

Dorofej grabbed the Highborn Long-Walker before he could get his hands on the Svet. "Tear you apart, Falmagon, he will. Keep your head."

"He burnt it, Dorofej. He burnt *Habërmani*!"

The High Priest stepped in between them, speaking to his daughter. Quickly, he opened her hand and gave her the *Ojenek*, their hands both cupping the moonstone.

"Take this, my daughter, and keep it safe," he said. "It will allow you to speak to these strangers from Melkorka."

Melyena closed her eyes, accepting the gift. "Thank you,

father. I will bring glory to our family and to the Svet."

The High Priest smiled. "I knew you would understand. Make haste! For glory! For Rujan!"

"For glory! For Rujan!" Melyena repeated.

Inhuman roars and howls of the Vulkodlak packed the streets of Sorod. Melyena turned her head with a snarl, and bolted toward the west. The rest shadowed her as best as they were able with Asgrim at the front.

The wolf-men were smaller than Bukavac, but massive to Branimir as they bounded through the streets, clawing and tearing at the centaurs. No Svet, whether it be man, woman or child, backed away from the attacking Vulkodlak.

Branimir peddled his feet, staying in front of Falmagon and Dorofej with ease. His eyes locked on the monsters that tore across the town like a sweeping river. The place was booming with the brutal growls and roars of beasts. Without doubt, the dead would litter the streets of Sorod this day.

"Move faster," Meleyena bellowed from the front at the humans behind her. She did not even bother turning her head. It was as though she could smell them falling behind. Branimir would believe it; none of them had bathed in months.

A Vulkodlak sprang into the streets in front of them, but was dropped by Melyena. Her arrow penetrated the wolf-man's eye socket as soon as its paws touched the dirt road.

Making such a shot while running had to be the best form of luck, Branimir decided.

Another beast approached the side of the party as they ran. Asgrim caught the Vulkodlak midair with the shaft of his two-sided axe. A guttural sound trembled Asgrim's throat as he flung the monster to the opposite side like he was tossing a hay, using the wolf-man's momentum against him. However, Asgrim did not stop with the deflection. He trampled forward and stamped the beast as it slid on its back. Hoof met skull several times, followed by the blade in his hands.

The hunger for blood surprised Branimir. The death

delivered was not quick or merciless.

"We cannot run forever," Falmagon shouted, already tripping over his feet, chasing the hurried Svet.

Melyena twisted her head and raised her eyebrows at the two men who had fallen even further behind in just a few moments. It was as though she had just realized that they were not Svet.

"The stables are beyond the gate," she said. "Come!"

Asgrim mumbled something in the Svet language to the High Priest's daughter before glaring back at the Highborn.

Branimir ignored the two centaurs. He was bothered that the situation mirrored the events in Arkaim, which had ended in terrible bloodshed. Now, once again, the group was running from imminent death. He did the only thing that had kept him alive before, and clung to hope.

Chapter XXIV

They fled beyond Sorod, into the Hyaendi Hills with Vulkodlak in pursuit. The sound of battle echoed in the wind. The sounds of beasts battling beasts resounded in their ears as the Svet of Sorod defended their home and the lands they considered holier than any other. While the Vulkodlak hit the city by the hundreds from the west, the fellowship followed the direction appointed by the High Priest and rushed to the east.

Branimir rode bareback upon Melyena, with his small hands holding tightly to her leather belt strap. She galloped at full speed, luk in her hands as she ran. The long black hair flowing down her back and head hit him in the face, catching awkwardly inbetween his lips. He spit out the hair, tucking his head against her back, and attempted to use his arm to shield his face. She ran with all the speed of a faering at sea.

Ahead of her was Asgrim, pushing forward, with a luk across his back and his own quiver of arrows attached to his belt. His strong arm carried a labrys, swaying heavily with every bound. The large Svet was full of force, dashing back and forth across Hyaendi Hills.

Lastly, covering the rear of the two Svet, sprinted a painted horse and a black mare, carrying Falmagon and Dorofej. The Highborn, riding bareback as well, clung to the necks of the beasts that pushed forward to keep pace with the Svet. It was said that the horse was a sacred animal to the Svet and to their god, Rujan. These animals were frequent visitors among the Svet, not held by any means, but seemingly at the command of the man-horse and woman-horse of the hills. It was as though they were kin, only separated by culture and civilization.

The Highborn had been fortunate that the High Priest had allowed for the two horses to be taken in order to keep pace with the quick Svet.

"Where to?" Melyena shouted over the clopping of her hooves.

"To the Dyndaer to the far east and south," Dorofej said loudly, his old frame clinging to the mare.

Melyena nodded and shouted instruction to Asgrim. The black-skinned beast at the head of the fellowship changed direction.

They had only traveled for about an hour when Asgrim slowed them to a stop. He turned to look back the way they had come.

"What is it?" Falmagon said. "Why are we stopping?"

"Vulkodlak have been giving pursuit since we left Sorod," Melyena said, pulling Branimir from her back with a single hand and setting him down into the grasses.

Falmagon tilted his head. "I don't see any reason why we should stop moving then. If anything, let us pick up the pace."

"No!" Melyena said. "The Vulkodlak do not tire like the horses. Besides, the Svet do not run from battle, Anshedar. Stay back with the Kras and keep the horses calm.

Asgrim and Melyena trotted forward to the top of a hill, their bows held in hand, stone arrows nocked.

Falmagon and Dorofej slid from the back of their horses, their hands grasping onto the mane of the animals. The Highborn intentionally turned the horses to face away from the Svet.

Falmagon complained, "How will we hold the beast still

without a harness?"

"Maharian horses, these are," Dorofej said. "I say, they will not stir so easily as those found on Kalamaar. Let the Svet do what they must, and hope that no Vulkodlak make it past them, yes?"

Branimir held his head, still aching. If the wolf-men made it past the Svet, they would surely die or the Highborn would die using *Koldovstvo*. Dorofej was far too old to even touch the craft, and Falmagon was close to it.

Branimir used his far-sight to watch the Svet. Already they were firing arrows at enemies beyond the hill.

Melyena fired arrows at twice the speed of Asgrim, but Asgrim's shots seemed to deliver more impact, the string stretching further back. The quiver emptied quickly as they pulled arrow after arrow from the holding bag on their right side.

As Melyena fired her last arrow, she backed up waiting for impact. The first Vulkodlak Branimir sighted over the hill came with the speed of a northern gale, the gray fur whipped back. It snarled and hurdled itself at the female Svet.

Melyena swung her luk as she would a sword, striking the Vulkodlak across the jawbone. Branimir heard the beast yelp like a pup struck by its master, before gnashing its elongated teeth at Melyena again. It struck at her forelegs, and she reared up, kicking both legs downward, striking the wolf-man's head over and over again. As each hoof hit the monstrous creature in the head, its body jolted and eventually went limp. Melyena continue to stamp upon the Vulkodlak to be assured that it did not stand up again.

"We must help them," Branimir finally said. "It is the right thing to do."

Asgrim had already thrown down his luk, and held the labrys in both hands. He had two Vulkodlaks advancing on him, one with a mangled eye and the other with blood already dripping from its chest.

The Vulkodlak was hungry for blood, hungry for death. It lunged, claws striking at the Svet as a man would in a fist fight. The second moved to the rear to sink its teeth into Asgrim's hide.

Asgrim was quick, using the butt of his labrys to strike the first in the forehead, making it stumble backwards. The centaur than twisted his upper body and flipped the double-sided axe, catching the blade in the chest of the second. The Vulkodlak was suspended, its rib cage caught on the blade. Asgrim tried to rip the blade free but it was caught.

The first Vulkodlak dove again, side stepping and biting at Asgrim's human body. The Svet roared, spinning his body and rearing. His hind feet struck the Vulkodlak in the chest, sending the beast sprawling onto its back.

With a snarl, Asgrim's muscles bulged lifting the Vulkodlak on his labrys in the air. The wolf-man howled menacingly as the bronze blade dug deeper into his midsection. With perfect timing, Asgrim rotated around again, slamming the Vulkodlak on his labrys into the one standing with the missing eye. The impact tore his weapon loose and he charged to finish the first.

More Vulkodlak stormed.

"We must help them, my Lords," Branimir said, looking at the Highborn on either side of him. "They will die."

"What can we do?" Falmagon asked. "They have gotten us this far, and are truly not needed to reach the Ash Tree. Dorofej knows the way. I say we ride onward and leave them to their fate."

"You are a coward." Branimir puffed up to the Highborn Long-Walker. "You have the power to help others and you do nothing! How can you call yourself, Highborn?"

Falmagon gaped at Branimir, shocked lining his face.

In the distance, Melyena swept up Asgrim's bow, and held it in her opposite hand, swatting at the advancing beasts that charged at her. As one locked onto her shoulder, she screamed.

Asgrim ripped the beast from his companion, crushing the skull beneath his massive fist.

"Branimir speaks the truth." Dorofej scowled. "We do not leave the Svet behind, unless you wish the entirety of their armies to come after us, yes? A race to be reckoned with, Falmagon, they are."

"I am not a coward," Falmagon struggled. "There is nothing we can do. We have no weapons and I am without *Habërmani*. Must I remind you that we still have Nedezhda to contend with at the Ash Tree. The *Eretik* may be there already!"

"Finish this, Falmagon," Dorofej said. "Strength, you still have, even without *Habërmani*."

Falmagon frowned. "I could kill myself, Dorofej."

"You are Highborn!" the old man screamed, his face shaking with absolute rage. "You are Anshedar! I say, does Branimir have better sense of those titles than you? How long has it been that you have diluted *Koldovstvo* through that crooked staff, Falmagon Sej? Forfeit glory for greed, you should not. If truly faithful to the Lightbringer, you are, then fight you must."

The gray-haired man, called the Highborn Long-Walker, tore off the patch that had long covered the gaping hole in his skull where an eye should have been.

His lip curled, shaking with fury, as he turned to face Dorofej. "You know nothing of my sacrifice. You have lived a thousand years or more, so you say, and still you send other men to their death. You ask me to readily throw away what you have long coveted." Falmagon visibly was shaking. "Sit back and idly watch, Dorofej. So be it!"

Before Dorofej could say a word in protest, Falmagon tightened the grip on his horse and galloped full speed toward the battle on the hill.

As the ground lifted and rocks fell, as stone melded into flesh, and *Koldovstvo* seared through the veins of Falmagon,

Branimir trembled in absolute horror.

The man, once younger than Dorofej, aged beyond reason. Hair whitening and skin wrinkling until there was barely hair or muscle left on the man. He slumped on the horse, clinging to the mane of the painted creature as he continued to wield the craft of the Highborn.

The Vulkodlak howled as they fell in their own blood.

Falmagon moved beyond Branimir's sight.

Bran trembled when realizing the power of his words toward Falmagon. In months past, he would have said the Highborn had never taught him anything. He was wrong. He, too, had learned how to lead others to their death.

Branimir did not think he would ever see the Highborn Long-Walker again.

Chapter XXV

Another two months had passed and the Season of Frost was heavily upon them. The first snow had blanketed the world, melted, and another layer of the white fluff had fallen again. The winds nipped at Bran's skin, chilled with the breath of the Seamstress of Nightmares, known as Marheena. She seemed to bless Nedezhda and the demons with every passing day, making it more difficult for the fellowship to find their way to the Ash Tree. Czern, the Gray-Clad, was seemingly allied with her. The days grew darker as the God of Darkness lengthened his gaze on the world. Together, Marheena and Czern prepared Maharia for death and decay.

The Hyaendi Hills had long ago faded, the Hrani Highlands had blended into the Dyndaer, and two weeks ago the mountainous region had completely disappeared. While at the peaks of the Hrani Highlands, Branimir had witnessed the sight of the massive, enigmatic forest. It stretched further than any forest he had ever seen. Tree towered next to tree, higher than any manmade structure, wrapping around each other like a bandage that could never be uncoiled.

Somewhere within this forest was the Ash Tree. Dorofej claimed he knew the way. They had no choice but to trust the old man, who claimed to have lived longer than Kinhar and Erzebeth together.

Branimir shivered, pulling the deerskin around his body, lips nearly frozen together. The deer that now served as his cloak had been eaten for their supper two weeks ago. At the time, when Melyena shot it down, Branimir had crossed his fingers, hoping it was not a Vucari transformed. He had to push the thought from his head to keep his belly full, and his skin warm. Now, all he could think about was how odd the spotted fur looked against his red skin.

"Be'er learns to like da cold, Kras," Asgrim rumbled in the broken language of the Anshedar. Dorofej had finally taught him some words after passing the *Ojenek* back and forth between him and the Svet had become tiresome, but the language was still considerably choppy. Branimir had wished they had continued to pass *Ojenek* between them to help in the communication. "Dis is mild to what wills come."

Branimir stared at the black-skinned centaur that towered above him, pulling the skin tighter. It smelled terrible, but did the trick in blocking the cold. "I will cope, my Lord."

Branimir's feet sunk into the icy slush as he stepped over another fallen branch. The leaves had fallen from many of the trees, and were weighed down by the dampness of the snow. He found himself somewhat grateful. A couple of weeks ago the leaves had fallen across the ground so thickly that he nearly had to swim through them to keep up with the rest of the party.

Even with the leaves fallen from the trees, Branimir could barely make out the sky above. The branches were so thick that there was barely any room for light to make its way through. The entire forest was murky, laden with fog and shadow.

The Dyndaer was as mystical and petrifying as anything Branimir had ever come across. The trees were black and grew in such a way that Branimir could not see far into the forest. This made it difficult to track location, especially when there was no set path to follow. There was foliage upon foliage, trees and warped vines from the moment they had stepped into the wooded forest. If they were lost, they would not even have the insight to know it.

"How much further to the Ash Tree?" Melyena said, lifting her voice so that Dorofej could hear her at the front.

Branimir shivered again at the sight of Melyena. The Svet remained without clothing across her chest, like her counterpart, Asgrim. Her flesh alone gave indication of how cold it truly was in the frost. Branimir decided the Svet were mad.

"I say, it lies at the third bend of the most eastern river," Dorofej said, licking his thin lips. He walked by foot through the woods, pulling his black robe around him tighter. He stood out like a sore thumb in the whitish landscape. "Pray that it is still there, we must."

Branimir was the first to stop in his footsteps, hearing the last of Dorofej's words. "What did you say?"

"Hold on," the voice of Falmagon boomed from the painted horse at the rear. Branimir had to agree with the man's shock. Falmagon was barely a skeleton beneath his aged skin. He was blessed to have breath in his body. He had no hair left on his scalp, and his fingers shook, gripping the brown mane of his horse as he tried to keep himself alive in the brutal weather. "Did I hear you correctly? What are you rambling about, Dorofej?"

The old Highborn turned, fingering his white beard in contemplation. "Did you not know the Ash Tree does not always remain in the same place, yes? Moves about the world from time to time, it does. Makes it quite hard for anyone to find it twice or three times for that matter, yes?"

Dorofej winked.

"This sounds like something we should have heard before leaving Kalamaar," Branimir claimed. He was actually becoming angry. "You play with our lives when you keep your secrets, Dorofej."

Falmagon started, "But Kinhar and Erzebeth—"

"Fortunate, they were, to find the Ash Tree where I had last found it. But limited, their knowledge was, making them quite poor leaders, I would say. Found myself reluctant to follow their advice, but another place to look for the Ash Tree, I do not know."

Falmagon curled his lip. "Speak up, Dorofej, I cannot hear you." The man held tightly to the horse, turning his head so that his flattened ears, drooping and wrinkled, could pick up the sound. He had said that the world was more muffled since the battle with the Vulkodlak.

"What are we talking about? Who are Kinhar and Erzebeth? Have we spent the past two months pursuing hearsay?" Melyena said in confusion, her fingers brushing against the arrows in her quiver that she had crafted at their evening campfires.

Falmagon lifted his voice, increasing the volume after each question. "Are you saying that we could have come all this way for nothing? That the Ash Tree could be anywhere? Even back at Kalamaar? The Seven Islands?"

Dorofej placed his finger to his chin. "That would be unfortunate, yes? Though unlikely, the entry to the Netherworld is rarely near an exit. The exits do not move about so sporadically, I think."

"Rarely? You think?" Falmagon fumed.

Dorofej replied, "Calm yourself, Falmagon, before you faint from exhaustion, yes? You are much too old for such heated rhetoric, yes?"

"This is ridiculous," Branimir howled, barely believing he sided with Falmagon.

"It is what it is." Dorofej concluded.

Branimir exhaled. "I don't think it is."

Falmagon grunted and coughed, giving clear indication of how old he had become. His single eye was barely noticeable. It made it seem as if both of his eyes were missing from their sockets. From what Branimir could tell, Falmagon was blind or nearly so in his good eye anyway.

Branimir still felt somewhat responsible for the Highborn

Long-Walker's deterioration, but the loss of hearing and sight had not humbled the man. His nonstop, brash behavior made it easier for Branimir to stomach his guilt, especially when knowing how Falmagon had treated him in the past. Besides, he knew that once they reached the Ash Tree, Falmagon could regain his youth.

Falmagon placed his hand on his cheek, completely distraught. "We must hurry. I cannot take much more of this place."

Asgrim responded, "Da horse ca'ot take much in dis forest, lest it will die likes da ot'er Anshedars did."

"By *Mulafell!* What?" Falmagon said, "Bad enough I cannot hear, but my reply has to come in fragmented drivel."

Asgrim roared, bounding toward the Highborn Long-Walker. The Svet's hand already reached for the labrys at his belt.

"Asgrim!" Melyena howled, stepping between him and the Anshedar. Falmagon nearly toppled off his horse at the sound, though the horse remained unmoving.

Asgrim stopped at sight of the High Priest's daughter.

The male Svet bellowed in his language at the other in guttural sounds that Bran thought would make the trees of the Dyndaer wither.

"We are here to bring glory to Rujan and to the Svet, Asgrim," Melyena said. "We will not blemish our kind in this tale."

"Den when da tale is done, I will kills him."

Melyena, who seemed to have a bit more sense about her, attempted to change the conversation. "How long have you been away from your Melkorka?"

Branimir responded quickly, "Nearly six months."

If any Svet could have been merciful or compassionate, the look on Melyena's face may have marked the moment in history.

Dorofej called out, "Come. The light of the day is wasting, yes?"

For hours, the five of them slipped between the trees, keeping their trail as south and east, as best as they could tell. Dorofej had clearly made their situation seem direr than previously thought, but none had any choice but to continue to follow the old Highborn. Despite his frustration, Branimir had come to the same conclusion as the rest. This was the only path that lay before them.

Wildlife was scarce in the Dyndaer, primarily due to the cold. Branimir spotted a couple of rabbits near midday, and pointed them out to Melyena, who cut them down. They were cooked immediately and then continued forward, worried to waste any time.

An hour later, Dorofej cried out from the front, "Whoa! We have reached a river." He hit his foot against the ice that sat on the surface. It broke straight through.

"Perfect," Melyena snorted through her enlarged nostrils. "If it doesn't hold you, it definitely will not hold us!"

"How wide is the river?" Falmagon asked, blind to the world around him.

"Doesn't matter," the female Svet said. "Anyone wades in that freezing water in this weather, and they will catch sickness and die soon after."

"Then we go around."

Dorofej shook his head. "Back north we would have to go, yes? I say, it would be another month before we reach the end. And many more rivers to cross, there are."

"There must be something we can do," Branimir said.

Dorofej fell to the glazed ground, covered in his murky robes. "The weather will grow colder at night, yes? A better chance of crossing, we will have."

"You wants us to walk ov'r a frozen river in da dark?" Asgrim questioned. "Dat is madness, Anshedar! We are barely making it in da li'le light dat we have!"

Melyena twitched her ears. "I do not hear a better idea, Asgrim. We cannot wait here until the Season of Warmth, can we?"

Asgrim grunted, twitching his ears. "Der is no honor in drowning, Melyena."

Falmagon huffed. "I have to agree with Asgrim on this one. I cannot see the way that it is, and rely on you four with eyes. How is this going to work if none of you can see in the dark? We should be spread out on the ice so that it does not give way, if we make it beyond the bank of the river. We could easily become separated, lost, or worse."

Melyena started, "We could connect ourselves together—"

Dorofej interrupted. "A rope, we do not have, and even if we had it, straight to the bottom, you or Asgrim would drag us."

"I can see in the dark," Branimir offered. "I could give direction and lead you each across."

"That could work," Melyena agreed. "It at least assures that we will know the fate of one another."

"That is real assuring," Falmagon nearly fell from his painted horse as Dorofej and Asgrim bobbed their heads.

They made camp for the remainder of the day and into the evening. Each took a turn sleeping on and off to gain some extra rest. Branimir, try as he might, had a hard time finding sleep in the cold.

Branimir felt enthused in the forest, every sight and sound overwhelming him in its elegance. He could not help but pinpoint each sound of the forest. The creatures, such as the dormouse, hedgehog, and many birds seen a month ago, were no longer active in the woods. Bran assumed that they prepared for hibernation. Yet there were still many others that continued to make the forest their home.

Shortly after huddling in the deer skin, Branimir sighted a fox close to their camp. It had scurried off before he could mention it, which was fine by him. He was still plenty full from the rabbits eaten that afternoon. He had also seen deer on the opposite side of the river, but they were well outside of the range of the luk.

"You said that you were the last of your kind, Kras," Melyena stated to Branimir. The sentence may have been a question, but it was said so matter-of-factly, that Branimir was uncertain.

He looked at Dorofej and Falmagon who slept soundly against the black trees, and then Asgrim, who treaded near the frozen river. "Yes, my Lady. To my knowledge, I am the last surviving Kras."

"How strange that must be for you."

"I suppose. I have tried not to give it much thought, my Lady. My duty has always been to the Anshedar and not myself."

"So you are a slave? I had thought that you were, but could not be certain. You speak so freely among the Anshedar."

"At one time, at Melkorka, I would have said that I was a slave. Anymore, I could not say what I am, but my priorities are the same," Branimir said. "My purpose is their purpose; my will is their will, as it has been for my father and his father before him. This is what it has always meant to be Kras."

Melyena raised an eyebrow, her ears lifting from beneath her dark strands. "Always?"

Branimir thought back to Illuard, to what the history of his people might have been. "Always for me, my Lady."

"You have surely known of other Kras," she said.

"I—I did, my Lady," Branimir stammered, "There were few of us who remained at Melkorka before…there was Mojmir…" Bran hesitated, realizing this may have been the first time he had said his friend's name since his death. "Poor Mojmir."

Melyena's face etched with concern. "What happened to him?"

Branimir's eyes glazed, the memory of Kinhar snapping Mojmir's neck flashed across his memory. "He didn't make it, my Lady. He did not survive the battle."

"You are brave," Melyena dipped her head, her dark skin crisped over with cold. "I hope you bring your people glory."

Branimir was not sure what to say. "You are brave too, Melyena."

"What do you mean?"

His face split into a crooked grin. He pulled at his nose nervously. "Bounding about without a shirt in these frigid temperatures. I do not envy you!"

Melyena laughed heartily, in a way he had never heard from either Svet. "Does it really bother you so?"

Branimir shrugged. "I've grown accustomed to it, I suppose. Just not natural for a lady to be showing off her… um…"

Melyena chortled. "They are called breasts."

If Branimir could have turned red, he would have in that moment.

Asgrim bolted toward the two. The ground shook as he stamped forward. His face etched in absolute fury.

Branimir quickly scooted backwards, frightened under the gaze of the massive male Svet.

Asgrim spoke in Svet to Melyena as he reached his hand toward his weapon. It was clear Branimir had done something to threaten Melyena or her honor.

He cowered.

Clear laughter followed from Melyena, who playfully kicked snow toward Asgrim. "I assure you Asgrim, the Kras and I will not be mating."

Asgrim looked at Branimir for a moment and then chortled as if he were measuring the Kras's worth, or maybe his diminutive size in comparison to Melyena.

Branimir's eyes were wide with disbelief, a grin splitting his own face at the thought. "Ha. I assure you that we will not."

The two centaurs chuckled again, pointing at Branimir with amusement. Then, without rhyme or reason, Melyena

slid her fingers along Asgrim's chest before trotting off into
the Dyndaer beyond Branimir's gaze.

Asgrim twitched his ears with delight and followed.

Branimir smiled.

Chapter XXVI

The ice was solid but likely not solid enough. Branimir could hear it cracking under the weight of the Svet.

"Hold!" he cried, from the opposite bank of the wide river. Getting across for him was as easy as running along solid ground. It was not quite as simple for his companions.

Asgrim took another step, and Branimir heard the ice shift beneath the surface.

"I said stop," he cried sharply, bouncing on the edge of the river, waving his hands as though any of them could see him.

"Listen to Branimir," Dorofej shouted with equal panic in his voice. "Lest we all meet a watery grave, yes? Come now!" The old man stood awkwardly balanced on one foot. His arms were stretched out as though he were attempting to fly, swaying back and forth at the far end of the line. The old Highborn was clearly fearful of taking any step in the pitch darkness without Branimir's direction.

Asgrim, twenty feet to the right, seemed less concerned. It could be he was having difficulty understanding the language, or maybe he did not care enough to consider Branimir, but he still did stop easing forward, even with Dorofej's warning.

Beyond him were Falmagon and then Melyena. Falmagon was crawling on all fours in his brown robes, bald head forward like a battering ram. The painted horse followed slowly behind him, moving at his command. Melyena was as cautionary as Dorofej and kept a large distance between her and the other three. It was only by chance she could hear anything Branimir was shouting.

"What do we do, Kras?" Falmagon yelled loud enough to wake the entire forest. Branimir guessed the man was minutes away from uncontrollably weeping.

Branimir's anxiety increased, doing his best to ignore the fact that he had never overseen anything before. If this were a less serious situation, he might have been laughing at how ridiculous the lot of them looked. Instead, he was nearly shaking out of his own skin. "Dorofej, put your foot down!"

The old Highborn did as he was told and heaved a sigh of relief as he regained his balance on the slippery ice.

"Now, Melyena move forward…slowly…and everyone else stop moving," Branimir said.

The female Svet did as she was instructed, her hooves clopping along the ice. The centaur was around twelve hundred pounds and stepping on ice that was barely hardened. If they made it through this, Branimir may believe a god was looking after them.

The ice popped and cracked again. She was only halfway across, just past the center of the river crossing.

"What is dat?" Asgrim yelled, holding firm with his front leg extended.

Branimir heard the ice loosen and fracture, with the shift in weight. "Get across, Melyena, and make it quick!"

The female Svet threw her weight to her rear and bounded forward, the ice shattering and breaking about her, while the other three remained unmoving, their faces stricken in terror.

"No one else move!" Branimir shouted frantically.

Melyena reached the tree line on the opposite side.

"I'm across!" she shouted.

"Good for you," Falmagon said. "The rest of us have

nearly pissed ourselves!" Falmagon turned his head to the side to yell at Asgrim. "By *Mulafell*, do you know how to keep your hooves steady, or do you have sheepdip for brains."

"What is dat?" Asgrim hollered, touching his labrys, but remaining still. Then, as if giving up on the meaning of Falmagon's words, the Svet said, "Gah! I will kills you, Anshedar!"

Falmagon shook his fist in the brute's direction from where he sat hunched on the ice, "Learn my language first!"

"Learn mine!"

"Shut up!" Branimir shrieked, scanning the cracking ice. "My Lords. I must think."

"That'll be new," Falmagon said under his breath, inching toward Branimir, directing the horse to follow behind him.

Bran disregarded the insult but considered letting Falmagon stay out on the ice a bit longer.

The ice groaned from the pressure as Falmagon's horse scooted closer to Asgrim's spot on the ice.

Branimir yelled. "Falmagon, you will kill everyone. "Hold steady. Hold your horse steady. Do not move!"

The blind Highborn flattened himself to the shelf atop the river. "I don't want to be out here all night, Kras."

The horse halted as well.

"Dorofej, you can come across."

As Dorofej walked carefully to the shoreline, Branimir slipped down to line himself up with Asgrim and Falmagon.

"Asgrim, you must move to your left and put more distance between you and Falmagon. The ice will give if you draw too close to his horse."

"I've made it," Dorofej said. "Nicely done, Branimir."

Bran called back to the Svet. "That is it, Asgrim. Just a little bit more." The male centaur stepped sideways over and over, putting distance between himself and Falmagon.

Ice crashed from where Melyena had been, water washing over the top of the ice shelf.

"Good," Branimir said. "Now, come forward, both of you, at your own pace."

Falmagon uttered curses as he wriggled along the frozen river. Asgrim moved with less subtlety, eager to get off the deathtrap.

The water from the broken ice shelf trickled down toward Falmagon and Asgrim. As it struck Falmagon's hands, he cried out.

"Ignore it, Lord Falmagon," Branimir ordered. "Just come this way."

The horse behind him whinnied and reared, the water sloshing past its hooves. Falmagon twisted onto his back and screamed at the horse, sensing its movement. "No!"

The ice shattered beneath the horse. Its legs breaking through the solid surface.

"Leave the animal, my Lord! Move!" Branimir yelled.

Falmagon, blind as could be, crawled on all fours. The ice broke away around him, the back of his feet sinking into the lake. He cried out.

"Falmagon!" Branimir screamed.

The old man's fingers dug into the ice, clawing desperately against the slick surface. Branimir dived onto the ice, grabbing ahold of the old man's clothing, pulling for all he was worth.

Branimir was not strong, but he helped provide enough resistance and leverage from the rushing waters so Falmagon could secure his grip. Slowly, the Highborn Long-Walker pulled himself back to the surface.

With all his strength, Falmagon scuttled forward as fast as he could. Branimir clung to the man's hand and pulled him, led him, to the bank of the river.

"Thank you," he mumbled, "thank you." He shivered, crumbling to the snow.

"My lord…" Branimir gasped, more from fright than exhaustion.

Dorofej pulled at his beard. "I say, might have been better

to go across one at a time, yes?"

Branimir shook his head at the comment. He should have thought of that. He was too dumbstruck to even respond to the old Highborn.

"Gonna need da fire," Asgrim said.

The Svet had barely let loose the words before Melyena cried out in pain. Branimir spun around to where the female centaur had been standing.

"Melyena?" Asgrim nearly toppled over Falmagon and Branimir in attempts to reach her.

Branimir jerked around to see three white-furred foxes approach Melyena, snarling. She bled from one arm.

As he made out the animals' brown eyes, Branimir said their name. "Vucari."

Asgrim cried out. "We ca'ot fight dem in da dark! Dey have eyes like da Kras."

The first and second lunged, easily taking chunks out of Melyena's forelegs and springing back before she could respond.

She cried out again, swinging her luk wildly at her attackers, having no idea where they were. She sniffed the air and swung a second time. Nothing.

"Dorofej," Falmagon groaned.

Branimir watched as the Highborn in the black robes stood, wrinkling his nose.

"Be quick, you must! My power is limited greatly," Dorofej counseled. Branimir barely believed it as the old Highborn wielded *Koldovstvo*. He had not touched the craft since Melkorka, since he had attempted to give life to Andrik Hjlavok and failed.

Blue and gold glowed in a swirling ball about the old man's hands, glowing heavily, and emitting light like the sun at autumn's twilight. Branimir stared through the immediate brightness, his sight adjusting with ease.

"I see the radiance of the light. Bring glory to the

Lightbringer, Dorofej!" Falmagon breathed.

The Dyndaer shown with more brightness than it may have ever witnessed as the light illuminated the expanse of the area. The dark trees became clear and the snow in the immediate area began to melt. The power was impressive to Branimir.

Each fox, white in color, stepped back, squinting its eyes as though they were staring directly into the sun. The animal on the far left had an arrow through its skull before it could react to the magic that circulated from the Highborn.

Melyena reached for another arrow after killing the white fox. Asgrim charged.

Another fox retaliated with a bark, springing forward. It leaped through the centaur's legs with striking dexterity.

Branimir could not believe what he was witnessing as the fox changed shape from beneath Asgrim. The white fur shed in a moment and the creature sprouted into a bear much like Erzebeth had done at Arkaim. Claws from large paws cut through the underbelly of the Svet.

The centaur snarled, leaping off the ground, before the claws could dig to his vital organs. Blood dripped. The first layers of his flesh fell away, blood dripping onto the frozen ground.

The bear twisted full circle, back to its four legs, and barreled at Dorofej with exceptional swiftness.

The other fox leapt at Melyena again, but quickly met the blade of the labrys as Asgrim crashed down for his landing. The creature was split in half, falling to the ground. Upon impact, the dead body shaped back into the human form of a naked Vucari.

Branimir marveled at Asgrim. He was truly a warrior at heart, ignoring pain and focusing on victory.

Dorofej rotated the ball of light in his hand and flung it forward at the bear bolting at him. The light, like fire in the kiln, seared into a cylinder and tore through the chest of the bear. The innards of the animal exploded through the back, near the spine, and the light went dim. The Vucari joined the other attackers in immediate death.

The battle had lasted mere seconds. Dorofej fell to his knees, coughing heavily.

"Dorofej, my Lord," Branimir squealed. "Dorofej, are you okay?"

The old Highborn lifted his blue eyes to Bran sputtering, "I still have my sight if that is what you mean."

"Oh, Dorofej," Branimir clutched the human. "I could not go on without you."

The old Highborn returned the embrace.

Falmagon said nothing, still shaking, his feet frozen from the river water.

"Asgrim!" Melyena stumbled to the centaur. "You are hurt."

"Eh, and you," Asgrim exhaled loudly, looking at the wounds of Melyena, "but we wills live to see tomo'ow! Dis journey is not yet done for us, Melyena."

Melyena nodded, placing her hand on Asgrim's shoulder. Her eyes drifted to the Vucari with the smoldering, fiery hole in its chest that gave minimal light to the area. Burnt flesh seared.

"The power of the Anshedar is great, Dorofej. If all Anshedar hold the potential of you and Falmagon with this magic, demons will not stand a chance in destroying this world. What can compete with such power in combat?"

Dorofej spoke softly, "If all Anshedar could do what we do, demons would not have need to threaten the purity of the world, yes? Already have stolen pureness, the Anshedar would have."

Melyena could not help but take a step back, weighing the implication of the old man's words.

Chapter XXVII

The Vucari were as thick as the trees in the early light. Branimir had no time to count their number as they swarmed around the makeshift camp near the riverbank.

Branimir plunged the kinzhal into the back of the bear's leg as it clawed and snapped at Asgrim in the midst of the Dyndaer. The animal roared, twisting to swing at him. Branimir ducked, the long claws narrowly missing his ears. Asgrim took advantage of the distraction and slammed the labrys into the side of the creature, ripping it open and spilling its guts out onto the snow.

Branimir disappeared again, and raced to Melyena who fought against a wolf. With the Highborn limited, he was doing all that he could to aid the centaurs in the battle.

He sped past Dorofej and Falmagon. The white-haired man had a makeshift branch that he held defensively over the Highborn Long-Walker, who remained completely helpless. Dorofej swung the branch at the animals as they ran by him, doing all that he could to keep Falmagon from being killed. Asgrim stood on one side and Melyena on the other, circling as they attempted to keep the Anshedar safe.

Branimir reached Melyena as she slaughtered the gray wolf before her with a point blank shot through the skull.

Melyena shot true, cutting down the enemy. Her quiver

was filled with arrows. Fox and owl and wolf crumbled under the stone-tipped arrows that impaled them through their flesh. As each animal exhaled their last breath, their body shifted and waned back to the human form of the Vucari, naked and bleeding in the snow.

It seemed that no creature who burst through the forest was safe.

Crouching, Branimir watched the snow owls that flew overhead. The large birds pummeled, spiraling toward the centaurs with fierceness in their large, brown eyes. As they neared the ground, they transformed into gray wolves and snow leopards and large bears.

Asgrim swung his labrys wildly, striking bear and leopard. The white frost turned as crimson as Branimir's skin. Centaur and Vucari each bled and it seemed that none would survive the day. Still, Bran had hope. After seeing the many Svet at Sorod, he knew that the centaurs were battle-trained and fought with the precision of any known warrior.

Melyena caught the first gray wolf that landed at her feet. She grabbed the beast by the back of the neck with her hand and threw it toward the frozen river. It howled as it crashed through the melting ice in the morning warmth. The current beneath the ice pulled the wolf down and under, out of sight of the Kras.

A leopard with thick gray fur vaulted at the female Svet immediately after, catching its powerful jaws around her neck. Blood spurted from her vein. She stood for only a moment before the large cat twisted its body and took her to the ground.

"No!" Dorofej cried.

"What is happening?" Falmagon shouted looking around unsuccessfully, hearing the constant ferociousness of the beasts that assailed them.

Melyena convulsed on the ground, clawing at the beast on her neck. Her hands reached for the cat's eyes, its neck, anything to pry it loose before her life slipped away.

"They will kill us," Branimir said to himself. "They will kill me." His body shook with emotion. He could not believe what he was doing. There was blood on his hands.

Branimir sprang over her midsection, and slammed the kinzhal deep into the neck of the snow leopard. It scrambled frantically as it released and pulled away, its sharp claws nearly catching Branimir in their grip as it fell over into the snow. It took Bran's weapon with it, lodged in the thick flesh.

Branimir forgot his weapon and covered the puncture wounds on Melyena. He urgently tried to hold back the flow of blood. It gushed and pulsed through his small fingers.

"I cannot stop the bleeding—"

She gurgled, her luk fallen from her hands, her chest heaving. Scratch marks lined her torso and several pieces of flesh gaped across her body. Her hooves twitched as her life fled.

"I cannot stop the bleeding, my Lady!" Branimir wept, pushing with all his might on the wounds.

Branimir watched her eyes flutter, her ears lying flat against her head.

"You cannot die!"

"Branimir!" Dorofej swung his branch, connecting with the snout of a wolf that snapped at him.

He had not even heard it come at him in the chaos.

Branimir squealed, dipping his head down on the woman Svet. He could nearly hear her heartbeat slow.

Dorofej stood between the gray beast and Branimir, swinging the branch as though it were a stave, keeping the animal at bay as best as he was able.

Falmagon crawled behind Dorofej, following the old man's footsteps, not having enough strength to stand.

"It is over," he said.

The wolf clutched ahold of the branch by its teeth and ripped it out of the old Highborn's hands. Dorofej gasped in surprise at his own weakness. His muscles shook and shuddered. He could not be frailer than what he was without being in the same state as Falmagon.

Dorofej did have a chance to respond before Asgrim barreled through and struck the wolf with his labrys.

"Stay behind me!" he boomed.

The Vucari circled them. There were several dozen with their brown eyes pinpointed on the enemy against the riverbank.

The Svet roared, his sharpened teeth barred at the beasts who threatened them.

Branimir looked into the Dyndaer past the Vucari. Something stirred beyond the trees that he could not quite make out. There were footsteps, lightly falling on the snow.

"Something else is coming," he said. "Be ready, my Lords."

"What more?" Dorofej said under his breath, more to himself than any other. He stood in front of Branimir and Falmagon with his arms spread protectively. Asgrim stood beyond him.

Half a dozen men and women burst through the brush. Bright blue eyes and light hair was quickly masked by light blue orbs springing up around them as they prepared for battle.

The Vucari changed focus and attacked these other humans. Branimir noticed they greatly resembled the Highborn and Northmen of Kalamaar.

"By *Mulafell*, what's happening?" Falamagon asked.

The roar of a windstorm emanated from the heavens, mixed with falling shards of stone and fire and ice. The humans manipulated the elements as the Highborn would with considerable power. Air picked up animals flinging them from the riverbank, fire tore through others, and ice and stone pounded them into pulp.

Few Vucari made it past the display of the craft of *Koldovstvo*. Those that did bound around the elements hit the blue orbs only to be thrown back by an unseen force. Lightning was flung from the orbs, tearing through the creatures, taking their lives.

Branimir was somewhat pleased to see the young faces of the men and women that wielded *Koldovstvo* show signs of aging as it would be with the Highborn of Melkorka. Branimir could not imagine holding such power without having a cost.

Faces had added wrinkles, hair color changed, and skin drooped, depending on the spell that was cast. The men and women worked together to blend their magic, and to destroy the Vucari.

As the battle ended, a few Vucari scattered off into the forest, still in their animal shapes. The men and women released the orbs and approached the group huddled around Melyena's fallen body. Asgrim stood defensively with a sense of fear in his features, the labyrs raised. He was prepared to die.

Falmagon begged, "Someone please tell me what is happening?"

"Believe it, you would not," Dorofej smacked his lips and dropped his hands, where they had remained suspended the entire time.

Branimir kept his hands fastened on Melyena's neck, although she had surely already passed to the Beyond. He could no longer feel her breathing.

"I am Valya Shelagin of Shayol Domier. These are my companions," a man said flatly, stepping in front of the rest. The individuals on either side of him did not budge. "Identify yourself. You clearly are not the Vucari."

"Shayol Domier…" Falmagon said hastily, looking around at the voice that spoke. He tried to pull himself up and failed miserably, falling back to his knees. "Falmagon Sej from Melkorka upon Folkmar from the Seven Islands of Forghar. I am friend to Kinhar Sayan. I need to speak to Moreth Eanbald."

"Kinhar, you say?" Valya said. "I have heard of the name

more than once. If you know of him, where is he?"

"Passed from this world, he has some time ago, Valya," Dorofej responded, taking measure of what was being said before him.

Branimir easily took hint that the old Highborn did not want to be where he was in this moment.

"And, who are you?" Valya asked.

"I am from Melkorka, called Dorofej, a name you should remember well, I imagine. Here is also Branimir Baran who has come with us from Melkorka, yes?"

Valya raised an eyebrow. "A Kras?"

Dorofej lifted his bushy eyebrow in return. "Yes, he is. Asgrim Garoar and Melyena Rogov of Sorod are the Svet before you, and aid to Melyena we would value before our yammering outlives her life."

Her warm blood still flowed through Branimir's fingers. "She is gone, my Lords. She is already dead."

"Brought back she can be, if not too far gone," Dorofej said. "*Koldovstvo* can still save her. Do any of you have the sacred blood? Make haste!"

One of the women lifted her voice. "We are familiar with the savage Svet of the north. We will not give aid to their kind. Let her die."

"It is quite questionable you even travel in their company, Highborn," Valya spoke steadily, squinting his eye suspiciously.

Branimir gasped, "You cannot be serious."

Asgrim howled, throwing his labrys down and pushing past Dorofej. He spoke heavily, screaming in the language of the Svet. Branimir barely moved out of the way before the large Svet fell to Melyena's side.

The beast roared in sorrow as the crimson liquid flooded from Melyena's neck, the skin already pale. He lifted the human half of her body and hugged it closely to his chest.

Branimir noticed the nod from Valya about the time Dorofej shouted in defiance.

A male behind Valya wielded *Koldovstvo* lifting three stones from the ground. The stones were flung through the air with enough force to crush Asgrim's skull before he knew what had struck him. The Svet did not have a chance to cry out before his breath fled from his lungs. Asgrim's fell dead atop of the High Priest's daughter.

Branimir scurried in shock back to the two Svet, touching them lightly. Only yesterday, he had shared conversation and joy with the two centaurs, and now they were dead. They had found their way back among evil men.

With a heavy heart, his fingers traipsed along Melyena's skin. Soon, he found *Ojenek* held in her fingers, and returned it to his pocket.

He would keep it safe.

"Why?" Dorofej cried out, helpless against the many who faced them.

Valya grinded his teeth, clearly not used to being questioned. "We are Anshedar and Highborn. They are Svet. Svet cannot be trusted, being both reckless and inherently stupid. The beast would have turned on us sooner or later."

"The way of the Highborn, this is not. The way of the Anshedar, this is not," Dorofej said, clenching his fists at his sides.

Falmagon opened his mouth once more, curving slightly in a smile, mocking Dorofej. "But, the way of the *Kadari*, it is. The old ways will come to pass, and the Lightbringer will lift up the chosen. We will rule over this world and all the lesser creatures!"

Valya nodded in respect to the blind Highborn. "You must be familiar with Kinhar. You speak of the wisdom that he taught many years ago before the Vucari lost their way."

Dorofej's thin lips quivered. "What of us? I say, will stones be thrust into our skulls as well?"

Valya shrugged in disinterest. "You will come to Shayol Domier. Patrician Moreth will decide your fate."

Chapter XXVIII

The cold chilled Branimir to the bone throughout the half day that it took to travel to Shayol Domier. He desperately hoped it was closer, but it seemed luck had left the fellowship some time ago. Despite the bitter weather, drops of sweat still slid down the back of his neck, causing his black strands of hair to stick to him like a wet cloth. The walk had not been strenuous, but he still had uncalled-for perspiration. Without a doubt, the *Kadari*, as they were called, made him nervous.

Gripping the fur around him, the frosty wind sputtered against his flesh. The makeshift cloak flapped wildly around him. He shivered and kept his eyes on Dorofej in front of him. The cold was the worst.

Branimir's eyes burned in the stinging, dry air. His pupils wanted to water, but the tears would not come, and so he was simply left with the sensation of pinpricks on the whites of his eyes. He wanted to cry for Melyena and Asgrim or even Kinhar and Erzebeth, but no tears came.

The far-reaching sky was hidden beyond the branches, giving little light and giving a pure bleakness over their path. Bran took in the group who held them captive, not bothering to look for an escape. Branimir have been many things, but a hero was not one of them.

Valya stopped the group of them as they approached

the gates of Shayol Domier. The home of the *Kadari* was not anything Branimir would have expected it to be. The wooden gate was massive. It was made up of two, inward-swinging doors and looked sturdier than Melkorka. The gate was three times the height of any man, giving reason to believe it was crafted from the trees of the Dyndaer. From the wear on the wood, the place had to have been built over half a century ago.

Matching banners flapped at the top of stone towers. They were marked with the image of the sun, the same sign found at Melkorka. The golden, dancing swirls was the symbol of Dahz, the ruler of the golden sun and Protector of Men. It was no surprise to Bran that it was found here as well.

Palisades lined the outside walls in hand-dug trenches, preventing any beast from charging Shayol Domier down without impaling themselves first. Men and women walked along the top of the walls, their heads peering over the top watchfully for any enemy that may approach their holding. The fence stretched thirty feet in either direction before twisting at rock towers that were made up of flat stones. The rock towers were accessible from the walkway around the fencing. Branimir gawked at the structure.

"Looks like we made it back," one of the *Kadari* men said with a smile, slapping a female next to him on the back.

She grimaced from being jostled, eyeing the lithe man while rubbing her mouth as though she were scrapping off dried saliva. Branimir noticed she barely turned her head toward him.

The man continued in his talk, paying no mind that she had not responded to him. "We are returning to camp like snow in summer or rain in harvest. Moreth will be pleased. Though, it is awkward being here after being gone for so many weeks," he said seriously. "You know, the world makes sense in its telling of how things should be. We do not use a whip on a horse, nor do we place bridles on donkeys," he shook his head despondently, "and yet, here we come, shaped by the gods, living our lives as though we should be equivalent with the idols of children's dreams. Not sure we all can be what we want to be, you know?"

"Good that you recognize your plainness, Artemiy," a thin smile twisted on the lips of the woman. "And to think, I had always thought you to be more conceited."

Lowering his eyebrows, Artemiy responded as though reciting a verse from an ancient text. "In the end, Alyona, the arrogant are always caught in the schemes they devise. If I were prideful I would never prosper."

Suddenly, Branimir noticed Alyona was looking at him with her purplish eyes. The young woman inclined her head slightly, not even looking at the man as she talked, a hint of satisfaction in her smile. "It is still to be determined if we are presently," she nodded her head toward Shayol Domier, "thriving in life or heading to our demise."

A larger man behind the two of them dropped his jaw slightly, turning his head to match the cold eyes of the woman. "What is meant by that?"

Artemiy seemed equally shocked. "This is a blessed prospect for each of us, sister. Be sure your words are not wicked; it will only bring despair upon us. The Lightbringer shines down upon us this day! Do not hex us!"

Branimir was sure he heard Dorofej harrumph under his breath.

Alyona swallowed, appearing less robust than she had a moment ago, retracting her statement. "I do not know what I mean."

"Ah," Artemiy lifted his voice as though he were addressing all of them. "Do not fret. Alyona speaks outside of her knowing. It has long been a common occurrence." The crooked grin on his half-haired face returned.

Branimir turned back to Valya, who had signaled to a handful of sentries at the opening.

It was probably just a bit past midday, and already there were lanterns hanging around the area, adding to the pale light. As they moved forward, barely making it twenty paces, a man approached dressed in a bulky, black, wool cloak. His shoulders were broadened and his triangular features were steadfast. He did not appear to be a man that was easily manipulated, having odd strands of crystal white hair despite his middle-aged face. He scanned the group, particularly Branimir, so it seemed, before fixating his eyes on Valya. He dipped his head with reverence.

"We come from the depths of the Dyndaer with prisoners and wish to speak with the Patrician," Valya directed.

"Naught worthwhile, Valya," the man muttered as though he despised the chore of giving details. He offhandedly brushed the cold off his outer cloak. "There is no place for prisoners. If your intent is to hold them captive here, may I suggest you kill them instead? Last night, Aravdur reported he seen a human figure westward of the palisades. Said the woman walked like death, never touching the ground. Delkarv was with him and said he saw nothing. Mayhap, it was just in Aravdur's head, but it has the Patrician jumping at ghosts and not in the mood for audience."

Valya scowled.

"Nedezhda." Branimir whispered, grinding his teeth.

They did not come all this way to be cut down. Why was death always the answer, no matter the question?

"Fie!" The guard paused, his eyes squinting at Dorofej, Falmagon, and Branimir. His eyes lingered over Branimir a few extra seconds before continuing. "Then again, they may provide the men something more to do besides freeze. A tournament, perhaps? Seems suitable for the Kras, at least. Teach a lesson, I would think. Besides, some entertainment would be welcomed before we are all neck high in frost."

"There will be no tournament, Orgath, and this Kras is not one of our own," Valya's mouth tightened as though he were upset that the man's tongue was flapping so loosely, but he said nothing of it. "These men claim to be from the Seven Islands and Highborn. Patrician Moreth will see them."

The guard raised his eyes in surprise, but kept his mouth shut. Without a word, he turned and steered the lot of them through the wide angled doors into Shayol Domier. No other humans at the gates or within the palisades said a word as they passed through Shayol Domier.

The inside of the stronghold stretched beyond what Branimir could see, primarily due to the many Highborn who were scattered throughout the area. There had to be hundreds of men and women. Many fires were burning brightly with the Anshedar gathered around them for warmth.

In the center of the structure was a keep that sat below the walls. There were several small buildings constructed of the same stone as the tower, possibly a guardhouse or armory of sorts. There were cottages and workshops scattered along the fences on the inside that stretched beyond the keep with the long wall that marked the boundary of Shayol Domier. In addition, there was a large garden that ran on either side of the keep, wrapping around the building out of sight.

Even with all Shayol Domier's splendor, this was not the reason Branimir stopped walking.

"Kras…" he whispered to himself. Among the Anshedar, the *Kadari*, there were many Kras, possibly half the number of men and women. The red creatures scampered across the area at the beckoning of their masters. He had never seen so many. "Kras!"

He nearly jumped, turning to Dorofej. The old man had a half smile under his beard, sharing the joy with Branimir. He was not alone after all.

"Move, Kras," Alyona said behind him, pushing him forward to keep pace with Dorofej.

"Don't touch me," he muttered. He turned to face the woman.

Alyona lifted her hand to strike Branimir, but showed surprise when he did not lower his gaze and did not back away.

"Lay a hand on him, my Lady, and my wrath you will experience a hundred times over," Dorofej intervened.

The woman halted her movement, unsure of how to respond to the threat.

"Come, Branimir," Dorofej directed.

None of the Kras who worked in Shayol Domier seemed to notice the scene. They did as the Anshedar told them. They were as much as slaves upon Maharia as they would have been on the Seven Islands.

Bran followed reluctantly. He asked Valya, "Why is the keep so small, my Lord,"

"It is not small, Kras. You are awfully brave to speak to me as an equal. I have not seen the like from your kind. Perhaps, the Highborn were not strict enough with you at Melkorka."

Dorofej interrupted. "Mine to discipline as I see fit, this Kras is."

Valya snickered. "We will see what the Patrician says."

"This way," Orgath instructed. The guard nodded to a full-bearded, bulky man sitting on a bucket near the keep doors. "We need to speak with Patrician Moreth."

"Not sure if he will see the likes of you, but you can try," the man laughed, his ale-shaped belly shaking softly with his chuckles.

Branimir hitched his cloak around himself again as they stepped inside the keep. He wished he were better at ignoring the cold. Perhaps, if it were simply cold, he could ignore, but not with the wind that sprung through his bones like a wraith.

The keep doors opened. At the top of the stairs stood a giant stone statue holding a massive hammer. Based on the constant reference of Dahz's hammer, Branimir could only guess that it was supposed to be the sun god. The craftsmanship on the statue was perfect, even down to the single hairs of the pointed beard.

Three light brown stone pillars lined either side of a substantial staircase that led downward to the thick wooden doors of the underground keep. In between each of the pillars hung imposing tapestries of Dahz, like those that hung at the gates.

"The White-Clad," Artemiy explained.

"Familiar with Dahz, we all are," Dorofej said.

Falmagon made a face. Branimir was certain that the man was frustrated by his lack of sight. He was likely the only one of them that would truly appreciate the glamour of the entrance hall.

Valya moved to open the second set of doors ahead of them and the ground changed from dirt to red brick. Red bricks had been stacked against the dirt walls, but it seemed that they had run out of the material mid-development. Still, Branimir could only guess that the ceiling above was over seven feet thick with the downward slope of the stairs into the room.

This place was grander than Melkorka.

As soon as they stepped through the doors, two sentries stepped out of the shadows. Each of the Anshedar, apart from Dorofej and Falmagon, fell to both knees and bowed their heads with their palms firmly set on the red stone. The guards patted down Branimir and the two Highborn men, ignoring the members of the *Kadari*.

Falmagon cried out in surprise as the hands started touching him, but did not draw back. Branimir smiled to himself, enjoying the spectacle, nearly laughing out loud as their hands scanned his smaller body. He found himself lucky that he no longer carried the kinzhal.

"Welcome back, Valya," the nearest guard clamped a hand on the man's shoulder. "You were gone longer than expected. I assume that this is the one they have been waiting for." The blue-eyed man eyeballed Dorofej.

Valya rose to his feet with a snort. "Forgive us. We do not

have time for idle talk."

"Think nothing of it," he chortled. "Be on your way. I am sure that the Patrician will be eager to hear of Kinhar's adventures."

Moving past the guards, Branimir could see the large square room. It was about the size of a small hut. There were five doors evenly spaced on the south, east, and west walls and torches along the walls. Branimir could see well in the dim light. He noticed thin red lines formulating paths just thick enough to walk on in a single file line across the dark brown floor. The lines connected at the center of the room at a blue-painted circle. In following each of the red lines, Branimir found they all led to one of the doors on the walls.

"Do not stray from the lines," Valya muttered under his breath.

"What lines?" Falmagon asked.

Branimir took the bait. "What happens if you step off the path, my Lord?"

Valya did not miss a beat. "Take a step and you will find out, Kras."

"What lines?" Falmagon said louder, waving his hands.

"Hold onto me, Falmagon, yes? Lead you along the path, I will." Dorofej offered.

Valya grunted. "This way." The man turned down the fourth path heading to the north. When he reached the solid wooden door, he paused for a moment, and then knocked four times before pushing it open.

The other *Kadari* followed without hesitation as though they had walked the path a hundred times over. Branimir followed behind Dorofej and Falmagon, who took their time reaching the end. Falmagon held onto Dorofej's dark robes with both hands, following his instruction.

"Put your feet heel to toe, yes? Slowly. That is it!"

The room they were led into was no smaller than the previous one, and it held just as many doorways, these immediately led into open hallways instead of being blocked by a typical wooden door. Six red brick pillars stretched up to the ceiling, surrounded by limestone walls. Between these pillars was a large crimson rug covering the red brick floor. Candles and torches lighted the walls. The room was decorated heavily in interwoven tapestries of Dahz comparable to the ones Branimir had seen outside.

"How large is this place?" Branimir said to himself in wonder. It made Illuard look like nothing but a hole in the ground.

Dorofej whistled, as though that were answer enough.

At the end of the woven rug sat a single throne, more decorated than that of the King of Kalamaar. Facing the throne stood a tall man in a blue shimmering cloak.

The Anshedar of the *Kadari* bowed again with palms firmly on the ground in the same manner as they had outside the door.

The guard from the front gates spoke first. "Valya returns with his scouts from the Dyndaer. They have come with prisoners from across Strega's Deep, Patrician."

He turned around giving full view to his scarred face. "This is not Kinhar or Erzebeth. I was told Kinhar had come. Who are they?" The man's voice was deep with a slight rasp, as though he were getting over a recent sickness. However, it did not keep it from echoing in the sizeable room.

"They say they are Highborn from Melkorka." Valya answered. "They said they know Kinhar, Patrician. They have insisted that they speak with you."

"Speak with me, huh? If this is true then tell me where is Kinhar," Moreth said with a curled lip, turning and sitting on his throne. "Moreover, tell me why demons lurk on my doorstep?"

Falmagon did not move, the torchlight reflecting off his bald features. His voice lifted at equal level with Moreth. "I am Falmagon Sej of Melkorka, and I speak as the new spearhead of the Highborn, by commendation of the former."

"Kinhar put trust in you?" the Patrician asked, outwardly startled by the news.

"Without question," Falmagon said boldly.

Dorofej said nothing against the brash proclamation.

"I am Patrician here, Falmagon, and it is best that you not forget it. It was decided that I would rule here and Kinhar at Melkorka. Now, where is he?"

Falmagon paused. His unseen eyes looked in the direction of Moreth as though they were two beasts ready to kill for the fresh meat that lay between them.

The Highborn Long-Walker continued with a half sneer on his face. "Kinhar Sayan is dead. He was murdered by Nedezhda Mager, an *Eretik*, who has risen beyond the dead after receiving her sentence at Melkorka."

Moreth clicked his tongue on the roof of his mouth. His knuckles grasped the sleeves of the throne, nearly turning white. "You mean to tell me that the Highborn killed one of their own?"

"Yes," Dorofej whispered before Falmagon could respond. "Exactly what he means to tell you, it is."

Moreth nodded. "With what did you take the head of the *Eretik*?"

Branimir could not believe Moreth was so calm. Moreover, he was surprised at the familiarity the Patrician had with the ways of the Highborn and the Anshedar, especially when so far separated.

Falmagon spoke dully as though he were tired of repeating himself. "Her life was taken with a copper dagger called *kaelandur*. Kinhar said that you would know all of this, Moreth. He said that all of you had taken the *Kalamyr Oath* at Shayol Domier. Were we mistaken to have come here? Thus far, we have only been identified as enemies and guarded like rabid hounds."

"We could not know who you were for certain," Valya

interrupted, defending his actions.

Branimir gulped.

"Of course, I took the oath. We all have," Moreth said, ignoring Valya's attempt to give any excuse to Falmagon. "But, I did not think the old fool was rash enough to actually attempt what he has done. He talked about this years ago, but showed no sign of making the sacrifice. In truth, I had thought he had either given up or died. Alas, there is no turning back now."

Falmagon heaved a sigh of relief while Dorofej smacked his lips.

"Using *kaelandur* was a delicate task, which Kinhar obviously botched if the victim, this Nedezhda, still walks upon Aenar," Moreth said. "Nothing in the task should have brought her back from the dead."

Branimir scrunched his nose. He rarely heard anyone speak of the world, Aenar. People rarely had seen much beyond their own homes. For Moreth to use the name freely suggested the Patrician may have been as old as Kinhar or even Dorofej.

Though, it was the thought of Nedezhda's death being a deliberate act that chilled his spine. This ritual somehow was meant to give power to the *Kadari*. What more power could the Highborn be after? They already had found a way to escape death with the Ash Tree.

"The ritual plainly was not done correctly when Nedezhda was slain." Moreth scratched his head in thought, spewing questions. "She was knelt facing east of Dahz's last light? Her hair was burnt outside of any Anshedar's sight before her beheading? The cut was clean through her neck?"

Falmagon faltered, "The first and third were completed beyond doubt, but Branimir had lit fire to her hair outside of the sight of Highborn. I could not guess at the exact timing."

Branimir's knees nearly gave out as he heard the Highborn speak. Their words indicated that it was he and Mojmir who had caused Nedezhda to come back to the world for her revenge. His mind raced back to those moments when he returned from Melkorka. Kinhar had been insistent that he had tarried in his task.

Branimir's mind swirled! Was he guilty of all this atrocity? All this death? It could not be the full of it. Nedezhda had said at Arkaim that magic had been used to create *kaelandur*. That had to be the true cause.

Branimir opened his mouth to object, but stopped as Moreth continued.

Falmagon cleared his throat. "Kinhar wanted Branimir to stand before you so he may be judged for his mistake. If the *Kadari* are going to rule this world, we must have justice on all living creatures."

"I will not pass judgment on this Kras," Moreth said, not bothering to even look at Branimir. "There is little that we can do about what has already come to pass. The *Kadari* must listen fervently to the Lightbringer to lead this world. Our feet have been set in motion."

Kinhar had planned to have Branimir executed for completing the ritual incorrectly. His stomach churned at the realization.

Falmagon opened his mouth to protest, but Branimir cut him off, taking the attention off him. "What is the *Kadari*? I don't understand."

Moreth entertained his question. "The *Kadari* are Dahz's chosen that will rule over this world. We have the wisdom to give guidance. Those that know the *Kadari* way understand that it is our purpose to help all living creatures accept the will of Dahz, without question, so that they may find themselves in the Thrice Ten Kingdom in the Beyond. The *Kadari* will keep the races of Aenar out of the Netherworld forever, weakening Marheena and her demon armies."

Branimir had heard the Highborn speak of Thrice Ten Kingdom a long time ago. It was said that traveling through the Thrice Nine Lands and beyond the Netherworld would lead to a paradise, to the Beyond, to Thrice Ten Kingdom.

Bran reasoned, suddenly realizing why Dorofej held such rage toward the sect. Even now, Branimir noticed the dissatisfied look on the old Highborn's face. "You will take away people's choice of gods…their free will to worship?"

Falmagon answered, "If that is what it takes."

It was Artemiy who spoke up next. Branimir had nearly forgotten that so many of the *Kadari* were in the room with them. "Where is *kaelandur*?"

"Nedezhda has it," Falmagon spoke.

Alyona nearly screamed. "How did she get the weapon? We are doomed if she holds the weapon from the ritual."

"What? Why?" Branimir screeched.

"Destroy the Ash Tree with the blade, she believes she can," Dorofej said.

Moreth answered. "If Nedezhda believes this to be true, we must as well. If the Ash Tree is destroyed, it would kill us all."

Dorofej asked, "It was said that there is a woman, possibly undead, that walks beyond your walls this past night, yes? Nedezhda, it is, yes?"

"Yes," Moreth said. "From what you tell me, I am afraid that Nedezhda is already within the Dyndaer.

Dorofej smacked his lips. "To rid Aenar of the Ash Tree and bring demon hordes from the Netherworld, she comes. She wishes to kill us all."

"She must be stopped!" Valya bellowed. His scouting crew raised their voices in support.

"We will cut her down again," the Patrician said, "but first, I imagine these two men would like to have their strength returned to join in the battle."

Falmagon's eyes lit up at the suggestion.

"What do you speak of, Moreth," Dorofej said, intentionally leaving the title of Patrician to the wind.

Moreth paused and then decided not to correct the old

Highborn. "We keep barrels holding the Water of Life here at Shayol Domier for the *Kadari* to replenish their strength. You take a drink and you will be returned to your youth, but maintain your knowledge. You see, the Waters of Life are not far from here, giving us unlimited power and strength against those who would stand against the Lightbringer. The *Kadari* have long been blessed by the Lightbringer."

"Is that so? Take a drink, I might." Dorofej spoke as though it were the first time he had ever done such a thing.

Moreth signaled to a couple *Kadari* who hurried to fetch drinks for the Highborn. They returned a moment later, each holding a clay cup brimming with a watery liquid.

"Please, drink," Moreth said.

Falmagon wrenched his hands together hungrily for the taste of immortality.

Chapter XXIX

"I do not understand, my Lord. Why cannot I stay with Dorofej and Falmagon. Will they be okay?" Branimir asked as Valya led him back toward the courtyard of Shayol Domier.

"Your loyalty to your masters is commendable, Kras," Valya said. "But you speak far too much. Some conversations are not meant for your ears."

Branimir rubbed his cracked lips, trying to understand. He had overheard nearly every conversation that the Highborn had ever had, whether it was important or not. Branimir frequently stood in the shadows, almost like a keeper of history, taking in the accounts of the Anshedar who he served. To not be a part of that history was almost painful.

"I understand, my Lord," Branimir lied.

"Good," Valya said. The two of them stepped into the courtyard from the keep.

"Run along but do not venture too far. The Patrician may change his mind about your judgment," Valya muttered, adjusting his cloak. "You may stay with your own kind until you are called upon."

"When might that be, my Lord?" Branimir asked.

"Soon or never," Valya said with ice on his breath. "It does not matter. Your time is not your own to be measured, Kras."

Branimir dipped his head, watching Valya speed back into the keep and shutting the door behind him. Branimir stood alone.

"Where did you come from?" a Kras asked, who formed in front of his eyes. The creature was as red as Branimir with similar dark hair and black, oval eyes. Outside of the male's flattened nose and high cheek bones, he looked very similar to Branimir. They were even the same height.

"I am Branimir Baran from Melkorka," Branimir introduced himself. "I am from the Seven Islands of Forghar."

"Where's that?" the creature scrunched up his nose.

Branimir took a deep breath, somewhat surprised that the Kras did not know about Melkorka. "It is…a long way from here. It is where the Kras come from."

"What? You know where we come from?" the Kras smiled wide, showing his own crooked teeth.

Branimir nodded solemnly. "Yes. Do you not?"

The Kras shook his head, scooting closer. "We were told that we were created by the Highborn, but we did not believe it. Not really."

"That you were what—No, the Highborn did not create the Kras," Branimir scoffed.

"Oh, you must come with me. You must tell the others what you know. They will be so thrilled." He snatched Branimir's hand and pulled him through the courtyard.

Branimir could hardly protest as the Kras firmly yanked him to and fro past the Highborn who walked through the open space. In just a few moments, the Kras brought him to a small door that angled downwards, encased in stacked stones.

Branimir was dragged down a stone staircase to a dirt path in dark tunnels. He noticed that no lights were lined in the damp hole, which, of course, mattered very little to any Kras. His escort pulled him past several tunnels and rooms carved out of the earth. He saw a few Kras roaming about the enclave, staring at them as they flew by.

Within seconds, they stepped through a doorway leading to what appeared to be a common area. There were so many Kras that it was hard to make out much more in the room than small red heads bobbing. At the far end, Bran found small wooden plates and bowls filled with goo resembling food. The dishes were being passed around to the several hundred Kras. The commotion was deafening to Bran. They had come right during mealtime.

"Shanna! Lona! Come here!" The Kras shouted at two female Kras who passed by them. "He says our kind came from a place called Melkorka."

Branimir licked his cracked lips. Women of his own kind walked toward him. Real women! What would Mojmir think if he were standing here?

Branimir started to clarify, stammering as the females approached him with half-crooked smiles. "Well—"

"You know where we come from?" one of them said happily, clapping her hands. "We knew the Highborn could not have created us?"

His escort chimed in. "I know, right? We have never seen them create anything. They only destroy."

"Oh Shanna, isn't it exciting?" said the other female. "Who would have thought there were other Kras in the world."

"I am actually the only one left," Branimir said. "At least, as far as I can tell. I thought I was the only one until I came here."

"Oh, there are lots of us here," the male said, bouncing from foot to foot, full of excitement.

"What happened to all your people?" Shanna placed her hands on her cheek.

Branimir felt overwhelmed, "There were many battles that we died in, and…well, how many of you are there exactly?"

"Around five hundred," the male answered.

Shanna leaned into Branimir, touching his arm. "Died! Oh, my! You are a warrior?"

He flinched at her touch. "I—"

"Oh, he is a brave warrior from a distant land. Killed hundreds, even thousands. It is likely there were even more. It is hard to count once you start getting so high, you know?" the male said with a firm shake of his head.

"How do you know, Potap?" Lona tapped her foot at the red male.

He raised his hands in the air definitively. "Because we were talking before you two came over. Tell them, um… what did you say your name was…Branimir."

Branimir's pale eyes swelled. "Yeah. I wouldn't say, I mean, I have killed—"

"See! See! He is a warrior that has come to lead our people to freedom," Potap claimed.

"Are you sure?" Lona pursed her lips, "He is awfully unsure of himself."

"I am not!" Branimir claimed.

"You don't want to anger the warrior," Potap warned with a raised finger.

"Shut up, Potap!" Lona raised her hand as though she were going to slap him.

"Put your hand down!" Branimir demanded, stepping between them. "Our people are not violent toward others, unless, well—unless we have no other choice!"

Potap and Shanna sighed in admiration.

Lona faced Branimir boldly, her voice suddenly full of spunk. "Who are you to command me, Branimir? You are not a Highborn. You are not Anshedar."

Branimir looked around the courtyard, wild-eyed. More of the Kras in the area had begun to gather around. His people circled around Branimir, males and females by the hundreds. They scattered from the hallways, shouting at others in their rooms.

Branimir took a deep breath. He had never seen so many Kras in all his life. It was likely his father and grandfather had never seen the like either.

"Well?" Lona stamped her foot.

"Tell her, Branimir," Shana urged, her large black eyes looking up at him.

Branimir reached in his pocket. He felt something smooth.

It was his shiny stone!

"I hold the stone of our people, the *Ojenek*, from *Eevaltti*, the distant city of our people, called Illuard," Branimir cried out into the room. "This stone gives me the right to command the Kras, the ancient *Ojenan*; the Red From Beneath the Mountain!"

The crowd of Kras gulped and awed and cooed at the grandeur of the moonstone. The light from within flashed brighter than the dim light of the Dyndaer.

"*Ojenek*" was whispered among the Kras. Many of them stared helplessly at the shiny gem, their hands reaching toward it as though they would give their lives just to touch it once. The power of the moonstone was incomprehensible.

Potap shrilly hollered. "Bring him a plate of food!"

In a moment, slop on a plate was thrust toward Bran.

He took it awkwardly, looking at the zealous faces of his people. He had never felt empowered before. He was a god among these Kras who had been sheltered from the history and knowledge of the world, and of his beloved people. He was overwhelmed with a pity that he had never experienced before.

Lona was the first to kneel on one knee, eyes raised to the shiny stone that Branimir held in his free hand. The rest followed quickly.

Branimir looked around nervously, thankful that there were no Highborn. From the size of the Kras's quarters, it was likely none could fit without crawling.

"What are we to do, Warrior?" Potap raised his head.

Branimir gulped, looking at the many eyes of the Kras who watched him. There was only one thing that he could offer them. It was what every living creature wanted, whether they were aware of it or not. It was what the *Kadari* planned to steal away.

Branimir licked his lips, his squeaky voice holding the authority of a King, saying words that he had never thought he would hear, especially from his own lips. "We are going to be free. All of us! We are going to make our new home, deep in the Dyndaer, and without the Anshedar."

Whispers flooded the courtyard of Shayol Domier as his words spread among the ranks of the Kras.

"Is that possible?" Shanna said, as baffled as the rest that gave sight to Branimir.

Branimir manipulated the words he had heard Dorofej say in the past. "Every living being has the right to carve their own path. The Kras are no different!"

Voices of approval were heard among the crowd and Branimir could see heads nodding. He smiled, feeling the power of leadership.

"How, Warrior?" Potap wondered.

"This night, when they are asleep in their beds, you will disappear from sight. Each of you will run and hide in the forests, the Kras way! The Anshedar will not be able to find you if you do not want them to. You will head north to the Hrani Highlands, and we will make our home in the mountains."

"You will come with us, Branimir?" Shanna asked in a worried voice.

Branimir assured her, resting his hand on her shoulder softly. "I will come for you when I am done with my quest. I have a commitment that I must see through to the end, for the sake of the Kras and for the world,"

"Why don't you come with us?" several cried out in argument.

Branimir took a moment to look around at the many Kras. "Because, I am a warrior."

Chapter XXX

"Stop it, you daring man," a woman leered in a drunken slur, slapping Dorofej's hand away from her layered skirt.

Branimir watched in amazement.

Dorofej was draped in his insidious robes as black as storm clouds, ragged as any robes from the long journey he had taken. He raised his head to the young girl, the tufts of his dark red hair bulged from his hulking hood. His face was young, shaven, and all features of age had left him entirely.

"Not only was my body rejuvenated, but so were my boyish desires, yes?" Dorofej laughed. "Come now, this man may die tomorrow in glorious battle. Give him a raucous night to remind him why he is fighting, yes?"

Laughter erupted around the table in the small wooden cottage near the eastern wall of Shayol Domier.

A handful sat about in the room drinking from the barrels of ale and wine that were sitting in the cottage. Branimir noticed most of the individuals, including Artemiy and Alyona.

A strongman, who had identified himself as Dobromil, cackled, "This man has a way with women, does he not? I would not have believed the old man had such spunk in him."

"If he even looks at Alyona wrongly, I'll knock him upside the head," Artemiy threatened, not amused by the redheaded man, sipping on his tankard.

"Meh. Leave him be," Alyona chortled. "I can take care of myself. Besides, he is cuter than any other man at this forsaken place."

"It's not forsaken, sister," Artemiy wallowed in his chair, slapping the table.

Branimir noticed Falmagon holding his stomach, giving sign that he had been doubled over for some time to the point that his abdomen was beginning to hurt. Both of his perfect blue eyes watered, watching Dorofej with absolute amusement. "You do have quite the charm on the ladies, Dorofej. I would have never guessed that you had it in you."

"A charmer I am, yes, with women both in and out of the cloth?" Dorofej chuckled.

Branimir wrinkled his nose with disgust. "What do you mean, my Lord?"

Trying to understand Dorofej was like meeting a stranger for the first time. He was nothing like he was in his frailty. Then again, Branimir did not recognize either of the men in their fledgling bodies. Falmagon had two eyes that actually worked.

By and by, he ignored the two of them for the most part, sipping on his own drink. The hope he had given the Kras that afternoon would soon be known. In due time, the they would be escaping into the Dyndaer away from the clutches of the Highborn. Forever.

"Suggestion is determined by the amount of plum in the veins, Branimir. Full of it, I am." Dorofej's laughter continued to ring.

The cottage roared in laughter with the man. Wooden flutes and a string instrument played in the background as more alcohol was passed around to those that united together in the establishment. It was not an alehouse, nothing like the *Kal'bane*, but it suited the purpose for the evening.

"Never has this man spoken more truth," Falmagon garbled, slapping Dorofej on the back heartily.

The unnamed woman winked at Dorofej. "Just keep your hands to yourself, and we will see where the night leads, eh?"

Dorofej puckered his lips and whistled, ending with a satisfied smile on his young face. The man had likely not experienced this type of frolic in nearly a century. He danced in his chair, twisting his head back and forth, whistling with the tune of the pipes.

Branimir could not blame Dorofej for enjoying himself, but he felt that the man had forgotten a piece of himself in the change. The Waters of Life had transformed the old man into his younger body nearly instantly. It was not long before Dorofej was bouncing around Shayol Domier, shouting and carrying on like he had just found a priceless treasure.

Branimir did not recognize him in face or spirit. The wise man's concerns of all that had befallen them had seemingly fled his mind.

"Dorofej," Branimir nudged him, "you may want to hold back on the plum."

Dorofej scrunched his face at Branimir as if trying to remember him. His hand ran through his red locks several times, his eyes spacy and jaw drooping halfway open. Slowly, he sat down his tankard of wine. "You are more than right, Branimir! There is evil afoot, yes?"

Branimir nodded.

Falmagon raised his voice, "Let Nedezhda come! I have never felt so alive. A lifetime of *Koldovstvo* flows through my veins. I will cut her down and take back *kaelandur* to be used for the glory of Dahz and the *Kadari*!"

The men and women in the tavern shouted approval at the Highborn Long-Walker.

Falmagon raised his hands. The flutes and strings continued to play as the dark-haired man began speaking the *Kalamyr Oath* passionately. The crowd of Anshedar men and women that gathered around him smiled in recognition of the words.

Held fore'er by a simple word,
To defend against the impious,
Ne'er to kneel nor fall or lured,
Lest blood and death descend.
Beyond wealth and a princely home,
Trust held for'ever unto the Sun,
We war, we worship, we roam,
Lest blood and death descend.

The *Kadari* within the cottage raised their voices alongside that of Falmagon with the second verse. Dorofej and Branimir watched in absolute trepidation.

Rise above the frail and weak,
Fore'er standing beyond frailty,
Let all men hear us speak,
Till blood and death descend.
Feel the warmth of the White-Clad,
Blessing the Highborn in eternal glory,
Let none meander or fall gad,
Till blood and death descend.

As the last word boomed from the voices in unison, the music silenced. The Highborn clapped and hooted in recognition of their unified faith.

All except Dorofej, who seemed suddenly sober, staring at those who held the power of *Koldovstvo*. Branimir saw the flicker of reason flutter across the man's vision. Dorofej's blue eyes darted about the room like an animal caught in a snare. Whatever effect the Waters of Life had on his mind was slipping.

Falmagon shouted into the cottage at the many that whooped in admiration. "Bah! Are we not Highborn? Are we not Anshedar? Why do we stay hidden in this stick castle when evil sifts through the Dyndaer? Who said they had seen

Nedezhda the *Eretik* during the night outside the gates? Let us find her and her hordes of demons and cut down the lot of them!"

"Aravdur was the one that had seen the woman. Said she was like a wraith, a ghostly demon, and as pale as death," Dobromil shared.

"Where is this Aravdur?" Falmagon asked.

Marina answered, filled with vigor, "He is a little red brood. A Kras. Likely, he is back on watch outside on the wall. We can find him easily enough."

More shouts of encouragement sounded with clinks of tankards as they downed more of the alcoholic liquid.

Branimir tried to hide his look of fear. If the Highborn went looking for the Kras now, they may find that there were none left in Shayol Domier.

Valya, who sat near the back, stood, lifting his tankard high. "Falmagon Sej, you speak like the Patrician himself, like a true spearhead. You say that Kinhar had chosen you to take his stead, to lead the *Kadari* on Melkorka. I cannot dispute from what I have seen and heard. You take action with enough force to cut the path to glory. In truth, your words hold the truth that each of us have longed to hear."

The *Kadari* clapped in response, agreeing with the bold man who spoke for them like they were mindless children.

The idea of seeking Aravdur fled from their mouths and their minds. Branimir sighed relief.

The man continued, "Why hold this power if we cannot shape this world? What can stand between the *Kadari* and the rule of the kingdoms of men, especially when such strength is at the forefront?"

"There is nothing!" Falmagon cried out, rising from his chair. "I am your spearhead and will be your Patrician as Kinhar desired, if you would have me. What say you?"

The roar of approval that sounded from those in the cabin was silenced as quickly as it had begun. The door creaked open from the rear before slamming shut behind Falmagon.

Moreth, the Patrician of the *Kadari*, walked forward. He scanned the room nervously, before eyeing Falmagon with a quivering lip. His hands shook as though he had been chopping wood for half his life without rest.

The silence was as still as the grave. The Highborn Long-Walker glared at Moreth with the fury of a thousand warriors.

Moreth showed no sign of violence, speaking with a quaking voice, taking a deep breath between each sentence as though it could be his last. "I give you hospitality. I share the secrets of immortality with you, because you are Highborn and therefore, my brother. I gave you back your life like it had never been taken. I welcome you with open arms and your repayment is treason against me! For a thousand years, I have walked this earth and given direction to men where none could be found. To each of these, even in this room, I have given everything. Never have I given to a man as treacherous as you, Falmagon Sej."

Falmagon raised his hand, as though he were about to lift stone through the floor, to obliterate Moreth where he stood.

"Hold!" Moreth commanded, his voice having the authority of the gods. "Do not strike down your own, lest you curse the *Kadari* for eternity. You have already witnessed firsthand what happens when you lay waste to those of your own house, Falmagon. I had given warning to Kinhar before he made his schemes and he would not heed it. Be the wiser."

Falmagon swallowed, saying nothing.

"It is clear to me that my leadership has come to a close. My ... my brothers and sisters have accepted you as their leader and wish me discarded from my position."

"Patrician Moreth—"

"Silence, Valya! I have already heard you speak, and you have been bound by your words under the Lightbringer," Moreth said. "I will leave you to your fates under the direction of Falmagon Sej, and I pray he can offer the *Kadari* what you think I obviously could not."

Falmagon stood all the taller, physically accepting ownership of the hundreds of Highborn at his back, "I will lead to glory. I will give rise to Melkorka beyond anything the world has ever seen. I will bring Dahz, the Protector of Men, more honor and glory than he has ever received. We will have his full blessing from our sacrifice, from our offering, and from the blood of evil that we spill, in His name. You can hold me to that! Tomorrow we go to the Ash Tree. Tomorrow we put an end to Nedezhda and this madness!"

"Hear, hear!" the *Kadari* raised their tankards.

"That is a story I will have no part in." Moreth opened the door and stepped into the darkness.

Chapter XXXI

The following morning was as frigid as the day before while the Highborn prepared in the courtyard. The world was gray and bleak like a shadow on a grave. If ever a curse had seemingly befallen the world, now was the time.

"Where are those little red broods?" Valya said with a flick of his tongue. How do five hundred Kras just disappear?"

Falmagon snorted. His raggedy hair was wilder this morning than usual. His eyes locked onto Branimir, who stood close to Dorofej's dark robes.

Branimir turned his eyes away, his hands stuffed in his pockets. The Highborn Long-Walker had to know what had taken place. Branimir trembled, fearing the punishment to come.

"You tell me, Valya," Falmagon said. "Why does the single Kras of Melkorka stand ready to fight at our side and those of Shayol Domier flee in fright? Have they no wits about them?"

Valya turned his gaze away from the Patrician. "Maybe so. They are not accustomed to having demons at their gates."

Falmagon snorted. "It would serve them well to be cut down by the Bukavac while they tried to route like scared children! Let us hope that we find their mutilated bodies along our path."

"May very well be that they are already dead, yes?"

Dorofej smoothed his robes and rubbed his temples in a circular motion. "Slaughtered them whilst we slept off a drunken stupor, the *Eretik* may have, even within these walls."

"Dorofej, don't be a fool! Where would the bodies have gone? And why would they not have done away with us as well." Falmagon said.

"Don't shout, yes? Aching terribly, my head is."

"It is no matter whether the Kras are here or not. There are plenty of Highborn at our backs and with the Waters of Life, we will win this battle with ease." Valya reasoned.

Branimir hoped that the Kras were well beyond the reaches of the *Eretik* and the *Kadari*. They were the last hope for his people's survival.

Falmagon shook his head. "You know nothing of the Bukavac or Nedezhda."

"I have fought the Vucari for two decades, Patrician. I have some understanding of difficulty."

"Not like this, Valya," Falmagon muttered.

Dorofej clenched his red hair. "Shouting, you are."

"Maybe you should not have drunk so much wine," Valya said, peering at Dorofej and shaking his head.

"It would not have improved his thinking," Falmagon said, his hand moving as though he were wanting to slam a staff against the ground to finish the insult. He did not seem to notice that *Habërmani* had been lost.

Dorofej's eyes glanced toward the woman from the night before, wearing her split skirts, walking nearby among the Anshedar. "Worth it, a hundred times over, it was."

"By *Mulafell*," Falmagon turned toward the gate. "Get us to the Ash Tree, Valya, before my mind is branded with images I cannot erase."

"Of course, Patrician Falmagon. It is not far," he replied.

Several hundred Highborn moved through the Dyndaer Forest. With no organization, they moved through the dark trees, through the underbrush, toward the Ash Tree. The sound of their feet on the earth was like drums to Branimir, who walked up front with Falmagon, Dorofej, and the scouting party of Valya. The rest, none known to Branimir, trailed behind their new Patrician.

Dorofej seemed to sober as they moved through the trees of the Dyndaer, or at least his complaints of noise lessened considerably. As the distance to their location shortened, Valya instructed them to be at the ready.

It did not take more than an hour to reach their destination. The thick, tall trees of the Dyndaer did not sway or change in any way as they moved through the forest. There was no clearing. The Ash Tree suddenly just became visible through the haze of the forest as if it was where it was meant to be among the trees.

The over-sized Ash Tree melded in a dismal pool of dark water that was unlike any pond Branimir had ever seen. It sprung toward the heavens, brimming with leaves as large as Branimir, and plush fruits, and flowers more decorated than any ever seen. Its base was wide and the expanse of the branches was wider yet. The roots of the tree spiraled in and out of the waters that simmered like they were hovering over a furnace beneath.

Surrounding the edge of the pool, the metaphorical door to the Netherworld, were the Bukavac, their bluish flesh melding with the fog of the forest. Their crafted blades of death were clenched in their hands, hacking at the many roots of the tree, tearing it asunder from the world of the living. Their numbers were equal to, if not greater than, those of the Highborn.

Close to their number, stood the *Eretik* with *kaelandur* seized in her hand. Nedezhda barked orders at the demons beneath her, demanding that they work quicker. Half of the Ash Tree was already dismembered, lopsided in the Waters of Life.

"For Dahz," Falmagon mumbled.

"For the Lightbringer," Valya reiterated.

"For the Lightbringer," many more echoed.

At the sound of their murmured voices across the two-hundred-yard expanse, Nedezhda flung her head up from where she stood. Her lips curved in disgust.

Her mouth formed words that were unheard, her greenish, mucky hair clinging to her cheekbones as they rose and fell. Branimir still could not take his eyes off the black stitches circling her neck.

The moment of demons facing the living could have lasted an eternity. The Highborn stretched out among the trees, a low hum of whispers of encouragement. The Bukavac turned and stepped away from the waters, their roars reactive to the enemy. Any sounds of the forest in the cold months were deafened.

As the Bukavac sprang forward on their clawed feet, Falmagon's hands moved quickly, mending the dust of the ground into the air. A storm of sand erupted from the floor of the forest to slow the charging demons.

"Attack!" He screamed at the legion of *Kadari*.

While the Anshedar wielded *Koldovstvo*, Branimir took a step back, feeling as though he was not meant to be here in this moment. He suddenly wished he was among his own kind in the Dyndaer, hiding from the bloodshed that would soon follow.

This battle was beyond him. The Bukavac charged, tearing through the trees, their blades were deadly shadows in their hands, cold and menacing in the layered snow and ice. The Highborn screamed and bawled glories to the Lightbringer as they heaved stone and wove vine, laid fire and felled ice. This was a war for the divine or those close to it, not the meek Kras.

Branimir did as the Kras do, and faded from sight, clinging to the nearest tree within the Dyndaer. He was a warrior, perhaps, but he was not a hero. He definitely was not a fool.

Branimir cried out as the first Bukavac reached the Highborn ranks. It swung a labrys, wildly missing Dorofej who had pulled ahead of the other Anshedar. The redheaded Highborn twisted his body, embracing his renewed agility, lost for so long in the years that had passed. Dorofej laughed wildly as though battle was his voice and death was his song, reaching out to embrace *Koldovstvo*.

Branimir was nearly frozen, watching Dorofej wield magic beyond the skill of any other Highborn. The black mage grasped onto something deeper than the physical world, tearing through dimensions unknown to the living, touching the sacred world beyond anything known to any Highborn. The Bukavac froze in response to the unseen magic. It was as though the beast were living within a dream, a nightmare, deep within its mind.

Dorofej jumped, the air around him suspended him, and flung his body toward the beast that stood twice his height. In his hands, two swords purely made of fire formed, lashing and blazing, hungrily reaching for the icy skin of the Bukavac. Dorofej fed his weapons, plunging them into stone-like flesh of the Netherworld demon. In its daze, the demon did not utter a sound, but simply collapsed, absent of life.

Branimir bit his tongue as he watched Dorofej free the flame swords and rush into the masses of demons that assailed with a glimmer of madness in his eye. *Koldovstvo* flowed through him with minimal aging effects as though his body were accustomed to the current of the craft, like a river bed to the flow of water. It gave him far more strength than any of the other Highborn. Branimir was almost certain that Dorofej could lay waste to the entire army with his power, if he so chose.

Dorofej was not alone though. Falmagon flung his rocks and raised his strong-walls, controlling the movement of demons toward his army, giving example as to why Kinhar had once called him prodigy. Valya used similar magic, maintaining walls of air, constructing unseen barriers to protect the Anshedar as they manipulated *Koldovstvo*.

The *Kadari* stood close to those they were familiar with bringing on their own wrath through *Koldovstvo*. They cried out to one another as more Bukavac raided their fortifications, overcoming their own barricades, made of the air and the twisted trees of the Dyndaer.

"Dobromil!" One *Kadari* man screamed before a demon fist collided with his skull. His head caved inward.

"No!" Artemiy shouted.

Dobromil, the strongman from the tavern the previous night, charged at the demon. He crafted a mystical sword from stone out of the earth while he sprinted. In a fluid moment, he stabbed it through the gut of the demon. Bluish white blood spewed over his hand as the demon roared.

A second Bukavac came from behind, quickly grabbing Dobromil's leg. He pulled him from the ground and sunk his teeth into the man's calf. Dobromil howled in agony, the massive man feeling the fangs scrape against his bone. He lost consciousness mid-scream.

Artemiy was on the demon as quick as maggots on decaying flesh. Artemiy did not hesitate. His hand clasped over the demon's face and a fireball released upon impact. The demon's head was hurled backwards from the impact, singed and blackened beyond recognition. The demon would not roar again.

"Artemiy, watch out!" A *Kadari* woman screamed, forming the earth into a shield to take the impact of a sword swinging at the young man's head from another Bukavac that entered the area. The shield shattered from the blow, but Artemiy was saved. He reared back in time for Alyona to lift the beast with wind and fling it back the way it had come.

Falmagon smashed another advancing demon to mush with a solid stone from some distance away. The pasty guts of the beast splattered across the foliage. There were so many battles ensuing within battles that it was difficult to keep track of them all.

Highborn and Bukavac circled one another, cutting down one another as though they were ancient enemies destined to wage war with the other.

Branimir struggled to watch every action of the battle as Highborn and demon clashed. At any moment that it seemed the humans gained the upper hand, several more Highborn would fall to waste on the battlefield, from either a deathblow or from crippling themselves with *Koldovstvo*.

Falmagon stepped beside Valya and Dorofej, beginning to resemble his older self. "We must reach the Waters of Life to replenish our energy. We must kill Nedezhda."

"Push forward!" Valya ordered.

The Bukavac slowed in their advancement as the Highborn collided with the beasts. The area was falling to pieces, trees laying over trees, grasses burning, snow melting, and corpses well within its mix.

"Nedezhda!" Falmagon shouted.

The pale woman sneered, firing a shard of ice through the skull of a Highborn who advanced toward the Ash Tree. Blood splashed from the back of the skull of the long-haired woman. Ice shard after ice shard was loosened from Nedezhda's hand and the Highborn fell.

"I should have killed you when I had the chance, Falmagon," she shouted. "A mistake I will not make twice!" The ice shard meant for the Highborn Long-Walker skimmed by his head.

Falmagon, Dorofej, and Valya rushed through the trees dodging the projectiles, crimson blood and pale blood painted the ground beneath them as they struggled to reach Nedezhda. They flung fire and stone, only to be met with more ice and water from the *Eretik*. No blow seemed to land, but the sounds of battle forever echoed.

As they neared, two women rose from the waters on

either side of Nedezhda. Their hair was a blue wave, laced over their bare skin. Their eyes resembled the iris of a flower, shimmering like crystal.

Dorofej stopped immediately, throwing himself to the ground in a curled mess.

"Dorofej!" Falmagon slowed.

Valya pushed forward, flinging currents of air at the strange creatures.

"Stop!" Dorofej raised his hand toward Valya and Falmagon.

Dorofej was too late with his caveat as one of the females raised her hand at Valya and a cylinder of light pulsed into the man's flesh. In an instant, he was swallowed by nothingness, gone from sight, gone from existence.

Falmagon hit the dirt, giving no sign of caring for the slain Valya. "What are they, Dorofej? Speak to me!"

"Vila!" he hissed.

"The maidens of Marheena," Falmagon gasped, pulling himself behind a tree before another cylinder of light volleyed through the Dyndaer. "They exist!"

The Highborn around them screamed as their companions vaporized from existence through the magic of the Vila. Nedezhda only fed their fear by dropping balls of ice from the sky that caused the ground to quake. Along with the ice storm came a cloud of shadow sifting through the forest eating away at the flesh of the living. Flesh melted and tore from bone. Men and women screamed in agony.

"We cannot lose, Dorofej!" Falmagon said hastily.

"We are losing!" Dorofej shouted back.

"You must take her into the Netherworld and kill her eternally!"

Dorofej, in his new-found youth, looked at Falmagon as though he were mad. "Why me?"

"You have lived beyond your time, old man, and it is time for a new order to rule over this world."

"You mean the *Kadari*, yes? Stand for it, I would not!"

Falmagon grabbed ahold of Dorofej's dark robes, pulling him so that their noses touched, "This is the way that it must be. Have I not suffered enough. You must do this in the name of glory!"

Dorofej glowered, his red hair burning as bright as his eyes were cold. "Your glory is not the glory I seek, Falmagon Sej! Asking me to sacrifice myself, you are!"

"Have you not asked the same of me?" The Patrician roared over the screams of the dying that began to flee from the Dyndaer. Men and women crawled and weaved through the trees in absolute terror of the Vila and the *Eretik*.

"Your sacrifice—"

"Do not waste your fancy words on me, Dorofej the Highborn! You claim to care for this world and the people within it, but what have you sacrificed? What greater thing could you give than your life? End this! I have seen you wield *Koldovstvo*. Only you have the power to end this madness!"

"Bah!" Dorofej had tears in the corner of his eyes. Even in a lifetime of living, he wanted death no more than the next man. "So be it!"

Darkness enveloped Dorofej, as dark as Czern's breath, expanding around his body, hiding the murkiness of his cloak and placing him within the deepest shadow.

Branimir screamed, overhearing their words.

Dorofej was going to die!

The Highborn stepped away from Falmagon with a sneer. "If you bring blight to this world, Falmagon Sej, every drop of blood that has dripped by your words or at your hands, I will come back and see to it that you taste it!"

"So be it!"

Focusing on *Koldovstvo* with all his strength, Dorofej charged toward the water of life in the shroud of pitch, like dragon fire. Reddish yellow light dimmed over his body as his skin began to mend itself with every aging affect that impacted his flesh. The Vila screeched at the haunting visage, releasing ray after ray of imminent death at the ancient Highborn. As every ray approached, time appeared to stand at a still, as Dorofej twisted, and leaped, and rolled out of harm's away.

"Dorofej!" Branimir shouted. "Don't do this!"

The Kras ran toward the redheaded Highborn with every intention of saving the man that had kept him safe. He twisted in and out of the Bukavac, avoiding the massive weapons that swung about, cutting down the fleeing Highborn. Battle cries of man and beast echoed in the cavern surrounding the Ash Tree. The echoes would sound for eternity.

"Dorofej! Stop this!" Branimir screamed.

Branimir was answered by gnashing teeth of a Bukavac that swiped him off the ground. The beast squeezed his delicate body. Branimir could feel his bones crack.

A stone sword plummeted through the Bukavac's neck cavity. Blood gushed. Branimir's bones had not yet completely snapped.

Branimir fell to the ground with the demon crumbling next to him. Branimir crawled along the dirt, unable to climb to his feet. He paid no heed to Falmagon who had saved him.

Branimir pushed forward toward the Waters of Life after Dorofej.

Dorofej hit the waters like a tidal wave. The sound that escaped between his thin lips was a war cry from the depths of his stomach. It may have very well been the sound of death itself.

The blackness around Dorofej was extinguished as he pulled himself onto the roots of the Ash Tree. He swallowed a mouthful of water, replenishing his strength and any youth he may have lost. The Vila screeched as he flung himself through the air toward the *Eretik*. In a moment, he stood next to Nedezhda.

His icy eyes matched hers. "Time for this to end, yes?"

Nedezhda leered. "With pleasure, Dorofej."

She plunged *kaelandur* into the roots of the Ash Tree.

Dorofej bellowed in horror as the tree began to wilt. It smelted and crumpled into the boiling black waters. "No!"

The ancient Highborn leaped at Nedezhda, tackling her into the Waters of Life. The dagger was loosened from the impact, still clasped in Nedezhda's hand.

Branimir dived after him.

Kaelandur fell into the waters, out of reach of any outside of the pool. Falmagon ran to the edge yelling and cursing for what may have been for Dorofej, but what was more likely for the copper dagger.

Nedezhda screamed and flailed her arms as they sunk deep into the black void. Dorofej held fast to the demon woman as she clawed at him.

Branimir caught grip of Dorofej's robe. He would not let go. He could not let go!

The roots of the Ash Tree mapped their descent to eternal death, to the Netherworld.

Chapter XXXII

Branimir Baran grunted, his body aching from head to toe. His face was freezing against the solid ground beneath him. It was as though he were lying on solid ice. His body felt like he had been buried in the snow for hours, although he was certain that he could not have been unconscious for more than a few minutes.

Branimir had experienced the cold from Kalamaar to the Hyaendi Hills, but never had he known this type of relentless cold.

"What have I done?" Dorofej's voice echoed nearby.

Branimir turned over on his back, his eyes fluttering open slowly. The world was a daze, blurry and bleak. His eyes fluttered several times before he gained focus.

Above him was a pool of water, suspended in the air, with massive roots stretching like columns down to the world around him. Not one root touched the ground, and yet, it seemed to have no end. The pool of water was beyond his reach, an eternity upwards, but as clear as the clearest lake on the brightest morning.

The world around Branimir was covered in ice, over hill, plain and mountain. The frozen water was shaped into miraculous glaciers, sharp and menacing to the eye. The distance was filled with darkness, and although he would usually be able to see, his vision was blocked with a frozen mist. With the smell of rotting flesh pulling at his nostrils, he had to consider his limited sight a blessing.

"Arrgghh," Bran moaned, attempting to spring to his feet, only to fall back to the ice. His body was broken and bleeding. The wounds were deep, hidden beneath his flesh. He could feel it as readily as it were on the surface.

"I am not dead," Dorofej realized out loud. "The dead do not know pain, yes?"

Branimir turned to see the man cradled, knees clutched to his chest. He pulled at his red strands at his scalp, rocking slightly. Branimir was not sure if Dorofej was expecting an answer from him or not.

"No, I imagine they do not," Branimir said. He wheezed for air as though he were sucking it through a blade of grass.

For a moment, he thought that Dorofej had not heard him. It was possible that the old man had suddenly gone mad. It was possible that his voice was too weak. Branimir hoped that it was neither. The thought of living for an eternity with a madman in the Netherworld was beyond frightful, nearly as chilling as death.

The redheaded man spun his head around on the ground, looking at Branimir. He was only a few feet away from Dorofej. His blue eyes stared into the pale ovals of Branimir, and quickly he crawled across the frost.

The time that it took Dorofej to reach Branimir seemed to be an eternity within an eternity. When he finally did reach him, Branimir could have sworn another lifetime had passed by him.

With a grunt, Dorofej pulled at him, falling on the small body of the slave of Melkorka. He put his head to Branimir's body. In a moment, outside of time, Dorofej sobbed over him.

"Why did you follow me through, Branimir Baran?" Dorofej blubbered over the body. "Why did you follow me? This was my fate!"

"I could not leave you, my Lord," Branimir said, cringing at the weight of the man.

Dorofej lifted himself and ran his hand through Branimir's wet, stringy hair. "Served the Highborn for so long, the Kras have, sacrificing so much. None have ever done so as gallantly as you, Branimir Baran."

Branimir could barely look into the blue, gentle eyes of the Highborn.

"You are hurt, yes?"

Branimir nodded, suddenly realizing the measure of his injuries. He would not be able to continue.

Dorofej raised his hands to bring healing to the Kras's body.

"No!" Branimir commanded. "You will need your strength, Dorofej. You will need to find your way out of the Netherworld and back to the land of the living."

"If I do not mend you, you will die," Dorofej said.

A tear touched Branimir's eyes, "I…I know. It's okay." Branimir coughed, blood spilling over his lips.

It was worse than he had thought.

"Death comes for most—"

Dorofej tried again to touch *Koldovstvo*.

"Please! You must let me go. I…need to find…my wolf skin."

Branimir smiled as he referred to Dorofej's fable that had seemed to have been told so long ago. Branimir was finally going to be released of his duty.

"A warrior you truly are, Branimir," Dorofej said before turning his head away in anguish. "I would not have done this had I known?"

Branimir coughed. "You have done nothing, Dorofej."

The man was speechless. Branimir followed his gaze to Nedezhda who also was lying on the ground. Branimir's eyes focused on her pale skin against the ice several feet away. Her dark hair flattened against the ice, like moss against bark. Not an eyelash even flinched on the woman. She was motionless as though she had died again.

"This cannot…"

Dorofej cut himself off, not finishing the thought. Branimir lifted his head slightly, watching the Highborn move to the body of the undead woman carefully. As though brimming with rage, collective of the thousands of battles the man had fought, he screamed. It may have been for what Nedezhda had done to the Ash Tree, Aenar, or even how her actions had led Dorofej and Branimir to their fates.

Branimir was certain that Dorofej's wrath stretched beyond Nedezhda. Kinhar had lied. Falmagon had betrayed. The Highborn were lost! The *Kadari* would take control of Aenar and Dorofej was trapped for eternity in the Netherworld with the dead and the demonic.

No matter what the reason for igniting the fury, it was clear. Dorofej needed release for his ire.

The ancient Highborn lifted himself up over the undead *Eretik*, not bothering to check for breath. With a sneer, he made a fist and struck the woman in the cheek. She did not respond. He struck her again in the stitched neck. Bones broke. Flesh bruised.

"Dorofej! Stop!"

Dorofej ignored Branimir. He hit Nedezhda repeatedly until his knuckles were bloodied and his skin was torn. Lastly, without any hint of where he found it, Dorofej pulled *kaelandur* from his robe and plunged it through the chest of the *Eretik*. The demon never stirred, never fought.

"Dorofej," Branimir sputtered blood over his lips once more. He tried to wipe away the liquid that dribbled down his cheek. It was pointless. He could not even raise his arm.

When Dorofej had finished, Branimir could no longer recognize the woman that had been killed with *kaelandur*, executed at Melkorka. The face was sunk in and broken, the stitches around the neck loosened, and the white pale liquid spread across the ice.

Dorofej spread his arms toward the waters above him and

screamed again.

Branimir wanted to cry, but even that would take strength that he did not have. Hearing the man's laments, the ultimate defeat of the heart, shredded Branimir's hope. Dorofej knew there was no escaping through the Waters of Life.

From where Branimir lay, he could still see the Ash Tree and the fragmented roots. He had no understanding of it. He had seen the Ash Tree destroyed before sinking into the frozen Netherworld. Even if the Ash Tree had survived through some miracle, the entrance was never the exit and the exit was never the entrance. It was in the darkness of the frozen Netherworld that Dorofej would have to find his path back to Aenar.

"You … must find … a way." Branimir struggled to keep life in him.

Dorofej stood to his feet slowly, and moved away from the corpse of Nedezhda. The Waters of Life swelled and bubbled outside of his reach, taunting him with every gurgle.

"You must…save…your strength." Branimir said.

Dorofej wept, stumbling to the red creature. "Understand, you do not, Branimir Baran."

"Tell me."

The Highborn gripped *kaelandur* forcing a smile through the tears. "Your concern, it is not. Maybe in another time, another place."

"No matter how long it takes, you must find your way out of the Netherworld. Do not lay down. Do not rest. No matter the pain or the regret, you must cling to hope." Branimir gasped for air.

"Do not cry for the lost. You will find me in the world after this. For you, there is still glory to be had."

As the words slipped with Branimir's last breath, he saw a glowing light.

DYNDAER

Book 2

The Kaelandur Series

Thrice Nine Legends

Prologue

Age-old promises kept Dorofej alive. At the outset, he could not say how many years had passed. Time and space were distorted in the realm of the dead, but the stint had not caused him to stumble in his walk. Upon returning to Aenar, even after a thousand years, the Highborn found the world had not changed. Men were still enthused by power and gain, leaving sagacity to those who retained ideals but had nothing to show for it. Still, he had his promises.

"Another storm is coming. We should find shelter." Sulanna Maelthirren spoke in the tone of a true diplomat. Her voice was terse, yet gentle. At one time, she might have been found within the fastened bodice of a noble. Now, she wore the strapping armor of a soldier.

In the preceding months, Dorofej found Sulanna had the knack for speaking her mind, whether one wanted to hear it or not. Even now, her words served as a fair warning when considering the dimming light that gave shadow to the Hyaendi Hills.

The middle-aged man who led them responded. "Nowhere to go out here but forward."

Thunder rumbled overhead.

Dorofej disregarded the imminent storm. His companions were far more interesting. Sulanna and Alden had inadvertently educated him about what he had missed during the past millenia when he had been traversing the Netherworld.

Sulanna tightened her cloak, her brown hair falling against her cheek. "There is no chance of reaching Eldhaft this eve, Alden. We are over a hundred leagues out. Be sensible."

Alden gazed over his shoulder, letting the horse guide him. "Sensible? The only cover you will find out here is your horse's ass. Look around you. There is nothing but dirt and grass, woman."

Sulanna glowered at the warrior.

He pressed, "Besides, we have nearly reached the outer bounds of the Svet territory. I'd rather not spend another night risking our necks sleeping in the lands of the centaurs."

The belly of the sky was gutted, adding weight to his words. Rain pattered down into small puddles around the clopping hooves of their horses. Their stamping reminded Dorofej of the centaurs. He had learned the Svet were nearly slaughtered to extinction by the Northmen in past years. The thought still made his stomach upset. The centaurs may have been fierce, but it did not discount their goodness.

Sulanna centered herself on her mare. "These are their Holy Lands, Alden. You cannot hate them for protecting what is rightfully theirs."

"I can hate what I wish. The savages should have been cut down years ago. Maharia was given to the Anshedar."

"Given? Men took Maharia by force, slaughtering thousands."

"With the blessing of Svarog."

The woman tilted her head, squinting at the man ahead of her. The spear on his back bounced in rhythm with his horse's clopping feet. "Do not bring your god into this."

"You cannot ignore Svarog forever."

"I'll acknowledge the gods when they do something worth acknowledging." She shot back with irritation.

"Svarog will see to His children, my sweetness." Alden spit harshly and then licked the driblets of saliva from his lip. "Listen, I will not be sleeping on the ground tonight. My frame is too old and my ass cheeks too wrinkled. Riding this gelding for weeks has likely caused what little hair I have left to fall from my head."

To make his point, the warrior threw back the olive-colored hood of his cloak. His receding hair sparsely covered his scalp, covering just the tips of his thin ears.

A chilled wind advanced from the rear.

Dorofej held his black robes and watched Alden. The warrior had no less hair than when they had left Tamarri, but even in the failing light, Dorofej could see the scabbed cuts along Alden's arms. The blemishes joined many scars, which staggered his wrinkled skin; some were fresher and deeper than others.

Sulanna did not stumble over her words. "I do not see any gods helping us, Alden."

The man swiftly pulled his hood over his head, seemingly frustrated for not getting the hoped-for reaction from the woman. Alden spoke again, but this time his words were directed at Dorofej. "What do you have to say about this?"

Dorofej adjusted his hood, to keep his tufts of red hair dry. He could not agree with Sulanna, who had no belief in the gods. Nor, could he side with Alden, who had a misconstrued understanding of them. "I say, there is more than one god by far."

"That isn't the question, Dorofej." Alden spat again.

"It wasn't? Oh, I do apologize. I must have been distracted by the rain, yes?"

"You are kidding me?"

Sulanna scoffed. "Leave the boy alone."

Dorofej grew silent again, taking the advantage of his dark robes to slink back into the darkness.

"Fine. I'll let it be, but he is not a boy. He is a young man and should learn to speak his mind once in a while. He cannot spend all of his time with his nose in a book," Alden muttered.

A few seconds later he added, "We will press forward until the storm lets up or we find shelter."

The lightning flanked them, snagging the sky, as they meandered west. The jagged earth was layered in small patches of greenery through the muddied soil with tall grasses stretching in every direction across the swells in the land. With each step forward, the rain only thickened.

In the many leagues that passed, as the hours of darkness further set, there was no disrupting the melodic tune of raindrops, besides that of the horses' hooves stamping through the mire. Hill and hill again, they traveled over, rising and falling in their saddles.

"For honor, for glory," Alden uttered in a whispered prayer. Dorofej barely heard the words against the metallic sound of Alden's belt knife sliding from its scabbard. Even in the dark, Dorofej saw the loosened bracer hanging from Alden's forearm, and the sharpened blade slicing through his sensitive flesh.

He had to turn his eyes away.

Dorofej had learned the warrior cut himself as penance and would not stop until he felt he had brought glory to Svarog. Dorofej had attempted to explain to Alden the nature of the gods, of Svarog, but the attempts were futile. In time, he discovered Sulanna had spent the better half of a decade attempting to convince Alden of his irrationality. It did not do any good. The man was beyond help. Of course, this was not Svarog's way. Nor was this the way of the Anshedar. This was Alden's way.

The Highborn did not look again until he heard the blade return to its holding. Alden's blood washed away with the downpour, dripping from his fingertips.

Sulanna interrupted Alden's continued prayers, which had given undertone to the falling rain for the past mile. "I do not understand why anyone would hide this relic here in the North. Maybe the old Anshedar who Ivarr speaks about buried it, during the War of Shayol Domier."

"The War of Shayol Domier, Third of Frost, Month of Falling Leaves, 124 CE, it was, when demons last walked upon Aenar," Dorofej's whistled from the rear, welcoming the conversation. He was eager to take his mind off Alden's life-threatening pastime. "That battle was leagues to the south. Further than either of you have traveled, yes?"

"The mysterious, all-knowing Dorofej," Sulanna mocked. "There surely is some use to those books but I was not asking for a history lesson."

"Sweet Sulanna, through history we find the road to our destiny, yes?"

Sulanna turned to him sharply. "Either of you men call me sweet again, or any variation of, I will run you through personally."

Dorofej tittered with amusement.

Sulanna bit her bottom lip and tried again. "Seriously, what of the relic? Any ideas as to what we are looking for exactly?"

"We are searching for what is called *kaelandur*, yes?" Dorofej said. "The power to bring the demons back to Aenar, it possesses."

Sulanna raised her eyebrow, "And what exactly is this *kaelandur*?"

Alden coughed, finally joining the conversation. "No one knows."

"Then why were we sent after it?"

"Would you like to ride back to Tamarri and ask, my swee—"

"Alden means to say we do not know, yes?" Dorofej flashed his white teeth in a smile with the break of lightning, interrupting the balding warrior.

Sulanna glared at Alden, nearly reaching for her belt knife to follow through with her threat. She grimaced. "I certainly cannot imagine what would be buried in these hills."

Silence ensued.

At the bottom of yet another hill, a small, wooden farmhouse seemed to rise magically from the earth. The dark clouds lightened, though the rain continued, giving enough light to roughly see the terrain. A faint glow of a lantern's light radiated from a second-story window on the eastward side of the building, barely casting an outline of the diminutive home. A tattered fence of thin branches shaped the land around the place. Strangely enough, the structure stood alone with no outbuildings for livestock or farming equipment. Oddities such as these briefly slipped through Dorofej's mind, but was forgotten in anticipation of a warm fireplace.

The barking of dogs erupted into the night air, announcing their arrival. A small smile lifted on Sulanna's face. "I stand corrected. It seems your god has finally decided to do something worthwhile."

Alden ignored the sarcasm. "Something does not feel right."

Sulanna heatedly pushed back the soaked strands of hair from her eyes, attempting to regain a bit of composure. "Are you suggesting we refuse the mercy of your god?"

"Svarog does not simply give mercy to those who ask. We may be fools to seek sanctuary at this farmhouse."

"We are fools to sit here in a downpour discussing this nonsense," Sulanna barked with frustration. "We have been traveling in the rain for hours."

Alden met her unblinking eyes in complete wonderment. "There is something amiss, Sulanna."

"You are amiss, Alden," Sulanna retorted.

Alden frowned in defeat, "You are going to get us killed."

Dorofej followed them down the hill, watching the noble woman sitting high on her horse as though the edge of any sword was too dull to leave a mark on her throat.

Dark shapes distinguished to be the barking dogs ran toward them. There was a mutter from Sulanna indicating there were two in number. In a matter of seconds, the animals sprung over the fence and were next to them.

Even in the heavy rain, it was easy to tell these were nothing but ordinary dogs. The three riders ignored the mutts snapping around their heels and at the legs of their trained mounts. A couple measly dogs were not threatening.

Drawing near, Dorofej could see shadows through the window bouncing off the walls from a lantern's light. The shaggy animals jumping about his feet continued to snarl and yap, creating a great ruckus. Though, the booming voice of a man caught his attention as the narrow door at the front of the home opened.

"Jorwarg! Worlack! In the name of Marheena, stop…!"

The silver-haired man who stepped out into the rain appeared at least twenty years older than Alden. His face was wrinkled and unkempt with coarse patched hair that could not rightly be called a beard. He wore a white shirt with the collar untied and short brown trousers. Once seeing the riders, he froze barefooted in a mucky puddle of rainwater, holding his bulky body up with a fat branch in one hand. In his other hand, a lantern hung from his fingers swaying as his staff settled itself in the loose sludge.

In a moment of silence, Alden and Sulanna stared wide-eyed at the older man as he did back at them, his mouth crooked with his jaw dropped. He could have very well been the oldest man in the world.

Dorofej tugged back the hood of his robes. He was uncertain whether the man's words regarding Marheena had been a curse or a prayer. As if understanding the unknown, the yipping dogs became eerily quiet, and trotted off around the back of the house.

Sulanna introduced them. "I am Sulanna Maelthirren and these are my companions, Alden Forgaaf and Dorofej Creighton. If you would be so kind, we seek shelter from the storm."

Dorofej nodded at the made-up surname he had given himself upon returning to Aenar. Fortunately, it had been accepted by strangers with little question about its origin.

The stranger's brow wrinkled as though he were seriously distressed by Sulanna's words. His expression hardened, lips curling into a sneer. "Bohumir is my boy! You cannot take him from me."

Sulanna loosened her long knife from her belt. "I do not know any boy named Bohumir. We simply need a place to rest for a few hours."

"Bohumir Mager? You know Bohumir Mager!" The man spouted in laughter, tilting his head backwards.

Alden turned his head sideward to speak into Sulanna's ear. He was loud enough that all could hear him. "He is mad."

"Maybe not," Dorofej muttered.

She ignored them both, nudging her horse a step closer. "These rains do not show signs of stopping anytime soon…"

"Curse you!" The man croaked, his laughter abruptly ceasing with a sinister gaze resting on Sulanna. "Curse you and the foul rain!" Then, under his breath as if asking a question, the man spat, and whispered feverishly.

Dorofej leaned forward to try to grasp the words. They sounded ancient, familiar.

The lantern flying toward Sulanna's chest stole away his concentration. He watched as she dived from her horse, avoided the object, and landed in a grimy puddle.

The man reacted before Dorofej or Alden had a chance. He bolted to Sulanna's side with his staff raised over his head. In no way did the movement appear to offset the older man's balance. Sulanna, who acted more on impulse than anything else, rolled out of the away to avoid certain death. Then, with a quick sweep of her leg, the she took the aggressor off his feet.

He landed with a thud, the staff bouncing far from his grasp. His white shirt was dirtied, covered in both rain and mud. With a bestial snarl, he spun onto all fours like a rabid animal and rushed the noble woman again.

Sulanna cried out. She scurried backwards to regain her footing, fighting to pull her dagger from her belt.

From the side, Alden had dismounted from his gelding. With expert timing, he stepped forward and kicked the charging man sending him sprawling backwards once more. The old man clamored in the mud. Alden did not waste any more time, lifting his spear and pointing the tip at the fallen foe.

"Find salvation in this life or the next, it is your choice," Alden sneered. Sulanna pulled herself to her feet, finally yanking her dagger from her belt.

The man rolled over in the mud, gasping and wheezing. The white shirt was barely hanging on his body, torn down the front, staying in place with caked mud. He glowered, trying to stand, only to slip to his knees again. Alden kept his gaze on the man, allowing the stranger to stand erect.

He shifted his full attention to Alden and his spear. He spoke in huffs, "Marheena will smolder the lot of you!"

None of them had a chance to respond.

The stranger spun around the spear with inhuman dexterity. He had not taken more than three steps before Sulanna flung her dagger, the blade sinking into his neck.

Blood spurted to the sound of his horrific, gurgled scream. With a jolt, he staggered, crawling back toward the entrance of his home. His blood mixed with the moist earth.

"No," Dorofej inhaled. He raised his gaze from the dying body to see a small boy in his sleeping garments standing in the doorway. The boy did not return the look, but instead stared in shock at the dying man who had fallen near the doorstep.

"Father..." the boy was barely audible through tears.

The man struggled, raising his arm toward the boy, who rushed to him. The son fell to his father's embrace, weeping uncontrollably. The father cupped his hand on the young boy's cheek, and in a curdled moan stammered, "Bohumir, my son. Come with me."

With his remaining strength, the old man pulled a dagger from the back of his belt. In a moment, too quick to respond, the father sunk the blade into his son's chest. The father crumpled in a heap, lifeless. The son spurted blood from his mouth, his face aghast in bewilderment.

"Dorofej!" Sulanna cried, running to the boy's side.

He threw himself off the horse and ran to the doorstep, his eyes locking on the copper blade within the boy. He knew it well. "Take the dagger and quick, you must be." Dorofej kneeled, peeling back the eyelids of the boy called Bohumir.

Sulanna jerked the dagger from the cavity of Bohumir's chest. Dark red blood spewed from the wound. "Save him!"

"His spirit has not fled from the body. Time there may be." Dorofej was delicate in his movements.

Dorofej caught sight of Alden, who was kneeling in the mud a few yards away with his bracer dislodged. His belt knife was clutched in his left hand as he cut another gash into his forearm. It may have been a third cut, possibly fourth. He could not tell from the overwhelming amount of blood streaming down his arm. The old man's prayers to Svarog for forgiveness were choked and difficult to understand. His words were suffocated through gasps for breath, through tears and mucus. The warrior was lament with grief.

He spoke to Sulanna, "Go to Alden."

The Highborn's hands touched Bohumir, covering the wound. Blood flowed freely over his steadied hands. A glow of red and yellow glowed beneath the boy's skin as Dorofej manipulated his craft, *Koldovstvo*, ever ancient and powerful.

From the corner of his eye, Dorofej saw Sulanna rush to Alden. She grabbed him, screaming, all noble equanimity was lost, "Stop this, Alden! No god is worth this!"

Alden shouted back. "Let me go, Sulanna! I must save

him with my sacrifice!"

"No, Alden," she pleaded, "Think for yourself."

"You must let me go. I must do this."

Sulanna clutched the powerful man's arms in defiance.

From the depths of his gut, Alden bellowed. With merciless strength, he picked Sulanna off the ground and flung her to the side. She spiraled into a roll, slamming her face hard against the wet ground. Mud splattered into her eyes and covered her hair.

Determined. Gasping for air. She rolled against the sludge.

Dorofej winced, knowing he could not help. His task was too important.

Alden cut himself with more intensity. His prayers were screams. Pleas. He was going to kill himself.

The boy suddenly twitched beneath Dorofej's trembling hands. The black mage cried out, "He will live!"

Alden dropped the knife, his arm shreds of flesh hanging from bone. "Praise Svarog! For the Kingdom and glory."

Dorofej joined Sulanna in the mud, knowing not else to do, and wept.

ABOUT THE AUTHOR

Joshua Robertson was born in Kingman, Kansas on May 23, 1984. A graduate of Norwich High School, Robertson attended Wichita State University where he received his Masters in Social Work with minors in Psychology and Sociology. His bestselling novel, Melkorka, the first in The Kaelandur Series, was released in 2015. Known most for his Thrice Nine Legends Saga, Robertson enjoys an ever-expanding and extremely loyal following of readers. He counts R.A. Salvatore and J.R.R. Tolkien among his literary influences.

www.ingramcontent.com/pod-product-compliance
Lightning Source LLC
Chambersburg PA
CBHW071231190726
48292CB00007B/2228